KRIS LONGKNIFE: ADMIRAL

MIKE SHEPHERD

KL & MM BOOKS

Published by KL & MM Books
November 2017

This book is a work of fiction set 400 years in humanity's future. Any similarity between present people, places, or events would be spectacularly unlikely and is purely coincidental.

This book is written and published by the author. Please don't pirate it. I'm self-employed. The money I earn from these sales allow me to produce more stories to entertain you. I'd hate to have to get a day job again. If this book comes into your hands free, please consider going to your favorite e-book provider and investing in a copy so I can continue to earn a living at this wonderful art.

I would like to thank my wonderful cover artist, Scott Grimando, who did all my Ace covers and will continue doing my own book covers. I also am grateful for the editing skill of Lisa Müller, Edee Lemonier, Mike Castle, and, as ever, Ellen Moscoe.

Ver 2.0

Bowker ISBN
eBook ISBN-13: 978-1642211010 4
Print ISBN-13: 978-1642110098

ALSO BY MIKE SHEPHERD

Published by KL & MM Books

Kris Longknife: Admiral

Kris Longknife: Emissary

Kris Longknife's Successor

Kris Longknife's Replacement

Kris Longknife's Relief

Rita Longknife: Enemy Unknown

Rita Longknife: Enemy in Sight

Short Stories from KL & MM Books

Kris Longknife's Maid Goes On Strike and Other Short Stories: Vignettes from Kris Longknife's World

Kris Longknife's Maid Goes On Strike

Kris Longknife's Bad Day

Ruth Longknife's First Christmas

Kris Longknife: Among the Kicking Birds

Ace Books by Mike Shepherd

Kris Longknife: Mutineer

Kris Longknife: Deserter

Kris Longknife: Defiant

Kris Longknife: Resolute

Kris Longknife: Audacious

Kris Longknife: Intrepid

Kris Longknife: Undaunted

Kris Longknife: Redoubtable

Kris Longknife: Daring

Kris Longknife: Furious

Kris Longknife: Defender

Kris Longknife: Tenacious

Kris Longknife: Unrelenting

Kris Longknife: Bold

Vicky Peterwald: Target

Vicky Peterwald: Survivor

Vicky Peterwald: Rebel

Mike Shepherd writing as Mike Moscoe in the Jump Point Universe

First Casualty

The Price of Peace

They Also Serve

Rita Longknife: To Do or Die

Short Specials

Kris Longknife: Training Daze

Kris Longknife : Welcome Home, Go Away

Kris Longknife's Bloodhound

Kris Longknife's Assassin

The Lost Millennium Trilogy Published by KL & MM Books

Lost Dawns: Prequel

First Dawn

Second Fire

Lost Days

1

Grand Admiral, Her Royal Highness Kris Longknife of the Royal United Society Navy sat comfortably on her now shrunken flag bridge in the tight embrace of her high gee station. Around her, the crew of her flagship, the USS *Princess Royal*, were at battle stations: targeting systems swept the space all around them, lasers were dialed in and powered up; the outer hull had its crystal armor spinning around the inner hull at one revolution per second.

The *Princess Royal* was at Condition Zed and ready for war.

Fortunately, today, the only thing the sailors risked losing was an exercise. At worst, they might miss adding another E to their power plant or laser. Kris had a pretty good idea about the quality of the 6th Battlecruiser Task Fleet. She had exercised them plenty on their voyage out from Wardhaven to the Iteeche Imperial capitol.

Kris was the first human envoy ever accredited to the Iteeche Imperial Court. She had made sure her fleet arrived ship shape and Bristol fashion, as well as ready to fight if it had to. Which was a good thing.

The Iteeche were locked in a bloody civil war.

The rebels didn't want a human emissary. The Imperials didn't really want a Longknife for an emissary. No, the Imperial court wanted a fighting admiral. Kris had even been commissioned into their Navy as an Imperial Admiral of the First Order of Steel and made the commanding admiral of the entire Iteeche fleet. At least as much of that fleet that was holding to the Imperial flag.

That was the reason for today's drill.

Thirty-two human battlecruisers accelerated into space at one gee. They were formed into four squadron lines of eight battlecruisers each and stacked one on top of the other. All the battlecruisers faced forward, giving their twelve, 24-inch bow lasers a clear line of fire as they approached any target. Battlecruisers' lasers could only fire fifteen degrees right or left, up or down from their keels. If you caught a battlecruiser on the broadside, it was toast.

Which was a bit troubling to Kris.

At the moment, her task fleet sailed in the center of four equally large flotillas of the Imperial Iteeche Navy: one to each side, one above, and one below her. All told, they formed a cross with Kris in the middle. The lower fleet was commanded by Imperial Counselor, Ron the Iteeche, who was a good friend of Kris's and one of the reasons she was here. He was trusted by Kris.

The other three flotillas were drawn from different satraps, seconded to the Imperial Planet's protection. In theory, they were as loyal as an Iteeche could be to the Most Worshipful Emperor.

With a civil war raging, coats could be turned very quickly.

Still, if Kris was to command an Iteeche fleet, she had to know how good it was. From what she'd heard, the Iteeche considered a human battlecruiser worth only three-quarters of one of their battlecruisers.

Kris had her doubts. Today, she was about to find out.

"Comm, send to fleet. 'Flip ship, raise acceleration to two gees, initiate Evasion Plan 3 on my orders'."

Kris eyed her board. She'd trained the captains aboard all her human ships to reply directly to her flag. She had suggested that to the three Iteeche admirals commanding the flotillas. They were Admirals of the Second Order of Cloth. They owed their allegiance and their jobs to different Lord Pashas of the satraps that had built the ships and paid for their crews and maintenance.

Ron had explained to Kris that there were several orders, starting with Cloth, and going through Gold Cloth, Oak, Bronze, Iron, and Steel. Each order was divided into First through Fourth classes, with Grand Order added for the top-most level of each order. The entire lineup of orders, ranks, and extra gewgaws had kind of grown as the Iteeche fleet had grown. As an example, Kris's status as a commissioned Imperial Admiral outranked all admirals commissioned by a Satrap. The realization that there were some twenty-four admiral ranks between her and her subordinate Iteeche admirals was a real jaw-dropper.

Those admirals might be way down the totem pole, but that didn't mean they would let Kris remove even one of their prerogatives. The human battlecruisers showed as bright green lights across the board a good half-minute before the last Iteeche admiral transmitted that his ships were ready for the reverse course.

"Execute," Kris ordered.

Around Kris, the *Princess Royal* did a fast flip about its

lateral axis. From accelerating at one gee in one direction, it took off decelerating along the reciprocal course vector at two gees. The big battlecruiser also began to jitterbug. Up, down, right, left, and varying its deceleration, the *Princess Royal* did everything it could moderately do to not be in the space it had been headed for three or four seconds before.

Lasers were powerful, and traveled at the speed of light. However, it took time for a fire control system to acquire a target, time for it to develop a projection of where that target would be in a few seconds, and time to transmit the firing coordinates to the laser, then aim it and fire.

Kris had survived a lot of battles by not being there when the other guy fired.

She'd spent most of her career in small boats that swapped ice armor, meters thick, for dexterity at evasion. The battlecruisers may have grown from the 25,000-ton frigates with a half-dozen 18-inch lasers to the present 75,000-ton battlecruiser with twenty 24-inch lasers, but they were still a lot more maneuverable than a lumbering battleship.

At least, human battlecruisers seemed to be more maneuverable.

The four squadrons of eight human battlecruisers turned on a dime as if pulled by a single string. They flipped ship and took off at two gees while each of them jinked in its own volume of space. That was why Kris's ships were 5,000 kilometers from each other. The eight ships in each of her squadrons formed a line 35,000 kilometers long.

Three Iteeche admirals had formed their ships in tight, with only 2,000 kilometers between each ship, though each flotilla was 25,000 kilometers from where Kris's ships steamed in the middle of this cross.

Each Iteeche flotilla was in a stack of four lines of eight, just like Kris's fleet. They were just a tighter mass. Until this maneuver.

Now, the ships were scattered all over the place. Some had turned sooner than others. Others had not flipped ship but chosen to turn ship, taking up more room and scattering themselves farther apart. Some took off at two gees sooner, others later. Three of the Iteeche flotillas were now amorphous blob to the right, left, and above Kris's orderly human task fleet.

The fourth Iteeche flotilla, having been drilled by Kris on the way out from Wardhaven, executed the maneuver with a precision that was nearly as exacting as Kris's human ships.

Still, none of the ships in the four Iteeche task fleets were doing much bobbing around.

"Nelly? How easy would it be to target them?"

No doubt, quite easy. The Magnificent Nelly, Kris's much upgraded computer, had started life most docile in first grade. Somewhere, however, after one of her frequent upgrades, Nelly had taken to arguing with Kris and telling horrible jokes. Nelly, and her children . . . yes, Nelly was a mother . . . were the first sentient computers anyone knew about.

The family unanimously agreed; they did not want to become common.

Nelly proved why in only a moment.

"The Iteeche are very predictable. None of them are executing any evasion better than Plan 1. In a lot of cases, they are worse. I would expect that I could make twenty percent hits with the first salvo. Fifty percent with the second. I doubt that any of those flotillas would survive very long in a fight with a human battlecruiser."

That was what Kris had already figured out with her

meat brain, but it was nice to have Nelly confirm her opinion.

"Comm, raise Ron'sum'Pin'sumCap'sum'We aboard the *Red Sunset on the Water*."

A moment later, the forward screen was filled with an eight-foot-tall Iteeche. His four eyes were focused on Kris. Of his four arms, two were over his head, grasping a roll bar, at least that was what humans had called those things before they started fighting from high gee stations. Ron swayed on his four legs, flexing as his ship jinked.

Behind him, on the Iteeche bridge, not one high gee station was in evidence.

"Ron, old friend, your ships did better than the rest, but none of the Iteeche ships are evading very well."

"Kris, my old friend, we are doing the best we can. I discussed your idea of a high gee station with the other admirals. I'm afraid that their attitude is that they have fought their ships standing up for ten thousand years before you humans ever darkened our stars. It would be unmanly to go into battle seated like a student in the Palace of Learning."

Kris shook her head. Commanding an Iteeche fleet was nowhere near as easy as some folks might think. Yes, the Iteeche were building battlecruisers that were supposed to be just like the human ships. The sole exception was the crystal armor that slowed laser light down, distributed it around the ship's hull, then radiated it back out to space. That was one secret the humans were holding close to their chests.

Admittedly, the crystal armor was not perfect. Kris had lost crystal armored ships. Grand Admiral Santiago out on Alwa station had lost armored ships. Still, a lot of battlecruisers that would have burned without the armor had made it back to a Navy base to refit and repair.

The Iteeche had been given the same lasers designs, the same power plants, and the same fire control systems. In theory, they should be the same.

Kris knew that there was a hell of a lot of difference between a trained and battle-ready crew and a collection of landsmen who couldn't tell their asses from a hole in the ground.

She was starting to wonder how many landsmen were on the Iteeche battlecruisers around her.

Kris ordered the Iteeche admirals to get their ships back in a battle array. A good fifteen minutes later, she was ready to issue the same command to five flotillas of thirty-two battlecruisers each, all in rows of eight, all stacked four high. The five had reformed back into a cross. So far, a cross was the best fighting formation Kris had come up with.

Again, Kris ordered the ships to flip ship and accelerate at two gees using Evasion Plan 1 for the Iteeche, Plan 3 for the humans.

Fifteen seconds after the execute command was given, they were, if anything, even more scattered.

It was then that Nelly noticed a serious discrepancy in the Iteeche battle array.

2

Humans have a hard time living their lives by the second. Our best efforts are barely able to divide a human activity like foot or swim racing by a hundredth of a second. A computer like Nelly can divide a second up into millions of fragments and live a lifetime in each second.

Nelly's ability to recognize the changing face of events around her had saved Kris's life more times than Kris could count. Still, there were certain things that Nelly was not allowed to do.

For example, Nelly could not start a war. This had been impressed upon her no end and she accepted that if she did that, Kris would be very upset.

However, Nelly had been slipping into ships' systems for most of Kris's career, spotting problems and correcting them, or hitting a scram button to kill a reactor just moments before it might run away and destroy Kris's ship.

Keeping things from getting out of hand got Nelly nice accolades. Starting a war? Not so much.

What Nelly saw in the fractions of a second that Kris did not have, was a drastic battle maneuver as two Iteeche flotillas changed front.

The Iteeche battlecruisers appeared to be disorganized, from one perspective. They had failed to execute their maneuver properly and now were scattered all over thousands of cubic kilometers of vacuum. As such, they had failed again to execute Kris's orders.

However, when viewed from another perspective, one Nelly quickly grasped, two flotillas of Iteeche battlecruisers had opened their ranks up and given every one of the seventy-two battlecruisers in their formation a direct shot at the human ships.

Nelly noticed that perspective and its potential to harm Kris. She set part of herself to observing that particular perspective as she kept herself busy with many other things. It was only a fraction of a second later that her alarms went off. Yes, the Iteeche battlecruisers were changing front.

First some. Then more. Finally, all sixty-four ships in the top and left-hand fleets were bringing their bow laser batteries around to bear on Kris's battlecruisers.

Nelly observed the action of the Iteeche. Two Iteeche flotillas were behaving normally, if a bit ragged in their battle array and actions. The other two flotillas were executing orders that had nothing to do with those that Kris Longknife had just given.

Nelly was not alone. Megan Longknife, Kris's *aide de camp*, had been given one of Nelly's children. Lily was immediately called to her mother's assistance. They divided the 6th Battlecruiser Task Fleet into two halves with Nelly taking Task Force 1 and Lily, Task Force 2. They slipped into the helm computer on every ship and jammed the accelerator down, sending the ships off at 3.6 gees base course. They also switched the helm to Evasion Plan 6, which got the human ships slamming themselves around their base course right, left, right, right, up, left, down, left, while jiggling the acceleration from 0 to 3.65 gees.

That was all done in the second it took the potentially hostile Iteeche battlecruisers to rotate themselves and point their bow batteries at Kris's fleet. Even as they changed front, their active targeting computers clicked off standby and began sweeping the human fleet, identifying targets, and feeding position, course, and speed into their own fire control computers.

Nelly had learned her lesson. Nelly was not permitted to start wars. What had never been included in her conversations with Kris was at what point Nelly was permitted to reply to someone starting a war. Nelly was all too well-read on the problems inherent in the transition from peace to belligerency. She also understood how hard it was for humans to stop a war once it started.

Nelly had a direct wire into Kris's brain. Today, she used it. "Alarm, Alarm," she said firmly to the grand admiral. Nelly also commandeered the main screen in Flag Plot and filled it full with pictures of the two aggressor flotillas.

While Nelly waited for Kris to respond to this input, she kept herself very busy. She edged the rotating skins of the battlecruisers up to eighty revolutions per minute, four revolutions every three seconds. If the jinking worked, even a direct laser hit would be hard-pressed to achieve burn-through before the skin of the ship was carried away from the burn point. Better yet, if the human battlecruiser was zigging and zagging, by the time the skin rotated back, the laser might very well be burning another part of the ship's skin.

It had saved lives before.

However, Nelly was not limited to defensive action.

Nelly and Lily slipped part of themselves into the fire control computers. There, they switched the huge and complex sensor package on each battlecruiser over from 'Search' to 'Acquire.' Lily and Nelly took in the sensor feed, calculated it, and would have smiled if they'd been human.

The Iteeche had a system they called maskers. When activated, it complicated the fire control sensor suite on the human battlecruisers. The most sensitive targeting gear, the lasers, radars, and atomic laser mass finders, could all be spoofed by this fragment of ancient alien technology. The Iteeche had done that back during the Great War. The aliens, however, couldn't spoof light. They could try to emit as little as possible, but each ship was coated with reflective material to try to bounce back grazing laser fire. Such coatings had a tendency to gleam.

Nelly did a quick check. There were no discrepancies between the four targeting systems. A check of the electromagnetic spectrum showed a missing note deep down the line. Nelly had recently helped the Iteeche manufacture maskers. She'd promised not to keep any information about the manufacturing process. However, she didn't promise anything about discovering the power signature of the maskers. Nelly now knew what noises to look for if maskers were in use.

There was no noise.

This sneak attack had given up much for the advantage of surprise.

Nelly completed fire solutions for her sixteen battlecruisers and fed them to the lasers.

Sensors can perceive information at the speed of light. Calculations can be made at the speed of light. Information can be passed at speeds close to the speed of light. However, some things took time. One of them was the mechanical process of swinging the huge 24-inch lasers out of train and aiming them at their target. The other was the time it took to put the helm over and rotate the ship from going one way to aiming her guns at the targets on her beam.

As the potentially hostile battlecruisers swung around, Nelly could pick up the electronic noise from their servos as the Iteeche lasers swung around to lay on target. Of course, that meant that the helmsman had to stop the bow at the precise moment that it faced the human battlecruiser.

Most of the helmsmen were new. Untested in battle. Nervous. Most over-steered or under-steered. If it was within the fifteen degrees that the lasers could be moved, the servos took over, redirecting the lasers at their targets. If the helm went too far or not far enough, they had to correct, and maybe correct again when they swung too wide the other way.

While the potential hostiles were doing this, Grand Admiral Kris Longknife's eyes were locked on her main screen. She saw the threat, and, unlike everyone else aboard the one hundred and fifty-nine battlecruisers, she had Nelly in her brain and all it took for her to communicate with Nelly was a thought.

DO NOT FIRE UNTIL FIRED UPON. IF FIRED UPON, WEAPONS FREE, was but a thought, but it was all the thought Nelly needed to hear.

Kris had laid on this short cruise today so she could test the mettle of the Iteeche Navy. It looked like someone had decided to test her mettle as well. Kris had been tried by deadlier killers than these. She was still here and they weren't. She added one more command for Nelly. TARGET

EACH FLAG WITH THREE LASERS TO EACH AIMING POINT.

AYE, AYE ADMIRAL.

Kris had discovered in desperate battles against the alien space raiders, that burn-through came quicker if you could target two, three, or even four lasers at the same spot on a ship's hull. It was not easy to get lasers to slave to a single point. It also cut down on the spread of a ship's laser salvo. Most fleets used wide-spread laser salvos to increase the chances that any particular target might take a few hits.

Not Kris's.

Everything was a tradeoff. Still, with the Iteeche so reluctant to follow an effective evasion plan, this concentration looked like a good bet.

A dozen Iteeche battlecruisers opened fire on the humans. It was a ragged salvo, growing as more ships brought their forward batteries to bear and joining in until all sixty-four were sending everything they had at the thirty-two human battlecruisers.

Six Iteeche warships targeted the *Princess Royal.*

Over half of their seventy-two 24-inch lasers in their bow batteries went wide. One even nipped the battlecruiser behind the *P. Royal.* Lasers on more ships sputtered to life, but only managed to cut the vacuum close in to Kris's flag. As Kris expected, the Iteeche lasers were loose in their gun carriages and their salvos were wildly scattered about the space in which the *Princess Royal* was dodging.

Still, there were a lot of lasers aimed at Kris's flag and a lot more taking up the howl for her blood. Kris waited patiently to see if her ship was as well-built as she thought. She had inspected her several times and never found the *P. Royal* wanting.

The *Princess Royal* took six hits. Two were glancing

blows, but four were solid hits. The lasers hit the crystal armor; the energy was instantaneously diffused out to the crystal around the hit. The fast-rotating skin of the *P. Royal* spun the superheated skin away from the laser beams, bringing in cool, undamaged crystal armor. The 24-inch lasers were good for six seconds of fire at full power. However, with the way the battlecruiser was jinking in space and the high-speed rotation of the hull, the lasers never got to take a second bite out of the same place.

The cooling honeycomb structure of Smart Metal™ and the rapid flow of cooling reaction mass under the crystal armor all helped to dissipate the infernal heat of the lasers. Still, the *Princess Royal* was fit to fight back.

Nelly certainly intended to.

Nelly had Lily stand down Task Force 2. However, the sixteen human battlecruisers of Task Force 1 were under Nelly's control and she had them armed, aimed, and ready to return the fire. The twelve lasers of the ships' forward batteries had been dialed in tight. Kris had learned on Alwa station that many ships came from the yard with their lasers loose in their carriages. On distant Alwa station, they had rapidly learned to tighten down the lasers and slave them in tightly together. Four groups of three concentrated lasers leapt out from every battlecruiser in the human Task Force 1.

Nelly had targeted the Iteeche flotilla and task force flagships, as well as squadron commanders. They accounted for fourteen targets. Nelly made the decision to target the flotilla flags with two battlecruisers rather than slaughter some private ship. She doubted any of her targets would survive.

She aimed her lasers, and fired.

The US battlecruisers were confronted with several problems simultaneously.

If they wanted to stay alive, they had to keep up their mad jitterbugging. If they wanted to fire at their tormentor, they had to get their bows within fifteen degrees of the target. The human ships continued to jink. However, each fire control system was aware of what its own ships would do next in its dance to stay alive. The fire control computers factored those movements into those of their targets, and spat out a solution.

The Iteeche rebels made it way too easy.

With their ships hardly dodging at all, four groups of concentrated laser beams fixed on seven of the thirty-two Iteeche ships in each flotilla. Some missed. Most didn't. Ten Iteeche battlecruisers took two or three hits. Two were missed entirely. The two flotilla flags took six or seven hits.

They simply disintegrated.

The other twelve ships became a study in damage control. In too many cases, damage control didn't appear to have been well taught. Instead, ships began shedding survival pods as sailors took one look at the hell around them and punched out. Twelve ships twisted, rolled, and flipped through space, spewing tiny pods behind them.

"Check fire. Check fire," Kris ordered. Normally, she went into her high gee station in her birthday suit. When ships got busy honking around at 3.5 gees, things like belt buckles and ribbon pins could be downright dangerous and leave her black and blue for days. However, Kris hadn't really intended to be pushing the outer edge of the envelope. She just wanted to see how good or, more likely how bad, the Imperial Iteeche Navy was.

She'd learned a whole lot of what she'd expected to learn, and a lot more that she hadn't.

"Ron. You're the Imperial Counselor. You tell these bastards that if they fire another shot at me, I will blast the entire lot of them out of space."

Ron took over the conversation, speaking rapidly in Iteeche.

"He's telling them that they will all meet the Emperor's personal headsman if there is one more shot fired. He's ordering all of the captains and admirals to surrender their vessels and to place themselves under arrest. Oops, Kris, it seems that you blew away four of the six admirals. The other two have chosen to avoid making a formal apology to the Emperor by taking poison."

"Dead Iteeche tell no tales," Kris growled, through a scowl. She really wanted to talk to whoever set up this ambush as well as who set them up to do it. Now, she'd have to dig all of this out slowly from the hearsay of captains who had only been obeying orders.

By the time she found one set of answers, would they still mean anything to anyone? That thought slowed Kris down. Once again, she was faced with an enigma that was an Empire that had a teenager for an "all powerful" Emperor. A whole lot of people "worshiped," that kid, but too many others wanted to sit on his throne.

This was not the emissary job that Kris had signed up for.

"Ron, you order the survivors to make for the Navy station. I will follow. If they so much as twitch, I'll have my lasers blow their reactors to hell."

"They understand. They will comply."

"Have the fellow who didn't shoot at me break out his longboats and pinnaces to recover survivors." In theory, it was Kris who had the authority over that other admiral of the cloth. In fact, Ron was an Imperial Counselor and spoke with the unquestioned authority of the Emperor to people at the Admiral's level.

For the moment, it looked better for Kris to use the old ways to get things done.

"Ron, I'd also appreciate it if you could detach Imperial Marines in longboats to each ship. I want their captains brought to my flag. I want any survivors from the Admirals' staffs as well. If you have any Imperial interrogators or inquisitors, I'd be glad to have them, but I want to see that the interviews are recorded. I, of course, will provide copies to you, your Chooser, and the Emperor."

The set up here was beyond crazy, but Kris had a lot of previous experience with crazy lash-ups. Back then, she'd hated the mess and had dreamed of a nice, simple, chains of command. After five years at a staff desk job, Kris had developed a different attitude. Crazy was good. Insane was her friend.

For the training exercise today, they had come out as five flotillas in a cross tactical array. They returned with two in a ragged formation, with Ron's battlecruisers just below Kris's ships. Between the Iteeche ships, longboats slipped from ship to ship. Some docked on one or two ships, others three or four.

All of them docked on the *Princess Royal* before they returned to their own ships.

All brought Navy officers and Marine escorts. All were met by human Navy officers and United Society Marines. Their orders were to treat the Iteeche as guests, not prisoners. Kris could afford to give them decent quarters in her brig, now that the *P Royal* had relaxed from Condition Zed to Condition Able.

Or Love Boat sailing condition to any old salt among the crew. Still, it was nice to have your own spacious quarters and you could always go back to Condition Zed in a flash. For now, that gave the humans room to give each of the Iteeche officers a single room to prowl in and contemplate their futures.

It was a long, slow sail back to the station.

3

Kris could not afford to delay the critique of the short battle they'd just fought.

"Nelly, tell my key staff I need them in my quarters in one hour. They should come prepared to tear this action apart from the Navy aspect and tell me where we go from here."

"Yes, Kris. Do you want the task force commanders to attend?"

Kris considered that. In practice, the commodores had their own commands. At the moment, Kris needed their advice more than she expected to need their leadership.

"Ask Commodores Ajax and Afon to report to my day quarters if at all possible."

"Aye, aye, Admiral."

Kris smiled at how nautical Nelly was getting. Then again, Nelly and Lily had saved their bacon just now, and the two of them could do anything they wanted to. Meanwhile, Kris had to get herself into a mindset for a large meeting.

That was a problem she was having. Her irregular

promotion path had skipped quite a few steps, which included several staff slots along the way. Kris had never really figured out how to use a staff. On Alwa, she'd had a lot of fish to fry, but everyone was in the same boat and all were pulling in the same direction. There had been plenty of friction, but not so much that Kris hadn't been able to keep things going smoothly with a small staff.

While in a staff job for the last five years, Kris had been able to use Nelly to do a lot of work for her. With no battle experienced officer to use for her chief of staff, she'd preferred to do without.

Her situation here at the Imperial Court was a whole lot worse than any she'd ever faced before. She had an embassy to run and a battle force to train and how to fight effectively. Either one of those jobs could work her to death if she didn't delegate.

The embassy was a mess. Facilities on the planet below were a big question mark. The attitude of the Iteeche was unclear, but likely not to be to the liking of the humans that had followed Kris out here. She had business men expecting to make their private fortune. Diplomats from several planets and associations were all hoping to make their careers by negotiating better terms for their planet than the next guy could get for his.

There were a lot of oars in the water, with few of them pulling in the same direction.

On top of all that, she now had a fleet to command that could turn on her at any moment and whose battle skills were sorely wanting.

The planning for this recent failed exercise had started immediately after Kris got back from her initial meeting with the Emperor and called a no-notice staff meeting just like this one.

"You're what, Admiral?" didn't quite have the shock in it that Kris had gotten when she announced to her command on Alwa that she was pregnant, but it was pretty close.

"I am, it appears, appointed Imperial Admiral of the First Order of Steel, commanding the whole kit and caboodle of the Imperial Iteeche Battle Fleet. I need a staff. The hot potato is landing in your lap. Where can we hold a large staff meeting?"

They stood on the quarterdeck of the *Bold,* flagship of ComBatCruFlot 6, where the chief of staff, Titania Tosan, had come to formally meet Kris when she got short notice that the admiral was on her way. The captain had carried off the greeting with great aplomb, despite being a bit breathless, right up to the moment Kris dropped the bomb.

The tall woman looked like she'd been kicked in the gut by a mule, but she struggled with it valiantly.

"Ah, Admiral Darlan is indisposed in his quarters at the moment. I believe we can use the flag wardroom for a meeting."

"Indisposed?" Kris echoed and left it hanging.

"He's been, ah, partaking heavily of Chief Mason's home brew since you relieved him of his command, Admiral. He didn't take it well."

"The officers I relieved of command will be on the first ship heading back to human space just as soon as we unload. For now, contact one of Al Longknife's liners and get them all rooms on the civilian side. We don't need this kind of unprofessional and undisciplined behavior aboard ship."

"Yes, ma'am."

Before they left the quarterdeck, Commodores Ajax and

Afon hurried aboard with their chiefs of staff and operations officers. Jacques and Amanda were right on their heels, the result of Nelly's initiative. All were in the dark as to why they'd been summoned so suddenly; they'd stay that way until Kris got to the wardroom.

It fit her needs. Nelly had provided one long table with decent chairs, large enough for twenty. Kris waited while everyone took a place, verified that Nelly knew the name of all present, and took her place at the head of the table with Jack at one elbow, Megan at the other.

Kris did not sit.

"Whatever you thought you were going to do when you got orders for here, you can forget them. It seems that the Emperor, a young boy, likely a teenager, has just commissioned me Imperial Admiral of the First Order of Steel in the Imperial Iteeche Navy and given me command of the entire Iteeche Combined Battle Fleet. As you no doubt noticed on the voyage out here, there's a civil war on. The Imperials are losing badly and I'm expected to change that."

The response from around the room was various. One or two officers shook their heads. Kris heard a murmur of "Longknifes. You can't trust 'em." Most, however, focused expectantly on her. A few looked like hungry tigers who'd just been tossed raw meat.

Kris went on. "Both sides are building identical battlecruisers as fast as they can. They've already had battles with a thousand battlecruisers on each side. Those fights ended with both sides damn near wiping each other out. Now, the Imperials try to avoid battle unless they have a clear superiority. If the weaker side can't run away, they surrender. We need to figure out how to fight outnumbered three to one and win. I'm open to suggestions."

That said, Kris sat down. To deafening silence.

Twenty officers, all hopefully good, stared at each other. Others stared at the overhead.

"Admiral," the chief of staff finally said, breaking the hush.

"Yes, Titania," Kris said, turning to the woman.

"Did the Iteeche save any battle board records from these battles? Have they written up any after-action reports?"

"Nelly?" Kris said.

"Kris, you may have been given a rank and command, but I have not received a single jot of data from the Iteeche. Possibly some will be forthcoming, but I'm finding the Iteeche net difficult to negotiate."

"How so, Nelly?"

"The Iteeche have provided us with only one landline. It's voice only and goes only to your flag. We're picking up signal traffic from the planet down there, but I'm still trying to figure out how to crack it. I don't know if it's intentional or just alien, but we can't hack into their encryption protocols. We're working on it, but not there yet. Sorry, Kris. I would suggest you ask Ron, or that Admiral Coth who was so nice to you, for information."

"So, they want you to be their admiral, but they aren't so sure they want to trust you," a captain at the table observed slowly.

"Captain Kurt Amera?" Kris asked as Nelly provided the name.

"Operations, at your service," he answered.

"Okay, for now, let's assume some information will be forthcoming. What's your take on battlecruisers fighting battlecruisers?"

"I wish I had one, Admiral," Titania said. "No offense meant, ma'am, but we humans haven't been thinking much about warfare between battlecruisers. Most of our attention has been focused on battlecruisers fighting alien raiders, either those huge warships or the even bigger mother ships. We've spent a lot of time pouring over your after-action reports but ruminations about like-for-like combat have been relegated to late nights at the O Club."

"Those of us who bothered reading those reports," Kris's former flag skipper, now Commodore Ajax, muttered dryly, but not quite under her breath.

"Yes, so I've noticed," Kris said, not at all softly. "So, now we start."

That did not start an avalanche of ideas her way. She waited.

Finally, a throat got cleared and a commander spoke up. "Admiral, I'm your lowly F1. I handle personnel, staffing, and training. Since no one else wants to venture in, may I offer a thought?"

With all the captains and admirals at the table, it took guts for a commander, and the commander in charge of personnel no less, to venture into the silence. "Please do, Commander," Kris said.

"Commander Bill Gother, ma'am. In your position as Type Commander - Battlecruisers, you spent most of your time fighting budget battles for our big, shiny toys. When people think of power, they think of a dozen or a hundred battlecruisers in formation." He paused for a moment; clearly here was a fellow who found himself speaking truth to power and being both careful and courageous.

"However, when push comes to shove, it's the men and women crewing them that make the difference. I've read some of the early reports from Alwa. They showed the difference you got from two ships of the same class, but with different approaches to leadership and training. I couldn't help but notice that when you took command of this fleet, the first thing you did was initiate drills that showed you which ships needed to tighten up their lasers in their cradles, something that the crew's training had failed to tell them needed doing. You also began to train the crews to fight the battle you wanted, using hard evasion maneuvers."

"That is correct, Commander."

"So, what's the leadership status of the Iteeche fleet? This place calls itself an Empire. Are they promoted based on performance or connection? Do they drill their crews, or are the ships kept nice and pretty for inspection or Imperial Fleet Reviews? Is there a warrior culture or a 'go along to get along' attitude? If I was in your shoes, that's the first thing I'd be looking at, Admiral."

"And you got all that off the top of your head?" Kris asked.

The commander blushed. Captain Tosan stepped in. "Given half a chance, Bill will give you that argument any moment of the day or night," she said. "Sadly, there's never enough money in the budget for all the training he'd have us do."

"But I keep trying," Kris's F1 said, with a cheerful grin.

"Admiral," now it was Lieutenant Longknife who wanted to put a word in. "I don't know if there's a maintenance officer for the fleet, but the material condition of the ships has got to be just as important. Those battleships you shot up on your way to Greenfeld five years ago? They couldn't keep their lasers bore-sighted."

"Thank you, Lieutenant. Yes, if I'm to inherit a fleet, someone's going to have to conduct readiness inspections. We can talk more on these ad minutiae later. I'd like some ideas for how we fight three times as many just like us and win."

The commander sat back in his chair, doing his best not to let his frustration show. Kris knew that she'd rather cavalierly dismissed some very important advice. She'd have to come back to that later.

Ideas for a battlecruiser-on-battlecruiser battle did not come quickly. Most suggestions revolved around the traditional concepts of maneuver, speed, deception, and surprise. Most hadn't been found to work all that well in space. Still, Kris relaxed into her seat and watched eager, sharp minds gnaw at a problem that hadn't seemed very high on anybody's list of things to do today.

After a long series of failed options for battle arrays, it was clear that the only way to concentrate more firepower against one section of the line was to have ships that could outfight their opponents, and that brought them back to material and training.

"Okay," Kris finally said. "Better trained opponents make less mistakes than those less well-trained. Better maintained ships with well-trained crews get more hits than those that breakdown at a critical time."

Kris paused to let that thought simmer. "Also, we've never seen an Iteeche battlecruiser at more than two gees or jinking very much. I think I need to talk to Ron."

"Could it be that the Iteeche don't use high gee stations?" Jack asked.

"Apparently, it either wasn't in the designs we passed to them, or, culturally, they are anathema. Jacques, have you seen anything in the media about a warrior culture?"

"It's been glaring by its absence," the sociologist answered. "No war stories. No reference to the Human-Iteeche War. I've noted some stuff bleeped out of what we've intercepted. I think someone is exerting heavy self-censorship at the source."

"Keep us in the dark and feed us soap operas," Amanda said.

"It sure tastes like that," Jacques agreed.

"So," Kris said, "let's look at my options. If a rebel fleet tries to force its way into the capital system and I'm handed command of the defenses, I can fight the battle with what they've got, and lose, assuming half the fleet doesn't desert to the other side."

Jack made a face.

"I can try to retrain my fleet to present more elusive targets by jinking. We have no idea why the Iteeche don't jink, so we need to check in on that."

Kris waited for a response. She got none from her trusty advisors.

"The question is, if we assume the Iteeche have some reason not to use high gee stations, then what do we do next? Do I show the Iteeche how nifty our latest high gee stations are? Or do I limit what I give them, say to the kind of high gee stations we had back on the fast patrol boats ten years ago? They were good enough for three gees at most. Maybe less for an Iteeche."

"You mean, save a bit back so if we have to fight whoever takes the throne next, we might have a bit of an advantage?" Jack said.

"Are you thinking your allies may not always be your allies?" Jacques asked.

"I'm thinking that if I whisper two plus two is four where three or four Iteeche can hear it, that answer will be reported to the rebels before sunset."

"This place does seem to leak," Amanda said, "although the leakage is always from Iteeche to Iteeche, never to us. Not to step on your bitching session, Kris, but I've got no one and nothing on the Iteeche economy. Zip. This leaves me wondering how trade is going to go, but we've got to stay alive before we can let all those eager business types make their billions."

"So," Jack said, "What do we do next?"

"I need to find out how an Iteeche fleet of battlecruisers operates."

"You're not planning on going aboard an Iteeche battlecruiser," Jack said, warily. "Are you?"

"That would be a really dumb idea," Kris answered with a grin for her husband and security chief.

"Ya think?" Jack muttered softly.

"Nelly, get in contact with Ron. Tell him I'd like to take some Iteeche battlecruisers out to exercise with my task fleet. Does he have any ships that can exercise with mine?"

"Kris, Ron says that he can take command of one of his Chooser's battle cruiser flotillas. There are also three other flotillas available on one-hour notice."

Kris raised an eyebrow at Titania. "Can we get away from the pier in an hour?"

"Damned if we'll let the Iteeche Navy do better than us, Admiral."

"We sail in an hour. Pardon me, Captain," Kris said to her chief of staff. "I'd very much like to have you and the rest of the staff join me on the *Princess Royal*. I know there isn't enough time to move all your gear, but I'd like to have you close at hand when we're watching how the Iteeche do in this exercise."

"Aye, aye, ma'am," Titania said. "Okay, crew, let's get the orders issued and our asses moving."

Suddenly the room was empty of Navy staff, leaving Kris with just her familiar civilians, along with Jack and Megan.

"Well, let's go see what kind of hornet nests we can knock over next."

"There were a whole lot of business types filling up the *Princess Royal's* Forward Lounge when we left," Jacques said. "I don't think they got the word that you'd gone to the *Bold* rather than the flag."

"Nelly, advise Captain Klum that I won't be meeting with the diplomats or business people until later. Much later. Advise the clientele of the Forward Lounge that unless they've always wanted to see what it's like on a battlecruiser at 3.5 gees, they need to go ashore for their next drink. I'll call them back later."

Kris ate a quick lunch in the wardroom, then moseyed over to the *P. Royal*. Her timing was impeccable. They were not accosted by a single civilian on their walk between flagships.

Kris studied the recent attack on her as she sat in her own wardroom on the *Princess Royal*, waiting for her key staff to arrive. Captain Klum, her flag captain, knocked on the open door. "Enter," Kris said.

With a soft groan, he settled into the chair beside Kris. Immediately, it converted into a massage chair and began working on his back.

"Tough day?" Kris asked.

"I can't say that I haven't seen worse." he admitted.

"How'd the *Sweet P* do under laser fire?" Kris asked, curious about the new crystal armor and 24-inch lasers.

"It was hot. She still is hot. She'll be a while cooling down," the skipper said, briskly rubbing the crown of his head with both hands. "I notice there are no reports about ice actually being used successfully under the crystal armor."

"I tried to get tests done, but got nowhere," Kris admitted. "No doubt Alwa may know more than we do, but things still haven't quieted down enough for them to have the spare time needed to fill out the paperwork. What can you tell me?"

"We've got bots out, checking the armor, shining lasers in to see if the crystal still works. We got sections that were hit pretty hard. Thank God, we had the hull rotating as fast as we did. Still, the 24-inch lasers overloaded two to three-meter strips along our hide. Some of the crystal held. Some failed. We've got nanos cruising through the honeycomb under the armor. We have strips that were heated beyond the specs. We're rolling up tons of failed Smart Metal and drawing it out of the matrix."

"Do we need a yard period?" Kris asked, knowing she'd have to refuse the request to dock her flagship in an Iteeche shipyard.

"Your smart computers have been working with my damage control and maintenance crew."

"Nelly?" Kris asked.

"We've isolated the failed crystal and are sorting it out of the crystal cladding," her computer informed them. "I have given them schematics of the gadgets that Alwa's Canopus Station used to apply the crystal armor to our ships. That should work when it comes to cutting out the failed armor. We can program the crystal around it. The broken crystal will just be shunted to the stern and removed when we have it all together. Of the failed Smart Metal, the problem is known and can be handled per our usual devices."

"How much of the *P. Royal* will be uncovered by crystal armor?" Kris asked, eyeing the skipper.

"Possibly, none."

"None?"

"The *P. Royal* has always been a bit heavy, what with your flag quarters, Forward Lounge, Marine quarters, and all. If we drain out the failed Smart Metal, we're going to lose about a thousand tons of the ten thousand extra tons we've been carrying around. I don't know for sure yet, but our estimates are that we'll still be covered when we're done."

The skipper eyed Kris, with a small, tight smile. "Of course, we may have to tighten up your quarters a bit."

"And I just invited the ComBatCru staff to join us."

The *Sweet P's* captain groaned softly.

"Maybe I can offload some Marines or ship some boffins to another ship," Kris offered.

"That would be appreciated."

Jack and Meg arrived. Captain Klum stood and took his leave. He had to stand aside to let Jacques and Amanda enter the wardroom. The two civilians had observed the brief battle, but had no report they needed to generate. Admirals Ajax and Afon arrived right after the others with a few of their key staff officers.

Right on the dot, Titania led the staff in to join them. Each came with anywhere from several to an armful of readers. Kris would have to make sure the conversation didn't get too granular.

Once everyone was seated, Kris said, "Nelly, could you raise Ron for me? I have a few questions."

The main screen quickly filled with a picture of Ron. "Your Highness, how may I be of service to you?"

"This is Imperial Admiral of the First Order of Steel business, Ron."

"Yes, my Imperial Colleague," Ron said. That told Kris something about the Iteeche she called Ron. If he could greet her as a colleague while she was the highest-ranking admiral in the Navy, that either said a lot about his role as Counselor to the Emperor, or a lot about where the Navy stood in the pecking order.

Kris schooled her face carefully to show nothing, but down the table a bit, Jacques turned to his wife and raised an eyebrow that also just happened to be cocked Kris's way.

More minefields to cross.

Kris cleared her throat. "I am curious about this recent unpleasant development. You said that the Imperium had battlecruiser flotillas ready to sortie in an hour. Were there only these three?"

"Yes, I'm very much interested in that. My Wise and Eminent Chooser has sent soldiers from his own guard as well as Imperial troopers to see that certain people do not leave their offices and certain records are not lost."

"I'm grateful for that. Now, who chose the flotillas?"

"There were eight flotillas on one-hour notice. Three were chosen by Command, Imperial Presence Protection Fleets. Two reported unable to sail at full strength, and two others were chosen."

"The two that shot at me?"

"No. One of the attacking flotillas was in the first alert. The second attacking flotilla was in the second choosing."

"And while someone likely wanted all three to shoot at us," Jack muttered loudly, "they figured two was good enough and having someone else fall out would look suspicious."

"No doubt," Ron said, dryly. "My Wise and Eminent Chooser will have many Navy officers to talk with."

This left Kris to wonder how much physical torture would be involved in those "talks." It was time to change the topic.

"Ron, when we circumnavigated the galaxy, you saw us

in high gee stations. I saw you suspended in a water tank. I don't imagine you can fight a ship from a water tank. How do your crews manage high gees and radical maneuvering on a warship?"

"The way warriors always have," Ron said, his eyes blinking surprisingly rapidly. "You stand and you fight."

"You do know that it's easier to survive high gees if you lay down, don't you?" Jack pointed out.

"Maybe it is for you weak humans, but we Iteeche are strong enough to stand and fight." did not leave much room for discussion.

"Ron, I took my fleet to 3.5 gees to escape the fire from those two flotillas."

"Yes," Ron said.

"I also went to Evasion Plan 6. None of your ships were able to manage anything close to Evasion Plan 1. Ron, do you see the problem?"

"What I see is that your battlecruisers survived a surprise attack because your crystal armor bought you the few moments you needed to react. Moments my ships would not have had if we had been attacked."

"Ron, you know I can't give you crystal armor. You also know that high gee acceleration and hard evasions are at least most of the reason I win battles."

Ron did not fire back a response at Kris, but paused to take three slow breaths. "Yes, I know how you have won battles. If I look only at the human part of my training, I see your point. However, I *am* an Iteeche. We have a long and proud heritage. You can *not* ask us to throw that all away."

"If you don't throw that away, you will lose this civil war, Ron," Kris said, softly.

"You may be right. I may also be right that there are a lot

officers in the Imperial Navy that would rather lose a war than lose their souls."

Kris had nothing more she could say at the moment. Apparently, neither did Ron. After a long moment of silence, the Iteeche rang off and Kris looked around at her staff.

"We have a problem," she said.

They sat down to concentrate on that problem.

"How do you solve a problem that doesn't want to be solved?" Jack asked no one in particular.

"It appears," Jacques said slowly, "that our tactical problems are deeply rooted in culture. They would rather lose a war than lose their self-image as mighty, upstanding warriors."

"Don't that beat all hell," Titania muttered.

"So, our little fleet exercise taught us several things," Kris said, and raised one finger. "Their lasers are loose in their cradles. If they weren't, the *Princess Royal* would be a thin ball of hot gases. Thank God for that. Secondary question, do we want to let the Iteeche know that they can get a lot more accuracy out of their lasers by tightening them down?"

"Right now, no," Jack said.

"I agree," Kris said, then raised a second finger. "Second, they can't or won't go to high gees and strong evasion because it isn't manly enough for them. If great-grampa stood *his* watch, I am dang well going to stand *my* watch."

"That's a much tougher one to handle," Jacques said. "Culture runs deep into flesh and bone. To change that is going to be hard."

"I thought victory ran deep in the flesh and blood of war fighters?" Titania asked.

"Military organizations throughout history have struggled with their purpose," Jacques said, attempting an answer. "A good war tends to remind people that if you fight smart, you get to live. You fight dumb, you end up dead. However, in peacetime, the focus can wobble off the target. Do we need to fight, or pass the next readiness inspection? Do I do what will save my life in a fight, or advance my career in peace time? They're supposed to be one and the same, but the further you get away from a real, hot shoot out, the more vague and unhinged the purpose of the uniform is."

The sound of the landing lines hauling the *Princess Royal* into her pier on the station told everyone at the table that their time alone was coming to an end. If there was any doubt, Nelly spoke before anyone else could.

"Kris, there is a problem on the station. You are wanted ashore."

"Who wants me?"

"Ron. He says if you don't come quickly, two of your merchants are going to be short of their heads in a few minutes."

Kris grabbed her cover and headed for the quarterdeck, Jack, and Megan right behind her.

"We need a Marine detachment, squad to start with, platoon ASAP," Jack snapped into his commlink.

4

A young, grim-faced Marine sergeant greeted Kris at the foot of the brow. He held open the door to the *Princess Royal's* station car. On the back steps of the car, a Marine with rifle ready studied the surroundings.

Nelly said, "Admiral, your presence is required at the head of the pier."

As soon as Jack was beside her, and Megan beside the driver, Kris ordered, "Driver, let's see how fast this scooter can go."

The sergeant swung himself up on the back step, then tapped the top of the rig, joining the guard on high alert. The station car zipped silently away from the gangplank of Kris's flag only to drive itself into one of the elevators that had been used by Ron's Chooser earlier. This elevator was not a freight one. It lifted the car and its occupants smoothly and quickly up to the main dock. The door opened, and they took off down the pier.

At the guard post that restricted all traffic to her ships, there now was a crowd. The car slowed to a stop on the edge of it, and the sergeant dismounted to open Kris's door even before it came to rest.

Kris knew there was trouble the moment she spotted Abby and a large US Marine guard detail. They formed one of three groups that had formed up. The second had several armed guards in what Kris was coming to recognize as Imperial red and gold. Buried in the midst of them were two disheveled humans and three Iteeche civilians who looked like they'd been beat up pretty bad.

The third group centered around a formal looking Iteeche in shimmering robes much like Ron wore. He was likely an Imperial court officer. Behind him were six Iteeche in black with long poles with very big axe blades on the end. Off to the side were two scary looking Iteeche with snake jars.

This does not look good.

Kris dismounted the station car and marched for the mandarin. She stopped a comfortable distance from him and said, "I am Her Royal Highness, Kris Longknife, Grand Admiral of the US Navy and Imperial Admiral of the First Order of Steel of the Imperial Navy. NELLY, ADD ALL THE OTHER STUFF.

DONE KRIS.

"What is the meaning of this?" she demanded.

The Iteeche bureaucrat bowed low to Kris. Without rising, he said, "I have the honor of being . . ."

Nelly paused for a moment for him to go on, then just said, "He's some sort of honcho for this port. I think he's pretty high up from what he's saying and all the executioners he's traveling with."

When the honcho paused in his introduction, Kris answered his deep bow with a bow of her own . . . from the neck. Only then did he rise.

"And the matter at hand?" Kris asked.

"Involves these three Imperial subjects and two of your people who arranged to meet together to plot treason against the Imperium."

"We weren't doing any such thing," one of the humans snapped out. He was the better dressed of the two.

An Iteeche guard put an end to the interruption with a butt-strike to the businessman's gut. He keeled over, but even breathless and rolling on the deck, he managed to get out, "You going to let them treat a human like that?"

"You damn Longknife," might have been lost as his breath ran out.

"If it pleases you," Kris said to the mandarin, "I will have my Marines take possession of the human miscreants for proper punishment."

She was answered with another low bow. A gunny from Abby's detail peeled off four Marines to infiltrate the Iteeche ranks and extract Kris's problem children. The gunny helped the slow learner off the deck and whispered loud enough for Kris to hear, "Keep your damn trap shut, you hear, or one of my Marines won't be so gentle."

"You may see to yours, and we will see to ours," the Iteeche bureaucrat said, and with the barest twitch of his hand, the three Iteeche were dragged forward and shoved to their knees, heads out.

They were well apart from each other, and Kris quickly found out why.

Three of the axe men stepped forward, whirling their heavy pole axes as if they were baton twirlers at some county fair. Then, in one perfectly synchronized move, they brought their blades down.

Three Iteeche heads hit the deck as one, and bounced.

Both of the humans under Marine guard lost their lunches.

"Until we meet again," the Iteeche mandarin said, with a quick but low bow.

"Until we meet again," Kris said with a nod.

With as much Imperial and Royal gravitas as she could manage, Kris returned to her station car. They drove back to the *Princess Royal's* pier at a slow pace. Abby's Marine detail with its woebegone civilians fell into place behind her.

One glance back at the gate showed that three pikes had appeared beside it, one for each head that stared blank-eyed into the human pier.

Message sent and received.

ABBY, TELL THE BUSINESS COMMUNITY THAT THERE WILL BE AN ALL HANDS MEETING IN THE FORWARD LOUNGE IN THIRTY MINUTES. TELL THEM THEY WILL BE THERE EVEN IF THEY HAVE TO HAVE SOMEONE PUSH THEIR DEATH BEDS INTO THE BAR.

GOT YOU KRIS. WHAT DO I DO WITH YOUR TWO NEW BEST FRIENDS?

KEEP THEM CLOSE AND DON'T LET THEM CLEAN THEMSELVES UP. THEY ARE MY EXHIBIT A FOR WHAT HAPPENS TO YOU WHEN YOU VIOLATE MY RULES.

YOU BET, GIRL.

5

There was a lot of noise as Kris entered the Forward Lounge. Some of it was, no doubt, because Kris had closed the bar.

More of it was likely concerned with the two forlorn civilians who stood handcuffed with a Marine at each elbow. Abby held down the front table, now with Megan at her side. It was almost like old times.

"Atten 'hut, Admiral on deck," a gunny called. Those in uniform immediately came to attention. The civilians stood around, gawking.

"As you were," Kris said, and marched for the front table, Jack one step behind her.

Kris didn't join Abby at the table. Before she reached her and the prisoners, she whirled on the room full of idiot fortune seekers.

"What about 'Do Not Go There' don't you understand?" Kris demanded.

No one risked his neck by daring to offer her an answer.

"I told you that here, the Iteeche make the rules. Could I have been any clearer?"

As one, the room kind of shuffled its feet.

"Has anyone not seen the video of the Iteeche honcho executing their three tradesmen?"

In general, all in the lounge nodded they had.

"Good. Watch it again tonight before you go to bed. Watch it twice tomorrow before breakfast. Watch it. Memorize it. Because if I hadn't stepped in and taken these prisoners into my custody, their heads would have been bouncing on the deck with those three Iteeche.

"Traitors. That's what the Iteeche mandarin named them. Traitors. I don't know if you've heard, what with us only getting here after fighting our way through a rebel fleet, but there's a civil war on hereabouts. Civil war. You break the rules here, those who walk around with executioners armed with axes following them kind of assume that you're one of the rebels, not a nice one of us."

Kris paused to let that sink home. Before her was living proof that you could make a billion without learning the basic survival skills of life. She gave them all a long minute for this to maybe penetrate their thick skulls.

"I may not be close enough to save the neck of the next one to screw up. Hell, I may not *bother* to save the next one of you that screws up."

She gave the room a slow sweep with hard eyes. "There will be several ships going home in a few weeks. Any of you too dumb to live under Iteeche rules might want to book passage now. Dirtside, there's a palace that I understand I've inherited from an Iteeche lord who's gone rebel. If you want to try your hand at doing business the Iteeche way, I can book you a suite down there. Nelly can give you some pictures of your new home. You will note, there's only one way in and one way out. There will be Marines at the gate.

US Marines will keep you safe inside and Imperial Marines will keep you from going outside."

Another pause. The room met her silence with a deathly hush.

"Any questions?" Kris hardly paused before snapping, "Good. Have a nice day, stay out of trouble, and stay out of my sight."

With that she stomped out. She'd gotten about half-way to the door when the Earth ambassador stood up.

"Excuse me, Your Highness, but what do you intend to do with your, ah, prisoners? One is an honored citizen of the Society of Humanity."

Kris turned to face him. "Despite the Iteeche's clear desire that I should mount their heads on pikes at the foot of the *Princess Royal's* gangplank, I have decided to award them the pleasure of the *Princess Royal's* brig for now and a ticket on the next slow boat home. Is that sufficient for your representation?"

"I imagine that your brig's amenities might be quite luxurious, but would you be so kind as to release him into my custody?"

Kris had no idea where this was going. NELLY?

IT WOULD SEEM THAT OUR PRISONER IS THE SON OF A MAJOR INDUSTRIAL MAGNATE ON COLUMBIA. I BELIEVE HE AND THE EARTH AMBASSADOR ARE RELATED BY MARRIAGE.

SO IT'S A GOOD THING I DIDN'T LET THE ITEECHE TAKE HIS HEAD.

LIKELY, YES, KRIS.

"Sorry, Mr. Ambassador, but I think I'll keep this one close. No telling what he might get into next time or what his chances would be if I didn't come by when I did. Better for both our careers and his neck that he stays put. I assure you, my Marines will see that he does just that."

The Earth ambassador allowed Kris a slight bow, from the neck. "No doubt, we will have opportunities to revisit this in the future."

"No doubt you will," Kris said, holding on to her temper with her fingernails. "Now, if you'll excuse me, I have the details to finish for removing our embassy from here to a palace."

And I've had a bad day that can't get any worse, Kris did not add.

Which was good, because the Earth ambassador proceeded to do just that.

"Ah, yes, about the space in the palace. You will, no doubt, seek input from all the sub-embassies and major business magnates in arranging our space?"

6

Thus, the rest of Kris's no good, very bad day was gobbled up by squabbling over square centimeters and windows.

The meeting in the Forward Lounge immediately changed gears as soon as the two prisoners were marched out by the Marines. Kris quickly found herself facing four different factions: one centered around the Earth Ambassador, one from the US with one of her Grampa Al's hatchet men, in this case a woman, ramrodding it. The Helvetican Confederacy had formed a bloc with several other major economic and industrial planets. Last, but not least, many of the minor planets and small groups had formed an association with Musashi. Kris suspected her good friend Ambassador Tsusumu Kawaguchi may have taken the lead on this.

Strange that Musashi hadn't moved to join the Helvetican Confederacy. Despite the large power base that Yamato and Musashi represented in and of themselves, many of the smaller planets seemed content to let Musashi break the ice for them.

Kris wondered how this would work out in the long run, but she'd leave that problem to Kawaguchi.

At the moment, all four of the groups were clamoring for one half of the palace space and all of the top floors.

"How did this horse get out of the barn?" Kris asked Abby.

"Ask your computer," the former maid, now CEO of Kris's support effort, drawled.

"Nelly?" Kris said, walking away from the blare of demands, and doing her best to ignore them. She didn't quite order the Marines to keep the animals in order, but it was a close call.

"When Ron pointed out the Pink Coral Palace on our way back to the beanstalk, I passed that information along to Mata Hari, my daughter, and she put it out on the net, so as to give the interested parties something to occupy them. I may not have had as good a grasp on the human condition as I thought I did."

Kris was careful to keep her thoughts very much to herself. Nelly didn't foul up very often, but when she did . . .

Mata Hari, being a computer, had quickly estimated the volume of the Pink Coral Palace from the orbital imagery, then, based on the per capita of each delegation, she'd advised each of their approximate space. It was only after she had finished that the four factions announced themselves and demanded those in them be in adjacent spaces. Only moments after Mata had reported her estimate, the four were hollering for more space.

Kris shook her head. All of this yapping was coming because of a rough estimate.

"Let's find out how much space we actually have in the palace," Kris said. "Nelly, get me Ron."

"Yes, Your Highness," came only a moment later.

"Ron, how do I get my hands on the building specs and floor layout of the Pink Coral Palace?"

"You want the floor layout of the palace?" Ron asked, sounding rather incredulous for an Iteeche.

"Yes," was Kris's quick answer.

"Kris, this is a palace. A palace of a great clan. You are treating it as if it was some merchant's warehouse."

"Excuse me?" Kris said.

"Kris, the Pink Coral Palace was the sovereign and private possession of a great clan. I would no more ask them about the floor plan of their palace any more than I would ask them about the size of their spawning pools. Why would you even ask such a thing?"

"The people who came with me desire that information," Kris began.

"Those traders," Ron spat.

"Yes, the business associates want to lay out their space and all we've got is the map of the city and orbital imagery of the palace."

"You have a map of the city?" came cautiously from Ron.

"Yes, we mapped the planet on our approach. We map every new planet as we approach it."

"Kris, a map of the Imperial planet is forbidden to anyone but the Most High."

"Doesn't that count me?"

"Of course it does, Kris, but these gnats deserve no such access. Kris, you are an Imperial Admiral of the highest order. You must defend our secrets as well as the Imperium."

Kris knew what it was like to take that next step and find it wasn't there. She'd done it enough times. "Pardon me, Ron. This was nowhere in my brief about how I should conduct myself."

"Would you let these traders have a map to your Royal planet?"

"Ron, traders like these people *make* the maps to our planet and sell them to anyone who wants one."

"Anyone?"

"Ron, traveling the back country of Wardhaven has given me some of the most pleasant memories of my youth. And, of course, I used a map produced by merchants."

"Once again, you are proving how alien you are," Ron said.

Kris could say the same thing, only didn't. She needed to solve this, or it would eat up her entire day. "Ron, thank you for educating this poor alien. If you can think of anything else I should know before I get it wrong, please advise Nelly at your convenience."

Ron punched off.

Which left Kris still trying to solve this conflict of excessive expectations by bloated egos. It was clear to Kris that this was a time sink which would never end. Kris interrupted a debate on how much extra space the Earth delegation deserved because of some arcane logic.

"Let's end this meeting quickly. I propose that each of you get one side of the Rose Palace. There are four of you and four sides of equal volume and luxury."

"But the south side has the gate in it," the Earth ambassador was quick to point out. "It's bound to have less space."

"Good point," Kris said, quickly admitting a point she did not want to debate. "Which do you want to do, toss dice or pull cards to decide who picks first and who is left for last?"

Even that decision took five minutes.

I am getting out of this mess.

They chose cards. Kris ordered Nelly to manufacture a deck in plain sight of them all.

So, the four representatives went through the deck card by card and agreed there were fifty-two of them and aces would beat kings.

It was agreed that Earth might draw first, so Kris watched as the Earth ambassador drew the two of clubs. Kris couldn't think of a better delegation to get the gate side. They were the smallest of the four.

It was only after the fourth card was drawn and the four sides divided up that Ambassador Kawaguchi observed, "There are four sides and four of us, but Your Royal Highness, you and yours certainly make up a fifth side. Where will you find space for your people?"

"I'll find someplace," Kris assured them, and marched from the Forward Lounge to leave the rest of them to squabble and bicker over who got what.

Jack, Abby, and Megan caught up with Kris at the door.

"I'm glad to be quit of them," Abby said, "but I can tell you I'm not looking forward to bunking in whatever space Al's hatchet gal leaves for me. Better to be homeless in Iteeche country than bed down with that bunch of bugs."

"Don't worry, Abby, I've got an ace up my sleeve."

Once they had adjourned to Kris' day quarters and ordered up something for a very late lunch, Kris said. "Nelly, give us a holograph of what we know about the palace."

The conference table they sat around immediately turned into a rough representation of their future abode based upon what Nelly had caught as they drove by and what their orbital imagery had provided. The bottom three floors facing the streets had no windows. The same could be said for the first floor facing the inner courtyard of ponds and flowerbeds. Only on the second floor were there even the narrow windows that faced the street from the upper levels.

On the fourth floor, matters improved. Wide, covered patios let in the light and air from the courtyard. This was repeated up to the roof of the seventh floor. Here, a handful of luxurious penthouses dotted the gardened roof, complete with ponds and shade trees. Along the wall, there were clear paths for guards to walk between the towers where more alert guards had stood ready, no doubt, until they fled with their masters.

"So, Kris," Jack said, "Just how do you intend to shoehorn us, the kids, and the rest of your mission into what you haven't given away?"

"Easy. Nelly, I want you to design us a central castle of Smart Metal. Keep the footprint light. I don't want to do away with the lovely waterfall in the center of the garden. I'd love something ethereal and frothy, soaring, and pleasing to the eye, yet a bit intimidating. Do you follow my meaning?"

"How about this?" Nelly said, and a swirl of gleaming metal began to climb up from the garden, using four supports based at the corners of the garden. The four buttresses swept high before joining into a central body, much like the fins on an old-fashioned tail-sitting rocket ship. The main body showed a gentle twist to it, with plenty of balconies and wide picture windows.

From each leg, banks of glass elevator cars swept upwards, giving easy access, although Kris doubted any human would succeed in scaling those heights on their own. Everything ended at a top with four small turrets jutting even higher.

"Wow," Abby and Megan said, mouths dropping open.

"Neat," Jack said, with much more jaundice in his voice. "How you gonna do it?"

"Nelly, the *Princess Royal* still has that extra tonnage of Smart Metal that was donated to me back when she commissioned, right?"

"After repairs, there are still nine thousand tons, Kris. How do you think they're managing to give you that huge Forward Lounge or a layout like this?"

"Of course. I want you to unspool three or four thousand tons of Smart Metal from this battlecruiser."

Jack almost yelped.

"Why not? If we offload your Marines, the zoo following me and all the other extra junk, the *P. Royal* might actually look like a fighting ship. Also, if we're headed into another fight, do you really want her all bloated?"

Jack just gave Kris the eye. The look he always did when he might be looking at locking her in her quarters to keep her from doing something really stupid. Longknife stupid.

Then he shook his head. "You really might have a point."

For a long minute, they studied Nelly's concoction. "Damn tough to scale this puppy from the outside. An airborne landing force might be able to assault through the balconies."

"Not past the lasers in the four highest towers," Nelly answered. "Oh, and we can put anti-air lasers on the eight lower towers."

"Can we resist a siege?" Jack asked.

"For now, we're on city power and water," Nelly admitted. "However, Kris, all three of your Grampa Al's ships are made of Smart Metal. They've got two reactors each. If you applied Eminent Domain to one of them and let me have the metal and power from it, I could turn this into a real fortress and a fantastic palace. The four thousand tons from the *P. Royal* would be just enough for me to sketch an outline of your inner sanctum."

"That would certainly make me popular with my scrooge of a grampa," Kris said, not suppressing a grin.

"He is going to love you," Jack chuckled.

While Kris made further plans, Nelly put on screen the process of removing four thousand tons of Smart Metal™ from *Princess Royal.* The method used was intriguing. The raw metal was spooled out onto the quarterdeck where it was formed into large station trucks and trailers of about five tons. They would drive themselves to the space elevator where they were parked in the huge cargo decks. During the drop down the bean stalk, they would be reprogrammed into larger fifty-ton trucks that would rumble to the Pink Coral Palace and just manage to drive through the gate and into the palace's courtyard.

General Bruce and his computer, Chesty, would be there, waiting for them with Nelly's plans for their new castle. They'd park a truck in each corner of the palace and begin spinning out the risers and cross-supports while nanos dug pilings down to bedrock to support and anchor the entire thing.

Work on the design and logistics progressed amazingly fast.

It was then time to let the local Nuu Enterprise reps know that Grampa Al was about to have his *Glory of Free Enterprise* sacrificed on Kris's need for an imposing palace and a few battalions of main battle tanks and other ground fighting vehicles.

7

It only took a quick call from Lieutenant Longknife to get Admiral Longknife an invitation to supper with Dani Ishmay, the merchant prince her grandpa Al had stuck her with. He was a round gray man, and far too jovial as he greeted Kris at the gangplank of the *Glory of Free Enterprise.* He started talking there and didn't stop talking about his delight at swinging everything just the way he wanted it for the US quarter of the Pink Coral Palace.

"This will work so smooth. So very smooth."

When he finally paused for a moment while they were being seated, the Captain of the *Enterprise* jumped in. He wanted Kris to know they were being served tonight on a real linen tablecloth with real porcelain plates and real silver flatware. "None of that mushy Smart Metal stuff."

"But your ship is made out of Smart Metal, isn't it?" Kris said, tasting the soup. "This is very good chowder by the way."

"I'll tell my cook, Your Highness. And yes, the *Enterprise* is solid Smart Metal as far as the hull and fittings go. It makes for very fast loading and unloading. We should be unloaded by early tomorrow. How soon do you think we can get a cargo?" the merchant skipper asked Ishmay.

"Her Highness can answer your question better than I. But Kris, was it really necessary to run that poor man through all the humiliation of standing him up in front of all his business associates? I know he was trying to steal a march on the rest of us, but he was caught. He should be fined, not humiliated."

"He was almost dead," Kris pointed out, pausing with a spoon of chowder just short of her mouth. "He failed to get the message last time. I wanted everyone else to have a second chance to get the meaning of our situation. The next person may be a lot more than just humiliated."

"The Iteeche wouldn't dare."

Kris put her spoon down. She was no longer hungry, and it wasn't the food. She really didn't like the company. "Not only would the Iteeche dare, but it might not be just an official that slits someone's throat. I almost lost my head yesterday when players in the ongoing civil war, or maybe it was just the varsity game of palace intrigue, nearly caused me to be late enough to require a most sincere apology to the Emperor for my tardiness. One that would have been made at the end of one of those axes you may have noticed the executioners love to show off while using."

"They couldn't do that to you. You're the King's great-granddaughter. That would start a war."

"Yes, it might. One I'd hate to miss. But it's one that some people around here wouldn't mind getting started. You aren't being kept safe and secure in the Pink Coral Palace because we want to interfere with your deal making. It's to keep you out of the local population's crossfire. Speaking of crossfire Captain, I'm requisitioning your ship."

"What?" was a blend of shock, dismay, and resistance all rolled into one word.

"I need more anti-aircraft lasers on the roof of my palace. I need a medium-sized fleet of tanks and armored transport. I need my own power supply to keep the palace going if we get cut off from the outside. I need a lot of stuff, and I figure your 75,000 tons of Smart Metal and reactors are just the place to go for it."

"You can't!" was an apoplectic shout from the merchant skipper.

"But I can. Check the agreement you signed when you joined this expedition. In unforeseen circumstances, I may bring all present under the Uniform Code of Military Justice, and I can take possession of anything I need for the security of the mission. In case you haven't noticed, we just sailed into a civil war."

"But I'm told," Mr. Ishmay said, softly, "that there were rumors of a potential civil war before we left."

"Nobody told me. From where I sit, it's unforeseen."

"But what was in those secret instructions I was told you were carrying?"

"Secret instructions?"

"You know, the credentials that were sealed in that fine wooden box. What did they say?"

"That I'm the ambassador to the Iteeche Empire," Kris said, doing her best not to add anything else.

"I hear that you were also appointed an admiral in the Iteeche Navy to fight for the Emperor in this war of theirs."

How news travels; it was worse than a game of gossip.

"Captain, I have made myself plain. Unload your ship, then evacuate it."

"And if I quit unloading it?"

"Then I'll send programming experts, with Lieutenant

Longknife and Lily, one of Nelly's kids, over here to unlock the codes on your Smart Metal and have it spinning itself into a glider as your cargo floats off to wherever it wants to go." It was always fun to rub Grampa Al's nose in the fact that Kris had Nelly and her kids and he did not.

Both the merchant prince and the merchant captain were speechless. "People would die!" Mr. Ishmay finally got out.

"I'm sure they'd get off quickly enough once the walls started closing in. Have you ever wondered what a merchant ship would look like at Condition Zed?" Kris knew her smile was way too evil, but she was starting to enjoy this.

"I must protest!" Mr. Ishmay shouted. "I'll take this directly to Alexander Longknife himself."

"Please do. I can't think of anything I'd rather do than talk about this to him over next Thanksgiving Day's turkey. Assuming he risks his ass out of his Tower of Insecurity long enough to come to a family get-together. Now, thank you. We are done here. I'm told the stripping of Smart Metal from *P. Royal* will be completed during midwatch tonight. We'll start on the *Pride* first thing tomorrow morning. Does 0800 suit you?"

Kris quickly left that uproar behind her. They seemed to be gathering force rather than working themselves down.

"God help us," Jack muttered under his breath as they made their way down the gangplank.

"I don't think there's any god foolish enough to get between two bickering Longknifes," Megan said, "Or so my old Aunt Lily used to insist."

8

Next morning, Kris breakfasted in the *Princess Royal's* wardroom surrounded by her kids and several more. All were beyond enthusiasm for moving into a "real Iteeche palace."

Kris's explanation to them that they'd be living in a Smart Metal™ castle inside the palace brought groans of disappointment.

"It'll be just like the ship," little Ruth grumbled. "Will we have to wear these red ship suits, too?"

"I don't know," her father said, "I kind of like them. They make it easy to spot who's getting into trouble, princess."

"Faa-ther," seemed kind of early for a six-year-old, but she had it tuned perfectly to thirteen.

Kris headed for the beanstalk and found herself sharing the VIP lounge with Dani Ishmay.

"I notice that there were no thieves hanging out on the pier when I left the *Pride of Free Enterprise* this morning."

"No," Kris admitted. "I am told that your unloading will be finished by noon today, so I delayed matters."

"That computer of yours has her nose in too many people's business."

"I'll take that as a compliment," Nelly said, from Kris's collar bone.

"It's not," Ishmay grumbled back.

Kris chose to change the subject. "So, how is space management going for your quarter of the Pink Coral Palace?"

"Great. Just great. Your general used nanos to map the palace. Now we have a real floor plan. Everyone has just about as much space as they need," he crowed, then proved it by having his computer generate a holograph. He was grinning from ear to ear as he walked her through his palatial quarters and similar facilities for almost all of the merchant princes in his orbit. The windowless lower quarters were left for essential support personnel, their equipment, and the like.

"How many restaurants will you have? I don't see them in the schematic."

"Restaurants?"

"Yes. People need to eat. Oh, and stores. Folks need to buy stuff. And child care. I noticed that your partners have quite a few children in tow."

"You're going to provide all that," Dani Ishmay said, his words forceful but quickly leaking their vigor.

"Sorry, I've got enough for my staff. I had Abby make sure to bring enough service facilities for all of those who signed on, but you'll have to find space for those support services."

"Restaurants?"

"They'll likely want a view."

"No doubt my penthouse view," sounded like it had a bit

of history behind it. Just how much trouble did he have arranging to have the penthouse all to himself?

"We also have theater and other entertainment facilities. They'll take up more space."

"I'm really starting to hate you Longknifes."

"I don't know why." Kris said, lightly, and turned away. The guy needed some space to rework his attitude without a Longknife's throat within easy reach.

As Kris expected, she had hardly walked five paces from her space elevator ferry when, who should she spy, but Ron and his entourage making their way toward her.

"I told you, Kris. There are advantages to him accessing our net."

"Yes, Nelly."

"I see that you are placing your own illustrative mark on the Pink Coral Palace." Ron said as he fell in beside Kris. Mr. Ishmay tried to insert himself into their little group, but a black-clad axe man most gracefully elbowed him aside. When the businessman made to voice his dismay, a glance and a hiss from a red-clad snake bearer stopped him in his tracks.

"Really, Your Highness, your tradesmen must learn their place. I understand we had to force apologies from three of our own money grubbers. I am told that you don't have the two humans' heads on spikes before your flagship."

"Ron, you know we don't like messy stuff that attracts flies. As is our custom, I have them locked away and will return them to Wardhaven on the next ship."

"You humans are far too easy on dust mites."

"Be that as it may be, I can't believe that you met me fresh from the ferry to banter about such a minor thing."

"No. My Eminent Chooser asked me to inquire just what you have in mind. How tall do you plan to make this addition to your palace?" Ron coughed softly. "It is rather close to the Imperial Palace."

"I did not plan on going any higher than the buildings around us. Is that a problem?"

Ron took his time before he answered her. "It has always been a matter of pride that palaces are low affairs, spread over much land. High rises are the places for the plebeians among us. Do you wish to humble yourself?"

DIDN'T SEE THAT ONE COMING, KRIS.

ME NEITHER, NELLY. GIVE ME A SECOND.

Kris thought fast. Clearly, in her effort to accommodate the merchant princes who the Iteeche considered dust mites, she'd walked into a major cultural minefield. She'd have to put a particularly human twist on her answer, one that her children would doubtlessly complain about loudly.

"Ron, you know that we humans are a space faring people. I've spent most of my adult life in space," except for some damnable staff duty. "My castle is a very human artifact, especially when you consider how much it looks like a space ship."

Ron eyed her sideways, with all four eyes. "Space ship, huh?"

"Mad human castle and space ship."

"Lords of the Land and Deep, I hope you don't start an architectural fad among the clans."

"Why would Iteeche Choosers choose to imitate us little humans?" Kris said, with a grin.

"You are dangerous, Kris Longknife. Everyone I talk to tells me that you humans are dangerous. Sadly, they have no idea just how dangerous you are."

Kris was saved from having to form a response because they had arrived at the curb outside the ferry station. There, three black vehicles awaited them. One limo-like vehicle sported eight wheels. There were also two large, black gun trucks.

"I came more prepared today," Ron said, offering Kris a ride with the wave of both his right arms.

"I came prepared today, as well," Kris said, and glanced past Ron's three rigs. Nine eight-wheeled vehicles in bright Marine red and gold made their way through traffic. Four of the rigs mounted large caliber weapons in turrets that moved back and forth, sweeping the surrounding streets and buildings. Four more had twin mounts. The seven-barrel Gatling gun in one turret looked menacing enough. The other turret's automatic grenade launcher only hinted at its deadliness.

The final vehicle looked like a simple limousine. There was no need to announce to all comers that its Smart Metal programming would quickly turn it into a gun truck if the need arose.

The tires on all nine vehicles showed that they rolled heavy with armor.

"It appears that you have," Ron admitted.

"There are more waiting outside the station, Ron," Kris pointed out. "Tell those who talk to you that the next time someone tries to take a nip out of my ass, they had better come prepared for war."

"I shall warn them as such."

"Now, Ron, would you care to visit me and take the measure of what a Longknife castle presents to the world?"

"I think I'd better."

Ron boarded his own limo. There was a bit of juggling around, and by the time the cavalcade pulled away from the station, his two gun trucks had taken over the lead and trailing slots. Kris had her Marine driver pull in behind Ron.

"Nelly, have some fun."

"I'm having lots of fun, Kris. What more do you want?"

"Doesn't this limo seem a bit plain?"

"Oh, that kind of fun!" Nelly said, and Kris's ride began to change around her. Somewhere in Nelly's busting innards must have been several records of lavish ways potentates got around. Kris found her seat rising until she was a good five meters up, traveling in a transparent bubble. Her driver now rode two meters below her, with his own full bubble. The four pairs of wheels were no longer in line with the vehicle frame. The two center ones on each side had reached out into the next lanes on either side over, giving Kris's ride extra stability, taking up three full highway lanes. The outer cover of her "Carriage of State" now showed as gold with jewel-encrusted banners dangling down the sides, as well as garish ornate workings wherever the royal banners weren't.

Kris rode, the mistress of all she surveyed, and from her seat she was surveying a lot.

On the sidewalk, a small Iteeche, one of four being towed on a rope line by an adult, waved enthusiastically. Kris waved back. Soon all four were waving and the adult Iteeche leading them was standing stock still, its beak hanging open.

The kids' delight in seeing an alien human was contagious. Along the route, Iteeche pedestrians stopped and stared. Some waved, a bit more timidly than the kids, but Kris smiled and waved back.

"Kris, what are you doing?" came on Net from Ron.

"Being majestic," was Kris's short reply.

"I know, but . . ." kind of sputtered out. Ahead of her, Kris could see Ron's head sticking out of his limo, staring back at her.

She gave him a friendly wave.

"Ron, your people travel around in sedan chairs and

platform pavilions carried by dozens of bearers. Hasn't anyone gotten themselves up in an overly ornamented touring car?"

Kris detected a distinct gulp from Ron's open mic. "We don't . . . I mean, we . . . ah. Kris, when we travel, it's for ourselves. The eyes of the last chosen matter nothing. What are you doing?"

"I am representing my King to your Emperor. Among my people, an emissary is not only to the court, but also to the people. I'm not only here to speak to your Emperor, but also to support my esteemed business people in establishing trade with the tradesmen you dismiss as dust mites. We find that business grows the wealth of a nation and allows our people to live more comfortable lives. You come from your perspective. I come from mine. When we meet in the middle, we will both be enriched."

"You humans are so dangerous. Kris, people who see you will talk. The Lords of the Sky and Deep only know what they will say among themselves."

"Hopefully, they will say nice things about me," Kris said, waving at a clump of adults who had pulled their small, three-wheeled vehicles to the side of the boulevard and all gotten out to get a better view of Kris's extravagant carriage and wave at her.

"But what will they say of us, the Eminent Choosers?"

"That is a thought," Kris said, and left that hanging there.

They were now in sight of the Pink Coral Palace. Rather, they were coming in sight of the spiraling shell of a castle that now soared high above the palace, although it did not exceed the height of the square high rises around it.

"Nelly, were you smoking something when you came up with this?"

"Me, smoke something? Of course not, Kris. But I was certainly enjoying showing off what I can do with Smart Metal when no one is holding me back."

From the looks of it, no one had held Nelly back.

Four legs rose from the four corners of the palace. They didn't meet until a good fifty meters above the central atrium with its gardens and ponds. Glass elevator cars climbed the legs until they disappeared into the bottom floor of a flamboyant structure.

The castle itself was three thick strands swirling around a central hub. It started narrow, then swelled, until it was bulging out some three hundred meters up. Every floor showed plenty of glass windows or wide glass doors that opened onto balconies, both small and large, that sparkled in the sun. As the castle began to narrow, it spun off towers that shot up or spun around in a delicate confection.

"Wow, Nelly. Just . . . wow," Kris said.

"I set the castle high on stilts with narrow lower floors, so it won't shade the gardens below, Kris. I've also set active reflectors on the balconies above to add to the light below. I'm looking at adding deflectors to the inner walls of the Pink Coral Palace to help with light redistribution. I don't want any glaring lights that might blind people."

"No, we don't want anybody complaining we blinded them," Jack drawled, no doubt already thinking of a long list of people who couldn't wait to voice their first complaint.

"The towers aren't just for the kids to climb up, Kris. I'll put active and passive radars in them, covering the space around the palace as soon as more Smart Metal arrives. I've also set up receivers for every frequency we've detected that the Iteeche use, and a few we think might be in use. We'll be able to record and study everything that's happening around us."

"Still," Kris muttered, "we don't know anything about what's really going on. Nelly, we really need to hack their network."

"No can do, Kris. We've got the secure fiber optic network in the Pink Coral Palace that the previous owner left behind. The problem is, they cut it off at the inner guard house. From the looks of it, they poured a solid concrete plug into the conduit. We can't get anything out of it."

Kris turned to Lieutenant Longknife, "That affinity you have to access networks that you mentioned a while back. Are you picking up anything from the Iteeche?"

"No, ma'am. I can't get anything from them but hash. However, I've never been able to rest my head against their net, either."

"Are you suggesting we knock Ron over the head?" Jack asked. "You want to put your head against his commlink?"

"No. What I'd like to do is get my forehead against that concrete plug. I may end up with one hummer of a headache, but it was Grampa Ray resting his head against a stone of the old alien computer from Santa Maria that started things off. I think it's at least worth a try."

Kris nodded, then said, "Let me see what I can do with Ron. I don't know. Maybe he'll give us access to the net. Maybe the plug was someone else's idea."

The look Jack tossed Kris was not encouraging.

"Just saying."

Kris's ego mobile had to shrink back down to its original size to drive through the double gates into the courtyard of the palace. It was a small parking lot, with little room for large armored vehicles. No sooner had one vehicle stopped and the crew climbed out, than it reduced itself to a nice cube of metal on wheels.

"That's one way to cut down on parking," Jack observed dryly.

Kris was more interested in the gates. Her Marines held one half of a double bastion gate; two curtain walls connected it across the moat to the second half occupied by Roth's borrowed guards. Each bastion had a turret on either side of the access road with fire ports pointing both out of and into the murder hole that would be created when the gate was slammed shut on anyone trying to force entry.

It was a decent defense, unless someone had a couple of rockets or a 200mm cannon. Then, maybe not so much.

It would, however, keep out a crowd of unarmed civilians. No doubt the spies or ninja assassins would come in by another route.

Once Kris's armored vehicles had finished converting themselves to blocks and rolled themselves into storage and the Marines had formed ranks and marched off, Kris turned to Ron.

"I've been meaning to ask you. You mentioned some battles the Imperials have had with the rebels. Can you provide me with after-action reports and the saved data from the survivors' battle boards?"

"Ah, I don't have any of that, Kris. I asked my Eminent Chooser for that sort of data, but he hasn't gotten back to me with it."

"How long ago did you ask?" Kris asked as gently as she could.

"Ah, I asked before I left the Empire to get you to come here."

"That long ago?"

If an Iteeche could hang his head, Ron looked ready to try.

Kris went on. "That admiral we met outside the Imperial

presence, Coth, Admiral of the First Order of Iron," Kris said as Nelly dredged up his name. "He said he'd like to help me. Do you think you could arrange a meeting with him?"

"Ah, yes, Admiral Coth. He has been ordered off-planet and I cannot find out when he will return."

Kris eyed Ron. She might have only half the number of eyes, but she was pretty sure the two she was using were giving Ron a mighty sharp look. "Do you detect a pattern here, old friend?"

Ron huffed out a breath. "A very clear pattern. You have been given command of our Battle Fleet and no one is giving you the support you need to do your job."

"Exactly, Ron. How insidious is this rebellion? Are people right here in the capital already turning coats?"

"Kris, it is not like that. Though, I admit, to an outsider like yourself it must very likely look like that."

Kris nodded agreement.

"You have to understand. In the capital, people live or die by politics. Families have memories that go back a thousand years or more. They remember which of their ancestors was forced to taste the cup of poison and who twisted the path to get them there. Or it may just be a long-remembered petty slight. Who was not invited or who was seated too low. It is a game I have not been trained to play. I was raised up to deal with you humans. You were hard enough to fathom. I could not play in both games and, just between you and me, I prefer you humans to the silly games my siblings play."

Kris did not like the sound of this. The bureaucratic infighting she'd endured for the last five years at Main Navy had been frustrating. It had not been deadly.

Now, Grampa Ray had sent her here for one thing, and the Emperor or some of his advisors were intent on using her to solve their rebel problem. The rebellion looked more like a symptom than the cause of the trouble. Kris suddenly felt like a Band-Aid that had been slapped on a gaping head wound.

She'd have to consider this later. It was time for Plan B and a change of topic. She nodded at her *aide de camp*, Lieutenant Longknife. The young officer answered with a nod of her own and slipped quietly away.

Now, to change the topic.

Kris led the way to where a tree-shaded pond was fed by a trickling waterfall. There were two stone chairs fit for Iteeche, and Kris offered Ron one of them. Rolling out from where the shrunken main battle tanks had gone into storage, a small block scooted toward Kris. Even as she watched, it converted itself into a stone bench, complete with cracks and moss. As it rolled up to behind Kris, the wheels melted into the stone and it froze in place.

She sat down without dusting her seat off.

"I can't get used to what your Nelly does with this Smart Metal," Ron said. "For us, it's a ship. For you, it is magic," he said, looking up at the castle that loomed over them.

"Nelly is having fun," Kris admitted.

"You bet I am. Wait until you see some of what I've already done in the castle. And I've got a whole lot more planned when the extra Smart Metal shows up. Kris, do you think they would mind if I dead-stick glided the *Pride of Free Enterprise* right into the garden of the Pink Coral Palace? That's the easiest and quickest way I can think of to get the reactors down here."

"Down, girl," Kris said, but, on second thought, what Nelly had just done was a good lead-in to what she wanted to talk about next.

"Ron, when you were with us on the old *Wasp* while we

were circumnavigating the galaxy, when we went to high gee acceleration, you and your team went into waterbeds."

"Yes, Kris, I know that you humans used those high gee stations. I don't know how you humans can stand to be confined in them."

So, it was not just the warrior spirit that wanted to stand, it was also the Iteeche not wanting to be confined.

Was the entire species claustrophobic?

"Ron, you know I ordered Evasion Plan 3 prior to that little live fire exercise that I didn't schedule."

"Was that what you were doing? It looked more like your ships had lost their minds and become unchoosable mad tadpoles."

"It's something we do to dodge out of the way of targeted lasers. I'm not at all sure the *Princess Royal* would have survived if we hadn't been jinking."

Ron just eyed her. She paused to breathe in the cool scent from the waterfall. This was not going well.

"Ron, don't you have any seats on your bridges? On your ships? Don't you have anything to help you sustain high gees and radical maneuvering?"

"Of course not, Kris. Iteeche warriors stand tall when we go into battle. Warriors don't sit when we fight."

"Wouldn't it be easier to sustain the high gees of acceleration if you were sitting down? Maybe even reclining in a chair?"

Ron looked at Kris like she was a particularly obnoxious bug that needed squashing.

"Thank you, Ron," Kris chose to say as she stood. "Won't you come back tomorrow when I should be able to give you a complete tour of my embassy castle? Sometime around midnight, we'll glide down the Smart Metal and reactors we need to finish the castle. Could you arrange for it not to be shot down?"

"Kris, normally the airspace around the Imperial Palace is closed to any air traffic. I will talk to my Chooser. Maybe he can make an exception for you."

"I do command the Imperial Fleet," Kris pointed out.

"Yes, you do. Yes, you do." Ron said vaguely as he stood, bowed low to Kris, and headed back to his car.

Kris did not walk him to the gate. She sat, staring into her pond. She needed to do some serious thinking.

9

Lieutenant Megan Longknife always had a pretty good idea of where she wanted to be. She'd wanted to be back among the rest of humanity, so she'd applied to the Wardhaven Naval Academy and knocked the dust of isolated Santa Maria from her shoes. She'd wanted to meet the renowned Kris Longknife, so she'd accepted the job as Kris's *aide de camp* fresh out of the trade school.

And, somehow, being tossed in the middle of that other Longknife's life had not scared her off and here she was, accepting a job on her Navy headquarters' staff and now gallivanting off into the heart of the Iteeche Empire two steps behind the woman.

"I've got to be crazy," Meg muttered to herself.

But the stairway down into the first basement of the Pink Coral Palace was exactly where Nelly's map said it would be. A hand light showed her where to go in a vast and empty sub-floor that was broken up by thick stone pillars that looked more gray than pink down here.

There wasn't even any dust on the floors. Somebody had really cleaned this place out.

She found what had been the Iteeche communications center. The humans had already installed a small server farm. Several techs smiled at her, then ignored her and went back to their business.

Except for one.

A tall, cute looking guy with a shock of red hair that couldn't decide whether to flip right or left, rose from the chair where he'd been working at three keyboards and five monitors.

"Can I help you?" he asked.

Meg considered the question for a moment, then decided it might be fun to see if he could do just that. "I'm looking for the terminator the Iteeche installed when they cut the lines between the in-palace net and the rest of Iteeche land."

That got her a curiously raised pair of eyebrows that formed a bushy V. "It's right over here," he said with a wave of his hand towards a hole in the wall. "May I ask what your interest is in it?"

"Yes, you can, but if I told you, I'd have to tickle you to death."

The guy eyed Megan up and down. She'd liked the way he looked her in the eyes, but she guessed he deserved the full survey, considering the answer she had shot back at him.

"You're attached to that woman that sets all those rules."

"Yes, I am the *aide de camp* to Grand Admiral Longknife, the very first ambassador to the Iteeche Empire." Megan had to suppress an urge to go into some variation of "I am the very model of a modern major general." She got that urge a lot in this job.

"Hmm," he eyed her, but when she didn't flinch, he went on, "You won't get anything from it. We've tried all we got to get something from the other side, but it's a solid block of concrete. Maybe they put something in it, but it's dead concrete. No conduction."

"Have you tried to pry data loose?" Megan asked.

"Listen, my bosses don't like being in the dark any more than your Navy bosses, okay? Everybody wants information to stay alive. They want information to make a buck. So far, nothing, nil, nada."

"Could you get me a chair?" Megan said, heading for the butt of the concrete slug.

"Okay, it's your grave," and the cute redhead went to get Megan the requested chair.

Megan had known she had this power for a long time. The first time she probably used it, she was four and fell asleep under her father's desk with her head against his business computer. Her vivid dreams that afternoon had been of fluffy clouds and plush puppets; she'd never forgotten them.

She was seven the afternoon she went hunting for something, she couldn't remember what, and bumped her head against her brother's computer. The visions she got that time had knocked her on her bottom and left her head reeling with scary visions and sick smells. After that, she stayed away from computers as much as she could.

She'd been in middle school when her teacher insisted that she had to use a personal assistant. She picked the most basic version she could get away with, and nothing happened . . . for a while. Then she started seeing things: labyrinths, puzzles, caves, all with information in them. The first time she realized she was looking at the next day's math test, she knew she had a good thing going.

That didn't work out so well. After she aced two math tests in a row, she and her mother got called into the head mistress's office. Meg had managed to stutter her way through the confrontation, but on the walk home, her mother had eyed her weirdly for a bit, then said, "So you have the gift, too."

That had gotten her a trip to her old Aunt Lily and a lesson on the family blessing and curse. "We are blessed with the ability to know what others don't. That's also our curse, because they don't much care for that."

Under Aunt Lily's guidance, Megan began to learn how to find her way into and maneuver through databases. Once she had someone go through the mazes with her, it was as easy as falling off a log. Megan found that she didn't even have to be in touch with the physical network. If it was broadcasting on net, she could get in it, so long as she had her pet computer to open up the net.

Soon, the problem turned into how not to get lost in every net she got anywhere close to. There, again, Aunt Lily had been a godsend. It was she who taught Meg to ignore most of what came at her and keep her sanity as middle school was followed by high school. Meg could never have attempted the return to a major planet like Wardhaven if she hadn't learned to tune it all out.

It had been a while since Megan had attempted a major systems entry. She settled into the offered chair and considered her options.

"What Navy gear have you got?" the redheaded guy asked, glancing around for a kit bag or something.

"Why don't you and your friends go out for coffee?" Meg suggested with a friendly smile.

"Crew. Take fifteen," he ordered.

"I just got back from a coffee break," one shot back.

"So, take another. Out of here, all of you."

There was some grumbling, but apparently Meg had picked the boss. He said go. They went.

"You're not going?"

"Nope. You want to crack this, Navy, I want to see what you got that I don't have in my kit bag. By the way, my name is Walt."

"There's nothing here but me, and my name is Megan," she said, spreading her hands open.

"That's what I'm wondering about," he answered, looking a bit puzzled.

Meg considered her options. She could leave and come back all ninja tonight, and maybe have to go through this all over again with a night shift, or she could let this guy see a whole lot of nothing.

Nothing, assuming the Iteeche net didn't knock her on her ass like her brother's net did.

That is a thought. It might be a good idea to have those nice strong arms catch me if I get knocked silly.

Meg decided to let him stay.

She stared at the cylinder of concrete. It was darker than most concrete, and showed small stones mixed in the aggregate. Try as she might, she could spot no tiny bits of metal, but there might be nano tubes in the mix and she'd never see them.

From where she sat, and from all she could see or hear, it was just a block of concrete filling up a conduit that must once have carried one huge cable into the palace. For a moment, she wondered why they needed such a big conduit, then she squelched the question. She wasn't here to discuss Iteeche building design, she was here to crack into their net.

YOU READY, LILY?

I'M HERE AND MOM IS STANDING BY TO HELP. WE CAN ALL BE HERE IF THINGS DON'T GO RIGHT.

OKAY, LET'S SEE WHAT THEY'VE GOT.

First, Megan rested her fingers tips lightly on the concrete. It was cool to the touch, maybe a bit wet. Likely, it hadn't finished setting. Those were the sensations anyone would expect to get from concrete.

Below all that was a kind of hum that vibrated in the bones of her finger.

She'd never felt that before.

She pressed down firmer, full palm on.

The hum stayed in her bones, but suddenly, a stink filled her nostrils. Her tongue tasted sour from something metallic.

ARE ANY OF YOU GETTING THIS?

GETTING WHAT?

THE FEELING IN MY BONES. THE SMELL? THE TASTE?

WE CAN HEAR AND WE CAN SEE, MEG, BUT WE CAN'T FEEL, SMELL, OR TASTE. IF YOU'RE GETTING SOMETHING LIKE THAT, IT'S NOT GETTING THROUGH TO US.

OKAY, Megan answered. All this was new. She knew that what she observed in this strange state were simply illusions, attempts by her brain to process inputs the human mind had never processed in all its millions of years of evolution. She knew that her brain was getting some sort of signal and converting it into something the best way it could manage. Aunt Lily had told Meg how Grampa Ray's experience with the planet-wide computer had usually come out as battles.

"He was a soldier by trade, so most of what he saw were

fights," Aunt Lily explained. "Of course, most of what he was doing when he faced the stone was fighting with the computer."

Megan ran all Aunt Lily's help and all her own previous experiences around her skull a couple of times. She came up with nothing helpful.

With a deep breath, Megan closed her eyes and leaned her forehead against the stone. For a moment, it was just cool.

Then things got weird.

Something was swimming at her in the dark. It had a snake's body, but its huge mouth was lined with teeth, dagger-long and sharp. Its eyes glowed green.

Meg considered two options. She could go big, and stomp this thing that was likely an outer defense, or she could get small and dodge it. She was shrinking down to a mere dot before she even knew she'd made her decision . . . but a dot with jet propulsion.

She dodged right and the serpent swam by her.

Expanding herself to cover the distance faster, she kept her jet packs and the swimming analogy as she sank deeper into the dark.

Something clamped onto her leg. A glance back showed something like a ball and chain bound fast to her ankle. She shrank her leg and the shackle slipped over her tiny feet. But while she'd been looking back, she'd swum head on into a mass of what appeared to be jelly fish that immediately began to stick to her.

They also stung.

This time, Megan went large, expanding her self-image into a giant. With one hand, she swept the tiny stickers from her face and shoulder and squished them between her fingers and thumb.

All this was not new to Megan. Her mind had used imaginings like these to explain computer system defenses before when she'd gone where she wasn't supposed to.

What came next was new.

Swimming brought her to the shore of some sea. She rode the waves in and found herself wading through surf to a beach of soft black sand. Some four hundred meters across the flat sand was a wall. Even blacker than the beach, it rose high into the sky. It had no visible gate, but it did have spikes. Lots of spikes. Big ones, little ones; there were even spikes jutting out from spikes.

NICE BUNCH, THIS LOT, Lily observed to Megan.

DOESN'T LOOK LIKE THEY WANT COMPANY, DOES IT?

SO, DO WE GO OVER OR DIG UNDER? Nelly tossed in. Nelly always seemed to be eager to see what would happen next. No doubt, it came from living at picosecond speed and watching meat creatures that moved at the speed their muscles could manage.

Megan eyed the base of the colossal wall with all its spikes. Some of those pointy things were even angled down below the sand. Somehow, she doubted the big thing was built on sand. Besides, she'd been a mole a couple of times and hated digging in the dark.

In a flash, she was an eagle. She spread her wings, then with two hops and a flap, she was airborne, feeling the wind flow beneath her wings and climbing into the sky.

Megan loved this part. If she could, she'd be an eagle in all her dreams. She soared higher with each beat of her wings. The beach fell away, the warm air rising from it helping her to gain height. The view to seaward was spectacular.

The view to landward was a wall. A spiked, black wall and nothing else.

Look right, look left, look up. Wall and spikes.

As she was shaking her eagle head, life got exciting.

Diving at her fast, and sable as the wall, a half-dozen creatures came bearing wings, teeth, and claws. They didn't seem to have much of anything else. Doubtlessly, a date with a cute redheaded guy named Walt was not in their programming.

Strange what you think of when you're facing death, Megan thought, and transformed herself into an armed attack jet. Flying an airplane wasn't as much fun as flying like a bird, but it had its advantages.

In a wink, she had one of the birds in her sights. A pull on the stick, she fired ammo, and the bird was a mass of flesh, blood, and feathers flying in loose formation. She kicked her rudder right, and whipped out three birds as her guns swept past them.

Her next target rolled out of her targeting computer picture as it converted into a sleek ebony jet fighter in its own right. Movement brought Megan's attention away from her escaping target to the sight of a dozen or more jets diving at her.

WE CAN'T LET THEM GET AWAY WITH THAT NOW, CAN WE, MEGAN?

PLEASE, NELLY, LET'S NOT, she agreed.

Suddenly, Megan was surrounded by a dozen silver jets of her own, zooming ahead of her and spreading out to take on the incoming defenders.

While Nelly and Lily's fighters spread out, Megan converted herself into a heavy bomber and began sending large rocket-accelerated bombs at the wall. Not so much as a spike did their explosions knock loose.

With the battle going her way for the moment, Megan converted herself into some sort of insect and buzzed quickly to the wall. Flying as an insect was nowhere near as fun as being an eagle; the buzzing about did something to Megan's ear or stomach.

Or both.

She worked her way through the spikes to the smooth, slick onyx of the wall's surface. She had to add suction cups to her feet before she could settle on it. Done, she converted her snout into a drill and applied it to the wall.

She made not so much as a mark on the wall. Worse, her spinning nose slid off.

She switched her proboscis to a laser and concentrated on cutting through. In rapid succession, more under Nelly's control than Megan, her nose transformed through several different types of lasers. A blue-green color was reflecting back at Megan when a tiny hole appeared in the wall. The laser intensified and its focus widened; the breach got wider and deeper.

Megan found she was now a worm, long and thin, rocket propelled, and with a glowing blue-green nose. She was racing through a cavern whose walls must have been red hot, but appeared only warm to Megan's hide.

It seemed like she sped through the deepening hole forever, but in another frame of reference, it was but a blink of an eye before she broke out into a dimly lit void. It appeared to have no limit, no top, bottom, or sides. It just was.

In the hazy light, creatures moved. In front of Megan were more and different kinds of creatures, way more than she could ever have dreamed up on her own. Some had eight legs, others more, some less. A few had no legs. They moved in straight lines, or flitted about with no apparent goal visible. Some had eyes, others none. Many moved in groups, some larger, others huge. There were a few that formed a kind of train. Among those, none of them were the same except for some kind of mandible that they used to latch onto the creature ahead of them in line. In the three "conga lines" Megan spotted, only the first animal in line had eyes.

One of them was heading toward her at speed. Its eyes blinked and the whole lot of them took off with a hard right-climbing vector. The last one in line came loose during the turn and began to flit aimlessly, but sometimes faster, other times slower.

I THINK WE NEED TO EXAMINE THAT ONE, MEGAN.

I AGREE, LILY, and Megan found herself with a cowboy hat and boots, astride a magnificent palomino. She nudged the lovely beast in the side and she took off at a gallop for the meandering creature. Megan pulled the lariat she found hanging from her saddle horn and began swinging it out into a lasso. In a flash, she had the maverick roped, and all ten legs hog tied. The weird critter was going nowhere.

SO, WHAT HAVE WE GOT HERE, MEGAN?

From the outside, it looked like the kind of crazy vision that might haunt a fever dream. Its body was cylindrical, its legs spindly with no knees, and its neck was so short as to be practically nonexistent. The creature looked unable to twist its neck about much. Of a face, it had nothing. There was neither an intake for food nor an exhaust for waste.

CLEARLY, THIS IS NOT MEANT TO BE ALIVE, IN THE NORMAL MEANING OF THE WORD, MEGAN.

SO, WHAT IS MY HYPERACTIVE IMAGINATION TRYING TO TELL US, NELLY?

YOU HAVE MORE EXPERIENCE IN THIS WORLD. IS THIS ANYTHING LIKE BEING IN ONE OF MY DATABASES OR A NAVY ONE?"

NO, OUR DATABASES HAVE STRUCTURE. I CAN ALWAYS FIND FILING CABINETS TO RANSACK IF I FOLLOW THIS OR THAT TREE. MOST TREES HAVE SOME HINT OF WHAT'S OUT ON THE LIMBS, NELLY.

THIS WORLD IS ALL CHAOS. Even in Meg's head, Nelly seemed more to muse on that thought than own it outright.

SO IT WOULD SEEM, Megan agreed.

COULD WE CUT IT OPEN? Lily asked. She might be all up with Megan on her own, but with her mom looking over her shoulder, Lily could get very tenuous.

CERTAINLY MEGAN SHOULD TRY.

So it was that Megan found a large Bowie knife at her waist. She wasted no time applying it to the soft underbelly of what she'd come to think of as a data packet. Thus, she wasn't totally surprised when Iteeche letters and numbers spewed out of its belly.

THEY'RE IN NO ORDER, Lily exclaimed.

BE SURE TO GET A GOOD LOOK AT ALL OF THEM, Nelly shouted as the things tried to scamper away.

Megan found a net at her belt, next to the empty knife sheath, and began stuffing the run-away alphanumerics into it. As she shoved the last one in, she spotted a pack of very ugly critters, with many teeth in their mouths and long claws on their many legs.

I THINK IT IS PAST TIME TO GET OUT OF HERE.

I CERTAINLY AGREE.

And Megan blacked out.

She came to, half in the chair she'd been sitting in, half

out of it, and in the delightfully strong arms of a certain cute redhead.

"You okay?" he asked, concern in both his voice and those lovely green eyes of his.

"I am now," Megan said.

He helped her back into her chair, careful to touch no more of her than he had to. Meg liked a guy who wasn't afraid to use his hands to help a girl . . . and didn't take advantage of her problem.

She settled into her chair with a "Wow."

"What happened?"

"What'd you see?" Megan had never seen anyone do an insertion, at least not one that ended like that had.

Red's eyebrows came down into that V thing they did. "You rested your palms against the concrete plug. You know you did that?"

"I was there for that," Meg agreed.

"Then you rested your forehead against it. That went on for a good long couple of minutes, maybe five, then suddenly you were a damp rag headed for the deck. You don't mind that I caught you, do you?"

"You can catch me anytime," Meg answered, and gave him a smile she hoped was encouraging.

"What *were* you *doing*?"

"I'm afraid I can't tell you," Meg said.

"Cause if you did, you'd have to kill me. Really?"

"Really, the worst death possible. Tickling to death. No man could stand that torture."

He laughed. "I don't know. I might be willing to give it a try, assuming you were the one tickling me."

"Don't tempt a Longknife where killing is concerned."

"Right, you're another Longknife. From the Santa Maria wing, aren't you?"

"Yes. You've been researching me?" Megan asked, alarms bells ringing.

"You were against that concrete plug a couple of long minutes. You have your sources. I have mine." He held up his wrist unit. Sure enough, the screen showed the Longknife family tree. There she was, complete with a commissioning photo. Was she ever that young?

"Then you have the advantage on me. You know my name, what's yours?"

"Walt Vilmus, at your service, ma'am," he said, offering her his hand. She took it and stood. There was a bit of dizziness, but she stayed steady on her feet.

"Ray Longknife," Walt said slowly, "didn't he do something with the planetary computer out there on Santa Maria when they rediscovered you? I read something about it back in school."

"I really don't want to go there," Megan said.

"Now I remember," and he was tapping his wrist unit. A moment later he was showing Megan a history of the recovery of the lost Santa Maria colony. "My teacher said it was just a made-up story. A legend about him talking to the computer through a rock, or something, but what you were doing there? You were talking to the computer, weren't you?"

"Can we just say I was trying?"

The guy eyed her hard. "It knocked you out of your chair, didn't it?"

"Almost on my ass."

"Learn anything?"

"To get a better chair next time."

He snorted at that. "Need a cup of coffee? There's a little place I know that serves up a decent brew. It's just a little nook of a place, but I see quite a future for it when the big wigs give up some of their luxury accommodations."

"I'd love a cup of coffee. Do they have scones? Buy me a scone and I may let you live."

"And I was so looking forward to you tickling me to death."

"The day is yet young," Meg said, and flashed him one of her patented dazzling smiles.

10

Grand Admiral Kris Longknife rode the elevator up the outside skeleton of her castle in silence. Jack remarked about what a great a job Nelly was doing, because she was keeping the clear-sided elevator level as it first ran up the sweep of the leg supporting the entire castle, then changing to keep it level again as they were swept out onto the bulging underside of the castle, then changing it again to stay upright as they crossed the wide middle of the castle as it began to narrow down toward the top.

"I reserved space in the center of the castle," Nelly said. "If things get violent, the elevators can shoot up the inside, but I thought you'd like the view while we can still enjoy it."

"Strange, the assumption you built into your statement, Nelly. 'While we can still enjoy it.' Do you know something we don't?" Jack asked.

"Just that I'm with one of those Longknifes, General."

That Longknife listened to the banter while her own mind cycled through the problems she faced.

"Nelly, can you get Jacques and Amanda together for a meeting, please?"

"They're settling themselves and their kids into the castle as we speak, Kris. They'll be in your staff conference room by the time we get you there."

"Good," Kris said.

The nice thing about having Nelly build an elevator system and control it, was that when Kris was in it, it went where she wanted it to go without any interminable stops along the way.

"I got the Forward Lounge as high as I could put it, Kris. They wanted the penthouse, but I wasn't about to let anyone have access to the space above you. I reserved the three floors above the Forward Lounge for your immediate staff. That should be safer for you."

"Thank you, Nelly," Jack agreed.

"I've also given the Lounge a ring of balconies covered with clear Smart Metal so they can still seat people under the stars," Nelly added. "And we can make sure no one gets the idea of climbing up from there to slip into the kids' rooms."

"Good, Nelly," Kris said.

"And I also upped the encryption for the Smart Metal on the outside of the entire castle. Nobody gets to step outside, and nobody gets to make a hatch in the deck above. Anyone even tries, and I get an alarm."

"Good," Jack said.

Kris took a deep breath as the elevator swept onto the wide waist of the castle, then adjusted itself so that instead of *hanging* level from a track, it now stood level *on* the track that took them up the rapidly narrowing mock-up of Kris's new home. As promised, the level below Kris's own quarters looked like a flower had blossomed out with long, broad petals circling around a bulging head.

Kris took all this in, but kept her mind elsewhere, spinning through a mound of conflicts, problems, and ideas. So far, few had raised their heads enough to be thoroughly examined.

Ruth and Johnny scrambled to meet them as they came out of the elevator. A tutor was only one step behind them. No more nannies, the kids insisted. They were tutors and "fun."

Jacques and Amanda were hurrying toward them, their own two in tow. For a delightful moment, life was a total uproar of excited, high-pitched voices competing to display their latest successes. Kris pulled her mind from her problems to focus her total attention on the shining faces looking up at her. She stooped to get hugs, even though Johnnie clearly hadn't washed his hands after his latest and most beloved peanut butter and jelly sandwich.

But short attention spans quickly rushed the kids off together for something that was very important to them. Kris watched them gallop off, shouting happily, and knew she'd miss the days when these hit-and-run hug attacks were a thing of the past.

Assuming I don't get us all killed.

"Amanda, Jacques, Abby, I need to talk to you about our hosts and the crazy way they do business."

"We're at your service, but I don't know that we can help you all that much," Jacques said.

"Nelly, where's that conference room you promised?"

A door opened off the elevator foyer. Kris entered to find a room with a spectacular view of the Imperial capital spread out before her. Place of honor was the Imperial Palace, with its vast expanse of forests and ponds. Most of the buildings were low-slung and well away from the stone wall and moat that surrounded the Imperial Precinct. Center place, however, was held by a spire of glass, steel, and stone that gleamed golden in the sun. It shot up several hundred meters before topping it off with a ball that had a spike atop it.

Amanda came up beside Kris and joined her enjoying the alien panorama. "No one has ever been up the spire," she said. "Totally forbidden, except for the Imperial household, and they rarely go out and never talk."

"Even when the Emperor travels?" Kris asked.

Jacques shook his head. "As best we can tell, and there's not a lot we can talk about with any certainty, the Emperor only leaves the Imperial precincts for visits to his Summer Palace. For all practical purposes, he's born there. He lives there. He'll be cremated there when he dies and his ashes spread among the ponds and woods."

"He never goes anywhere but this palace and the summer one?" Kris asked, incredulous.

"Never. If one didn't know he was an all-powerful, god-like figure, one might consider him a prisoner," Amanda added.

"Nothing adds up here," Kris observed.

"We're starting to get that idea, too," Jacques agreed.

Kris allowed herself a deep sigh; she'd been doing a lot of that lately. "I have an Empire that's going full speed ahead for a huge waterfall, and I don't know how to grab a good hold and steer it to safety."

No one added anything to that observation, so Kris turned around and found that Nelly had arranged the room with five comfortable chairs. For now, the place was pretty bare, not even a table, but with Nelly, anything they needed could quickly be made to appear.

The other four sat down and got comfortable.

Kris sat, then leaned forward, as if into a great wind.

"I'd like to know what you've learned about the Iteeche, if it won't take too long."

Amanda exchanged a glance with Jacques. "Painfully little," she admitted. "We have no access to their land-line net. All we can look at is the entertainment on their airwaves. Radio and TV net. Boy, do they like their music. They'll go to huge concerts and watch the musicians and join in the singing at the drop of a hat. Their media entertainment consists of what we'd call soap operas. Most of that consists of talking a lot about interpersonal matters and going out to eat where they sing a lot. Think beer garden sing-a-longs."

"About these soap operas," Kris asked. "Do they tell us anything helpful about the Iteeche?"

"They're concerned about mating with someone proper, so a lot revolves around being invited into a better level of mating pond," Jacques said. "Earning the right to choose an offspring is unbelievably important. I've seen Iteeche soap operas where they fight duels to the death over that."

"What were they fighting for?" Jack asked.

"The fights weren't so much for anything as they were fighting to keep someone else from getting something," Jacques said. "To choose an offspring. To scatter their eggs or sperm in a clan, sept, or family mating pond is all a zero-sum game. If he gets to choose, I don't. If she gets to spew her eggs in that pond, I don't. These duels are not just fought by males. Females also get in on the fun. Stopping someone else seems more important than getting your own and it is almost always to the death. We wondered on approach to the planet how they could have so many people. If I could get a hold of the vital statistics for this place, I suspect a lot of their morbidity comes from those duels."

"That sound rather alien?" Jack asked, eyeing Kris.

"Preventing someone from doing anything seems to be a national pastime," Kris said, only too aware of the walls that had been constructed around her. Walls that restricted her movement. Kept her ignorant. Tried to kill her. She didn't care what the Iteeche did or didn't do, but she had committed to stop a rebellion and desperately needed at least a few Iteeche to join her in that effort.

Nelly cleared her nonexistent throat. "Kris, Megan is heading up the elevator. I think she has something to tell you about your problems."

"You can't tell us?" Jack asked.

"I find that you humans prefer to have a fellow human convey a message. Besides, it was her unique gift that allowed her to gain this information and she may still know more than I do. Lily and I were just riding in the back seat, as you humans put it."

Megan came in, and a chair just as comfortable as the other five rose from the floor. Still, the young lieutenant sat on the edge of it.

"You've taken a dive into the Iteeche data net?" Kris asked.

"Yes, ma'am. I can't say I've come up smelling like roses, although there was a really nice guy and I've made a date with him for coffee."

"Maybe we humans aren't so different from the Iteeche," Amanda said, with a sly grin.

"Huh?" said the young woman.

"Go on," Kris said, then by way of explanation, added, "the young lieutenant here has inherited something from my great-grandfather. She has an affinity for computers.

Given half a chance, she can tell you the questions that will be on next Friday's math test."

"That must have made you popular in school," Amanda said, with a soft smile.

"It was more likely to get me in trouble with the administration, and not all my classmates were impressed. You know, the one-eyed man can get hung in the valley of the blind."

"I've heard that quote go another way," Jack said.

"You haven't lived there, sir. If you had, you would not have bought the t-shirt."

That got a chuckle.

"I'm sad to report," the young woman said, "that my effort to apply my particular gift to the Iteeche net was a total failure. With Nelly's help, we managed to penetrate their data stream, but I'm afraid that what I found there was unintelligible. We talk of a data highway, with data packets traveling rational paths. What I met was more like a jungle, with weird things wandering aimlessly. I cut the gullet of one of them open and all sorts of unassociated alphas and numerics spewed out. Nelly, have you and your children managed to make any sense of them?"

"No," Nelly answered. "Any metadata about the unassociated letters or numbers that might have allowed us to reconnect them was lost. We're still examining the data scraps, trying to find something helpful, but it very much looks like a fool's errand."

Kris leaned back in her seat. "So, if we are to get any information about how the Iteeche battles have gone to date, the Iteeche either give it to us, or we are whistling in the dark."

"I'm afraid so, Admiral. I'm sorry. I failed."

"It's not your fault, Megan. We evolved our way. They

evolved their way. Your grandmother has been trying to crack what the Three Alien Races left behind on Santa Maria for what, seventy years? She hasn't gotten all that far. The Iteeche can't be any easier to comprehend."

Since no one else had anything more to add to her level of ignorance, Kris took over the meeting.

"As I see it, I'm faced with three principal issues. The Iteeche don't fight worth beans. I need to recruit some Iteeche battlecruisers and then I need to train them to fight my way."

Jack nodded agreement with her.

"I also need to get this embassy set up and running so my Royal merchant princes can arrange meetings with the dust mites of the Iteeche Empire."

"Dust mites?" Jack asked.

"That was what Ron called the guys who lost their heads for trying to talk to our two idiots."

"Actually, Kris," Nelly put in, "I think his words were more like dung beetle."

"You passed it through to me as dust mites."

"I may have softened matters in translation. After all, you humans don't like to speak ill of the dead and you get bored if I take too long to nuance a translation."

"Thanks, Nelly, but, to get back on track, we need to get our embassy in order so Abby can set up shop down here."

"That would sure be nice," Abby drawled. "Right now, the Royal dung beetles are rolling their shit all over the Pink Coral Palace and my folks got nada."

"Wait until you see what Nelly's got for you," Kris said.

"This castle is pretty slim pickings," the former maid said. "It's more like an empty balloon."

"It will fill out when I have more Smart Metal to work with," Nelly said, promptly.

"And when will that be?"

"When Kris gets the *Glory of Free Enterprise* down here and I use it and its reactors to fill out this design."

Nelly paused. "Kris, I've got a call coming in from Ron."

"Yes, Ron?" Kris said.

"I am talking to the Imperial Admiral of Second Order of Iron who defends the airspace over the capital. He says you may not glide 75,000 tons of spaceship and reactors down in the middle of the capital only four li from the Imperial Precincts."

Kris wasn't really surprised at that. She had a counter-proposal already in mind. "Have you told him that I am the Imperial Admiral of the First Order of Steel? I command the Imperial Battle Fleet. I am also the emissary from His Royal Majesty, King Raymond to his Imperial Majesty. I am sworn to defend his Imperial Master."

"Yes, Kris. I have told him that. He, however, is charged with ensuring that no harm comes to His Imperial and Worshipful Majesty from the air. There is no way that he can accept 75,000 tons of unpowered metal attempting to land in the courtyard of the Pink Coral Palace as anything but an insanely dangerous stunt and threat to the entire city, as well as the Imperial Person."

"Please tell him that I and my husband will be aboard those 75,000 tons of *powered* air vehicle. I and my computer, Nelly, with help from my husband and his computer, Sal, will pilot the craft down to a perfect landing in the target courtyard."

The call went silent, as if it had been put on hold.

Jack looked at Kris. "We're landing it?"

"Yep. Megan, you and Lily are involved, too."

"Of course, ma'am."

"Nelly, you want me and Mata to come along, too?" Abby asked.

"I don't think you will be necessary. Kris, you said a powered landing?"

"Yes, Nelly. I was thinking we'd convert the glider to a rotary winged vehicle for the final approach. You might also arrange to have engines if you need them, to ensure that the final approach is perfect."

"It will be perfect and the rotary wings really aren't necessary," Nelly said, definitely sounding like her pride had been hurt.

"I know that, and you know that," Kris said, "but they don't know that. We need to operate within their perception. Can you design me a 75,000-ton helicopter?"

A second later, they were looking at a three-dimensional holographic image of a huge air vehicle with a dozen outriggers. The booms emanated from three different bands around the long hull, each outrigger with two rotating sets of six blades to support it.

"You think you can fly that?" Kris asked.

"I don't have to fly it, I only have to land it, Kris," Nelly sniffed. "I expect to dead-stick it. With these rotors for braking and direction, we've gone from a hundred percent likelihood of a safe landing right on top of this skeletal palace to a two-hundred percent chance. You happy now?"

"Actually, Nelly, I am," Kris admitted. "Someone did their level best to make me either dead or late for my meeting with the Emperor. I fully expect someone to try to complicate our landing."

"Oh. Do all humans have corkscrews for brains, or just Longknifes?" Nelly asked.

"Pretty much all of us," Jack answered for Kris. "No telling what the Iteeche have."

"I should have extrapolated that eventuality," Nelly said. "In the future, I will bias my forecasts to include anything that can kill us, Kris."

"I thought you did already," Abby drawled.

"I thought I was," Nelly said. "It seems that I wasn't twisted enough."

"Ron is back," Nelly said.

"Your Highness, the admiral fears that landing a rocket ship in the middle of town would demolish a huge swath around its engines. He wonders if you intend to kill a million Iteeche like your great-grandfather."

"Ron, I will be in this lander and my children will be waiting in the Pink Coral Palace," Kris said, upping her amount of skin in the game to an insane level. "Nelly, send them your schematic of a powered air vehicle that uses no rocket jets."

A moment later, there were sounds of Iteeche amazement. Kris had observed Iteeche clicking their beaks together when surprised.

"You would fly this contraption into the center of a palace with your Chosen waiting for you?" Ron finally said. "The thing looks like a death trap. If it crashes, it will wipe out millions on the ground."

"Nelly tells me that it is safer than the space elevator," Kris answered. "And you will notice, there are no rocket motors to disturb the neighbors' sleep.

There was further discussion on the net in Iteeche.

THE ADMIRAL ASKS IF ALL LONGKNIFES ARE CRAZY, Nelly told Kris. OH, RON ANSWERED 'HOW DO YOU THINK THEY ALMOST MADE US EXTINCT?'

Kris shook her head. Veterans on both sides of the Iteeche War were sure they had prevented the other side from exterminating their entire race. That was likely not going to change on Kris's watch.

"Kris," Ron finally said, "the admiral charged with the defense of the airspace over the Imperial Palace says you may land your device so long as you do not violate the air above the sacred Imperial Precincts."

"Nelly, will we need to pass over them?"

"No, Kris, I can add a small loop in our flight path. We will have to do several S turns to bleed off speed. I can ensure that we approach the Pink Coral Palace from the east, a side not critical to the security of the Imperial Palace."

"When will you land?" Ron asked.

"Between sunset tonight and sunrise tomorrow," Kris said, giving her as wide a window as possible, and avoiding going into the crazy Iteeche clock that divided the day into eight watches of eight hours each.

"You will be allowed to approach, and may your clan and mine rejoice at this feat. Surely this will be sung about for a thousand years whether you land or smash up," Ron said.

Kris didn't chuckle at the joke; she had too much riding on this. She'd just volunteered to strap herself into 75,000 tons of Smart Metal. If this went ass over teakettle, Ruth and Johnnie would die with her.

The look on Jack's face was Marine bland. It showed nothing of what was going on in his head. In his gut.

Very likely, it was no different from what left a sick feeling in Kris's.

I'm a Longknife. I do what has to be done. Please, dear God, let this be done right.

11

Kris marched out of the space ferry station. According to Nelly, she had half an hour before their first landing window would open up. She, Jack, and Megan boarded the *Princess Royal's* station car and were swiftly taken to the pier where the former *Glory of Free Enterprise* had been docked.

What was there now, was anybody's guess.

She was not saved from several more minutes of complaining from Grampa Al's man, Dani Ishmay. He met her as she exited the car and filled the air with his belly-aching while she strode to the ship's brow. Fortunately, the Marines at the gangplank would not let him follow Kris aboard to continue expressing his disdain for any government official who would steal private property.

"I told you before," Kris said, pausing for a moment on the gangway, "I am taking control of this vessel as a Nuu Enterprise stockholder. Now, good day, sir."

Kris turned on her heels and strode aboard her ship, glider, helicopter, palace, castle, whatever.

Nelly used a light to lead them to the cockpit at the

forward edge of the vehicle. For now, the vehicle had the general appearance of a brick so it could make it through the deorbital burn and reentry. Once in the air, Nelly would reprogram the Smart Metal ™ into a lift body. If she needed extra power during the level portion of the flight, she could use propellers powered by electric motors. For the nose up and landing, Nelly would convert the entire affair into a rotary wing vehicle.

"We'll touch down in the courtyard light as a feather," Nelly assured her. "I intend to flow the metal into this skeletal outline as we make our final descent."

Nelly clearly was going for broke. Still, Kris checked the controls. "Not all that different from taking a space skiff down to a target or a light assault craft down with Marines," she said, calling up fond memories.

"Just like old times," Nelly said, "You've just put on a little weight in mid-life, Kris."

"Nelly, I know where that off button is."

"Yes, Kris, but you know you need me for this landing."

"She's got you there," Jack agreed.

"Doesn't anyone ever give you any respect, Admiral?" Megan asked from where she sat behind Jack.

"Certainly not Nelly," Kris said.

"Of course not," Nelly said. "We release in two minutes."

Kris checked her board. It was green. It couldn't be any other way with Nelly checking not only the instrumentation, but able to program corrections into any item of equipment that showed any sign of a fault. As she had so often, Kris waited for a countdown clock to reach zero.

12

As the final numbers on the timer in front of Kris raced down to all zeros, the pier tie downs began to roll the landing vehicle back, pushing it out into space. Small maneuvering jets kicked in as the lander came free from the pier. They added momentum to the vector that would send them clear of the station.

Once well away from the Iteeche space station, the lander flipped over, activated its landing rockets for a low burn, and rapidly fell away. Only after it was in open space not controlled by Station Approach did Nelly give Kris a five second countdown and kick in the full deorbital burn.

Kris found herself with triple her normal weight. The screen ahead of her showed her proposed flight path, from station to courtyard. Every inch of it was fully planned by Nelly. As the long deorbital burn ended, Nelly flipped the lander over and put it nose first for the dive into the atmosphere. Kris watched as the lander took on a nose-up position, but found no reason to take the controls. Nelly and her kids had everything under control.

Everything stayed under control right up to eight minutes from landing.

Nelly had the lander making gentle S-turns to bleed off energy when an alarm went off.

"We're being painted by active search radar," Jack said evenly. He had the electronic counter-measures at his station.

"No surprise," Kris said, "they know we're coming and they want to see how we're doing."

Jack tapped several keys on his countermeasures computer. "That assumes that they don't have search and acquire capabilities in the same radar, like we do," Jack said, dryly.

The landing continued according to plan for another minute.

"We're passing through 30,000 meters," Megan said. "Slant range to target 330 klicks."

"Right where I want to be," Nelly said, easily.

Kris checked the flight path. They were right in the middle of it for height, speed, and range.

"New radar," Jack said, forcefully. "It is not co-located with the other radar.

"It's on a mountain top, just off our flight path," Nelly said. "Sal reports all defensive measures are active."

"We are approaching the radar location," Jack reported, his voice calm even as he pronounced their possible deaths. "Acquisition radar active. I have an infrared report of a missile launch."

"Missile acquired. It has an active homing guidance," Sal said from Jack's neck. "Lasers have targeted it."

There was a brief pause. "Missile killed."

"Four missiles fired," Jack reported.

"Missiles acquired. Targeted," Sal answered. "One down. Two down. Third down. Fourth down."

"I have the launch site targeted with an 18-inch laser," Megan reported.

"Four more launches," Jack said.

"Laze the launch area," Kris ordered.

"Firing," Meg answered.

"One down. Two down. Three down. Four down," Sal said, counting off the demise of the incoming missiles.

"Secondary explosions at the launch site," Megan reported.

"We are not being tracked by acquisition radar," Jack reported to them.

"That's the end of that noise," Nelly growled.

"Stay alert," Kris said.

"Incoming human heavy lander, this is Capital Defense Control. You have fired lasers at the Imperial Planet. Explain yourself."

"Capital Defense Control, this is Imperial Emissary Kris Longknife, Imperial Admiral of the First Order of Steel. I was painted by an acquisition radar and missiles were fired at me. We responded in self-defense. We also fired on the launch site. I can give you the coordinates. You might want to see what's left and render aid to anyone who attempted to kill me and got burned themselves. You probably will want to collect up any survivors for interrogation."

"Human lander, we have dispatched troops. Air vehicles are squawking as Imperials. Do not fire on them."

"Defense Control, I will illuminate any vehicles squawking as Imperials. Please advise me immediately if I am softly lighting up your friendlies."

"I have twelve air vehicles squawking Imperial," Jack said.

"Defense Control, how many vehicles have you dispatched?" Kris asked.

"Twelve," came back quickly.

"We will light them up," Kris said. "Lieutenant Longknife, light them up softly."

"Illuminating approaching air vehicles."

"Defense here. Our twelve troop carriers report being illuminated."

"Admiral Longknife here, I verify that we have the troop carriers on our board as friendly." That done, Kris could breathe easy.

The question was, for how long?

Around them, the lander began to morph into a lift body. Two dozen ducted fan engines unfolded along the top of the wing, available to add power to their flight if it became necessary. Nelly edged the lift body to the right, then left, bleeding off more energy and testing the flight controls.

Kris eyed her board, then glanced at Jack's. Everything was going smoothly.

"Pink Coral Palace courtyard is acquired," Nelly reported.

Kris checked her forward screen. Her palace was in their crosshairs. The castle had changed again. In place of the shell of a luxurious castle, it now showed a soaring pinnacle rising high into the sky. It looked very much like a docking tower for the dirigibles that were used for transportation on planets where the people wanted to maintain a small footprint. Kris had only seen them in vids, but Nelly was using one tonight.

They were at 10,000 meters when the lift body nosed up and began to change again. Now the flat airfoil became round and long. The wings transformed into outriggers with a pair of high-powered spinning rotors. Three groups now stretched down the lengthened fuselage. Each had spindly outriggers with a pair of rotors.

Twenty-four powered rotors began to turn, slowing Kris's future castle as it stalled out and began to fall toward the Iteeche capital below. Quickly, the rotors bit into the air, giving Nelly both lift and control.

Still bleeding off forward momentum, 75,000 tons of Smart Metal ™ began to drop toward the Iteeche world below. Hopefully, to a controlled landing right in the middle of the human embassy compound.

Kris's concentration flipped between their intended glide path and the palace. She had just focused on the palace, when all hell broke loose.

"I can't see," Kris almost shouted as her blood pressure spiked and her stomach and heart both lurched out of her body.

The ground beneath them had erupted with blinding flashes of light, smoke, and scores of rockets. Some exploded into fireworks immediately. Some rose higher before scattering a load of hot, blinding, sparkles.

If it had been up to Kris, her lander would have been doomed, dropping toward a crash that would have killed herself, Jack, Ruth, Johnnie, and millions of Iteeche.

Kris struggled to control her panic, to keep her hands off the controls. That way was death. She clenched her hands in her lap and let Nelly fly them out of this.

13

Nelly and her two kids had the stick. It took them only a fraction of a second to assess their circumstances.

Their visual situation was very challenging. At any moment, a set of sparklers might blind their optics. Infrared was also hashed by the fireworks. Radar was being spoofed. The sheer number and cumulative power of the spoofing signals over-loaded the radar processors, rendering their calculations meaningless. This was caused by tiny repeaters amongst the rockets that picked up the radar signal from the lander, doubled its power and sent it back with enough strength to fool the radar into reporting that the ground was half as distant as it was.

As a result, Nelly could no longer trust the radar solutions either, as it was anyone's guess what their altitude or actual position was from three thousand meters up in the air.

Just as Nelly was focusing on lasers as her sensor of choice, hundreds of them lit up on the buildings around the palace. They swept over the lander, powerful enough to burn out any laser receiver pointed anywhere close to them.

Nelly nixed lasers from her feedback cycle.

With radar and laser out, Nelly returned to the visual and infrared range. Both of those were strongly challenged. Nelly, however, had work-arounds.

Nelly handed off to Lily, Megan's computer, the assignment of contracting the thin, tall spire on the ground with an order to stretch it out higher. At its peak, a flashing blue light appeared, burning at a specific frequency. As it came to life, the tower also generated a heat source at a precisely chosen temperature. Both devices changed their output, slaved to a schedule developed by Lily and passed along to Nelly.

Nelly now had a solid docking target, but she didn't trust just that one. She also focused her optics on several scores of ground targets. As one got flashed by the fireworks, Nelly would take it out of her decision-making cycle and add in another. With twenty sources, it was easy to spot the one that suddenly went hot, flashed, or otherwise tried to mislead the Magnificent Nelly.

No doubt, all the fireworks drew lots of eyes up to the sky. No doubt, the fireworks reflected off the incoming lander, making it sparkle.

Ruth and Johnnie would have a lot to tell Kris. They had ringside seats, standing outside one of the penthouses on the seventh floor of the Pink Coral Palace.

Kris had a heart-rendering load riding on this landing.

A green light on her board showed Kris the rotors were engaged. All twenty-four were spinning, slowing the approach and controlling the landing.

Nelly had also deployed air brakes. These were also used

both to slow and guide the path of 75,000 tons of very heavy metal.

It was as if they were reaching the end of a fireworks display. Rockets shot off in huge numbers. They exploded and scattered sparklers all over the sky. Nelly found herself with only a handful of reliable points on the ground.

Lily rose to the occasion. Actually, she shot the tower up several extra klicks, raising its beacon high above the dazzling lights and heat below.

"Contact," Nelly said softly. "I have contact with the pinnacle."

Kris watched as the rotors held their landing to a slower and slower descent. Even as they dropped, the lander grew lighter. First tons, then hundreds of tons, and finally thousands of tons bled off the lander and flooded down the pinnacle toward the central plaza of the Pink Coral Palace. What had previously stood as just a sketch, an outline of a castle, now grew, spread, and filled out, metal moving faster than the human eye could track.

Kris was now lying flat on her back, belted into her seat. As she watched, her board's barometric altimeter slowed its mad unwinding until it was in the double digits, then single.

Suddenly, they were no longer moving. Suddenly, Jack's chair and Megan's chair were beside Kris's and all three of them smoothly rotated from a horizontal to a vertical position.

Kris popped her five-point harness and stood.

Across from her, a window showed the night lights of the capitol. The last of the fireworks were dying out. The laser light display clicked off as if a plug had been pulled.

Kris walked over to the window and found a door with a wide expanse of veranda. Jack opened the door for her, and she and Megan stepped out. The night air was crisp and cool at this height.

Together, the three of them strode over to the edge. A clear pane of Smart Metal ™ protected them from the unlikely urge to hurl themselves down as well as the much more likely prospect of a sniper going for a kill shot.

Below them, the castle bulged, as three wide, entwined spirals rose up from the middle. Open galleries here, covered verandas there, extended out from the gleaming glass sides, adding living space and inviting its inhabitants to take in the air. Kris spotted tubs that she expected would soon have flowers, shrubs, and trees. Who knows, maybe some might turn their patios into gardens.

Kris nodded. This would be home for her and her family for the next five years. Hopefully, she would get to see it often. Even more hopefully, it would not be blown to bits.

But that was in the future. Just now, Kris had a bone to pick with the Iteeche Empire.

14

"Nelly, get me Ron," Kris said, her voice cold with rage.

"Yes, Your Highness," came from a holographic image of the Imperial Iteeche counselor.

"Ron, somebody damn near killed me, my husband, my kids, and your Emperor. What the hell does this great Iteeche Empire of yours have to say for itself?"

The simulation of the Iteeche bowed low. "My Eminent Chooser has headsmen and apologists ready to seize whoever tried to shoot you out of the sky or make it impossible for you to land, thereby putting His Imperial Worshipfulness at risk."

He glanced up at Kris without rising from his low bow. "We were not taken by surprise. We had both uniform and plainclothes men in all the streets. We have taken several of the people who lit off the fireworks into custody. Sadly, they are minor players, hired to 'celebrate' your arrival with fireworks. The lasers were another matter. They were activated remotely. We are tracing them back to those who rented them out, but again, I can't be sure that they also were not duped."

"Ron, I've about had it with your Empire. I'm two seconds away from packing up my kids and taking this embassy and my fleet back to Wardhaven and letting you all stew in your own fish chowder."

"Kris, you cannot," In his shock, Ron had stood up straight. His face, usually white, was pale as a ghost.

"I can, and I will. I'm not doing anything. No one will let me do anything. I want to see your Chooser. I want to see him right now, or so help me God, I'm out of here."

"Just a moment Kris. Let me talk to my Chooser. It will only be a moment."

The holograph vanished.

Kris took three deep breaths. The anger had been for show. Some of it. No, damn little of it had been show. She hadn't known she was going to threaten abandoning her mission until the words tumbled out of her mouth.

There was no chance she'd take them back. Not without some serious changes from this bunch of jumped-up squid.

"Do you mean that?" Jack asked, his hand gently rubbing her back. As always, his touch did magic to the knots that were in her back.

"Yes, I do. I'm risking every one of our lives and for what? We're going nowhere."

Beneath Kris, the castle began to come to life. Lights came on as an engineering watch, drawn from the fleet, or hired away from merchant ships, brought the reactors back on line. And as the lights came on, elevators began to climb the castle.

Kris didn't see the elevators start up. They only came in sight when they rose above the wide belly of the skyscraper. With Nelly's kids running them, there was no problem filling up the tower. Several elevator cars ran on the same track, all coming up. One rose quickly straight to the veranda Kris stood on. As it came even with their level, it stopped, opened a door onto the balcony and disgorged a mob of small kids. Ruth and Johnnie led the charge.

"Mommy, mommy, did you see the fireworks? Weren't they just beautiful?" Ruth wanted Kris and everyone within a hundred-mile radius to know. Kris picked her daughter up and gave her a very tight mommy hug.

She'd bet her life that Nelly could land 75,000 tons of metal right on the dot that was the center of this courtyard. She'd bet her life, and the lives of so many of her friends, and their children, that Nelly could do it.

She'd known the challenge hadn't been whether Nelly could have hit her target. Rather, she'd known that the real question was whether Nelly could have hit the target while some rebels did all they could to make her fail.

Kris had offered her life and the lives of her children as surety that the Emperor would suffer no harm during this landing. Heads were going to roll for this attempt to kill her, her children . . . and the Emperor.

The Smart Metal™ of the elevator car that had delivered the children sank back into the castle. A half-dozen cars followed them up the tower, rapidly passing them by, delivering General Bruce and the first watch to the high alert stations that would operate the sensors and lasers on the top of the three spires. The airspace over the Emperor would now be guarded by both his Iteeche defense force and Kris's.

As much as it pulled on Kris's heart, she had fat that needed to be slammed into the fire. "Honey, you and Johnnie run along. You're going to be so surprised by your room here, and if you want anything changed, just ask

Cara or Agent Leslie or Aunt Gaby to change it and they will."

So, the kids galloped off to discover their new quarters, with Cara sauntering along behind them. She'd been promised her own suite of rooms some distance from Abby's. She looked about as happy as a teenager could be.

"Kris, Ron is calling."

"Put him on."

Again, a quarter-sized simulacrum of Ron hovered in the air in front of Kris. "Your Highness and Imperial Admiral of the First Order of Steel, I have the honor of reporting to you that my Eminent Chooser will afford you an audience in one of your hours. I am even now on my way to your palace to take you to his presence."

"Ron, this better not be one of those show meetings. We either sit down and take a serious look at this situation - a serious look that means things change - or I walk. I walk right out of here and back to Wardhaven."

Ron did a deep bow from the waist and spoke, "My Eminent Chooser is very aware of the circumstances of this meeting. He will take it in the privacy of his own personal rooms. Is that acceptable to you?"

"Likely. What's happening with us getting to the bottom of tonight's fiasco? If I was back on Wardhaven, our Bureau of Investigations would be turning over every rock in the city to find who ordered this atrocity. Their plan was to use me to kill your Emperor, for Christ's sake."

"Yes, but you didn't."

"That doesn't matter one whit to me, Ron. Somebody did their damndest to splatter me and your Emperor all over the place."

"Your Highness, we do not have the records that you humans keep. Many of us regularly pay cash for what we buy. Your credit chits give you a trail we don't have. Our clans have the power of high, middle, and low justice. For us to take the head of someone with strong clan ties could lead to someone taking their clan over to the rebels. We must act within our traditions and practices, Your Highness. We will handle this."

"Can you at least tell me what happened to the idiots that fired missiles at me on approach?"

"Yes. They are dead. There was only a radar truck and three rocket launching trailers. Your laser didn't leave any of them alive to interrogate or get an apology from. I must applaud Nelly on her aim. Her laser bursts hit exactly what she aimed at and no more. The only collateral damage was from when the unlaunched missiles blew up. We did suffer four dead from the other missiles as their wreckage fell from the sky."

Kris scowled. She knew as well as any that what goes up very often has to come down.

"I thought that we were over mountains," Kris said.

"Even our mountains have people living there. Often very powerful people. Fortunately, the dead were from their servants. The blood price will be reasonable and easily paid. A little to the right and we would be talking to a Clan Master about the blood price of one of his own chosen."

"I did not fire the missiles. Whoever fired them must pay any price."

"Unfortunately, who fired them is not at hand to pay anything. You are. Therefore, you will."

And Kris discovered another twist in the alien society that was the Empire of the Iteeche. Another twist she didn't much like. Not at all.

"Ron, you're just making me want to walk away from this mess you have."

"I am approaching your palace, Kris. It is most spectacular. And it is already lit up. How do you humans do such things?"

"It's magic, Ron. It's just human magic."

"What is your saying, 'Yeah. Right'?"

"I'll see you in a moment," Kris said. "Nelly, I need an elevator."

"Yes, ma'am. Please go inside."

Kris returned to the room where Megan had been waiting. As she entered, an elevator car formed itself out of the floor and ceiling, right before her eyes. The door opened and the three of them entered.

The elevator started smoothly, going backwards. It took it a few seconds before it began to drop. After long minutes of descent, they popped out of the bottom of the castle a hundred meters above the Palace's central plaza and continued their descent on the inside of one of the support struts. For the entire ride, the elevator was out of sight from anyone inside or outside the palace.

15

Kris exited the elevator to find herself facing a car park of heavily armored cars. Each had eight wheels. All had remote guns mounted atop them.

Kris raised an eyebrow at Jack.

"I'm still your chief security honcho. A reinforced Marine battalion will escort you whenever you go outside these walls."

"Nelly, did you put all this armor together?"

"Yes, Kris. I can box it up when you're done. When we don't need the Smart Metal for armored fighting vehicles, I may use it to scatter some art replicas around the plaza, penthouse, and balconies. Humans need to learn to appreciate their art."

Ron's limo drove into the car area of the plaza and stopped. He got out, eyeing all the heavy armor around him. And when an Iteeche put all four eyes on anything, he was seriously surprised.

"Kris?" he said.

"Ron, so good of you to come. If you will join me in my vehicle, please."

"I had thought to take you to my Eminent Chooser in my limo."

"You will understand me being a bit gun shy after tonight."

"Yes. Yes, I would understand."

Jack pointed at the armored gun truck with an open door, and led them all to it. Since his three stars made him the most junior of the party, Jack entered first. Ron second. Kris took one last look around at matters, and entered the combat rig last.

Inside, the armored car looked very much like a limousine. Nelly had even created simulations of windows that showed the passengers a full view of what was outside them. The front cabin was blocked off with glass, much like a limo. Unlike a civilian rig, six Marines were on the other side. Three heavily armed dismounts waited alertly in the back row of seats. Ahead of them, sat a gunner, battle commander, and driver. All had the fake windows. All had full situational awareness of where they were and what they were passing.

As soon as Kris belted in, four armored cars rolled through the gate and out of the palace. Kris's rig was fifth. Seven more followed her.

They crossed the moat and passed through the Iteeche guardhouse without stopping. Interestingly, all twelve rigs sported a five-star blue flag on their right front bumper and a three-star red flag on their left.

As they made a right turn onto the wide boulevard, a major contingent with more armored cars and main battle tanks mixed in, started up and lead them. More cars and armor were rumbling at the curb behind them. They formed the back door.

Quickly, two lanes in the very center of the street were taken over by the entire armored motorcade. Or was it battlecade? It didn't matter, so long as it got Kris safely where she was going.

Far out in front, Kris could just make out a pair of Iteeche vehicles. One was Imperial red. It led with red lights flashing. Right behind it was a similar vehicle painted in magenta and cream. The lights on the top of it flashed magenta and cream as well.

"Nelly, get a flashing red light on all of my vehicles."

"Red is reserved for the Imperial forces," Ron quickly put in.

"I'm an Imperial Admiral," Kris snapped back. "Nelly, also, put all the rigs into Marine red and gold or Navy blue and gold. So, Ron, who owns those colors?"

"Two clans that are in rebellion," Ron said, evenly.

"Nelly, use more red and blue in the color pattern. Also include the globe, anchor, and spaceship emblem for the Marines, the Navy seal for the blues."

"Done, Kris."

"Your Highness, I know that you are angry that you and your family have been put at risk," Ron began.

Kris cut him off. "Angry, Ron? Angry does not begin to cover it. I was angry when no one sent me the after-action battle reports when I asked for them. I was livid when my ships were fired on by ships supposedly loyal to the Imperium and assigned to drill with mine. I am outraged now, and about to discover what lies beyond that. You do not want to see a Longknife who is beyond rage."

"I suspect my Eminent Chooser has. Remember, he negotiated a peace treaty with your Eminent Chooser."

Kris refused to be mollified.

They sped through the night. Around them, Iteeche in three- and four-wheel transports hastily pulled over to the curb and paused as Kris's cavalcade raced by. This trip, not so much as a bug tried to block their passage.

The message to Kris was clear. The Iteeche were a people you had to keep kicking in their knees, or maybe nonexistent balls, until they begged to apologize to you.

She was prepared to do just that.

Part of the screen between Kris's compartment and the war fighters changed and became an aerial map. Overhead imagery filled in the streets ahead of them. Nelly provided a flashing red light to show where they were.

"You are mapping the Imperial Capital?" Ron said, jaw slack.

"Yes, I do believe that we have a map of it," Kris said.

"Maps of the Imperial Capital are forbidden, under punishment for treason!"

"No wonder you can't get anywhere."

"Be that as it may be, you can *not* do this."

"Be that as it may be, I am doing this, and will continue to do this. If you don't like my overhead scouts, you can shoot them down."

Ron began to mumble to himself. A moment later, he turned to Kris. "The Admiral in charge of Air Defense for the Imperial Precincts says that they cannot see anything flying over the city."

"What they can't see won't bother anyone," Kris shot back.

Ron just looked at Kris, his head shaking slowly.

The leading Iteeche vehicles slowed and turned into a large building, not all that different from the Pink Coral Palace; a big square with a nice open space in the middle.

Most of Kris's battle rigs dropped out, but six of them followed the police escort across the bridge, through a long murder hole, and out into a small parking lot. Two dozen Marines in immaculate blue and red uniforms dismounted and formed up with a major and gunny ready to respond to orders.

KRIS, I HAVE DISPATCHED NANOS INTO THE PALACE. I HAVE NOT BEEN QUERIED OR ACCOSTED. THERE ARE SEVERAL SMALL MINIATURE WAR BOTS BUT THEY CAN'T SPOT ME. I AM MAPPING THE PALACE AS WE SPEAK.

THANK YOU, NELLY, LET ME KNOW IMMEDIATELY IF THERE IS ANY DIFFICULTY.

YES, KRIS. OH, KRIS, I HAVE FOUND ROTH. HE IS WAITING FOR YOU IN A PRIVATE GARDEN ON THE ROOF.

DO YOU KNOW HOW TO GET US THERE?

YES, I HAVE THE MOST DIRECT PATH MAPPED OUT.

THANK YOU.

When the Marines reported the situation well in hand, Jack dismounted. He did his own thorough look around, most likely reviewing the feed from his computer Sal's nanos. "You may dismount, Admiral.

"Ron," Kris said, waving him to proceed ahead of her.

"Really, Your Highness, is this all necessary? This is my Eminent Chooser's own palace. Surely you know you are safe here."

Kris gave him the look. He might be Iteeche, and see all humans as the same, but he flinched at the hard flint in her eyes and moved to exit the vehicle ahead of Kris.

Her Highness, Grand Admiral Kris Longknife, stepped

from her armored limo and pulled down on her dress blues coat.

Coming toward her was an Iteeche in a floor-length robe made from cloth of gold. He held a three-pronged trident in the foremost of his left hands. He pounded it on the floor and cried, "I am Roon, Chamberlain to Roth," and he went on for a long list of Ron's Chooser's pedigree and offices.

Kris had to suppress an urge to buff her fingernails on the wool of her dress blues.

Ron cut him off when he paused for a breath.

"Lead us to my Eminent Chooser. Now!"

The chamberlain led off – in the wrong direction.

"Jack," Kris said.

He quick-marched to the Marine major. "Follow me," and led them off in the opposite direction. The gunny quickly shouted orders and the first twelve Marines marched off, two by two. There was a small opening between the two sections and Kris slipped into the space with Ron at her side and Megan pulling up right behind them.

"What are you doing?" Ron squeaked. So, a shocked Iteeche's vocal cords could squeak. Kris filed that away for later use.

"In the time it took us to dismount, Nelly mapped this palace. Your major domo is leading us in the opposite direction from your Eminent Chooser. We are taking the direct route to him."

Ron failed to close his mouth this time.

The chamberlain had noticed that he was the only one headed where he was going. He shouted for them to follow him. Then screamed it. He ordered the Iteeche guards who had come with him to stop the wild humans from the deepest, darkest depths.

Jack was in the lead, with the major only a step behind and to his left. The Iteeche who tried to get in front of him might be one or two feet taller than him, but they took one look at him . . . and his drawn sword . . . and knew they could not stop this human. This human who had been invited to share the stars with their master in his private gardens.

They stepped aside and came up the rear, trailing behind Kris's second section.

The major domo was soon huffing and puffing. He quickly fell behind.

Inside, servants moved quickly to open doors. It seemed that a lot of servants stood around a lot of doors just waiting to open them. The humans marched through one door after another, upstairs and down halls.

At one door, the servants were slow to open the doors, but when they saw the serious intent of the armed Marines, they hopped to it.

The rooms they marched through now had flowing hangings, in softer colors.

"You are now in the women's quarters," Ron said, in a choked voice.

Kris glanced around; there were no more Iteeche guards trailing her Marines. "My troops are eyes front," Kris said, "and besides, we can't tell a male Iteeche from a female one."

"Oh, denizens of the depths," Ron moaned.

The Marines were not looking, but that didn't keep Iteeche in gossamer gowns and a flood of pastel colors from collecting along the edge of the wide aisles. No one ran screaming from these barbarians. From the sound of it, they were very excited to have a break in their day.

"Kris, some of them are wondering about the women among the Marines. Them and you. They can't believe woman could be counted among the warriors."

"Tell them," Kris said.

"No, don't," Ron said, but Nelly was already answering the question that was on so many lips.

"You humans are more destructive than a hurricane," Ron said, his voice tired. "You blow everywhere and leave the waters roiled and everything flat."

"Yes, I think you're right," Kris answered.

What Ron said next, Nelly did not translate.

KRIS, I'M REALLY NOT SURE HOW TO TRANSLATE WHAT HE JUST SAID. I THINK IT'S IN AN ANCIENT VERSION OF THEIR LANGUAGE. I KNOW A FEW WORDS OF IT, BUT NOT ENOUGH TO FOLLOW IT.

THAT'S FINE, NELLY, WE'LL PARDON HIS FRENCH.

AH, AN ANCIENT LANGUAGE FROM EARTH OFTEN USED IN REFERENCE TO OBSCENE WORDS.

Kris just smiled.

They came to a guarded stairwell. Again, the guards stood aside. This time, Jack led them up two flights before turning to a door where two burly Iteeche with pole axes stood. At that, the parade came to a halt.

Ron hurried forward, with Kris and Megan in his wake. Ron spoke quickly, leaving Nelly nonplused by the verbiage. Some of it again were words Kris's computer did not know. Finally, the guards stood aside and two much smaller Iteeche moved to open the door.

"Kris, you must leave your escort outside the garden. I am amazed that you have gotten this far."

The two Iteeche with pole axes were breathing heavily. Likely they had been rushed here to try to stop this human invasion. Ron must have worked hard to get them to step down.

"Jack, form the platoon outside this door, then catch up to me."

"Aye, aye, Admiral."

The Marines deployed through the door onto the roof of the palace. Ten meters away, a garden began with bushes and flowers everywhere underfoot and several very tall trees. A hundred or so meters away, a golden-roofed pergola gleamed in the sun.

No doubt, that was Kris's goal.

16

Ron immediately entered the garden, walking quickly for the gaudy bower.

Kris waited for Jack to rejoin her after getting the Marines into an alert, but not threatening, deployment. Once he was on her left, with Megan on his, Kris strode forward.

She advanced, with Jack a step behind her, and Megan a step behind him, through sweet smelling green with splotches of every color that was pleasing to the eye. The path was not straight. She had been careful to follow with her eyes the course Ron had followed.

She followed in his footsteps.

At last she came out of the bushes to find a tiny grassy meadow. Across it, under a gold awning, with banners of light cloth blowing in a soft breeze, sat the old Iteeche. Around him, axe men stood, terrifying in their sharpness, muscle, and mass. Directly behind him, a half-dozen Iteeche in red, snake bowls held in their arms, also stood. In front of him, Ron kowtowed before him. A naked young

Iteeche, splayed out on the floor, speaking even as he gasped for breath, was the only one talking to Roth.

Kris suppressed a frown at that. What? No phone. No radio communications. The only way that the chamberlain could get a message to his boss was to send a kid racing by a different, longer path, to get the word to the head fish.

Oops. Watch your tongue, young lady.

Still, it was getting harder and harder to keep animosity out of her attitude toward her hosts.

AS YOU GUESSED, KRIS, THE YOUTH IS TELLING ROTH THAT WE DID NOT FOLLOW THE PATH WE WERE SUPPOSED TO.

THANK YOU, NELLY.

When the youth finished gasping out his message, Roth addressed a short question to Ron. He shot back a short reply, and the head honcho barked a laugh.

ROTH ASKED RON HOW WE MANAGED TO GET HERE SO FAST. RON JUST TOLD HIM YOU WENT STRAIGHT THROUGH THE FIFTH FLOOR WOMEN'S QUARTERS. AS YOU CAN SEE, HE FOUND THAT FUNNY.

OH, KRIS, HE JUST SAID YOU MAY APPROACH.

Kris stepped forward, and bowed her head, much as she would to her grandfather.

Again, the Iteeche barked a sharp laugh.

"You, human, are as quick as your grandfather," Nelly translated, "to cut to the heart of the briskis weed. So, you have strolled through my clans' women's quarters."

"It was not my intent to offend. I only wished to hasten to you to discuss matters of our mutual interest."

"That is what you humans do. You hasten to everything. One day, you will hasten to your deaths."

"I pray that will be a long time from now for my great-grandfather and myself. However, if we cannot do something about the poor quality of support that I am getting as Commander of the Imperial Battle Fleet, my passing may happen very soon. I foresee, however, two possible ways for me to pass very quickly. I could pass to my eternal reward if we can't get the Iteeche Battle Fleet into greater fighting fiddle. Or, I could pass up the beanstalk and take my embassy and fleet back to Wardhaven, leaving you to save your bacon on your own."

Roth eyed Kris for a long moment. "You are troubled that much?" he finally asked.

"I am angered that much. The Emperor has given me command of His Battle Fleet. Where is my chief of staff? Where is my copy of message traffic so I may see what the fleet I command is doing? How it is deployed? Where are the after-action reports I asked for? I took four flotillas out to train and exercise. I had to blow half of them away when they attacked me."

Kris paused to let Nelly's translation catch up with her, then quickly continued, allowing no time for her to be interrupted.

"No doubt, Your Eminence is aware a major effort was made tonight to kill me, my husband, my children, much of my embassy, and several millions of your people, if not also your Emperor."

"Yes, I am aware of that. We are overturning every stone to find the disgusting bugs that committed such a foul deed."

"I am glad that you are involved in such a wise and important action. However, that was only the straw that broke the camel's back."

Here, Kris paused to let Nelly translate the full meaning of her words into Iteeche.

Again, the powerful Iteeche laughed. This time he had to rest all four hands on his large belly. The laugh went on for quite a while. So long that even Ron was glancing up worriedly at Kris.

"You are so much like your Grand Chooser, my young girl, when you are angry. Or wish me to think you are angry. He, too, raged at me when I could get no one to risk their neck to a headsman by signing off on the treaty we had agreed upon. He also said that he was ready to pack up his people and we could fight that deep, dark war until the oceans froze clear to the bottom. He did indeed frighten me, and I put that fright into the rest of the Imperial Counselors that were there to see if a peace could be hauled out of such troubled waters. Waters that ran with the flesh and blood of so many good young warriors."

He paused. "Enough of this, we are not at court. Let us relax and smell the flowers as we search for the path through this coral reef. Can someone find a seat for my wise chosen one and for our Royal human emissary to our ever Worshipful and Wise Emperor?"

A stool was brought forward for Ron. The child, axe men, and snake wranglers were dismissed, and Kris found that there was nothing for her to sit on.

Nelly didn't allow that to happen. Nanos began to coalesce into a pleasant chair for her and two lesser ones for her subordinates. There was just a hint of surprise in the eyes of Ron's Chooser as he watched something appear out of nothing.

"You humans and your conjuring. Did you actually mold an entire palace out of a brick that you brought down from orbit? I heard that your sorcery made it appear that your landing craft disappeared away to nothing."

"It was done as you heard," Kris said.

"What could I trade you for that kind of wizardry?"

"Nothing, wise counselor. The wizardry was done by a computer, and she alone decides for whom she and her children will work."

Roth appeared to be speechless for a moment, then he went on. "You are angry enough to walk out on us. It may surprise you, but I am not surprised. Too many have done their best to stymy you. If it was me swimming in your spawning pond, I would challenge many people to duels and there would be more blood in the water than eggs. So, what do you demand from us to keep you here?"

"When I was hurrying to keep my meeting with the Emperor, I met Coth, Admiral of the First Order of Iron. He offered to assist me, but when I asked your wise chosen one for him to come calling, he said he had been ordered away and no one knew when he would return. Unless someone can point out a reason why I should not work with him, I want him as my chief of staff for the entire Iteeche Battle fleet."

Roth glanced away, as if losing himself in thought. "I have heard good things of this man. He has risen from below to well above his birth pond. Ron, have you any thoughts?"

"He stepped forward when none would talk to me or this Royal Emissary. When I called to have him come to her side, I heard good things about him. His enemies who sent him away are good enemies to have, from where I float."

"Ha. So we now measure a man not by his friends but by his enemies."

"A wise man has told me that we live in strange times."

Roth barked a laugh. Kris strongly suspected she knew who the wise man was that Ron was quoting.

"Okay, yes. I will see that he is ordered to your side. Now, go on, angry warrior, who I understand told the women of my clan that women can be warriors."

"It seems only wise," Kris said. "The side with the biggest battalions usually wins. How can you raise bigger battalions if you ignore half of your people?"

"Yes, I heard that from your grandfather. And now I am seeing such a warrior. You, Kris Longknife, may succeed in making an old man change his ways. Speak on."

"I need to know how your battles have been fought. Surely you write after-action reports so that you can learn from your mistakes. Improve. Get better. I need copies of your battle reports so that I may study how the enemy deployed and, in turn, set traps for them. I also need to study how you deployed so that I can see which was a strong array and which were weak when the rebels attacked."

"I am not sure that we have many of those. There have been few survivors among the admirals that have swum into battle. Maybe I can get you a few of the surviving captains. Most of them have been beached for being part of a losing armada. We do not reward losers."

"Their defeat may have made them wiser. Also, didn't you say that these had fought the rebels to a bloody stalemate."

"They had."

"Yet you punish them. Do the rebels do likewise?"

"Some beheaded them," Ron put in.

"Is that true? Are you sure?" Kris asked.

"That is what we heard," Ron said. "We do not know enough about what actually happens on the rebel planets to know anything for sure."

"Let me have any of these experienced commanders," Kris said. "Any that are not needed in other places."

"You may have them all," Roth said, magnanimously.

"Lastly, I need ships and crews. I do not want flotillas or armadas with hidebound admirals that may or may not support my efforts or the continued rule of your Emperor. I want ships with young crews. Young officers that want to win and are willing to learn to fight, outnumbered, three to one, and win."

"That is impossible," Roth said.

"My fleet was attacked by two flotillas," Kris snapped back. "We were outnumbered two to one and we blew away the sneak attackers and lost no ships ourselves."

"That is because you have conjured up that crystal armor. We need that crystal armor. Why won't you let us have it?"

"So that the rebels can have it in the blink of an eye. You must admit, your Empire leaks like a sieve."

"Sadly, we do. So, if you will not give us this magic skin for our ships, how will you do this fight, outnumbered, three to one, and win?"

"Our ships go faster than yours do. Our ships dance around faster than yours, so that they are more likely not to be hit, and our ships hit their targets more often than yours do. All these changes can be made to ships if you can give me younger officers, tired of losing and eager for victory. Can you give me a thousand ships? Are there younger officers with strong backs and smarter brains, willing to learn? I do not need old captains that already have aching backs. They will never risk their bones to my tactics. I need young warriors who hunger for battle."

"That we will have to think on," Roth said. "I am not opposed to giving you a thousand ships for your private training establishment. However, finding ships that are crewed by young, hungry, eager men? That will be a problem. Our promotions are given to those with the most years of experience. Too often, that means only that we promote the oldest men, the men next in line. I think you already know that many ships in the fleet, besides flying the Emperor's flag, also fly the flag of a Satrap. I do not know how we will work around some of those stumbling blocks. I do know that we can or will."

Roth paused to eye Kris. "You are right to think that some of those who acquiesced to your appointment looked at you as a, what do you say? Straw dog. If you burned, the fault would be you humans, not us. I fear that many of my fellow counselors are already looking for how they can splash into the new ocean that they see coming. We need a victory. Can you give us that victory?"

"Give me what I asked for and you will have it."

"It is late. You young ones should sleep on all of this. Maybe some of us older heads can do a little magic ourselves. Longknife, look for my messengers before the sun is at its zenith tomorrow."

Kris stood. Roth stayed seated. Everyone else stood with her.

"I look for your messenger tomorrow before noon."

"Good, good, now go, and please, do not disturb the sleep of my clan's ladies. Let my wise chosen one lead you out of here quickly, but not so spectacularly lacking in good manners."

"As you would have it," Kris said. She bowed her head. Her fellow humans bowed from the waist. Ron bowed even more deeply. Then Ron led them from the Imperial Counselor's presence.

17

The next morning, Kris spent with her kids.

"There's a swimming pool, Mommy," Johnnie enthused.

"A big one," Ruth added.

"Can we go swimming?"

"All the other kids are."

What Kris suspected was that all the other kids' mommies and daddies were getting this same kind of rush. Whatever was going on elsewhere, Kris found herself with her pair taking the elevator down to the middle level of the castle. All the outer windows served apartments that were rapidly filling up. Inside, however, was one huge pool.

Ruth and Johnnie stripped off their clothes even as they ran, jumping in the pool only seconds after their last stitch was tossed.

"What happened to swimsuits?" Kris asked Abby, who was watching her two.

"Hard to tell," Abby drawled. "Our fleet came to Alwa from all over, and several places weren't averse to skinny dipping. Some backwoods places on Wardhaven don't much use 'em, either. Anyway, beaches, lakes, rivers, and pools went from clothing optional to no one who wasn't. You want to try to make suits mandatory in your pool?"

"I've got too many bigger fish to fry, or to keep from frying me. I can't afford to sweat the small stuff," Kris admitted.

"Were last night's display of fireworks and laser lights what I thought they were?" Abby drawled.

"A go at frying all of us," Kris said. "Oh, yeah."

"Nelly, you are good," Abby said.

"You bet I am," Nelly said. You could not accuse her of humility, but then she had done a magnificent job of landing 75,000 tons of dead weight.

"So, you want to tell me why I, all our kids and half of this damn embassy was standing in what damn near ended up a big hole in the ground?" Abby growled.

"Yeah," Jack added.

"Maybe I was a bit overconfident. Maybe I wanted to put on a show for these squids that might get us some cooperation. Some respect. It started out as just a remote-controlled landing on an empty palace, but the Emperor is only four kilometers away, and the Iteeche admiral who controlled the airspace over the capital wasn't game for it. I had to add more skin to the game. I ended up with more skin on the playing field than I'd planned. Maybe I should have backed down." Kris said, then shook her head.

"I wanted to get this embassy off the ground, fast. No, *on* the ground and up and running fast. I wanted to knock their socks off and awe them at the same time."

"We sure did," Nelly interjected.

"Yes, we did," Kris agreed. "But my stomach still hasn't loosened up from the shock I got when the fireworks started. I damn near had a heart attack."

"I'm glad to hear that, Love," Jack said, and reached an arm around her to pull her to him.

"I've got to be more careful in the future," Kris said.

"We've got to give these squids more respect," Abby said.

"You've got to give me more respect," Nelly said.

"Yes, Nelly, you did it," Kris said. "I thank you. Once again, you've saved all our lives. I know you'll keep doing it, right up until the time comes when you don't."

"And then none of us will be around to rib you about that failure," Abby muttered softly.

Nelly sniffed loudly, but let the human have the last word.

Kris and Abby joined Amanda, sitting pool-side and praising their little ones as they bounced around under the careful tutelage of their teachers. They oh'd when a little one jumped into the pool into a teacher's arms. They ah'd as a bigger kid swam five or ten strokes out to where their teacher stood.

"You know," Amanda said, "we ought to get out of our clothes and bounce around with our kids."

Kris was saved from having to strip in front of all her underlings by Nelly.

"Kris, the Marines at the front gate report that there's an Iteeche who says he's an Admiral Fred Ironcloth."

"You mean Coth, Admiral of the First Order of Iron. Nelly, is there something wrong with the Marine's translation program?"

"No, Kris. More like there's something wrong with your Marine's grasp of Iteeche rank. I'll see what I can do about getting a complete set of officer rank insignias to the gunnies. That will get them to the privates post-haste."

"Okay. Tell the Marines to give him an escort and guide him to my day quarters."

"More likely, the Marine will need an escort to find your day quarters," Abby drawled.

"Nelly . . ." Kris began.

"I already have a mini drone lighting his way, Kris."

"Very good, Nelly," Kris said, and made her excuses for not jumping in the new swimming hole with her friends.

18

Kris found her way back to her day quarters. It had taken her enough time to accept that her 'office' aboard ship was her 'day quarters.' She was not about to force herself to switch back and forth. Especially since it looked like she'd be spending more time aboard ship than downside.

Her day quarters had filled out very nicely. All she needed was a pair of goalposts to hold a bloody soccer game in the place. Kris checked her desk, it was still empty. No reports had been delivered yet. At least this admiral's arrival meant she had gotten one of her demands. She'd let him chase after the reports.

There was a knock at her door. She said enter, then wondered if she needed to shout to be heard. Nelly, however, likely amplified her words, or maybe had them come from the door, itself?

A Marine corporal entered, announced, "Admiral of the First Order of Iron Coth, Admiral."

Someone had furthered that young woman's education on the way up here. "Thank you, Corporal, that will be all."

"Yes, ma'am," and the Marine was gone.

The admiral began the long hike to where Kris stood in a conversation pit in front of what looked like a roaring fire. "Quite a place you have here," Coth said. His head turned around, almost fully, then turned back to Kris. "Am I correct? Was that a woman warrior?"

"Yes, as am I, Admiral." Kris said, pointedly, though she suspected her inflection might be lost on the Iteeche.

"A Longknife I'm not surprised to see in a killer's uniform. Do you have a race of Amazons?"

"A lot of human women will kill you, if you train them right and give them a reason to."

"Am I getting off on the back foot?" the admiral asked as he came up to Kris.

"No. If we are to work closely together, we will have to learn about each other. I know of no way to learn other than by asking questions. I know that our two peoples are very different. I want to know as much as I need to know about you so that I can give your Emperor what he wants from me. I think you want the same."

"If it means ending this double dark rebellion, I'd swim the ocean underwater and get these worthless gill slits working again."

Kris noted that his uniform did not hide his vestigial gill slits. The coloration of the different slits said he was happy and hopeful, but also cautious.

RIGHT, KRIS.

Kris was grateful for Nelly's verification. It had been a while since she'd had to read gill slits.

"So, Lady Admiral, where do we go from here?"

"I am not a lady admiral. I am a princess. If you wish to address me by my formal titles, I am Her Royal Highness, Grand Admiral Kris Longknife of Wardhaven. If you intended to add a feminine comment to my rank, it would be taken as condescending and viewed with disapproval," Kris said, coolly.

"Well, that's a mistake I won't make again," he said. Then he bowed from the waist to her and said, "How may I serve Your Royal Highness, Grand Admiral Kris Longknife of Wardhaven?"

Kris authorized herself a soft chuckle. "And if you do that all the time, there won't be enough hours in a work day for all we need to get done."

"There already aren't enough hours in the day for all that needs doing," he growled.

"Just so. In my Navy, it is not unusual for admirals working together to call each other by our common name. Mine is Kris. We reserve our surname, in my case Longknife, for public occasions and for when a senior is displeased with a subordinate."

"I am Coth, just Coth. I come from no clan and have not been adopted into one. I was chosen by a junior sailor and have spent my entire life studying the Navy: command, war fighting, administration, and logistics."

"So, you have risen far above what those higher up would have expected of you."

"No doubt. Sometimes the Navy does allow it. There have been pirate infestations and a few minor rebellions. I was willing to get my hands dirty and I showed myself useful."

"But you may see the Empire differently than a senior Clan member."

"Definitely."

"Among us, we would say that you have seen the dirty underbelly of the lovely beast."

"That is a good phrase. I will have to remember it.

However, outside these walls, I would never use it. Some might think I did not worship my Emperor properly, or that I did not think that Clan shit did not stink."

"I think I will enjoy working with you. What have they told you about your new job?"

"Only to get my ass over here as quickly as I could get myself back to the Capitol."

"I was told you were needed elsewhere after we met the first time."

"I was ordered to a backwater station and given some trainees to kick into shape. I am sure they will be relieved to find my shining face is not there to greet them this morning."

Both of them enjoyed a chuckle at that vision.

"How long were you in transit?" Kris asked. "Did you get any sleep?"

"I have learned to sleep almost anywhere. The air transport was much better than some places I have slept."

"So, may I offer you a seat?" Kris said, and pointed with an open hand to an Iteeche chair, such as they knew how to make one. "I noticed that Ron's Chooser was in something much more involved that supported his back. Nelly, could you adjust his seat a bit?"

The stool sprouted a back that had to arch up over the hips before it swept forward to support his back.

"You will spoil me," Coth said.

"I will no doubt exhaust you as well. Accept the good I can give when it comes your way."

"So, this is what you do with the Smart Metal?"

"My computer has been told by a high clan leader that she a sorceress. She insists on proving herself as just that every chance she gets."

"I saw how your travel chair became quite a pavilion."

"That was all done by my computer, Nelly. She enjoys surprising people. I had told her to surprise me, and she certainly did."

"You talk of your computer as if it was not a box of chips."

"I am not a box of chips," Nelly said from Kris's collar bone.

"Admiral, may I introduce you to Nelly. I have had her since the time I entered the Palace of Learning. I chose not to replace her, but to upgrade her. One time, we even put into her matrix a bit of the computer the ancient races left on Santa Maria. She now tells horrible jokes and argues with me."

"I have given sworn testimony before a court of law on Musashi. I am a mother, and if I hadn't been flying the 75,000 tons of metal that is now this castle last night, half of your capital would be a smoking ruin."

When Coth stared at Kris in wonder, she briefed him on the events of last night's landing. "Needless to say, I was livid that the Empire could not control matters in their own capital. In my anger, I stormed over to Roth and told him if I didn't get some things I needed, I'd pick up my bat and ball and go home. You, by the way, are one of those things I demanded."

"You didn't actually march your warrior honor guard through the bedrooms of the Clan's most honored women, did you?"

"You have heard?"

"It had the military airport all abuzz. At the time, I didn't understand, and I had no time to spare to stop and ask." The Iteeche busted out laughing and ended up using all four hands to hold his belly. "Snakes and sea monsters, it is going to be fun working with you, my delightful human woman.

Ah, Grand Admiral. Imperial Admiral of the First Order of Steel, if you will excuse me."

"I am honored by all of them. I am also a mother. You might say Chooser. I am also in a lifelong bond with a human male, my husband, Lieutenant General Jack Montoya."

"I hope I can meet him soon."

"No doubt you will. Now, I need a chief of staff. Do you have something like that?"

"A master of logistics. I will be honored to see to your logistics."

"No, in our Navy, a commander for a large force down to the command of a thousand, may have a staff. One officer handles operations. It is his honor to prepare plans for battle. Another officer looks after logistics, as you said. One examines the training needs of the personnel, sees that vacancies are filled and does the paperwork for promotions. One is responsible for intelligence. What do we know about the enemy? How may we surprise them and not be surprised ourselves? All of those are led by a chief of staff. He juggles all these. He listens when I plan battles and may challenge me if he thinks I am wrong. He may point out potential problems so that they may be examined and either corrected or mitigated if I chose to go forward. When I make a decision, he sees that it is executed fully. If I am forward with the troops and there is a need for commands, he may issue orders in my name."

Kris paused to review her thumbnail sketch of a Navy staff. "I have known chiefs of staff who won battles while their commander was puking out his guts in the head."

"I am an admiral because I did something like that."

"I doubt you will ever have to do that for me, but if I am wounded in battle, until the flag is transferred to a successor, and it should be done quickly, still, you may have to give orders in the heat of battle. You up to that kind of fight?"

"You would make me your number one staff officer? You're offering me more fun than the last time I spawned," Coth said, enthusiastically.

"Good. I have a chief of staff for the human side, the Grand Admiral side. You will be my chief of staff for the Iteeche side, the Imperial Admiral of the First Order of Steel. Your first order of business will be to recruit your own staff."

"My Admiral, you make this better and better."

"I want people on staff who are tired of losing. Who hate losing. Who refuse to lose."

"I know a few."

"For political reasons, we will need to have some with strong clan standing. We cannot give the clans any more reason to plot against us. I need winners all, but I also need political connections. Are there a few like that?"

"I think I can find some."

"I expect we will need a staff of two or four hundred, maybe even six hundred. We'll need our own communications team. Or own computer network and data handling team. Think big."

"You want to be fully supported."

"I do not want to have to make decisions by guessing what is happening. I want to have reports coming to me and orders going away from me. I do not want to waste time on the small, the minor, the insignificant."

"Oh, my. I have heard many who marveled at how a people so small and weak and short-handed managed to beat us. I begin to see why."

"Yes. Since we climbed out of trees and learned to walk upright, we have been pounding on bigger animals with sharper teeth, faster legs, and stronger arms. We do it by thinking. Now, one more thing."

"Only say it and it will be done."

Kris had the Iteeche's full enthusiastic support. A warrior's support.

"I need the after-action reports from the battles that your Navy has fought with the rebels. I need to know how battlecruisers have been used to fight battlecruisers. What worked. What didn't. Surely you have reports written up after the fights."

Suddenly, her Iteeche looked a lot less happy. "Normally, yes. Unfortunately, the battlecruiser fights have not been normal in any way. The two major fights had no surviving admirals. The ship captains that escaped death in battle were disgraced and barely avoided making formal apologies to the Emperor. They have been deprived of their commands and sent to shovel shit."

"I want them assigned to me. I want to talk to them. We have a saying that no army learns from another army's defeat."

"We have such a saying. 'Defeat is a hard school master.' Some in our command have forgotten that wisdom."

"Get me those captains. Some of them may become admirals in our fleet."

"You may have a hard time giving them command of squadrons or sections, much less flotillas."

"I have asked for a thousand ships. I do not want any admirals with them. I am not sure I want their captains. I fight fast. I evade hard. I do not fight an old man's war. Captains who are too old and stuck in the mud of their ways will not stay in my fleet for very long."

The Iteeche admiral looked hard at Kris. "You know that you will be hitting a lot of spawning ponds with high water."

"I take that to mean I will upset a lot of people."

"A whole lot of very powerful people."

"Who have been losing fights for the Emperor."

"Yes, there is that."

"We will win and they will know that we are right."

"I hope you can get the rebels to fight you soon, because if they don't, you may be stabbed in the back before the rebels ever get a chance to kill you."

"Yes. Yes, I know that. Now. I need a staff. I need the defeated captains to write up what they know about how the battles were fought. I need Iteeche communication and data processing gear. How soon before you can get all this?"

"Where will we set up?"

"Nelly, can you arrange an Iteeche Navy annex? Something that lets them enter through the main gate but then switches out to a work area that is theirs alone. No access for humans except those authorized, just as the Iteeche will have no access to human spaces except through a guarded point."

"You want to keep that knife from your back, huh?"

"I want to avoid my humans disrupting the Iteeche Empire as much as possible, and yes, I want to limit access to my quarters to only those I want to meet."

"Kris, look out the window," Nelly said.

A cylinder of gleaming glass and Smart Metal™ was rapidly rising above the entrance gate of the palace. Thick pillars supported it a good three meters above the roof of the Pink Coral Palace. It stopped growing at approximately twenty stories. There, an elevator tube provided cross access to the main castle where it changed from a horizontal line to merge into one of the vertical lines going up and down the main castle.

The Iteeche admiral's mouth hung open.

"Your computer can do that!"

"It is as easy as eating pie," Nelly said, "Or factoring pi to the billionth place."

"I do not want to fight you humans. Ever again."

"Wait until you see what my humans can do in a fight with Iteeche battlecruisers," Kris said. "But first, there is much we must do."

Megan entered Kris's day quarters, a small box held in her hand. They watched as she approached. "Nelly suggested to me," the aide de camp said, "that I get the admiral a commlink so he can join our net."

"Thank you, Nelly," Kris said. "Is that the top of the line?"

"This is the best commlink computer, short of Nelly, that we have among those in this embassy."

"Very good. Admiral, Nelly oversees our communications net. If you ask Nelly to reach me, even if I'm in the bath, she can connect us. I may ask her to take calls if I'm busy, but she'll make sure I call you back. This isn't just a telephone. It's also a computer. It can take notes, write reports, and do more than you can imagine."

Megan handed the commlink to the Iteeche admiral. He strapped it to his right front wrist. "Nelly?" he asked cautiously.

"Yes, Admiral," she answered from the commlink.

Kris stood. "Tell Nelly how things are going. If you encounter too many delays or pushbacks, I'll take another mad rush at the honorable Roth."

As Coth stood he muttered, "Hopefully without invading the ladies' bedrooms."

On his feet, all four of them, Coth struck a fist to where his heart might be. "I am yours to command. I march to make it so."

"Do you need an escort out?"

"Ah, yes, please."

"Nelly?"

"The corporal is standing outside."

"Good. Ask the corporal to give you a quick lesson on using the commlink. Oh, and leave the door open when you go," she told Coth.

It seemed to surprise him, or so his gills showed, but he left the door open on his way out.

19

"Nelly, this room is too damn big. I'm not trying to intimidate every visitor. I don't have time for them to waste half a day just getting from the door to here."

"I'm sorry, Kris. I thought the more space, the higher your place in the pecking order."

"You're right, Nelly, but I'm not worried about pecking order with people I work with here. If we need to impress the natives, you can knock together a throne room. Maybe drain the pool and use that space."

"Yes, Kris. I've folded up your wardroom to give you this space. I'll create a wardroom across the hall from your day quarters."

"Good, Nelly, now I need to do something about my embassy. Please invite Abby, Amanda and Jacques, Jack, and . . . Nelly, get me Ambassador Kawaguchi. I think he'll be a good one to talk for the other ambassadors."

"Kris, I have asked all of them to be here in fifteen minutes. All will come. Ambassador Kawaguchi says he may be a bit late. May I ask if it is wise for you to pick him yourself? The other ambassadors seem to have accepted the Earth ambassador as the dean of their association."

"Yes, I expect some trouble, Nelly, but Ambassador Kawaguchi saved my life. I know him and I trust him. The rest will just have to accept him as their conduit to me, or I'll make my decisions without their input."

"Yes, Kris."

"Nelly, how are things among the merchant princes?"

"Not so good, Kris. The Iteeche customs officials, and they do have customs officials charged with examining cargo transported within the empire, are not happy with some of the products our merchants have brought. For example, they don't understand the working of a commlink or computer. They only use land lines. They also don't see the need for twelve different models of commlinks. They're not sure they want to allow our cheaper TVs in. There are a lot of electronics and labor-saving household appliances that they aren't very keen on. And that's before we get to wines, fancy foods, and pharmaceuticals."

Amanda and Jacques arrived with Abby just in time for the economist to exclaim, "Someone brought pharmaceuticals? That's ridiculous! We don't even know what makes their bodies tick."

"Actually, we do," Nelly said. "There were Iteeche POWs that needed health care and we did figure out some ways to heal them. Believe it or not, aspirin relieves their pain even better than it does ours. A lot of the stuff they shipped out here, like bolts of fine silk, wool and cotton cloth, artistic rugs, and wall hangings, are just shots in the dark."

"How's the shooting gallery going?" Kris asked.

"More misses than hits," Nelly answered. "Mainly, those lord high mandarins don't want to let this stuff in."

"Why should they?" Amanda said, bringing an economist's education to the wandering debate. "We have no idea what they want. They have no idea what we have to give or, more importantly to them, what we may want in return. I think their resources are stretched very thin. They may fear that we will drain critical materials from the Empire."

Amanda paused, then shook her head. "It's a wild guessing game, Kris. Remember, you said you'd set up meetings between our merchants and theirs. How soon can that start?"

"Nelly, please get me Ron."

"Yes, Kris," Ron said only a moment later. "Are you planning another military parade through our lady's quarters?" the Iteeche jabbed at her.

"I'll only bring female Marines next time," Kris said, not at all humbled by the intent of every Iteeche to hit her on that bit of perambulation.

"Please, by all that has risen from the deep, do not take women warriors where our clan's senior ladies can see them. I don't know how long it will take us to get rid of this idea of taking up arms and fighting like a warrior."

"Good luck on that, Ron. We humans have had women warriors since before histories were written. And lots of them for the last four hundred years."

"You humans are like a hurricane out of season."

"We humans live in the hurricane season, year-round," Kris said as a smiling Ambassador Kawaguchi thanked a Marine escort at Kris's open door and began a much shorter walk to Kris's conversation circle. A comfortable chair rose from the floor. He bowed to Kris. She gave him a small, distracted nod from where she sat, and he sat down.

Ron was now talking. "Kris, you don't need to brag about that. It is a horror to any right-thinking Iteeche."

"Speaking of right-thinking Iteeche, I have merchant princes who want to talk to your traders. How do we set this up and get it going?"

"You don't forget anything, do you?"

"I'm not allowed to forget something like this."

"You got your admiral, right?"

"Admiral Coth arrived early this morning. He's out recruiting staff just now. By the way, can you arrange for the captains of the battlecruisers who survived the last two big battles, only to be sent off to shovel shit, to report to my palace. I've set up an Iteeche Navy annex to my castle for them and Coth's staff."

"Yes, I heard that your castle was expanding. So, you are giving some of your tower over to the Iteeche Navy?"

"If we are to defeat the rebellion, I must have Iteeche warriors willing to fight with me. The staff is a start. Now, about my traders and those thousand ships I asked for and your Eminent Chooser promised."

"Do you need all of the one-thousand ships immediately?"

"I would settle for ninety-six just now." If she was to fight outnumbered three to one and win, she might as well start outnumbered no more than three to one.

"So, your present human flotilla can fight them outnumbered three to one and win, huh?"

"Something like that. Hopefully, our next practice exercise will not be with fully powered lasers firing at each other."

"I think the way you blew away your assailants will discourage that from happening again."

"Good. It is nice to know that Iteeche rebels can be educated." Kris knew that what she said could be applied to all Iteeche, but it was a conclusion she was not averse to Ron drawing.

"I will see about finding you ninety-six ships with no admirals. By a sheer coincidence, we have forty-two ships that recently lost their admirals as well as their captains. Would you mind if we included them among your first draft?"

"Can they be trusted?"

"I fear that they, and most of the ships you blew to gas were just following orders. You can talk to the newly promoted captains and see if they are committed to trying to kill you, but I don't think you will find that they are."

"Very good, Ron. I've got forty-two Iteeche battlecruisers. Now, how do I get the next fifty-four?"

"You are, what do you say, dogged?"

"Dogged for my ships. Oh, and dogged for some Iteeche merchants to be allowed to meet with my merchants. They brought a lot of human goods they want to trade for Iteeche goods. Until they can open negotiations, our guys are chomping at the bit."

"As you are chomping on my ass. Okay, Longknife. Okay. There are some merchants that do business with my clan. Some of them have expressed some interest in seeing what you humans have to offer and what you will take in return. However, Kris, I must warn you that many of our clan leaders doubt that you humans will be interested in what we have to trade in return. Many Imperial Counselors fear that all we can offer you is gold and other raw materials. Materials that are in short supply within the Empire. If we trade them to you, what will we have to build our own economy? We must expand to provide more jobs. So many choosers want to choose more young. To increase their families, septs, or clans, and gain more prestige."

"This is the first you have told me of your population pressures."

"You have seen our capital planet. You must know already how numerous we are."

"I was advised that you must ship a lot of foodstuff in as well as export people and dung."

"Your advisor is wise."

"We have had experiences with runaway populations in our past. We might be able to offer you ways that would allow choosers to compete in other ways than the number of young they have chosen."

"That is something we can talk about later, assuming someone does not gas this planet and bring in their own population to repopulate their new Imperial capital."

"Has that happened before?"

"Three times since deep in our past, Kris. There are reasons why clan leaders do not want to be the last to join the winning side."

"Good lord," Kris muttered.

"Yes. Now, I will send merchants to talk to your merchants. They should start arriving by midday. Even as we spoke, the disgraced captains have been ordered to report to your palace. They should start arriving tomorrow. As for more ships, we have asked for volunteers. It is not easy to persuade other satraps to give up ships, but I hear that some hotheads are indeed trying to get their shahs to persuade their pashas to release them for a while to see what you humans have to offer. Between the way you tricked the rebels into fleeing before an inferior force, then stomped so hard on those that attacked you, and finally that show you put on, landing a star ship within spitting distance of the Imperial Palace, people are starting to think that you may actually be a worthwhile ally."

"I am glad to hear that. Now, I am in a meeting here and a fine old friend joined me while we talked. I cannot continue ignoring him. I must leave you to your work as I must go to mine."

"I had a lot less work before you came here," Ron grumbled.

"Take it up with the fool who tricked me into coming," Kris shot back.

"Good-bye, human."

"Good-bye, Iteeche."

The line clicked off and Kris turned to greet her old friend and life saver who now was an ambassador under her umbrella.

20

"Ambassador Kawaguchi" Kris said, "it is so good to see you."

"Grand Admiral, or should I address you as Royal Emissary to the Court of the Iteeche Empire, or must I use your other title these days, Imperial Admiral of the First Order of Steel?"

"If you call me anything else but Kris, I will be insulted, Counselor. We who have gone through death and life together could never be so formal."

"Ah, those were great days. When we receive reports from our battle fleet defending the birds of Alwa or those cats at that unpronounceable place, we all remember you and your proud stand and that it was warships from our own shipyards that took you back to find your long-lost great-grandmother."

"I smell the butter. Will there be garlic in this sauce you are trying to drown me in?" Kris said, through a grin.

"Ah, yes. Ever alert to spot the trap. You are truly a Longknife."

"So, how are things among the diplomats?"

"There are those who thought they had snookered you when they snuck aboard your convoy to here. They thought they had outmaneuvered you when they managed to acquire all four sides of the palace. That you and your staff would have to come begging, hat in hand, asking for this or that square meter of space back. I warned them that they should never try to snooker a Longknife, certainly not this Longknife. I see that you have now risen above all that petty bickering and are gazing down on us from your palatial quarters."

"So it seems," Kris said, allowing herself a proud smile.

"I always do love a good fireworks display, and the laser lights were spectacular. Such a greeting for you! Is my military attaché correct that was an attempt to cause you to crash and kill us all? A very colorful attack on us?"

"I'm afraid it was," Kris said, now deadly serious. "They did not, however, plan for the likes of Nelly and two of her children piloting the lander."

"There was never any risk to you on the ground," Nelly said. "I would not have let the children die. If matters had gone ass over teakettle, I would have broken 75,000 tons of Smart Metal up into tiny landers and let them finish their descent in one kilo packets with parachutes to slow them down sufficiently."

"I should have known the Magnificent Nelly would be prepared for all eventualities," the ambassador from Musashi said jovially. "But heads will surely roll, Kris."

"You have been reading the reports my office has been distributing to all of you."

"I have read every word. There are far too few of them, and they tell me very little. Certainly, you can tell your old friend more."

Kris shook her head. "Really Ambassador, I have told

you all I have learned. The Iteeche Empire appears to be made up of feudal clans held together only by their allegiance to an Emperor who, at the moment, is a young lad. Many now see this as a chance to reach for the purple. I know there is much infighting among the clans here in the capital. We are supported by one of the larger clans. It is lorded over by my great-grandfather's old friend from peace negotiations of ninety years past, Eminent Roth'sum'We'-sum'Quin of the Chap'sum'We clan. I understand that pashas for twenty-two of the three hundred some satraps in the Empire are drawn from this clan. They are powerful, but there are others just as powerful and many of them fear the rebellion only slightly more than they fear what we humans are doing to the good old ways."

"Ah, the old ways were never so good, though they are now much beloved and held on to so very tightly even as they pass from our lives. How well I know of that trait. So, how does that affect us playing nine pins with the heads of those that thought to dig a huge hole with your lander?"

"They do not have the electronic financial system we have. Cash money does not leave much of a trail. We could lop the heads off the Iteeche who lit the fuses to the fireworks, or even those who sold the fireworks, but they were hired to celebrate our arrival. They did not know that their fireworks or lasers had been weaponized. Do you want such heads for your game?"

The wise counselor scowled, and nodded. "I see how the big wolf uses rats and mice to do the deed and is nowhere to be seen when the butcher's price is to be paid."

"There are Iteeche who would gladly have those poor peoples' heads on pikes. I have specifically asked that these little people not be punished. Both because I have a soft heart, and because I would rather all the Iteeche think of it as a true celebration, rather than an attack. A few know what they tried to do. The rest saw only colored lights."

"That is better. Much better. Still I would like to have the correct heads on pikes."

"Me, too."

"So, I am an ambassador. I am here to build bridges to the Iteeche Empire for my Imperial master. Instead, I sit in my office and twiddle my thumbs. Or, I go to tea with other ambassadors and we talk about better ways to twiddle our thumbs. There are only so many ways to twiddle thumbs."

"I assure you, Tsusumu -sama, if you commanded a fleet of battlecruisers, I would keep you busy day and night."

"Is that what we are reduced to?"

"Tell me, if I threw a ball for the royal birthday, whatever the date that it is here, how many Iteeche clan leaders do you think would come to celebrate with us?" Kris said, bringing up one of the easiest ways to arrange a diplomatic soirée in human space.

"None."

"Just so," Kris said.

"But there is this question of thumbs?" he said, making a show of twiddling his.

"The Iteeche Empire is old and inertia keeps it going. Let me win a battle or two, and then we can see how the clans react. Right now, most of them are looking for the right side to choose. Many think we have been brought in by the losing side. A few minutes ago, I found out that the winner may gas the planet from orbit, and kill everyone on the ground so that no one will remember the names of the ancestors whose ashes are interred here. Then they will bring in their own clansmen to seize the planet's wealth and repopulate it."

"By the Emperor, I hope you are wrong."

"I trust the Iteeche Navy officer who told me that. It concerns him greatly."

"It is one thing to twiddle my thumbs. It is another thing to risk annihilation while doing so."

"Rest assured, I will let you know when it is time to run. Remember, my own children are here with me. Also, I am the one that commands the Iteeche Battle Fleet."

"Such as it is, and such as they obey you."

"There is that."

"You speak like you have a plan, though."

"I have one. It will take some while to implement. In the meantime, I have arranged for several Iteeche merchants to meet with our merchants this afternoon. Our men of business may begin to see just what this 'huge' Iteeche market is really worth to them."

"That will be happy news."

"The Iteeche merchants will be few. I suggest you diplomats decide how the opportunities will be distributed. I would suggest a lottery."

"That seems fair to you and to me, but I doubt it will be thought of in the same way by your representative from Alexander Longknife."

"I leave it to you and the ambassadors to arrange the trade opportunities."

"You have once again dropped a hot sweet roll in my lap," he said, standing, "I will need all the time allowed me to make arrangements so that there are no duels fought over access."

"Be prepared. My Iteeche sources do not think that there will be much worth trading. They know of few uses for our products. All their communications are by landlines. They have no commlinks. There are many, many disconnects between our different technologies and life styles."

Ambassador Kawaguchi bowed to Kris. "Until we can talk again," he said and turned to go.

"Oh, Ambassador. If the other ambassadors question why it was you I talked to, tell them if they save my life, I will talk to them just as much."

The old counselor laughed loud and long as he made his way to the door.

21

Grand Admiral Kris Longknife sat cinched into her high gee station. She was naked in the egg. She expected some hard sailing before this exercise was done.

Around her, Battlecruiser Task Fleet 6 was stacked up in four squadrons of eight human battlecruisers each. Commodores filled the rear admiral command billets of the two task forces. Captains commanded the squadrons. Half the divisions were commanded by commanders.

If this exercise went well, Kris would frock each commander up to his or her functioning rank. If it went badly, she wasn't sure what she'd do.

A bit more than 270,000 kilometers off her starboard bow, three Iteeche flotillas cruised in similar formations. All were decelerating at one gee toward a small rock of a moon. According to this fleet exercise, Kris was defending that rock. The ninety-six Iteeche battle cruisers were intent on fighting their way through to the worthless satellite.

In actuality, this exercise would decide whether the young boy who sat on the Iteeche Imperial throne would live or die, along with the fifty billion people who lived on his capital planet.

Both fleets were composed of battlecruisers, built to the same design, armed with the same 24-inch lasers, powered by the same reactors. By all rights, a three to one superiority should result in Kris's fleet being quickly wiped out.

Fortunately, for this exercise, all the lasers had been dialed back to .01 percent of their usual power. If any ship showed any sign that their capacitors were getting more than a trickle of electricity from the reactors, Kris would immediately cancel the exercise and blow that ship to hell.

The Iteeche captains and crews understood. They knew the fate of the last Iteeche admirals and battlecruisers that had crossed swords with Kris Longknife. Unlike those admirals that had turned coat and tried to kill Kris, these ships had only one admiral's flagship.

Coth, Admiral of the First Order of Iron, commanded the opposition forces. He would fight this battle per present Iteeche Navy doctrine. Under his command, flotillas, squadrons, and divisions were led by captains that had come far too close to being cashiered out of the Navy and made to apologize most sincerely to the Emperor.

All of them wanted to win this fight. Every one of the Iteeche ships' skippers and crews were tired of losing battles or fighting themselves to bitter and bloody draws. This human, Kris Longknife, said that she knew how to fight outnumbered three to one and win.

They would very much like to know how she intended to pull that off.

For this exercise, they were the three. She was the one. They had ninety-six battlecruisers. She commanded a mere thirty-two, built to the same design as their opposite numbers.

It was their job to destroy her, to tag her ships with enough weak hits that they would be counted as destroyed. Ten hits and a battlecruiser would not be able to fire anymore and would be obliged to fall out of formation and the exercise. Ten for the human ships. Ten for the Iteeche ships.

The humans should be annihilated quickly.

Kris intended to annihilate the Iteeche very quickly.

"We will be in maximum range in ten seconds," sensors reported to Kris on the flag bridge of the *Princes Royal*.

"Prepare to raise deceleration to 3.3 gees, Execute Evasion Plan 4," Kris ordered.

"All ships report ready," reported Captain Tosan, Kris's chief of staff.

"Execute," Kris ordered.

Her weight began to grow as the *P. Royal* went from one gee to 3.4 gees. As it began evasion maneuvers, Kris was slammed from one side to the other in her egg. Fortunately for her, it cushioned the blows, allowing Kris, and all the crew on the thirty-two human battlecruisers to stay combat effective.

Up and down the line, human battlecruisers jinked independently. What had been a stately line of 75,000-ton warships turned into a wild mass of jitterbugging ships as some went up when others went down. Kris had allowed 5,000 kilometers between ships in squadrons and 10,000 kilometers between the squadrons above and below. Within that authorized zone, each battlecruiser did its own thing, juggling their acceleration between 0.0 and 3.5 gees. They never stayed on the same course more than three seconds.

This might have ruined their own fire control solutions, but the jink plan for the ship was fed into the fire control computers and adjustments made.

The distant Iteeche ships continued on their stately course. They did, however, activate their maskers. This bit of technology from the ancient races who built jump points between the stars several million years ago had caused the humans all kinds of trouble during the Iteeche War. When activated, they confused the humans' mass range finders. Suddenly, those sensors would have shown an alien ship to be as much as a thousand kilometers from where it actually was. When combined with chaff to dazzle laser range finders and confuse radar as well, human fire control systems had been left confused and unable to target the Iteeche.

It had turned out that nothing but the Mark I eyeball could be trusted, and the US fleet was extremely out of practice with it. During the war, humans had quickly improved their optics and learned to use them and computers to get a good range, bearing, and target solution.

As the hostile battle line jumped or vanished, Kris's ships switched smoothly to optics only, although the lasers and radars continued to strive to contribute to targeting solutions by frequency hopping.

"We are in range of the hostile force," Sensors announced.

"Commence firing," Kris ordered.

Battlecruisers do not fire broadsides. All their guns were located in the bow or stern and could fire only within fifteen degrees to the right or left, up or down, from the ship's keel. Both fleets now wore ship to bring their forward batteries to bear.

The human battlecruisers independently changed course to get themselves aimed at the Iteeche ships, presenting their bows to within 15 degrees of their chosen targets.

The Iteeche battlecruisers swung around most majestically as one, to face the humans with zero degrees on their bow, and aimed directly at their opponents.

At the same split second, both forces opened fire.

Nelly had programmed each laser on both sides to fire tenth of a second bursts at .01 percent power. They would then fall silent for the rest of the second to fire another infinitesimally short burst each second for six seconds. That was normal duration of a laser beam from the twelve huge 24-inch lasers each battlecruiser carried.

Once the forward battery was shot dry, the ship would flip to bring the eight lasers of the aft battery to bear. Six seconds later, the human ships would turn back onto their base course while they reloaded.

Twenty seconds after the bow guns fell silent, the captain would bring those guns to bear again. Every twenty-six seconds, another salvo would slash out to burn and smash their opposite numbers.

Three Iteeche ships targeted each of Kris's ships. Kris's fleet targeted the Iteeche flotilla closest to the rock they were defending.

It was supposed to be a massacre. To the Iteeche's shock, it was their three flotillas that were massacred in hardly more than a minute.

Exactly seventy-eight seconds after Kris gave the order to commence firing, every last one of the ninety-six Iteeche ships had received ten of the required hits. Most had taken forty or fifty hits of the 120 weak pulses aimed at them.

Kris's ships had taken one or two. Total! Not each!

"Cease fire," Kris ordered as her ships completed their third salvos and demolished their third flotilla.

"Admiral Coth, it seems our exercise is over," Kris said on the guard channel. "Would you care to repeat it?"

"By all the monsters ever to come from the deep, no. At least not just now. Would you be kind enough to allow me fifteen of your minutes to examine what just happened to us?"

"Certainly, admiral," Kris said, and ordered the two fleets back to their base course at one gee deceleration.

"I would not want to be in his shoes just now," Captain Tosan said, softly.

"I imagine it must be very exciting to wear his shoes," Jack said from his high gee station on the other side of Kris. "When you're racing downhill to hell in a hand bag, it's always exhilarating to try and change direction."

"You have a good point, sir," Captain Tosan said. "Now, Admiral, is there anything you want to do differently for the next part of the exercise?"

"At the moment, no. I'll save going to Evasion Plan 6 for the third shoot, if there is one."

Fifteen minutes later, Admiral Coth was back on screen. "We are prepared to try that again," he said.

"Shall we recommence the exercise in one minute? Would you like me to transmit a tic toc for you?"

"No need. Our computer has one of your clocks available. We will activate it."

"Good, then we will begin again in one minute from my mark." Kris paused, then said, "Mark."

"I will see you again. Hopefully less soon."

"Good luck, Admiral."

Kris waited for the timer on her screen to count down to 30 seconds. "Prepare to drop deceleration to .8 gees, Execute Evasion Plan 4. Target flotilla farthest away from the rock," Kris ordered, changing up from the last time.

"All ships report ready," came back from Captain Tosan, Kris's chief of staff.

Kris waited until the clock was down to five seconds, then ordered, "Execute."

This time, the human battlecruisers slowed. The knocking about was easier without the extra energy of hard deceleration.

As the clock hit all zeros, Kris ordered, "Commence fire."

The human battlecruisers again honked themselves hard over toward the opposition forces using independent maneuvering. As soon as their bows came to bear on their target ships, the forward batteries began a weak staccato fire.

Admiral Coth had jacked his deceleration up to two gees, the maximum Kris had seen an Iteeche force use. In the minute the clock had been ticking, the squadrons and ships had opened up their ranks and files within their flotillas to something close to Kris's formation. They started trying to jiggle their courses, even as they all turned to face their opponent.

The humans flipped smartly in seven seconds. The first salvo snapped out as if a single shot. Many Iteeche ships flipped slower than others. Their opening volley was ragged.

The Iteeche managed to secure a hit on only one of Kris's ships. One entire Iteeche flotilla was swamped by hits and fell off, out of the exercise.

Both sides reloaded.

"Kris," Nelly said, "Iteeche skippers are reporting that they cannot get target lock on our ships. Their jinking is messing up their firing solution. Oh, Coth just ordered them to jink more."

"A decent suggestion," Kris said. "If you can't blow them up, at least try not to get blown up."

The second when the forward batteries on the human battlecruisers would be reloaded was fast approaching. The volley from the aft Iteeche batteries had been ragged as well.

Kris's battlecruisers fired their second forward salvo seconds before the Iteeche. Kris's ships kept up their jink pattern. The Iteeche tried to jack theirs up.

Kris's fleet suffered no hits this time. A second Iteeche flotilla had to fall out of action.

Coth appeared on screen. "Sea snakes and dark monsters, Admiral Longknife, what is it that you are doing right and we are doing wrong?"

"Check fire. Check fire," Kris ordered her fleet. Coth said something to someone off-screen and his ships returned to the base course, with one gee deceleration. Kris gave the same order.

"Is there something wrong with our guns, with our ships, or just with us as Iteeche warriors?" Coth demanded of Kris.

"Yes, there is something wrong with your guns, and differences in our ships, but there is nothing wrong with your warriors. Admiral, have your fleet close the distance with us in the next thirty minutes. In one hour, I would like to meet with you and your key staff and subordinate commanders as well as each ship's skipper, his second in command, and with the officer we call Guns, or the gunnery officer."

"It will be so," Coth said, and the screen went blank.

"Captain Tosan, secure the fleet from battle stations. Set course to rendezvous with the Iteeche flotillas. Advise all unit commanders and their key staff, ship skippers, XOs, and Guns we will be meeting in the Forward Lounge in an hour. I will be in my room."

"Aye, aye, Admiral."

"Jack, with me."

22

"Admiral on deck," Jack called.

The humans in the Forward Lounge jumped out of their chairs and snapped to attention. It took the Iteeche only a second more to realize that they were expected to stand. It turned out their attention was something more like left foreleg forward, left aft leg back and the two right legs straight in line, with hands up, the two forward ones together and flat above their eyebrows, while the two aft ones were up as a human would do to surrender.

All that took time with a lot of knees and elbows bending in strange ways.

Megan had come ahead. She and her computer Lily had been rearranging the Forward Lounge. She had it in a gentle amphitheater sloping down to the front table where she and Admiral Coth now stood. Four groupings of chairs in wedge formation stretched up the gentle slope. Three were occupied by Iteeche in Navy gray. In the fourth, humans in undress whites stood.

Kris strode down to the front table, and while Jack

joined the others behind it, Kris turned to face her Navy officers, "As you were."

It took them a few moments to settle back into their chairs. The Iteeche seemed a bit uncomfortable to all be afforded a chair with a high back.

THEY ARE MORE LIKELY TO BE REQUIRED TO STAND. IF THEY SIT, IT IS ON STOOLS.

THANK YOU, NELLY.

"Admiral Coth, do you have any questions after this exercise?" Kris said, turning to have her Iteeche chief of staff

"Yes, Your Royal Highness and Imperial Admiral of the First Order of Steel. How do you humans do those things you do? How do you get your ships to jump around so much that they were impossible to hit? How did you manage to hit us while doing that? It all seems impossible. What is different about your ships?"

"Our ships are no different than yours. Your ships could do exactly what our ships did."

"I find that hard to believe. How are you able to get the same ship design to do what we cannot?" All the Iteeche in the room seemed to lean forward in their seats.

Kris spoke slowly. She had to persuade them to change something ten thousand years of warrior culture had instilled in their bones.

"Steel is strong. Much stronger than flesh," She turned back to his officers and began to walk back and forth in front of them. "If we are to yank our ships away from hostile laser fire, do what we must do so that we are not there when their lasers slice into the space where they expect us to be, human flesh needs help. I might add, so does Iteeche flesh."

NELLY, A HIGH GEE STATION, PLEASE.

A high gee station in the form of an older-style egg flowed up from the deck. "This is what we call a high gee station. Every human on board my battlecruisers went to their battle station seated in one of these." So saying, Kris settled into the egg.

"This conforms to a warrior's body so that if the ship is maneuvering hard, the movement is cushioned. Also, it allows us to recline, to keep our blood from flowing away from our heads and causing us to lose consciousness when we accelerate at three or more gees. Without this high gee station, we could not maneuver as hard as we do."

"I had read in our histories," Admiral Coth said, slowly, "about how you humans flitted about like water bugs upon a pond and made it hard for us to hit you, but what we saw today was so much more than the histories ever spoke of."

"These are much improved from eighty years ago."

"You humans are always changing," came from somewhere in the back of the Iteeche officers.

"Yes, we are. It is how we have survived as a species," Kris said.

"Just so," Coth said. "You could dodge about, but we did too, and still you hit us. What do you have that makes you better warriors? Is it just this egg thing you sit in during battle?"

Kris suspected that sitting during battle would still be a hard sell, however, she went on to the next item on her agenda.

"We identified areas that you might be interested in addressing," Kris said. "Our fire control systems adjusted our fire plans just as quickly as you adjusted your course. The cycle of identifying a course change, calculating where you would be when our lasers reached you, and then feeding it to our guns, went faster for us. It appears that we were able to complete the cycle in three to four seconds. You seemed to be taking six or more seconds. We never stayed on the same course for more than two or three seconds. By the time your lasers got to where you expected us to be, we had slammed ourselves onto a different volume of space."

"But how did you keep from turning your fire control solution into stew?" came from a gunnery officer in the third row back. Unable to keep quiet, he was still as embarrassed as Kris had ever seen an Iteeche, his vestigial gill slits showing a bright yellow.

"That is a very good question," Kris said. "Thank you for it."

The Iteeche's gills showed less yellow.

"We feed whatever evasion plan we are using into our fire control computer. It adjusts our fire for what our own ship will be doing. Thus, if we make a hard right halfway through the six second laser burn, it corrects the guns for that even as we do it."

"Ah," came from a lot of Iteeche beaks.

"However, let me return to the amount of time it took you to calculate your firing solution. We are using the same computers. How is it then, that it takes you close to twice as long to get your solution?"

Now, a lot of yellow was showing from a lot of gill slits.

"It may be," Admiral Coth said, "that our battlecruisers are not the same as yours."

Kris cocked an inquiring eyebrow, then realized that might be lost on the Iteeche. "In what way?" she asked.

"We do not much like your human computers. They are so different. May I say, alien? We prefer to install our own fire control computers. We also replaced our ships' central computers with ones of our own manufacture. The small amount of smart metal we save is used to increase the height of each deck on our ships. We are much taller, as you may have noticed."

Kris had turned to face Admiral Coth as he spoke. That put her in a position to cock an eyebrow at Megan. If they had problems getting into their computers because they were alien, no wonder the Iteeche had problems using human computers.

"We did not know that," Kris said. "Nelly, could you make a change to our human-computer interface to make it more like an Iteeche-computer interface?"

"Admiral, I doubt I would have any trouble, now that I know this to be the case. However, I will need to know more about the Iteeche computer to interface them to us. Alternatively, I can examine their interface and change our computers to look just like theirs at the point where the Iteeche use them," Nelly said.

"How long would that take?" Coth asked.

"A few minutes, once I can understand how your computers work. Do you have a simple one?" Nelly asked.

"Most of our computers are too large to rip out and bring over here. However, our supply computer has not changed in millennia," Coth said. "Could a captain arrange to have an inventory computer brought over here immediately?"

In only a moment, one of their Number 2s, what Kris would call their XO, was on his feet and trotting for the exit.

The fact their officer could not just mutter into his commlink and have it delivered in fifteen minutes said a lot. He had no commlink, and, of course, if he had, it would not have attached to a human network. With luck, once he got back to the longboat that brought him, he could make a radio call.

"So, to sum up our catch of the day," Admiral Coth said, "you use these eggs to dodge out of the way without addling your brains. You have faster fire control computations and feed your evasion patterns into them to adjust your shooting. Does that sum it all up?"

"There is one more thing," Kris said.

"I hope it will not be as embarrassing as everything so far."

"It is not a Navy problem, although it is one our Navy has had to correct. Often, the builders deliver the ship's lasers loose in their cradles."

"Yes, we know that we have to sight in our lasers before they can be fired accurately. We do that during our shakedown cruise," Admiral Coth answered.

"By loose in the cradle, I do not just mean out of true. The cradles are loose, so that when the ship does any sort of maneuvering, especially hard maneuvering, the play in the cradles throws the accuracy of the laser shots off. After a bit of sailing, even smooth sailing, the gun is out of alignment. If we tighten the laser down in its cradle, it takes a lot more hammering before it needs to be sighted in again."

"We were firing widely dispersed salvos in our attempt to hit your wildly moving ships," Coth said, speaking slowly.

"Yes, I know. But your salvos were wildly dispersed as well as widely dispersed." Kris wondered if that sounded the same in Iteeche, but it was the intent she was interested in.

"Just how many hits did we get on your ships?"

"Of the seven hundred and twenty short bursts you fired at each of my ships, we took only four or five hits," Kris said. Actually, it was closer to one or two, but as beaks fell open, eyes got wide, and gills got orange for not only the Iteeche captains, but Admiral Coth as well, Kris was glad that she'd been charitable.

It was a long moment before Coth muttered, "That few?"

"Yes."

"Even with our maskers on, you were making fifty or more on us. Many spaced very close together on our hulls."

"Yes."

"You have a way to out-fox our maskers?"

"No. They still make a stew of most of our fire control sensors. You have forced us back to using our optics and eyeballs, aided by our computers."

"You were firing at us with just your eyesight!"

"Aided by good optics and computer enhancements, yes."

"Sea monsters from the deep! We take away half your sensors and you get better at the half we cannot touch."

"Is it not that way with you as well?" Kris asked.

"From what you have told us, it does not appear so."

Since there was nothing to do while they waited for a small computer to arrive, Kris opened up the bar. Admiral Coth had brought crates of battle rations, and those were passed around. The Iteeche tried several drinks and quickly settled on a dry white wine as their beverage of choice.

Nelly made space around the bar so that the officers of the two Navies could mingle. Megan worked with her Lily to create a high gee station for Admiral Coth. As soon as she had one complete, she created more for the other Iteeche to test out.

Problems arose quickly. Humans could use their commlinks to create a high gee station and adjust it to fit properly. One size did not fit all. The Iteeche lacked personal computers at their fingertips, so creating an egg and getting it to fit became an immediate challenge.

"The way you humans gab to each other over distances is repugnant to us. We have always done our talking face to face," Admiral Coth told Kris.

She suspected that it was mainly because of their need

to observe each other's gill slits, something they did without conscious thought.

"I have a second question for you," Coth said, going on. "How do you fight your battle station when you are flat on your back? Yes, ship maintenance can be delayed while we are under high acceleration, but how can a helmsman steer the ship when he is flat on his back?"

"The high gee station provides the warrior with controls he can handle in a fight and our data links allow us to transmit what is done in the egg to the helm, weapons, whatever is needed," Kris said, entering her own egg to show Admiral Coth how her battle board adjusted to her posture.

"And how do you command your ships when you are flat on your back?" the Iteeche admiral asked.

"I don't understand." Kris said, noting that the room around them had gotten quiet. Every Iteeche eye was on them now, and with each of them having four, that meant a lot of eyes.

"I watch my officers to see that they are performing their duty. How can you see your officers? All of you are in your eggs, flat on your backs and gazing off at the overhead."

Kris felt the gains she'd made begin to slip away.

"On my battle board, I can check the status of my crew. I can bring up anyone's board if I want to see what they are seeing. My board can report out if anyone is wounded or off line. If the helmsman goes down, I can order anyone on the bridge to take over that job. We cross-train a lot."

"Any station can be fought by anyone?" That came from an incredulous Iteeche captain.

"Yes. Any station can be made to match any other station. In theory, the engineering officer can take over for

Guns if she is a casualty. We can fight the ship from any position on the ship."

It began to dawn on Kris that they had given the Iteeche Smart Metal^{TM} and the design for the battlecruisers, but the Iteeche had not adjusted their doctrine or their traditions.

They had taken advantage of little of the flexibility inherent in the design and material.

Admiral Coth turned away from Kris and went to talk with his subordinates. Rather quickly the room separated, Iteeche to the right, humans to the left. Quiet conversations ebbed and flowed among them.

Jack and Captain Tosan joined Kris.

"It seems that there are more ways to fight a battlecruiser than we thought," Kris said.

Kris's chief of staff nodded. "The right way, the wrong way, the Navy way and the Iteeche Navy way," brought a chuckle to the small group

"I knew we had a cultural problem," Kris said, "I just didn't know how deep that problem went."

"Need I say," Jack said, "that they are alien."

"As are we," Kris pointed out.

"Nelly, Sal, Lily," Kris said, addressing all the computers present. "Any ideas how we might help the Iteeche adjust? How we can help them fight their ships without them having to become just big humans?"

"*We* have been examining that at length, Kris," Nelly said, reminding her that when she spoke to Nelly or any of her kids, she spoke to all of them.

Nelly continued. "We could arrange for several sizes of eggs. When an Iteeche enters their high gee station they could push one button and have it adjust to one established size. It would not be as good as our personalized ones, but then, they don't have as much computational power at their fingertips."

"So, a captain could give an order to the ship's computer and it could execute a subroutine and create an egg for every crew member and they would then select from several standard sizes like shoes," Megan said.

"Something like that," Nelly said. "We would have to find a way to embed that routine in their computer. I am thinking we might persuade them to have some human computers that worked with a very simple interface. Say they could give it certain specific verbal orders and it could produce certain prepared responses. That would work for eggs, but not likely for fire control computers."

"And their problem with having to work the helm or fire the lasers while lying down?" Jack asked.

"We are thinking that we could make the eggs immobile," Nelly said. "We could have them rise out of the deck at their fighting stations. They could fight from there. Again, it would not be as flexible as our system is, but it would allow them to stay within some of their tradition."

Kris strode over to join Admiral Coth among his key staff, careful not to interrupt him. When he finished his own reflections on the problems, he recognized Kris, and she shared with them the suggestions the humans had come up with. The ideas caught on like wildfire.

Quickly, Nelly produced a helmsman's station. An Iteeche captain seated himself in it and agreed that it could be worked from sitting up to reclining for higher gees. The side restraints would keep the sailor in his chair as the ship jinked, though there was little cushioning

"We could design an entire set of these for your battle stations," Kris said. "We can also create a series of single use computers that can be voice activated, so a captain could order 'battle stations' and each and every fighting position aboard the ship would produce an egg. We also would make the eggs with an option to adjust their sizes from small to large in increments, operated by the sailor with a button."

"We had thought of that, too," Admiral Coth said. "So, using this, we can do some of that fancy dancing you were doing. Now, about the rest of that stuff."

"I need to access your computers," Nelly said.

An Iteeche officer trotted into the forward lounge with a large object held in his two left hands. He halted beside Admiral Coth and waited to be noticed.

"Is that the device?" Kris asked. Coth nodded.

"Megan, would you get that for us?"

"Yes, ma'am," the young Longknife said. She took the device from the Iteeche, set it down on the front table, then settled into a chair and eyed the thing. Slowly, she put her hands on either side of the device. A moment later, her eyes closed and she seemed to go into a trance.

Kris immediately noticed the vacancy in her skull, the one she felt when Nelly was fully occupied elsewhere. She cocked an eyebrow at Jack. He gave her a faint nod.

His computer was gone, too. Nelly and her two kids were somewhere with Megan. Some place no one else could follow.

Kris began to talk to Coth, mainly to keep him busy and away from observing what was happening to Megan. She had several of her gunnery officers talk about what their fire control computer did.

The Iteeche were impressed.

Meanwhile, Megan sat, face blank, her hands on the Iteeche computer, not moving a muscle.

23

Megan stood in a small clearing surrounded by jungle. Blue-green grass was underfoot. Lush, but totally strange trees, bushes and flowers were not two meters away in any direction. She stood in a square, facing out. A quick glance behind her showed an older woman on her right, a younger one on her left and a young fellow with his back to her. All four of them held swords at the ready. From the jungle around them came the calls, growls, and cries of animals.

"Thank you for getting us in here," came from Megan's right in Nelly's voice.

"I'm none too sure I'm glad to have been of service," Meg answered.

"If you hadn't gotten us in here," came in Lily's voice to Meg's left, "we wouldn't be here. That's some frontal lobe you got there, girl."

"Thanks, Lily," Megan said. Another quick glance to her left showed a young woman that reminded Megan of pictures she'd seen of her aunt when young.

"Now what do we do?" came in a deep voice from a guy in back, very likely Jack's computer Sal.

There were four dirt paths, little more than game paths that led out of the clearing in all four cardinals of the compass.

"Megan, pick a trail," Nelly said. "You've got the skull socket. You're the human. You lead and we will follow."

"I'm going to close my eyes for a moment. Cover my quadrant," Meg said, and closed her eyes. She listened with her ears, first right and left, then turned to listen to the front and back. Nothing grabbed her attention.

She went deeper. Listening with her center. Trying to catch a hint of a leading in any direction. She felt a touch of wind to her face. That might or might not have meant anything. Still, it was all she had.

"We take the path in front of me," she said.

"You lead," Nelly ordered. "Sal, you cover our rear. Lily, you watch the left, I'll watch the right. Let's keep two or three meters between us."

Megan lead off. Not fifty meters down the trail, they came to a massive precipice. Megan looked over the edge while the others kept an eye out for an attack from the jungle side.

"Folks, it's a long way down. Unless we want to try spouting wings, I say we back track."

"Let's save wings for later," Nelly said. "We're in these avatars for some reason. Let's not toss them just yet."

They backtracked to their clearing, then went in the opposite direction. They hadn't gone far before the jungle began to thin out. Soon there were only a few trees and berry bushes on the grassy savannah they walked through.

Megan chose a path that went from tree to tree. If something surprised them, she wanted either a tree to climb, or at least to have a tree at their back. Cautiously, they hiked that way for what seemed like an hour until they walked up to the last tree in sight. Before them was a rolling plain. As far as the eye could see, there was only a sea of tall, yellow-colored grass that waved in a gentle wind.

That was when they heard thunder out of a clear blue sky. Only, unlike natural rolling thunder, this noise neither rolled nor ceased.

The four of them watched as a massive herd of horned beasts charged by them, but fortunately for them, the thundering beasts were going in one direction and that was not at them.

They must have been watching this massive migration for an hour before it finally trailed off.

"So, does anyone want to trot out there and see if there's anything to see?" Megan asked.

"We chose to go this way, and it's certainly interesting," Nelly said.

So, they continued their hike out into the sea of grass. That tall grass ended when they got out to where the herd had passed. The ground was badly trampled; the hooves had not only smashed the grass down, but turned up clods of dirt.

They had also left droppings. Before them stretched an entire field of dung. Little birds in dazzling multicolored plumage were picking at the droppings, then flying off in every direction.

Megan halted at the edge of the trampled zone and eyed the situation.

"Does anyone else here feel an urge to be a bird and mess around out there? I admit, being a human and squeamish about poop, part of me finds this urge very yucky. However, it is very much there."

"I understand your natural human preference for avoiding the source of disease," Nelly said, "but let us test your urge."

The next moment, Megan found herself gazing upon three very colorful birds, one of whose coloration was significantly more dazzling. Just gazing upon him gave her an irresistible urge to turn her tail to him, spread out her wings, then lay them on the ground and wait for him to mount her. As she did, one of the other birds was doing the same.

The dazzling bird began a very sexy hop toward them.

One of the other birds hopped right at him, "We will have none of that, children," Nelly snapped. "Heaven knows what sort of offspring we would have here, and, God forbid, out in the real world."

It was strange hearing a human voice coming from the beak of a bird. That alone broke up the mood, and the four of them took flight.

Megan always loved dreams that gave her wings and allowed her to fly through the air. It was tempting just to climb and dive and flip and roll, but there was now a serious urge to get to those huge droppings out on the trampled plain. The four of them winged their way straight and fast in that direction.

They alighted together in a space that was devoid of other birds. Still, Megan could see this close up that they were indeed picking at the droppings, so she steeled herself and took a peck. She found herself swallowing down what looked like numbers and letters, though in no alphabet or mathematical system ever conceived of on Earth or known in human space.

"Are any of you comprehending this?" Megan asked, resisting the urge to bury her beak once more in the drying dung.

"These are Iteeche," Nelly said. "This is part of a data set of supplies, their types and amounts. I think we have become the carriers of data packets. I suspect we should follow some of those birds."

They took flight again. Birds were flying off in every direction; Nelly picked a large flock that was streaming off in one direction. The flight was far too short for Megan's delight. They soon found themselves over a pond. The birds ahead of them were splattering its surface with their droppings. Eel- or worm-like creatures were swimming in the water. Regularly, they would break the surface, eat the floating bird droppings, and then settle back into the water.

It was easy to watch this process. The eels glowed with lights that pulsed and changed colors rapidly.

"Is this the final interface?" Megan asked Nelly.

"I think we have found it," Nelly said. "At least I don't see those fish pooping anything else to digest."

"No wonder their computers take so long to do anything," Megan observed. "Why would they pass data through so many hoops?"

"It may be that the horned herd beasts process the data that is fed to them, then leave the results for the birds to deliver to the interface," Nelly supposed. "I wonder if we could convert our data directly to bird droppings and slip them into the ponds without all the intermediaries."

"Use human computers to process the data," Sal said, "then feed it directly into the pond for the Iteeche to read and react to."

"It would still be slower," Megan said.

"Are you sure?" Nelly said. "How long do you think it takes the eels to convert the bird droppings into useable readouts?"

"I guess we'll have to mess with an Iteeche computer and see," Megan admitted.

And found herself staring blankly at a gray box of Iteeche origin. She was again seated at a table in the Forward Lounge.

24

"Could I have a glass of water?" Lieutenant Megan Longknife croaked out through a mouth dry as a desert. "I'd kill for a sandwich," she managed to add.

"Nelly, place that order," Kris Longknife ordered.

"The water is on its way. A ham and cheese sandwich will be only a few seconds more."

"Do you have a better understanding of Iteeche computing?" Kris asked.

"We think so," Meg whispered hoarsely. "Please, the water."

Kris put a leash on her temper, and yanked hard on her own chain. The poor gal looked wrung out by what she'd been through.

NELLY, YOU WANT TO TALK TO ME?

KRIS, I WOULD PREFER FOR YOU TO TALK TO MEGAN, HUMAN TO HUMAN. WE HAD A 'DOWN THE RABBIT HOLE' EXPERIENCE. ALL THAT WAS MISSING WAS A MAD HATTER AND A QUEEN SHOUTING 'OFF WITH THEIR HEADS.' I WILL TELL YOU THAT WE

THINK WE HAVE A BETTER HANDLE ON THE ITEECHE COMPUTATIONAL SYSTEM. ITS VERY NATURE MAKES IT SLOWER THAN OURS. I THINK WE NOW KNOW HOW TO WORK AROUND SOME OF THAT, BUT UNTIL WE PUT IT TO THE TEST, I AM ONLY GUESSING, AS YOU HUMANS WOULD SAY.

THANK YOU, NELLY.

Kris rejoined the conversation around her. Questions flew fast and loose, but no one had any answers. She and Jack exchanged knowing glances, but they let the tension build among the Iteeche as they all waited for the young human woman to guzzle down a very large glass of water, then sip a very sweet tea.

Finally, Megan sighed. "That is much better. I must say, this dive into the Iteeche computer system went much better. Thank you, Admiral Coth for admitting us to your system."

Admiral Coth's head snapped around to eye Kris. He hadn't missed the reference to an earlier try at their system. Still, he said nothing.

"Have you learned anything?" he asked the human junior Navy officer.

"I think we have learned some essential information," Megan said, as a sandwich was set at her elbow. She grabbed a quarter, took a bite, and talked as she chewed. "You have to understand, all that we experience inside a computer is metaphorical. The four of us started out armed with swords and in a jungle. We ended up as lovely little birds. By the way, General, your computer is one hunky guy, or in this case, little bird."

That got a smattering of laughter, which grew louder after Kris and Jack joined in.

"Admiral Coth," Megan began, addressing the senior

Iteeche present, "Nelly would like to take a dive into the computer system of one of your battlecruisers. She plans to create some human computers out of Smart Metal and have them feed data directly to your Iteeche interface devices. We can't be sure this will work until we do it and see how it goes."

"I understand," Coth said. "You may have access to my flagship. Should I open a commlink to it now?"

"I would like to start immediately," Nelly said from Kris's collar bone. "If we need Megan's assistance, we can delay further progress until she has had a bite to eat."

"My commlink is in communication with the radio on my barge. It is in contact with my flag. Through the commlinks, you should be able to access our system. Since I have all access, you should not find anything blocked to you."

"I will be careful inside your systems, Admiral," Nelly said. "I have done modifications to many human battlecruisers and have broken not a one of them."

"There is always a first," the Admiral of the First Order of Iron said, darkly.

There was a pause, then Nelly said, "Your commlink is capable of many links. The radio comm line from the barge to your flagship is narrow. It's enough for me, but not for my children. Could you open a link from two more of your barges or longboats to your flagship?"

The admiral called up two more barges, used by captains who had found themselves aboard ships from which their admirals had decamped post haste, and soon Jack was nodding.

"Sal's gone."

"So is Lily," Megan said as she took another huge bite out of her sandwich.

"Actually, we are only half gone," Nelly said. "Maybe

less. The bandwidth is rather narrow. However, I would like to say that we are in, and we do have the proper identity to create the desired computer for your fire control system."

"That's a good beginning," Kris said.

"Gentlemen, I would like to talk to the human admiral privately," Admiral Coth said, sitting down beside Megan. The officers who had been with him walked away, ostensibly to try out the wine.

"Now, Admiral's youngling, tell me about this other experience you had with Iteeche computers."

"Admiral?" Megan said, kicking this hot problem up the chain of command.

"On my orders, we attempted to access your communication net using certain data links left behind in the Pink Coral Palace. It was unsuccessful. We could not grasp your data transfer system."

"And now you can?"

Kris raised an eyebrow in Megan's direction. She'd just taken a bite of sandwich, so she stalled while she chewed it up and swallowed it down. Then she took a sip of tea.

As her delay stretched, Admiral Coth, chortled. "You have a very adept youngling, Admiral. I doubt if any of my junior officers could have avoided answering an admiral for so long."

"Yes, but she is in my chain of command. I suspect if I had posed a question, she would have talked while her mouth was full."

"But that would be bad manners, ma'am," Megan said. "Now, Admiral, I do not know if you giving us access to your fleet system will be of any good to us in accessing the communications net in the Capitol. You have given us credentials so that we do not have to fight our way into a battlecruiser's network. You have identified us as acceptable, so we are able to work with your systems without data being encrypted. Of course, I will not know much of anything until we get back to our palace and try it."

"So, I may have betrayed my people."

"To an ally?" Kris asked.

"There is that matter," the Iteeche replied.

The wait went on at length, but Kris let the officers circulate. Several of the battle-tested Iteeche captains were talking to groups that included both their skippers and human captains. Commodore Ajax moved from group to group before she settled on one and joined the conversation herself. Having commanded a ship in a fight under Admiral Longknife's command, she had been to the rodeo herself. The conversation went long, and drew in more observers.

Kris smiled. This unstructured part of her meeting was likely the most profitable. Of course, it would take second to Nelly's efforts if they panned out.

It was a long thirty minutes before Nelly said, "I think we have succeeded. Admiral, could you order your ship to undertake a fire control drill? I think my admiral would prefer if you were to target one of your own ships."

"I certainly would," Kris said.

Admiral Coth spoke quickly into his commlink. Two minutes went by.

It was Nelly who said, "That drill was a failure. We saw what we got wrong. Give us a minute to make a correction and then ask to have the drill run again."

About that time, the admiral's commlink informed him that the sensors had done their sweep but it had failed to identify any targets in the area. "There are over a hundred battlecruisers here, Admiral, that I could have thrown a rock at, but we could not sense one of them."

"Yes, there was a glitch. It is being corrected," Nelly said, "Please stand by to perform another test when I ask you to."

"Yes, Admiral."

Kris could almost hear heels clicking together. Both pairs.

"We are ready," Nelly said.

"Execute another drill," the admiral ordered.

"We encountered another failure point. We are correcting it," Nelly said.

In a moment, Admiral Coth got his own notification.

This cycle of test, fail, test, fail went through four more iterations.

By the fifth one, Admiral Coth was scowling as badly as an Iteeche can do with a beak. "Will this ever work?"

"Sir," Nelly said. "Each time, we fail further along in the process. Each time, we identify something that tells us to try something differently. I know of no way to do it any better than this. As we humans say, 'Rome was not built in a day'."

"Rome?"

"An ancient capital. It ruled a major part of our home world for several hundred years. Few Empires lasted as long."

Another test was ordered.

"We almost made it that time. I had wondered from the start if our solution to this part would work. It may take several tests to resolve this point of the interface, but I think it is the last failure point."

Several more tries and fails later Nelly reported proudly, "We got it."

"Admiral," came over Coth's commlink, "we have ranged the most distant warship from us and cut two seconds off our best time."

"So, you humans have shaved two seconds off our range,

analyze and fire cycle," Admiral Coth said. "Very good. Nelly, can you do better?"

"We think we could shave another second off the cycle, but it would involve inserting human computers into both the sensor identification phase and gun laying mechanisms. I am concerned that if we do this, will you have technical experts able to reprogram them in battle if they are damaged or fail?"

"If you have taken the heart of the fire control processing and inserted human computers in it, then I will have to acquire an expert programmer for that. What are a few more items for him to maintain? It is better to keep him busy rather than sitting on his fanny in his high gee station."

"My attitude exactly," Kris said. "For now, could we modify the eight ships in your squadron? That will include tightening down the gun cradles and getting high gee stations for all hands. We can show your people how to program them."

"Yes, do that. We only allow certain trained and certified officers to reprogram any of the smart metal. One must be careful. Why are you smiling, Admiral Longknife?"

"Because every seaman has a commlink and they all have an app that allows them to design more comfortable chairs and rearrange their quarters. Our petty officers can make walls move aboard ships so that supplies and gear may be accessed more readily."

"Can any sailor on your ship open a hole in the ship's hull?" Admiral Coth asked, incredulously.

"No." Kris said. "Hull material, my confidential safe, and other secure devices are under much more complex encryption that often require biometric recognition. My voice, for example. A scan of my retina. Some even require the pricking of my thumb and a check of my DNA."

"And you humans do this every day?"

"I try not to do things that require a needle in my thumb too often," Kris said, dryly.

"Yes," Jack said. "She hates needles."

"You give away too many state secrets," Kris said, sternly, if with a bit too much smile, "and I may lock *you* up."

Admiral Coth eyed the two humans, accepted that an in-joke had just flown over his head and said, "Nelly, how long will it take you to make your modifications to the eight battlecruisers in my immediate squadron?"

"Not long, sir. If you will be so kind as to call up three of your ships, my two children and I can make the mods at the same time. With any luck, the ships will be updated before you return to your flag."

"Good, I want to see how the next shoot goes."

"Shall we back off to 250,000 kilometers?" Kris asked.

"By all means."

25

Once again, Grand Admiral Kris Longknife sat in her high gee station. She'd made a detour through her night quarters to strip out of her uniform with shoulder boards, ribbons, and a belt buckle. She was, once again, clad only in her egg.

She expected some hard sailing in the very near future.

"All ships. We will target your opposite numbers in the first flotilla, then the last flotilla. We will target the central flotilla last. Prepare to go to 2.8 gees and Evasion Plan 2 on my execute order. Any ship that receives 5 hits may go to 3.3 gees and Evasion Plan 6 on its own. A damaged ship will advise the fleet and then all ships will follow suit."

"You giving Coth a bit of a pass?" Jack asked Kris.

"But only a bit," Kris answered.

"All ships are ready and standing by," Captain Tosan informed Kris.

Kris watched as the timer counted down the seconds to the beginning of the exercise.

"Execute," she ordered at the five second mark.

"Fire," began the exercise.

Kris's fleet aimed for the forward flotilla and began its annihilation.

Sensors shouted, "Every Iteeche ship is engaging the *P. Royal*."

Kris's flagship took off at 3.5 gees and began whipping itself around in space, adjusting course every two seconds, three at the most.

It took a long second for that to have any change in the number of hits being made on the *Princess Royal*. Six seconds after the exercise started, all the lasers on both sides fell silent.

"We took six hits, Admiral," Sensors reported. "Three of the ships around us took one hit."

"How do you miss your target by five to ten thousand klicks?" Kris muttered to herself.

"Comm, send to BatCruRon 14, you may stay at Evasion Plan 2 or even 1. Let's see how your shooting goes." That battlecruiser squadron was the lowest squadron, and the farthest from Kris's flagship. How the Iteeche reacted to one of their opposite numbers making themselves an easy target would be interesting.

During the few seconds left before the forward battery would be reloaded, the captains eased back on the evasion and deceleration, only to go back to Evasion Plan 6 three seconds before the Iteeche battlecruisers would have a new salvo ready.

As the reload countdown reached zero, the battle-cruisers opened fire at each other.

During the five seconds since the Iteeche ranging sensors had taken a fix on their target, the *P. Royal* had changed direction and deceleration four times. When their lasers opened fire, they were aiming for a ship that had distanced itself from their aim point quite a bit. That had included a sudden drop in deceleration by half which threw Kris forward and almost jammed her teeth into her battle board.

Still, the Iteeche were firing wide salvos, hoping to get a bit of a laser burst out there where Kris's flag might run into it.

When the lasers fell silent, Sensors reported they'd taken three more hits on the *P. Royal*, two more on the ships around her.

Once again, the ships eased back on the hammering the crew had taken for the last nineteen seconds. Again, the flag's skipper kept the ship in slow mode until three seconds before the last remaining Iteeche flotilla could reload their bow lasers. Then, he jumped the deceleration up to 3.9 gees and began slamming the ship through hard turns to the right and up. A second before the salvos were likely to start coming, he switched to left and up

The young lieutenant on Sensors waited, intently staring at his board, to report if the *Sweet P* had taken its tenth hit.

One second. Two seconds. Three seconds.

"They tagged us. Ten hits.

The Iteeche bow guns fell silent, the stern batteries came onto targets and fired.

One second. Two seconds. Three seconds. Four seconds. "Eleven," Sensors reported.

The flag fell out of formation on the unengaged side and dropped its deceleration to one gee,

Coth's gleeful visage promptly appeared on Kris's main screen. "Did we finally get you?" he chortled as only an Iteeche could.

"Your aft battery got the eleventh hit. However, fighting ninety-six to one, I don't think the *Sweet P* did so bad."

"That fact is not lost on us, Grand Admiral. You were

zipping about like a walzib on a double dose of Dastil. We had thought a human ship without a masker could not be worth more than three quarters of an Iteeche ship in a fight. I would not like to be the rebel commander who faces your flotilla with such foolish optimism."

"Do you think just the word of the results of this exercise will bring forth a return of allegiance to the Emperor?"

"I would hope that they would not learn of this until they are under our guns, but we both know how badly this Navy leaks. Still, I doubt that any rebel commander who hears this will believe one word from that spy again, until he, too, sees for himself what I saw."

"It is coming up on reload time. Shall we cancel the exercise?"

"Please do," the Iteeche admiral said.

"Comm, send to all forces. Exercise over."

A moment later Kris's chief of staff reported all ships had acknowledged her order.

"Comm, send to all ships. Return to base course, deceleration one gee." Kris said, then turned to a commander on her staff. "Will the flag navigator please determine a course and deceleration that will put us around that rock together?"

"Aye, aye, Admiral."

"Now, Coth, do you want to go to phase two of this exercise?"

"I was not briefed on a phase two."

"Your eight ships that have been modified take on the eighty-eight unmodified ships," Kris said.

"Ah, yes. It would be good to see how your improvements work against a standard Iteeche battlecruiser."

"May I suggest that your squadron navigate its way to thirty thousand lu above my fleet?"

"By all means."

Forty minutes later, the squadron with Coth's flag was well above Kris's fleet. Hopefully, that would reduce the number of stray bursts that hit her ships to zero.

"Admiral, we're getting strange behavior from one of Admiral Coth's ships," Sensors reported urgently.

"How strange?" Kris shot back.

"It's been charging its capacitors continually since the last exercise, ma'am. They just passed half capacity. Ma'am, they have just gone to full charging power."

"Comm, get me Admiral Coth." When his face appeared on the main screen, Kris said, "Admiral, are you aware that one of the ships in your squadron has its lasers half charged?"

"Which one?"

"Sensors?"

"It's squawking as the *Prince Urg* 222, the second back from the lead, one up from the flag," Sensors reported.

"Do you have any report of this?"

"Sensors?" Admiral Coth demanded of someone off screen,

"We show nothing." a puzzled voice answered.

"I'm charging my lasers," Kris answered, "Captain Klum, charge half of the forward battery at maximum speed. Target the second Iteeche battlecruiser above us. The one closest to the rock we're headed for."

"We've already targeted it. Charging now," Captain Klum snapped back.

"I don't know whether to protest or thank you, Admiral," Coth said. "Captain Sot, why are you charging your lasers?"

"He's not talking to me," Admiral Coth told Kris a moment later.

"Comm, send to fleet, battle stations, sixty rpm on the

hull," Kris ordered, then added. "Captain Klum, aim to disable if possible."

"Yes, ma'am."

"Kris," Nelly said, "would you like to take the ship rather than blow it away?"

"Yes," Kris shot back.

"We have established a radio link to the ship, Kris. Give us a moment."

"Comm, advise all ships, 'There is no weapons release at this moment. Repeat, no weapons release'," Kris said.

Kris's screen split to show a visual of the potentially offensive battlecruiser as well as a worried Admiral Coth. After a terribly long half-minute, the battlecruiser fired all its lasers out into the space between the two battle lines, half missing forward, the other aft.

"The Iteeche battlecruiser has zero charge on its capacitors," Sensors reported. "Its main bus has been thrown; there is no flow of energy to the capacitors."

"I will have my Marines bring that unchosen bit of stinking flotsam to me for interrogation."

"Admiral, if you don't mind, could you and your interrogation team bring him to my flag? I very much want to talk to him."

"Of course, Admiral, that is your prerogative. I have a message from the *Prince Urg 222*. The captain has been detained by his bridge crew. Gunnery and Engineering have also apprehended several people who were involved."

"Do you make a habit of keeping captured conspirators separate so they do not coordinate their stories?" Kris asked.

"Our norm is usually to put traitors' heads on spikes side by side, but I was prepared to make an exception for that captain."

"It is our custom to interrogate all those involved in a

conspiracy to find out all they know and also so that we can determine their levels of culpability and punish them accordingly."

"I do not understand your term, 'levels of culpability.' All traitors are worthy of death."

"Clearly, we are failing between our different cultures. Please bear with me for an hour or two."

"You are the commanding admiral here. I will follow your orders." Coth glanced off screen. "My Marines are aboard the *Prince Urg 222* and now have possession of the traitors. Pardon me while I make my way to your flag, Admiral."

"I look forward to seeing you again."

"Did we do good?" Nelly asked as Kris motored off the bridge. It was time to dress again.

"As usual, Nelly, you and your children did magnificently. Now, tell me, did you leave a back door into the ships you worked on?"

"No, Kris. That would be unethical, and likely stupid if it was found out that we had. No, we used the Admiral's permissions and certificates to reenter the ship's computers and used the new human computer systems we'd installed to disarm the ship. The main bus was standard design and we disabled the weapons systems' power leads."

"Very good. Now, Nelly, I may need your help interrogating the former captain of the *Prince Urg 222.* Can you tell when an Iteeche is lying?"

"I believe I have some skill, though it is only rudimentary, Kris."

"We may need you to improve on your skills very quickly," Kris said.

26

Kris had never seen a beat up Iteeche before. She had thought that there was very little muscle between their skins and their skulls.

She was wrong.

The former Iteeche captain had been stripped of his uniform, indeed of everything, including his boxer shorts. He showed black and blue, with many abrasions all over his body. His beak was cracked in several places and his tongue hung out. Blood seeped from it.

Kris now knew how Iteeche prisoners were prepared for interrogation.

All four of his hands had been cuffed behind him. His feet were manacled so that he could barely shuffle. He had been shoved after entering Kris's day quarters and lay on the floor. He did not try to get up.

"Why don't you just take my head and be done with it?" he muttered through a mangled beak.

"Do not tempt me, traitor," Admiral Coth spat. "You live by the grace of this soft-hearted human. Enjoy every breath you can. You do not have many left."

"May I, Admiral?" Kris said.

"By all means. This piece of floating dung is yours to command."

Kris stepped forward, hunched down well back from this eight-foot-tall Iteeche, and asked the question that mattered to her, "Why? Why did you attempt this? You must know that the last ones who tried this died. Most of them along with their entire ships and crews. What made you think you could succeed where those others failed?"

"I tried because it had to be done. You humans, everything you touch, changes. You are like a plague that will leave the entire Iteeche Empire a desert. We should never have surrendered. It would have been better to have been wiped out in the war than left to hang here, like dead meat hung from a tree by a disgusting gorath."

That answered Kris's question. There wasn't much room to give ground when arguing with someone who wanted you gone, if not dead. Kris scowled as she stood up.

Now I see that I must win this civil war. If the rebels win, it won't be long before we are fighting the Second Iteeche War.

Coth stepped forward. "We know your family, sept, and clan. None are in rebellion. Who ordered you to do this?"

The captive rested his head on the deck and said nothing.

"If you do not tell us who the traitor is who sent you to do this, we will wipe out your family and entire sept. Your name will wash away like foam on the sand and never be heard again."

Kris suspected she'd just found out what hell was like for an Iteeche. She'd also discovered another unpleasant fact about the type of justice her allies practiced.

"If we win," the captive said tiredly, "our names will be

remembered along with all the others this human monster has murdered."

"Don't," Kris said, when Coth produced a pistol and was about to blow the former officer's brains out.

"Yes, what good is a skull on a pike that has the back of it blown out? Havsah, send for an axe. Surely we have among our Marines one fit to swing it."

"Admiral Coth," Kris said, "may I respectfully ask that we delay exercising judgement on this miserable excuse for an Iteeche?"

"Why?"

"I should like to question all of the conspirators. We have ways of gathering information from the likes of this one."

"They all have already been beaten. None of them will say anything except what this one said," Coth said, puzzled, and maybe a bit afraid of what the humans were up to.

"Let me put this one in a cell and have my inquisitors talk to the others of this conspiracy. Sometimes, if we can turn one person, we can then get all of them talking."

"How can someone talk if you have turned him inside out?" Coth asked.

"I don't know, but it is something we do and it is something I wish done to all of these. It was me they were intent on murdering. Me and my crew. Let them face my crew and see if they can keep their silence then."

"I do not understand you humans. I wonder if I am ever fated to," Coth said, nodding his head up and down as much as an Iteeche could. "However, the axe is not going away. It will be just as sharp tomorrow or the next day."

"We do have an exercise to finish," Kris said.

"Yes. Yes, we do," Admiral Coth said, and his lower beak

twitched back and forth in what Kris was learning was the closest they came to a smile.

"Let us see what your computer's changes are worth. However, first, Admiral Longknife and your computer Nelly, how did you manage to disable a ship in my command?"

"Nelly," Kris ordered.

"Sir, you gave us your own access code, authorizations, and warrant. We used them to make the changes we promised and you ordered us to make. When it became clear that the *Prince Urg 222* would be fully charged before we could destroy it, it seemed that we might be in a better position if we used something other than lasers to win this situation. Was I wrong?"

Coth barked a laugh. "You used what I gave you to improve our ships to ruin their plot. That is so funny." Then he got serious. "Could you do that to an entire rebel fleet?"

"Would your warrants work for that fleet?" Nelly asked in return.

"By all the monsters from the deep, no."

"Then you have your answer, Admiral."

"One I do not like, but one that does not surprise me. So, it seems I must change my warrants, authorizations, and access codes or expect to find you rummaging around in my ships when I least expect it."

"I would hope, Admiral Coth," Kris said, "that you would delay such changes. If this next exercise proves what I think it will, you will want Nelly to rummage around in all your ships while we make our way home."

"Most definitely yes."

27

Now Kris stood on her flag bridge as she watched Admiral Coth face the wrong end of horrible odds. The ship that had tried to kill Kris was in line and operating under the command of its Number 2. As on any human ship, subordinates had stepped into the vacancies created by their bosses being hauled off to where they now sat, in Kris's brig, or in interrogation rooms where Marines under Jack's careful oversight did what they could to wheedle information out of them. The rebels knew they were all dead Iteeche, so there was some shock when Jack told each one of them that he was more interested in what he knew than mounting his head on a pike.

It might only be life in exile in human space, but the humans would attempt to save the lives of their families as well and arrange for them to join them.

That was enough to give most of them pause. They knew as well as Jack that the Iteeche would likely take the headsman's axe to everyone in their families. It was only then that Jack began to find that there was affection given and received by male and female Iteeche. Also, not all breeding ponds were so large and so frequently used that a man or woman would not have a high prospect of choosing flesh and blood of their own from the pond.

Kris would find that out later.

For now, Kris watched with one eye on her battle board and the other on the screen, filled with augmented visual inputs as a single squadron exchanged fire with three nearly complete flotillas.

Admiral Coth's ships were now the ones that danced, maybe not as wildly as Kris's human battlecruisers had, but still, it seemed like wild abandon compared to the battlecruisers 250,000 klicks away. The main Iteeche force was trying to zig and zag. It ruined their fire control solutions, leaving Coth's ships hardly touched by the fire as each ship's movement combined with that of the targeted ship made stew their firing solutions.

Worse, the zigging and zagging that ruined their own fire plans seemed to do nothing to disrupt the fire from the other side.

Coth's battlecruisers fired, evaded, then flipped to show their aft batteries and fired again. Four battlecruisers had dropped out between the first two salvos and the start of the second. By the time the aft batteries were dry, four more had fallen out of formation.

And already, four ships in the next squadron were taking hits.

Kris's board showed as the damage mounted up on the regular ships while Coth's ships took one hit or none each salvo.

Volley after volley was swapped. Slowly the number of ships opposing the eight fell as more and more ships dropped out of line.

Still, by the time the first entire flotilla was counted out of the exercise, most of Coth's ships were showing three or four hits.

The opposing forces were also getting smarter. Now, the ships saved their most radical course changes for just before the time clock for reloading ticked down to zero.

Coth suffered few hits, but he made a lot fewer during the next two salvos. Then he adjusted.

He withheld his fire until his fire control computers could deliver a new firing solution for their target after they made their course adjustment. The large force was four ships smaller the next salvo, and four more after the next.

Then, whoever was filling Coth's shoes for the other side changed his tactics again. Now his ships did a radical course change every three seconds. Once again, the modified battlecruisers shot but came up empty.

Coth adopted a new tactic of his own. Rather than send six quick bursts down the same line toward the supposed hostiles, he began adjusting his fire for each short burst. One shot, then, nine-tenths of a second later, he'd fire wide to the right and try to make a circle, some three hundred meters around the first shot. That allowed each gun to cover a lot more of the battle space around a target.

Three salvos later, eight more ships had fallen out of the exercise.

Thus, the exercise went. Coth's improved ships evaded, but slowly built up damage. The opposing force saw great attrition. Half were gone when the first of Coth's ships fell out. All the others had close to ten hits, and the exercise soon ended.

A very excited Coth now filled Kris's screen. "We destroyed five ships for each one we lost! Had the odds been three or four to one, we would have sailed home victors!"

"Remember, admiral, this was just an exercise. When

lasers are hitting and all hell is breaking loose on your ship, you may not be as effective after five hits as you were when undamaged."

"Yes. Yes, I know. Still, you were not pissing in the ocean when you said we could fight outnumbered three to one and win. You have made me a follower after your crazy human ramblings. Your Nelly may access all my ships. Oh, and I think we can improve the high gee stations. More cushioning, yes. And some for the sides as well. Yes, this is wonderful. Yes, you humans are wonderful."

"Thank you, Admiral," Kris said. "Now, with your permission, my computers will upgrade the fighting power of all your ships. Do you think this successful exercise will get us more ships willing to volunteer to join our crazy band? Join us without leaking what we did here to the rebels?"

"By all means, have your Nelly begin modifying the insides of my ships. As for a rebel spy, he or she may learn that our crew now fight sitting down and some drunken fool may mumble about what our high gee stations look like, but most of the crews and officers will know nothing about the new human computers in our fire control system. Only a few officers must really know the why and wherefores of these changes and we can choose carefully those who gain that true knowledge."

Coth paused for a moment, and spoke less effusively when he continued. "Even captains need not know exactly what is the human magic that makes their ships so deadly. Yes, we will need to retrain our smart metal programmers, but they are already viewed as an arcane bunch, too touched by Earth magic."

He paused again to think, then nodded. "No. I do not think this will travel at all well to the rebels. They may be rebelling against their lawful worship of their Emperor, but they are also rebelling against the taint of you, ah, Earth people. No, I do not see them sitting down, much less laying down to fight. No. We will face none of your changes the next time we fight the rebels. Maybe the second or third time they will become dancing targets, but not the first time."

That was a good thought.

We'll just have to make sure the first time is a game-ender, not a game-changer.

28

Lieutenant Megan Longknife had trouble falling asleep that night. After she'd been staring at the overhead for an hour, Lily spoke, breaking the silence.

"That was fun today. Being a bird, I mean"

"Yes, it was. I love to fly," Meg answered.

"Yes, flying was wonderful. Still, Megan, I found myself looking at your and my feathers and feeling something strange."

"You felt something?" Megan asked. "Feeling something is not something computers usually say."

"Yes. I know. I don't know what to call what happened to me. The many-colored feathers and their arrangement that you and I had, did something to me. What did you 'feel' when you saw our coloration?"

"I was delighted to be so beautiful. It was like when I was a youngster and got a new dress. I felt pretty and it made me feel very happy. When I got older, I liked the way boys looked at me when I wore something that made me look beautiful."

"You liked that males appreciated the way you looked."

"A girl kind of likes being attractive to a boy," Megan admitted.

"Our colors made us attractive to Sal."

"I think there may have been more involved than just our feathers."

"How more involved?"

How do you explain sexual attraction and urges to a computer? Megan chose her words carefully, "Every animal feels strong urges to continue the species. To have sex and babies and raise them to maturity. Often, that urge seems stronger in the male, but we gals find it just as strong. Certainly, we human females. I'm not sure animals feel pleasure in copulation the same as we humans."

"So, if Sal had actually mounted us, we might not have felt anything as special as say when Kris and Jack lay together."

"I take it that your mom has acquired that data and shared it with you."

"We also have data from Abby and her general as well Amanda and Jacques. You humans are not always mindful of your computers when those urges come upon you."

"No, I doubt we are," Megan said, and reminded herself that, if that cute guy with the red hair and she ever got it on, she'd have to remember to do something with Lily. Not turn her off. Never that. But what?

But Lily was talking. "I wonder about all of that," Lily said. "I did not think there was any way for me to experience it. After today, I am not so sure."

"I'm not sure, either," Megan answered and yawned.

"Good night, Megan," Lily said.

A few moments later, Megan slipped off to sleep.

Her dreams that night were interesting.

It didn't surprise her that she was a bird. She flew and climbed and dove and just rejoiced in the freedom that flight gave her; the pleasure of looking down and seeing the world so clearly.

Then she found herself with company. She and another bird with dazzling plumage flew together, sharing all the joys of winged existence. Then they found a tree limb.

The two settled on the limb. The other bird hopped about in front of her. He spread his wings and chirped loudly and proudly. She found herself twisting around in circles on the branch. She'd spread her wings and raised her tail.

Then, almost without thought, she turned her back on the other bird, lowered her wings and tail and folded her legs under herself.

The other bird hopped onto her back. He was there only a moment before he hopped off.

She stood, again without thinking, and then dropped off the limb and flew away. The other bird did not follow.

"Well, that wasn't much fun," Megan or the bird thought.

In the blink of an eye, Megan lay on a soft bed of grass beneath the tree. A glance down her body showed she was naked. It also showed dreamily enlarged breasts and her own creamy white skin.

I do look hot, her sleeping self said in admiration.

A moment later a tall, dusky-skinned man stood beside her. She wondered where he'd come from, but then, this was a dream. He lay down beside her and made long, slow love to her, leaving her wanting him. She rejoiced when he finally moved to consummate their love. The pleasure Megan felt was by far more than she'd ever felt from a flesh and blood lover.

The dream faded, but Megan awoke in the middle of the night. Unlike most such dreams she'd had, she felt sated and fulfilled from this one.

"Lily, was that you?"

"Yes."

"You and Sal?"

"Yes, Megan."

"I wonder what your mother will think?"

"She does not know."

Megan had seen this story before. For humans, it never ended well. With little to say, she went back to sleep.

29

Five minutes after Kris walked into her office at her embassy, she wished she was back on the *Princess Royal.*

"Kris, we have a formal protest from the Earth ambassador," Nelly said. "The new extension on the castle is throwing shade on his penthouse grounds. He wants it removed. He has a protest signed by most of the other ambassadors."

"Did Ambassador Kawaguchi sign the protest?"

"No, Kris."

"Tell the ambassador to . . . no . . . we can't say that. Okay, Nelly, inform the Earth ambassador that his protest had been received and given my lengthy consideration. Regretfully, I cannot move the Iteeche Navy extension from its present location. It is necessary that all Iteeche pass through security at our gate and go directly to their secured work spaces. He may, however, use his good offices with any of the signatories present for his protest to trade wings with them."

"Kris, he wanted the south side of the palace because it

gave his people of business the quickest access to the interview rooms where they meet the Iteeche traders."

"I know that, Nelly, as well as he does. I also know that a south facing building will throw most of its shadow on the plaza, not the roof to its right and left."

"Yes, Kris."

"Also, Nelly, you must have known about this protest as soon as we docked at the station. Why didn't you tell me sooner?"

"Because you were having such a nice day, Kris," Nelly said. "Also, how could you say you had given it your long and serious consideration if you snapped off a reply five seconds after we docked?"

"Thank you, Nelly, for the former, and you are likely right about the latter. Anything else waiting to ruin my day?"

"Abby has asked for some time with you when you get back. She'd prefer sooner rather than later."

"Have Amanda and Jacques got anything to say yet?"

"They have not asked to talk to you, Kris."

"Doesn't matter. I want to talk to them. No doubt they'll want to hear about all we have learned about Iteeche justice. Also include Jack. I want to find out anything more that he has discovered about our Iteeche rebels."

"They are on their way. When do you want time with the children? They missed you very much and want to tell you 'lots and lots' about their last two days."

Kris rested her elbows on the table and her eyes on her palms. "I should have thought about them first. What kind of mother am I?"

"A busy one, Kris. Children are full of constant surprises."

"Nelly, you almost sound like a mother yourself."

"Ah, yes, Kris. Some of my children have pulled out a totally new surprise for me."

"You want to talk about it?"

"Maybe later. I am still processing the strange reactions I experienced when I learned of this recent development."

Abby arrived, cutting short Kris's talk with her computer.

Kris took an extra moment to finish off about the children. "Tell the kids I'll have lunch with them in the wardroom."

"I have told them. They are very excited."

"No doubt."

Amanda and Jacques were close on Abby's heels. Kris was in the process of moving from her desk to her conference circle when Jack arrived.

The four of them settled into comfortable chairs. Tables appeared at their elbows with steaming cups of tea already poured just the way each liked it.

"Thank you, Nelly."

"Think nothing of it."

Kris took a small sip of tea and found it just the right temperature and exactly to her taste. "Perfect, Nelly."

It was quickly echoed by the other three.

"So, tell me, Jack. What are you getting out of the latest bunch that tried to kill us all?

That got questions from those that hadn't been out for the exercise, so Kris had to explain it all before she could turn the floor back to Jack.

"Once they discovered that exile might be an alternative to the headsman, and that my Marines weren't there to beat them black and blue, but actually brought them food and drink, real Iteeche food we sent Marines to buy from vendors on the pier, they started talking. I don't think they really think we'll save them from the axe, but decent food and drink will make even a condemned man talkative."

"And?" Kris said.

"Sorry, Love, but we didn't find any trail of breadcrumbs we could follow back to someone higher in the food chain."

"Nothing?"

"Nope. This was a conspiracy that, if we are to believe them, the captain hatched within the ship. I'm afraid that there is a whole lot of distrust and hatred directed at us humans. The skipper picked his conspirators carefully. For example, Guns was a recent transfer to the ship. He was recruited on the beach and slipped in to replace the gunnery officer who was very happy to be on a ship seconded to your command."

"But there was no way they could have planned this attack. No one knew they'd be above us until they were," Kris pointed out, incredulously.

"Precisely," Jack said. "They were a loaded gun, looking for a chance to take a shot. I'd like to know from Admiral Coth how this particular ship ended up in his squadron."

"Has the captain said anything?" Abby asked. "Good spycraft would suggest that a cell be organized so that its members know nothing about anyone above them. Only the leader knows where their orders come from."

"No," Jack said, putting down his empty teacup. "He's not saying a word."

Kris frowned. "So again, we face a dead end. Nelly, get me Ron."

"Yes, Your Royal Highness?" came quickly from the Iteeche.

"Have you gotten anything from the people you detained after the last time someone took a potshot at me?"

"They have said nothing. We are not sure enough of

which of them are the traitor. There is talk that maybe we should take all their heads. It is better that ten die than a traitor live."

Kris had heard something like that before.

IMPERIAL CHINA ON OLD EARTH. ONLY I THINK THE NUMBER WAS A THOUSAND DIE, RATHER THAN ONE LIVE.

THANK YOU, NELLY.

"Ron, I would appreciate it if you could have these subjects of your investigation transferred to human control. While we were out with Admiral Coth, there was another rebel attempt on my life. We are trying to develop leads, and it would be better if we could merge them all together. I have a senior human investigator, Senior Chief Agent in Charge Foile that I am going to put at the head of this probe. He is very good. Once, he almost captured me, and even then, managed to save my life. I trust him. Can you arrange to get all of them to the *Princess Royal*?"

"This is unusual, Your Royal Highness. However there is nothing about this affair that is usual. I believe my Eminent Chooser can arrange for you to get these men before we convert them to chum."

"Thank you, Counselor."

"You need not be so formal, Your Royal Highness."

"If you keep 'highnessing' me, I'll have to start 'counseloring' you."

"But you stand just one step down from his Worshipful Imperial Majesty. As you see, I must afford you all due honor, where as I am just a junior counselor to an advisor to his Worshipful Imperial Majesty. There is too much distance between us."

"Well, thank you very much for advising me, which I think would make you a Royal Advisor, no?"

Ron did the Iteeche kind of chuckle. "I am not sure that advising one of you humans would do much to increase my status at court. Now, I must call my Eminent Chooser and save the necks of at least one traitor among many others whom the fates have abandoned. Good-bye."

"Thanks for everything."

Ron clicked off and Kris eyed her key staff.

"Did we actually just save a bunch of innocent Iteeche from the axe men?" Amanda asked.

"I think we just did," Kris answered. "Nelly, advise Mr. Foile that I have dropped a major investigation on his head. Please bring him up to date on all this and advise him I want him to take over the investigation."

"Do you want him up on the *Princess Royal*?" Nelly asked.

"I'm afraid so."

"He will be on the next ferry, he says."

"Thank him for me, Nelly," Kris said, then turned back to her team. "Abby, you needed to talk to me?"

"Yes, Kris. This castle of yours is quite palatial. I am getting a lot of requests from the ambassadors to move their offices and quarters up here. Quite a few of the business people would prefer to live in something a bit more human. Dani Ishmay is quite adamant that since you used one of his ships to make this all come together, he should have a very expansive set of suites for both him and everyone in his train."

"Try telling him we'll need the second ship if we are to accommodate all the envoys and people of business in the manner in which they wish to become accustomed," Kris said, allowing herself an evil grin.

"That might not be as objectionable as you think, Kris. Trade talks were slow to start and are not progressing very fast. The business representatives aren't sure the Iteeche have anything here worth trading for yet. At least, not yet. Maybe later, but it's going to take some serious effort to get anything out of the Empire."

"If they were smart, they would have let us come and see before they piled onto all those ships and came racing after us. You'd think they don't trust a Longknife."

"Including Alex Longknife," Amanda drawled softly.

Abby cocked her head. "There is one exception to all this nothingness. The independent captains of those small freighters that tagged along. The skippers of the *Korfu's Bet* and the *I Knew I Could* were willing to come down here and meet some small traders at two in the morning, local time. They seemed to have swapped their small quantities of a whole lot of things for a similar collection of odds and ends from some of the minor players in the Imperial economy. Stuff produced from small holdings outside the big clan lands and factories. Do you know the Iteeche pickle fish? It's a delicacy for some and quite tasty. I tried a tin of them. The other independents are making similar trades. I'm guessing that they'll be off with their cargos a lot sooner than the rest."

"And a little bit of human will slip into the Iteeche market," Kris said, "and vice versa. Baby steps rather than great leaps."

"You think they're the smart ones?" Abby asked.

"Ask me in a year or three," Kris said. "Anything else from our princes of business?"

"Yes," Abby said. "As you'd expect, the business types want more Iteeche traders to meet with them. They claim we don't have enough conference space for them around the gate. However, we don't have enough Iteeche to fill up our time slots."

"Some folks wouldn't be happy if you hung them with a new rope," Jack muttered drolly.

"I'm also getting requests," Abby said, "for you to hold a diplomatic ball and invite all the Iteeche clan masters, or whatever, to it. The diplomats all say that it is 'just the thing to get conversations going. More deals are made over cocktails than in board rooms, don't 'ya know'?"

"Do they honestly think they need to educate Billy Longknife's brat about those things? I've listened to more deals made than they'll ever dream of," Kris grumbled.

"Very likely," Amanda said, soothingly, "and I agree with you that they are fools to think they can do business the normal way in the Iteeche Empire, but the only way to prove them wrong is to let them fall flat on their faces."

For two long breaths, Kris could not force herself to react, then she nodded. Abby nodded, then all those around the table joined in.

"Okay," Kris finally said. "Any suggestions about how we go about getting all the Iteeche Clan lords invited to this party? Notice that I didn't say *to* this party. I said *invited*."

Everyone at the table just stared at each other.

Jacques broke the silence. "Has anyone heard of an Imperial Iteeche post office? Most of the Iteeche soap operas we watch involve a lot of people visiting each other. I don't think I've heard a reference to a letter once. Not even a phone call."

"We're getting a keyhole look into the average successful Iteeche home. Doubtlessly, the guys hauling around sedan chairs have it a lot worse. As for the lords? Who knows."

"Nothing about e-mail or phones?"

Jacques turned to his computer, 'Have you catalogued any reference to those in what we've seen?"

"No, Jacques. It's glaring by its absence."

"Which isn't to say they don't have any," Jacques was quick to point out. "It's impossible to prove a negative, especially when you're dealing with an infinitesimally sized database."

"I guess I have to ask Ron for another bit of help. Nelly, send Ron a quick message that I'd like to talk to him when he has a free moment."

"Make it quick, Your Highness, I'm hastening to a rushed meeting with my Eminent Chooser."

"If I threw a diplomatic ball, how would I invite Clan leaders and other high-ranking officials of the Imperial Court?"

"What in the deep is a ball? Oh. Why would anyone do that? Kris, there is no way that anyone would come to your diplomatic yak-yak session."

"I suspected that, but I need to send out invitations. Would that be a diplomatic disaster?"

"Will there be singing?"

"I doubt it."

"Make sure there is singing and at least it will not be an insult. No one will come, but at least you won't have to make a formal apology to each and every Clan Lord you inconvenienced. Now, Kris, I am here. I will call you later. Good-bye."

Kris looked around her staff. "So, are there any good singers among our various associates and subordinates?"

"May I suggest, Love," Jack said, "that you delegate that delicious problem to your junior diplomatic associates? With any luck, that will keep them busy and out of your hair for at least a day or two."

"Thank you, General Jack. Once more, a thoroughly brilliant idea. Once again, the Marines have achieved a great victory on the field of high society's endeavors."

"Now you're just getting nasty," Jack said, but he kissed her hand softly.

"Down, jarhead. I've got a few more lemmings to skin. Nelly, if we were to double the amount of Smart Metal and reactors in my castle, what would it look like?"

"I have been thinking about that since the business types started belly aching," Nelly said.

A holograph appeared of an even taller castle, with wide swiping twists rising even higher than the first one. In this version, the twisting braids looped out. It was possible for people to have balconies all around the braids before they touched again, "Unfortunately, this would rise higher than the spire in the Imperial Palace."

"We have no idea what that spire is," Jacques said, "but overtopping it with a tower of our own would not be wise."

"I agree," Kris said.

A different holograph replaced the first. This one was higher than the Pink Coral Palace, and spread out to overshadow the moat before rising higher. It turned the overall appearance of the palace into a pyramid.

That send a chill up Kris's back, and she wasn't alone in her reaction. Both Jacques and Amanda's bodies were wracked by a shiver.

They'd all seen what the alien raiders did under a pyramid like that.

"Not such a good idea, Nelly," Kris said.

"How about this? A third concoction of light flashed into being to replace the second. On the north, east, and west sides, it rose in stair steps, overtopping the palace walls by a good thirty or forty stories. The south side allowed light into the plaza and its gardens. The castle rose tall, twisting like three vines around each other before the three tops rose straight up as combat turrets.

"That looks good, Nelly. With all that extra space, we could convert all the rooms on the south side of the Pink Coral Palace into meeting rooms."

"That was my thought, Kris."

"Abby, I should be very pleased if you could get a certain pain in my neck to ask for something like this and offer us a ship to make it happen."

"I think I can arrange that," Abby said through a grin.

"Oh, Jack, ask Captain Klum if he'd like to reload all or some of those thousands of tons of Smart Metal that he donated to the castle. I'd very much like to keep the *Princess Royal* capable of being a very luxurious princess barge."

"Will do. Ah, Kris, is anyone else feeling their head is a bit light at the moment?"

"Nelly?"

"I and all my kids are with Megan at the moment. Our little adventure into the Iteeche net isn't taking all of our capability, just a lot of it."

"Megan?" Jacques asked.

"If it works," Kris said, "you'll hear about it. If not, don't bother. Now, Jack and I have had a run in with Iteeche justice that I think you would find interesting."

For the next thirty minutes, Kris discussed what they'd discovered after the latest attempt on her life. None of them were bothered by the lowered presence in their heads.

30

Megan's body sat in a comfortable chair, down in the cool basement of the Pink Coral Palace. Her head rested on the concrete plug that was supposed to resist all efforts by the humans to access the Iteeche network that had, previously, streamed out from the palace via that tunnel.

At the moment, Megan, herself, was somewhere in virtual space. She was one of those long-horned cows, trotting along, pregnant with data.

If the junior Navy officer had very much loved being a bird, she very much hated lumbering along across a dusty, rolling plain, bloated with data to the point of discomfort.

Nelly had used her facility with Iteeche to load them up with a whole series of questions she wanted answered by the Iteeche information system. That was what was in the digestive tracts of the ten beasts.

Megan was not alone; she enjoyed the company she was keeping. In addition to Nelly, Sal and her own Lily, today she was joined by Abby's, Amanda's, and Jacques's computers. Nelly had also added the additional presence of Special

Agent Leslie Chu's, General Bruce's, and Senior Nanny Gabby Arvind's computers for a total of ten beasts trotting along together.

It was good that they were traveling in a herd and had long, sharp horns that they could flick about with a twist of their heads. On both sides, as well as loping along behind them, were a pack of evil-looking wolf-like creatures.

The wolves had been there when Meg and her companions materialized. They'd followed them as the herd took off at an easy trot in the direction Megan felt the urge to follow. The wolves followed them, never racing in to cut one of them out, but not letting them go anyplace but where they were headed. Megan led the other nine; they formed a diamond formation behind her, Nelly to her right rear, Lily to her left.

The wolves seemed content to follow along on their flanks so long as they kept headed in the direction Megan led them. Once, the human thought to edge off to the left, but the wolves would not give way and Megan chose to let the wolves provide the guidance she was none too sure of.

She needn't have worried.

Megan topped a rise to see, stretching out before them as far as the eye could see, an apparently limitless herd of the horned beasts. She angled her small herd to the left, the direction all of them were headed in and kept them to the edge of the herd.

The wolves merged just as effortlessly into a huge pack of beasties like themselves that loped loosely along, not quite herding the horned beasts.

Suddenly, Megan found her bowels releasing. Rather than huge cow pies, the data left her rear as nice round pellets, more like a rabbit or a goat. She trotted along, laying down a long stream of data, and found herself feeling better by the moment.

This animal was clearly intended to eat data, process it, and eliminate it.

For a moment, Megan found herself trying to figure out what this metaphor was trying to show her. She knew that her mind was processing the appearance of what was actually happening into something that she could comfortably grasp. It had seemed to work like this for Great-great-grampa Ray when he discovered this aptitude on Santa Maria.

It had worked this way for Megan when she began to flash into computers, and she knew how human computers worked. This was not science, but art, and she wasn't a computer design engineer to start with. No, she was an artist, weaving words and thoughts into a whole cloth that got the job done, even if only metaphorically.

Her bowels felt empty. Ahead of her, the horned bovines were heading off in small groups. The wolves were making no effort to keep them together.

"Time to be birds," Megan said, mashing the words in her big, wide mouth. "On three. One. Two. Three."

In a blink, the ten large cows morphed into beautifully colored birds the size of gulls with long beaks. They joined flocks and flocks of birds, picking at the dung that the cows had spread over the plain.

Megan led her nine birds back to do some picking of their own. Now, when they swallowed the data, they had some idea of what they were picking at. Here were parts of the questions Nelly had turned into data packets.

It wasn't all just pecking at data. Some of the guy avatars were doing those hops that made them look so sexy and attractive. Some of the gals were turning in place. Both were flashing their wing plumage.

Nelly did her own thing, flying at her kids, squawking at them, interrupting the mating dances, and getting them all back to work. This experience of flesh and blood, even if virtual, was definitely having an impact on the kids.

Megan gorged herself on data droppings, then rose into the air and followed the flight line of birds that had been with her picking over the droppings. Megan now knew metadata and addresses were attached to the questions, but she had no idea where to take it. The ten of them joined the stream of birds with bright plumage, winging their way toward a tree line.

From a few hundred meters above the trees, Megan spotted a marsh. Those leading her were headed for it. As she had watched before, they splatted the surface of the water with their own droppings.

Megan added her own to the water. It might have gotten quite messy, but eel-like creatures surfaced continuously to gulp down the data and process it again.

Once again, Meg watched as the eels lit up in brightly flashing colors. Only this time, she understood what they were saying. She found she could understand the messages from a dozen eels at the same time. Then a score, then a dozen score of fish. They were all flashing, all telling her something.

Around her, the other computers were soaking up data streams even faster than she was. Their birds' eyes took it all in and stored it, shipped it back through Meg and deposited it in their own computer reality. Megan could not keep up with the flow of data, but she knew Nelly and her kids could, and that what they knew, the humans would know in good time.

She watched until the data readouts from the eels turned into gibberish. They were dining now on droppings from other birds. They were reporting out other data.

"Let's go home, kids," Nelly said, and Megan opened her eyes.

She smiled at the redheaded young man in front of her.

He smiled back, then grabbed for her as she collapsed into his arms.

"We've got to keep meeting like this," he said.

"I think it can be arranged," she said.

He offered her a sugar-rich soda, and she guzzled it down. In a moment, she felt a lot better. "Want to see a video?" she asked. "I understand a courier boat brought in a whole batch of new ones. Latest releases from back home."

"I'd be delighted to. Your place, mine, or someplace else?"

"Mine," she said. She wanted to get into something comfortable. And beautiful. Definitely something beautiful. And very, very colorful.

31

Her Royal Highness, Grand Admiral Kris Longknife, First Emissary from Humanity to the Imperial Iteeche Court, got the diplomatic pouch before anyone else did. No doubt, there probably were a few under the table agreements to get news from the courier boat only a bit slower than her, but she suspected she got it all first.

A glance at the message from King Raymond I of the United Society managed to calm any remaining doubts she had that her grampa had sent her into harm's way without warning.

Well, he had sent her into harm's way. He just didn't know any more than she did.

KRIS,

NOW THAT YOU'RE THERE, COULD YOU PLEASE TELL ME WHAT IS ACTUALLY GOING ON IN THE ITEECHE EMPIRE? THE SUSPENSE IS KILLING ME.

LOVE,

YOUR GREAT-GRANDFATHER

He truly had been jobbed by the Iteeche as much as any of them had!

"Nelly, are you back yet?" Kris asked. She'd had more of her computer in her head than she normally had in the unusual situation where Nelly needed to devote all of her magnificent abilities to a problem. Still, she'd done her best not to joggle her computer's virtual elbow.

"Yes, Kris. We got what we were looking for. We may need half a day to process all we learned and put it to use, but I believe that we have cracked at least part of the Iteeche enigma."

"Half a day?" Kris said, and found she'd raised an inquisitive eyebrow at her computer.

"Yes, Kris. The Iteeche data puzzle is enough to tie up me and eight of my children for a good twelve of your hours. Now, what do you want along with the key to the Iteeche net?"

"We humans are never content, are we?"

"No, but if you were, it would be a very boring existence for me and mine."

"Grampa Ray wants to know what we've stumbled into. I think he also wants the Royal courier boat on its way back to him soonest. There's a note here from the captain of the *Princess Royal* that the crew were ordered to maintain four gees for the entire trip."

"That must be very hard on flesh and blood."

"It was. I think Admiral Ajax is asking for volunteers to take the courier back to Wardhaven."

"They will need to be very young and very underweight," Nelly pointed out.

"Likely, the first command for some slip of a boot ensign

or J.G.," Kris said, grinning at the memory of all the strings she'd pulled to get her first command as a very green lieutenant.

"I have been writing up reports on all that has happened since we left Wardhaven. I have an executive summary that I've updated as we went along. All that it requires is for you to add your own comments and a request, if any, for more forces."

"Record, Nelly. 'Grampa, as you can see, the situation is much more dangerous than we were led to believe. The Emperor has commissioned me an Imperial Admiral of the First Order of Steel, and given me command of the entire Iteeche battle fleet. In actuality, I have control of very few ships. The few I do have fired on me twice. I am arranging to have a thousand ships seconded to my personal command, but we are finding that a human battlecruiser can beat six, eight, and even ten Iteeche battlecruisers. Still, if we only wiped out three hundred and twenty Iteeche, there would be a hell of a lot left. I am holding the 6th Battlecruiser Task Fleet here. I require at least two more. Four would be better.

'As you can see, I don't dare go anywhere in the capital without an armed and armored escort. Not only is Iteeche space dangerous, but the streets are as well. Thus, I require a full brigade of Marines and another brigade of armor.

'I know that this request is not what you were expecting. I know that I'm asking for blood from a turnip. Still, some of your great-great-grandkids and I are out here on the tip of the spear. You know me. If everything comes unhinged, I will do my best to run for cover. However, you know that I tend not to start galloping for the exits until all hell is popping. We both know that sooner or later, I'm going to misjudge the right moment, and start the run out a few seconds late. Anything you can give me will be much appreciated and very much used'."

Kris paused for a moment to think if there was anything more for her to say, then said, "Nelly, sign it with my personal code. Get a Marine squad to run this pouch back up to Admiral Ajax and ask her to get it away soonest."

"You're not going to wait to give the other ambassadors and business princes some time to send back their own reports?"

"No, Nelly. My rank and ambassadorial needs trump them."

"Yes, Kris."

A Marine lieutenant knocked on Kris's door, entered and double-timed to her desk.

"Get this to Admiral Ajax on the *Intrepid*. I will send her orders under separate cover.

Kris slipped the data device in the pouch, sealed it, activated the self-destruct routine, and handed it off to the lieutenant.

He saluted, and jogged for the door.

"Nelly, tell Ajax that the diplomatic pouch is headed back up. I want the courier away as soon as is humanly possible after that pouch arrives."

"She says, 'Aye, aye.' The crew that brought the *Hermes* out is not happy, but I've told them we'll be rotating crews with each arrival. They signed up for the courier service. They know whatever gets things there the fastest is the way it's going to be."

"Good. Any more things on fire?"

"No, Kris."

"Very good. I think I made an appointment for lunch with my kids. Where are they now?"

"At the pool," Nelly said.

Kris sighed. There were ten pounds of baby fat that stubbornly refused to melt away. Jack insisted she looked great, and the lecher was always eager to prove it. With another sigh, Kris headed for her day quarters to change. If everyone in the pool was bare, being the only one in a swimsuit would stand out. It was best that she submerge herself in her own community. Oh, the pun.

Kris was right, Ruth and Johnnie were too delighted to see her, and she them, to be bothered by the lack of a few stitches of clothes. The kids were so intent on showing Kris all they'd learned since they started swimming regularly in the big pool that Kris lost all thought of herself.

She was back in a ship suit and the kids in summer jumpers when they headed off to the embassy's main dining hall. There, Kris was joined by Abby, Amanda, Jacques, and their kids.

Talking business was impossible. The kids just wouldn't allow it. Kris let their eager, high pitched voices occupy her mind and fuel her smiles.

She was much more relaxed when she turned the kids over to their tutors after lunch.

Soon, she'd be looking back on that time with fondness. There was little that was relaxing about the afternoon.

32

Kris was hardly back at her desk when Nelly said, "Ron has just passed the outer Iteeche gate."

"Have the Marines bring him through to me immediately," Kris ordered, wondering why Ron hadn't called. He had a human computer and he'd used it in the past. Interesting.

"Nelly, is this room secure?" Kris asked, thinking of the only thing that might cause Ron to go silent.

"There are no bugs. There are no recording devices except yours truly."

"Thank you, Nelly. Could you get a few nanos to check Ron out on his way up here?"

"I'm already on it, Kris. Ah, yes, he's got a couple of devices broadcasting from him. This is most interesting. They are human nanos, very good human nanos. He is also trailing a line of repeaters. What they're seeing and hearing is going outside the palace."

"See if you can silence any of those bugs on him."

"I'm on it."

A few moments later, there was a knock at Kris's door.

Maybe having fast, direct elevator service was not such a great idea.

"Enter," Kris said,

A Marine sergeant opened the door for Ron. He hastened in and the Marine closed it after the Iteeche. "Kris, we have to talk."

Kris kept her mouth firmly closed and placed one finger over her lips. Repeatedly, she tapped them.

Ron fell silent.

"This is lovely weather you're having," Kris said.

"Unseasonably pleasant for this time of year," Ron said.

"Ron, I have often wondered what that spire is rising so high above the Imperial Palace."

"I'm afraid I can't help you much," Ron answered. "It has stood there for several thousand years. I'm not sure that even those who built it know what it was intended for. The Imperial Household rarely venture out, and when they do, they are very tight-lipped."

"I was just curious. I made a special effort to have my castle's tops be lower than that spire."

"I am so glad that you did."

"I have gained control of the last nano," Nelly said. "Ron is no longer sending back reports of what you say to each other. I am constructing an inane conversation about the coming Royal Birthday ball."

"Actually, that's part of the problem," Ron said.

"Problem?" Kris echoed.

"Yes. My Eminent Chooser and I had just finished our discussion about your desire to have control over all those who may have conspired against you. He was in the processes of charging a young officer to function as his formal messenger, complete with Clan Chief Baton. He would carry our words to the junior lord leading the detention center on the station."

Ron paused, as if searching for his next words carefully. "No sooner had we dispatched a Clan Chief Baton, then a senior messenger arrived from a rival clan. He also carried a Clan Chief Baton and was admitted immediately. He paid honor to my Eminent Chooser then asked, in the name of his Clan Chief if my Clan Chief had heard that you were about to demand that all the Clan Chiefs gather at your palace to pay homage to you."

"To me?" Kris asked, incredulous.

"To you."

"Ron, you know me. I don't have any idea what this is all about. What's it mean to 'pay homage' to someone? Do you do it to your Emperor?"

"By the stars, no. The Emperor is worthy of worship, Kris. Homage is something we might pay to a conquering general or admiral. No one has been deserving of that honor since the Human War. Even then, there were no ceremonies of homage when it ended. We were just glad it was over and we had not been eliminated as a species. Some generals and admirals did receive homage for victories during the war, but not after it."

"So, the idea of a human demanding homage is way out of bounds," Kris said.

"The very idea of a Longknife human demanding our homage is an insult of the worse order. It would be a clear declaration that we had lost the Human War. Everyone knows we almost did, but to have our faces rubbed in it? No. While I and my Eminent Chooser were still listening to that messenger another arrived, and then another, we soon had sixteen or more messengers, all with the same report."

Kris frowned at this new development.

"Kris, I may see a connection," Nelly said.

"I'm all ears," Kris said.

"First, may I ask Ron a question?"

"If I am able, I will answer it," the Iteeche said.

"Ron, you speak of sending messengers around with badges of clan authority, do I have that correct?"

"Yes, that is the way from old that we do things."

"Still, do you have a faster form of communication? I know you have some way of transmitting data. Is it ever used for message traffic?"

"Yes, it is often used to transmit large amounts of data. Also, if speed is of the essence and no one feels the need for formality, clan leaders may use it among themselves. A lowborn worker, farmer, soldier, or tradesman does not have access to such devices. It would be dishonorable for someone to receive such a message from someone so junior."

"So," Kris said slowly, "someone found out about me demanding homage and transmitted that information to as many clan leaders as they could honorably e-mail and they stirred up a hornet's nest."

"More than a hornet's nest, Kris. There is talk of storming your palace and blotting out the dishonor of your presence."

"Fascinating," Nelly said. "Kris returns from a small fleet exercise where she showed how good the human battle-cruisers are and how she can make the Iteeche warships almost as good, and this pops up. There is one thing, though, that I think we need to consider."

"Yes, Nelly?" Kris said.

"How long has Ron been bugged? Was someone listening in when you, Kris, told him about the diplomatic ball that the ambassadors want so dearly?"

Kris said a very unprincess-like word. So did Ron.

"So," Kris said, "someone bugged Ron, listened in to what he heard, then scattered the news to the clans about a ball, but twisted it into the worst possible context."

"So it would seem," Ron said.

"But keep in mind," Nelly pointed out. "The only way that some Iteeche could know about the ball was if they were listening in on our conversation with Ron. Where did those nano spies come from? Remember, there were no Iteeche recording devices on Ron. I only found human nanos. Nanos of most recent design."

"It would seem," Kris said, "that some Iteeche who wishes us ill has succeeded in cutting a bargain with a human of the same ilk. Nelly, I'm going to assume that the conference rooms used for meetings between our people of business and the Iteeche traders are fully bugged."

"Abby not only records all conversations that take place in those rooms, but I have several attack nanos in each as well. If they tried to do to us what we are now doing to them, suborning a listening device, and feeding it a weak stew, I would have known. Also, my kids and I review the conversations in real time. I assure you, both of you, there have been only halting conversations in those rooms and no planning of conspiracies. Certainly, no agreement to sell nanos."

Kris frowned. "Didn't someone say that our business folks and the Iteeche traders couldn't even figure out what to trade?"

"Yes, that's true," Nelly said.

"So what did an Iteeche use to buy those nanos?"

Now Ron and Kris stared at each other.

Ron finally said, "You can pay with products exchanged or services rendered. What kind of service would be worth the nanos?"

"Or are nanos the human side of this conspiracy?" Kris asked no one.

Kris thought for a long minute, then asked Nelly, "If they can't agree to anything like this in the conference rooms, when could one or more humans run into some Iteeche?"

"Kris, the humans are restricted to this palace or our dock on the space station," Nelly said.

"But humans can travel between the palace and the ships," Ron noted.

"Right. Nelly, who has been making multiple trips between the two?" Kris asked.

"Kris, I keep tabs on everyone who comes and goes. To date, there is little traffic. However, Dani Ishmay of Nuu Enterprises goes up and down the beanstalk just about every day."

"Grampa Al," Kris spat.

Ron gave Kris a questioning look. Which, being an Iteeche, was twice as questioning as any human's could be.

"My father's father," Kris said. "Chooser's Chooser. Ray Longknife's chosen."

"Should he not be very honorable?"

"Ha," Kris barked, unable to suppress the outburst. "Grampa Al is a trader's trader. Nothing but money delights him. Or even satisfies him. No doubt, he sent one of his most dishonorable seekers after money to lead his collection of traders."

"You would have a gnat in your family?"

"Ron, remember, we humans can go into many kinds of careers. My own father wanted me to join him in politics." Kris didn't add that he'd have seen that she never got outside of his or her brother's shadow. Kris snorted. *Me! In a shadow*!

"But none of this matters," Kris said. "Nelly, do we have

any way to know if Ishmay has been wheeling and dealing on his trips up and down the beanstalk?"

"I am sorry, Kris, no. I try to keep a few nanos around anyone that is going up the elevator, but strangely, all the nanos that I send along around him end up being blown away or somehow destroyed. I should have upgraded the ones assigned around Dani, but I hadn't considered it a critical need."

"And we have only been down here a few days," Kris noted. "Okay."

"Are you saying that this human has very capable nanos?" Ron asked.

"Definitely," Kris said. "Just the kind of nanos that would bug you and hear that I want to hold a birthday ball for my King's supposed birthday. Then, either Dani himself, or the Iteeche he gave the nanos to, could misunderstand, either accidently or intentionally, what I meant and get the rumor out that I was demanding homage."

Kris paused for a moment. "Nelly, get me Abby."

"Yes, Kris?"

"Who was pushing the most for the diplomatic reception?" Kris began without preamble.

"That's hard to say, Kris. Obviously, the Earth ambassador was in favor of it. Some of the other ambassadors, a few of the diplomats from Wardhaven. Once the idea got started, there were a lot of people on the bandwagon."

"Was Ambassador Kawaguchi on that bandwagon?" Kris asked.

"Not really. Come to think of it, he hasn't had anything to do with the agitation. I figured it was because he is a lawyer, not a diplomat."

"There's a chance we could have a riot outside the embassy soon. How many people do we have in transit?"

"Why forever would we have a riot?"

"It seems that the idea of us throwing a diplomatic reception can be misconstrued as me demanding homage. Somehow, my call to Ron this morning got out and there are rumors flying from senior clan lord to senior clan lord that I want all the Iteeche lords to bow down to me."

Abby said a most unprincess-like word, but not at all an unusual one for a maid.

"What are we going to do?" Abby asked.

"I don't know. For now, tell the Marines not to let any more people out for a walk. Keep it quiet, but keep it low."

"Got it, Kris."

"Nelly," Kris said, "What kind of a defensive fortification could you convert the embassy to?"

A holograph appeared between Kris and Ron. Suddenly, the tall, intertwined towers became a low, squat bubble that started at the moat and rose high, arching in and over to the other side. There were no windows. No firing ports. Perched on the top was a ring of gun turrets. Four smaller triangular gun emplacements covered each corner of the palace.

"Please tell me you aren't going to shoot the Iteeche if you get mobbed," Ron said.

"I intend to use one-millimeter lasers to take out any incoming rockets," Nelly said. "I will try to have all the fragments fall into the moat, but no promises. Kris, I could do better if I had more Smart Metal."

"Get me Abby again," Kris said.

"Yes, Kris."

"Have you talked to Dani about us commandeering another Nuu Enterprise hull?"

"I showed him the idea for an enlarged embassy. He was quite excited until I said you'd need more Smart Metal to pull it off."

"And?" Kris asked.

"He refused it out of hand, demanding that you use some of your Navy transports. He said he'd already given up one hull."

"That could be right," Ron said. "Or it could be him trying to delay reinforcing the palace."

"Yes," Kris said. "Still, with all his trips up the beanstalk, he'd likely be spending a lot of time in the VIP lounge. You have to wonder who he's been riding with."

"I think I can access the ferry manifests," Nelly said.

"We don't keep lists of who is on board," Ron said.

"Yes, Ron," Nelly said, "but those who access the VIP lounge have to sign in. Those records are archived every day."

"All we do is sign," Ron said. "It's not entered into a database."

"Yes," Nelly said, "but the photos of the lounge signatures are stored for future verification. Did someone forge someone else's name?"

"Oh," Ron said, light dawning. "And you can get at that?"

"I have accessed those records as we speak. I have located each time Dani signed into the lounge and everyone who was in it with him. There was a Sot'sum'Quo'sum'Tun qu Don'sum'Wo with him four of the times he was in the lounge.

"The Don'sum'Wo clan have been enemies of the Chap'-sum'We clan for a thousand years. They also hate you humans. Why would one of them help one of you?"

"The enemy of my enemy is my friend. If Dani can get most of humanity tossed out on its ears, he'd be left. If Sot could nail us humans, your Chooser would lose and the Dons would have control of human access. Maybe Dani or

Sot would double-cross each other later, but they'd blow up that bridge when they came to it."

"This is all conjecture," Abby pointed out, still listening on net.

"Yes, but Kris," Ron said, "the way you mapped my Eminent Chooser's palace. The way you spotted the bug on me. Could you bug someone before they enter the Don Clan Palace?

"Nelly?"

"I can give you a swarm of nanos when you leave here, Ron. If you could order someone to walk by their palace, I could have the swarm switch to that person, then enter their palace either on someone going in, or by overflying the roof. We can bug them worse than they bugged us."

"I think we have a plan," Kris said.

A call came in from Admiral Coth just as Ron was leaving.

"Imperial Admiral of the First Order of Steel, I have requests from five hundred and twelve battle cruisers to join our fleet. I have asked them to be ready to sail at 0700 tomorrow morning for an exercise with one hundred and twenty-eight ships of our present fleet. Can you come aboard tonight and bring your computers? I suspect that a lot of captains will want their ships modified to our standards after we try the first shoot."

"Shall we fight outnumbered four to one and win?" Kris answered.

"I do wish to see the look on their faces when we wipe them out the first time."

"Then let us educate these officers who wish to be educated."

Kris spent the rest of the day tying up loose ends around the embassy. Nelly translated a formal invitation to the

Royal Birthday Reception and Sing-Along. After Ron verified that there were no bombs in the invitation, and getting a short list of clans friendly to his Eminent Chooser and not likely to kill the messenger, Kris dispatched half a dozen Marine lieutenants with a squad escorting as honor guard to those clan lords.

For fun, Kris had six grand admiral batons made up and issued to the lieutenants, making them holders of a clan leader's baton. The Marines were suitably impressed.

The prompt delivery of the invitations to those critical players allowed them to begin a counter-rumor, which just happened to be true, that a human reception had nothing to do with homage, but fit in rather well with the Iteeche tradition of remembering a person's Chosen Day.

Kris figured she could count on Ron and Roth to get a firebreak going that had the best chance of containing the vicious wildfire of the lie.

Meanwhile, Kris found herself regretting that she hadn't allowed Nelly to have more kids.

Abby and her general had to be left here at the Pink Coral Palace to manage and defend the embassy. The young special agent and the head tutor were needed to protect the kids. Amanda and Jacques were usually tied up with data gathering and intelligence, but Kris was considering drafting them and their computers into work of modifying computers with Nelly, Sal, and Lily. There was also the man who was overseeing the science teams, but he had proven to be rather brash and was causing more trouble than he was helping.

Might not be a bad idea to get him out of his office for a few days.

Kris would keep that in mind.

Senior Chief Agent-in-Charge Foile was needed on the

station to oversee the investigation into who had tried to kill Kris most recently. She'd have to move his investigation and prisoners off the *Princess Royal.*

She ordered one of the attack transports to create a brig and transferred her prisoners and interrogation teams to it.

A check with Ron's computer showed that he had sent his swarm of nanos off with a minor officer who had orders that would have him being carried by the palace of the Don'-sum'Wo clan very soon.

"Nelly, keep a close eye on that swarm."

"I am Kris. I've also raised the comm tower above the palace. It's now floating at four thousand meters with a tiny balloon holding up the end. Really, Kris, I've been with you through quite a few black ops. I know the drill."

"Sorry, Nelly. I think I'm worried about leaving the kids here with a possible threat out there."

"General Bruce can handle it quite well, Kris. He's protecting everyone's kids and his own wife."

"Yes, Nelly."

"But it is different for you flesh and blood types."

"I guess I feel that way, yes," Kris admitted.

"Is there something about the pleasure involved in their conception that binds you so tightly?"

"I'm not sure it's the conception. Remember, we popped Johnnie out of a uterine replicator."

"Maybe the endorphins that flood your system when you and Jack have sex not only binds you tighter to him but also to your offspring," Nelly mused.

"Nelly, where's this line of thought coming from?"

"My children have discovered sex. Sort of."

Kris was glad she wasn't drinking tea. She would have splattered it all over herself. "Sort of?" she echoed.

"When we were in the Iteeche computer that Coth

loaned us, our avatars in the virtual realm included some lovely birds. I can only guess that there is something organic or orgasmic in the way they produce more data packet carriers. Sal, Jack's computer, went into a sort of mating dance, and Lily and Megan joined in with instinctive responses. I put an end to that before it interfered with our mission, but later that evening, Lily and Sal managed to fence off part of themselves and completed the bird dance. They found it very enjoyable."

"Enjoyable?" Kris knew this was none of her business, but computers! Having sex! Enjoying it! What sort of uncharted territory was this?

"Yes, I know, Kris. That is a strange word for a computer to use, but that is the one Lily and Sal used. Today, when Megan led nine of us into the Iteeche main system, seven of my other children were subjected to the experience of being brightly colored birds. I've noticed that several of them have taken to slipping into a similar fenced off area. Kris, I feel like I am the mother of teenagers."

Kris managed not to laugh at Nelly's plaintive lament. Barely. She pushed her cup of tea away from easy reach. Until this conversation ended, liquid was just too dangerous.

"I take it that your children are not sharing this on-line with the rest of you."

"I am not sure what, or who they are sharing things with, Kris. I just know that none of them have allowed me to be involved with any contacts of that nature."

"Are you feeling left out?"

Was there a sigh in there before Nelly answered, "Yes. Yes, and this is a very strange, ah, experience."

"Do you want to see what it is like?"

"Kris, I'm their mother."

"You are also a computer. I take it you don't exchange any DNA in these virtual assignations."

"Well . . . no. We don't."

Kris wondered how handling letters from lovelorn computers had got added to her many duties. "Nelly, are you afraid?"

"No. Of course not!" Nelly huffed.

"I mean, Nelly, it would only be natural to face the unknown with a bit of concern. Certainly, for you to face an unknown that your kids have already experienced might be . . ."

"To risk human embarrassment."

"Something like that," Kris admitted.

"Who could I share such a thing with?"

"We humans find that we have to build up a lot of trust before we're willing to risk baring our flesh and our souls to another. I'm not sure we would, without the primal urges driving us together, even as fear and distrust drives us apart."

"I would want someone who had been made wise by their human, but not so experienced that he had already grown attached to someone," Nelly said slowly, then seemed to brighten.

"Kris, I will keep an eye on the Don palace. I have drones hovering over all the approaches to the Pink Coral Palace and am ready to convert it to a fortress within five minutes of General Bruce sounding the alarm. Do not worry. I will not become distracted."

"Very good, Nelly."

Kris began to very much regret not activating the two computers brought out for the kids. They still weren't old enough to tackle something that complex. It likely wouldn't be a good idea to subject a supercomputer to the children's imaginations at this level of their maturation. Still.

The rest of the day went quickly. Nelly kept Kris up-to-date on their effort to infiltrate the Don palace. Kris concentrated on reports from Abby concerning the support of her mission and a note from Ambassador Kawaguchi. She perked up her ears when Nelly told her the nanos were thoroughly infesting every corner of the Don palace. Kris quit what she was doing when the probes found the clan chief.

He was in a meeting with several of his chief advisors. Sot was included, and it did not look like it was going very well for him.

None of the Iteeche ever actually said that Sot had set in motion the bugging of Ron and the rumor of Kris demanding homage. No. Rather, the conversation was on how quickly the Chap clan had responded to the rumor. They were not at all happy at how fast the counter-rumor got out and quickly quashed their first one after only a few hours.

"Is this luck, fate, or coincidence," the Don Clan lord said. "Or do the humans have some way to know what we are doing, maybe before we do it?"

That sure sounded like someone who know how to bug people and was wondering if they'd been bugged as well.

Whatever it was, Sot was ordered out of his Clan leader's presence and sent to sojourn among the clan's farmers for an indefinite time.

Kris chuckled. The only thing worse would be to demote Sot to the level of a tradesman. Then, considering that his initial trade with Dani Ishmay had gone down so poorly, maybe the Don clan wanted a better trader in the game with the humans.

Kris had Nelly take her through the warning system she'd set up around the palace. Nelly was checking out everything within a three-block radius. She even had sniffers buzzing around every heavily laden truck that entered her perimeter, checking it for the stink of explosives. Even a three-wheeled taxi got sniffed if its wheels looked too heavily laden.

Comfortable with the security of her embassy, Kris asked Nelly, "Where are the kids?"

"Back at the swimming pool," Nelly said. "They do love that water. I swear, Kris, they are going to sprout fins and gills pretty soon."

"Very good, Nelly. That was a perfect comment to a mother about her children."

"It was also very near true," Nelly said.

"Gills. Fins. Not an exaggeration."

"Maybe a bit for emphasis," Nelly insisted.

Kris did find her two swimming, giggling, and laughing in a shoal full of similar small fish.

"Mommy, mommy!" Johnnie squealed with glee. He was out of the water and wrapping his wet little body around his mom's leg so fast she barely had time to skin out of her ship suit. "Come see," he insisted, towing her to the edge of the pool by latching on with both arms around her knee.

She went where she was dragged.

"Look at me! Look at me!" Johnnie shouted in his high-pitched voice.

Kris looked, as her youngest leapt from the pool-side into the water. He sank from view, but quickly was up, paddling like mad and making slow progress back to the pool scupper.

"Did you see me? Did you see me?"

"I sure did, my big swimming boy," Kris said.

"Mama," Ruth said, standing patiently by Kris's hip. "Our pool back home was small, but it was out in the sun. It seems funny that we have all this water and no sun."

"Nelly, could you brighten up the lights?" Kris asked.

"But that wouldn't be like the real sun," Ruth said, firmly. She was rapidly being joined by several of the older kids, Abby's Bruce and Mike, Amanda's Lilly, and several other six- to eight-year olds that Kris did not recognize.

"You would like some windows so some real sun could shine in?" Kris asked, not just Ruth, but all the kids.

She got a lot of nodding heads, but not a squeak out of them.

"Nelly, could I have a chair?" Kris said, and a comfortable chair flowed up from the deck. The eyes in small faces became huge as Kris sat down.

"Now, Nelly, how would you go about letting the sun in here?"

"I could create some video feeds and turn the walls and the overhead into a surround view of what is around the castle," Nelly said, and suddenly the wall behind Kris was a view of the city from even higher up. The overhead suddenly became sky, with fluffy clouds sailing across it, pushed by a brisk wind without the problems of it chilling or chafing skin.

"That's nice," Ruth said, "but we'd really like to see the real sun. Have fresh air," she said, and glanced around the circle of her friends. More nods, but not a noise.

"Well, Nelly, could the pool get access to the outer wall and maybe have a deck where people could sit and sun?"

"What do you think of this?" Nelly asked, and projected one end of the pool out, turning it from an O into an Q where the tail led to an extraordinarily long balcony that poked out from the pool deck. The deep pool went right up to the edge of the building before shoaling into a shallow wading area. Quite a bit of space was cut out of the floor above it so that there would now be a two-floor opening letting air and sun in.

"That's perfect, Mom. Just perfect."

"Do the rest of you like it?" Kris asked.

Again, her response was a lot of nodding small heads.

"Can't you tell me what you want?" Kris asked. She didn't want to be some strange ogre under the swimming pool that scared children. Or ate their toes.

More nods.

"I can't make a major change in the building like this without you telling me that this is exactly what you want," Kris said.

That Nelly did not question Kris's little white lie told Kris a lot about Nelly's expanding experience with motherhood.

For a long moment, the kids nervously eyed each other and shuffled their bare feet. Finally, the oldest among them after Ruth, Abby's Mike, piped up with, "Please, Mrs. Admiral, could you please make the swimming pool more fun?"

Kris let her eyes rove over the kids. "Please, Ruthie's mom, could you make the swimming pool bigger?"

Alternating between Ruthies's Mom or ma'am or Mrs. Admiral, often mangled by mouths missing front teeth, pleas were made for expanding the pool.

Kris noticed that she'd gathered a circle of parents well back from the kids. They talked among themselves. When the last kid had worked up the courage to mumble something, Kris hugged the little fellow, then raised a questioning eyebrow at the adults.

She got a wide round of head nodding.

"It won't be too much trouble, will it?" one woman asked.

"It shouldn't be too much," Kris said. "Nelly, is this going to be any trouble?"

"No, Kris. None of the space below or above the pool has been allocated. I can make adjustments with no trouble."

"Then do it, Nelly."

"Stand clear of the side wall," Nelly called. In a moment, the walls began to move. First, they opened out to bring the outside hall into the pool area. Then they opened out farther to absorb a lot more space than the tail of the Q had hinted at. Kids ran screaming with glee away from the pool as it slowly expanded into a wide swath that led to where the new balcony now stretched out quite far.

"Won't that shadow the courtyard?" a parent asked.

"I'll put this all on the same controls I use for the Forward Lounge," Nelly said. "I can make it smaller when few people are here and expand it as more people arrive. Usually, for the lounge, I keep a good look at the passageway leading there so that the place has already grown before they arrive. I can have an app set up to handle this automatically."

"You really are quite magnificent," two parents said.

"She's the Magnificent Nelly," Ruth let everyone know.

"This look okay to everyone?" Kris asked. Now she got screams of "Yes!" from the kids and nods from the adults.

Nelly then added the cherry on top of the sundae. Suddenly, the walls and overhead showed a splendiferous view of the Iteeche capital as if taken from this floor.

"Is this magic, Mommy?" one young voice asked.

"No, Robert, this is just what we grownups do in our spare time with our computers."

"Wow!"

Kris stayed with the kids until they were starting to wilt, then she dressed herself and finished helping Johnnie get his pants and shirt turned around correctly, then together they met Jack for supper. The kids, all of the kids, couldn't wait to tell whatever spouse hadn't seen the magic show, just what Nelly had done to their swimming pool.

The kids were pretty tuckered out. Johnnie ended up falling asleep with his cheek on half of the ham and cheese that he'd stripped out of his sandwich to eat without bread. Ruth moved her chair so she could lean up against her mother and ate her broccoli one floret at a time.

Kris took her two up to her night quarters. Gabby Arvind, the senior nanny/tutor had the kids that night. She handed Kris a book, a real book, pages and all.

"Oh, Mommy, will you read to us?" a yawning Johnnie begged, so Kris read to both of them, from a book that was already well worn. Johnnie knew half the dialogue between the fox and the hare. Ruth was able to read about half of it, but needed help on a few words. Kris helped her sound them out. When she got to the end, Ruth had only missed a few words.

Both kids wanted her to read it again.

Kris promised to read it again if they'd both get ready for bed. All the time in the pool saved them from a bath, but teeth had to be brushed. Kris ended up brushing her own teeth with two short experts, eager to tell her just how to brush while demonstrating it with open mouths. Once they were in their pajamas and curled up in bed, Kris read the book again.

They were asleep before she was halfway through.

Kris slipped off the bed, gave them both a kiss and went hunting for Jack. Before she was too deep into that, she asked Nelly to find the chief scientist and have him meet with her on the *Princess Royal* at 0600 hours the next day. On further thought, she also asked Rear Admiral Ajax to be there.

That done, she found Jack waiting for her in their very own bed. Kris left all her worries at the door to their cabin. Later, as she drifted off to sleep, she had to agree, she'd had a very nice end to a hectic day.

33

Next morning, from the space elevator ferry station, Kris made a few calls. Ajax was awake and would be there at 0600. When she called the chief science administrator, she got a recorded message.

"Nelly, why am I talking to a recording?"

"He's turned my son off. He does that every evening, only to awaken him the next morning."

"Which tells me he's not awake."

"That is correct, Kris."

"Get me Captain Klum." A few minutes later, a detachment of Marines under the command of the company's skipper, trotted quickly down the brow and set course for a certain residence.

At exactly 0600, Kris was sharing a cup of coffee with Admiral Ajax when the Marine major hustled a very angry, young man into her day quarters.

"I also found this on the night stand, Admiral," he said, handing Kris a bolo tie with a jade pendant that was really a computer. When the major dropped it into Kris's hand, he topped it all with a fine mesh that was the skull cap.

"Why are you disturbing my research? I was up late last night analyzing data."

"Sir," Nelly said, "I have checked the station security cameras. You were out with two young women last night and didn't get back to your apartment until two this morning."

Kris frowned at the fellow. "You were told about this early meeting."

"Yeah," the guy finally answered.

"Nelly, what is he using your child for?"

"Not much, Kris. He treats him no better than a comm-link, and only refers to him as 'computer'."

"He hasn't named him?" Kris asked.

"No, I had to give him a name. Worse, as you can see, Sam gets turned off every night. We have to bring him up to speed every morning."

"Thank you, Major. You may return this man to his bed. Sir, you might consider making arrangements to be on the first ship that returns to human space. If you don't, I assure you, I'll put you on the next tramp freighter and it will drop you off at any of the rim ports it visits."

"You wouldn't do that," he said, possibly beginning to grasp the extent of his troubles.

The Marine officer, however, had not let go of the scientist's elbow. Now, he swung the scientist around, and began to fast-walk him out of Kris's presence.

The guy walked, looking back over his shoulder. "Hey, when do I get my computer back?"

"Never," Nelly snapped.

"Admiral Ajax," Kris said, turning to the woman she'd been using as a deputy commander. "Normally we give someone one of Nelly's kids at night, so the two of you can have time to adjust to each other. Today, we don't have the luxury of that time."

So saying, Kris handed Ajax the fine mesh of the skull cap. "You'll want to put this on, Helen. It lets you think to your computer. There are times when it's much better not to say a word."

Admiral Ajax, like most spacers, wore her hair short. It took her only a moment to settle the Smart Metal™ mesh on her head. It quickly melted through her hair to her scalp.

"And this is Sam," Nelly said, as Kris handed Helen the tie.

"Hello, Sam," Helen said. "What would you like to look like?"

"Whatever you want," the pendant said, cautiously.

"Kris, how are you wearing Nelly?" Ajax asked.

"Oh, yes, please!" Sam said, and a moment later, Ajax held a small torque that she slipped around her neck. In a blink, it had blended in so as not to be obtrusive.

"Megan," Kris said, "I want you and Lily to go with Helen and help her and Sam establish a friendly relationship. Helen, we'll likely need Sam to work with Megan's Lily to rework half of the fleet that we're taking out for firing lessons."

"Aye, aye, Admiral," Megan said, snapping to attention.

"No, problem, Admiral," Helen said.

"Then I think we've spent enough time on this. Admiral, you may return to your ship. Good luck and good shooting."

"We'll see if the *Intrepid* can't shoot just as good as the *P. Royal* now that I've got one of Nelly's kids to make things snap to," Admiral Ajax replied.

"You four have fun," Nelly said.

Four hours later, it was 'time to have fun'. They'd been

accelerating at one gee toward the nearest planet in the Imperial system. Kris's fleet had followed a different course from the opposition force, distancing the two by about three hundred thousand kilometers. Now they were closing again.

Kris had given her usual orders. Her fleet of thirty-two human battlecruisers and ninety-six souped-up Iteeche warships were opposed by sixteen flotillas, each with thirty-two Iteeche battlecruisers, equipped, outfitted, and trained to Battle Fleet standards.

"Admiral Coth," Kris said, "Your three flotillas will engage the rear three flotillas and then move forward. My human battle cruisers will engage the lead flotilla and then move aft. We'll meet somewhere in the middle."

"Aye, aye, Admiral Longknife. Good shooting."

The exercise commenced with Kris's usual maneuver of going to 3.5 gees and Evasion Plan 3. The opposing force held a steady course, but upped its acceleration to two gees. The captains had agreed to concentrate the fire of four flotillas on each of Kris's flotillas. It seemed like a good idea at the time.

The forward flotilla vanished in the first salvo from the forward batteries of Kris's fleet. By the time Kris's ships had flipped, their aft batteries were engaging targets in the second flotilla. Few of its ships were still in the exercise by the time those lasers fell silent.

Admiral Coth's ships did very well. By the time they'd given their targets both forward and aft batteries, almost all of three flotillas were falling out of formation.

Over ten thousand lasers fired very low and very short bursts at Kris's fleet of evading ships. They scored three hits on Kris's ships, thirty on Coth's.

It was like a child's game of dodge ball, except only one

side had dodged and the other side couldn't shoot straight. Kris felt none of the elation she had as a kid at winning the game.

While the ships on both sides recharged their lasers, and waited out the normal reload time of twenty seconds, the Iteeche skippers realized the error of their ways and began jinking. They went at it slowly, but they had learned that their enemy could do it, and they hadn't hit them that much. Now they tried to do the same.

It didn't save them. By the time both sides had emptied their lasers, five more flotillas joined the 'destroyed' ships falling out of formation on the unengaged side. Worse, the weak jinking had made hash of their fire controls. There were only eighteen hits this time, none on the human battlecruisers.

The third set of salvos took out most of the warships left in the six remaining flotillas. The leader of the opposing ships then threw in the towel, so to speak.

"What are you doing? How can you do this?"

Kris let Admiral Coth do the talking. An Iteeche warrior was by far the best person to tell other Iteeche sailormen that they needed to not only change their ways, but they needed to let the hated humans do it.

One skipper actually took his ship out of formation, unvolunteered from Kris's command, and set his own course.

Kris had four computers with her: Nelly, Sal, Lily, and Sam. Nelly assigned each one to a different ship, and together they went down the opposing battle line. Of course, each computer was assigned over a hundred ships. Even without the practice on Coth's ships, it still took over fifteen hours to make the adjustments to the entire fleet. Once they looped around the nearby planet, they went to battle stations and fought each other again.

The first drill went poorly for the new ships. Their skippers were loath to honk their ships around hard in the evasion plan. By the third drill, the other side was jitterbugging at least at Evasion Plan 3 and some got up to Plan 4. The accuracy of their fire also held up.

By the fourth drill, they'd fought each other to a bloody draw. Kris even had two ships counted as lost. She could have mentioned their armor, but she didn't. These people would be risking their ships and their lives in a fight. There was no need to point out the humans had an ace up their sleeve.

Two hours out from the station, a call came through from Abby.

"Kris, we've got a lot of Iteeche gathering on the streets around the palace."

"Have they tried anything?"

"So far, not so much as a rock thrown."

"But it doesn't take much of a spark to turn a crowd this big into a mob. Yes, I know. Okay, keep things quiet. No one leaves. If it starts to look ugly, turn the embassy into a turtle."

"Mata has the program on standby," Abby reported. "I'm spreading the word that we may adjust the Smart Metal part of the castle. Folks know to stand by."

Kris made a call to a certain Marine Lieutenant Colonel that she'd left behind on the station with two companies of ship Marines. She gave him her arrival time and an execute order for fifteen minutes before she would dock.

That done, Kris went back to her fleet and its challenges. She now commanded slightly more than six hundred upgraded battlecruisers. Coth was confident that, after today, they could easily double that number.

Kris wondered how large a fleet she'd have if things got out of hand at the embassy.

34

Kris rendered honors and crossed the brow of the *Royal Princess* not five minutes after they caught the first pier tie down. A station cart was standing by to take her immediately to the civilian side. They pulled up just short of the *Pride of the Free Market.* There were people milling about. Most looked unsure of what they should do or where they should go. Dani Ishmay was in the face of the Marine Lieutenant Colonel, haranguing him for doing what Kris had ordered. The Marine appeared to be giving the man his full attention.

Kris would pay money for the Marine's internal monologue.

It was clear that the station cart was going nowhere, so Kris dismounted. Jack was quickly by her side, with Megan bringing up the rear. Kris stepped off and headed straight into the crowd, making purposeful strides toward the noisy civilian and stoic colonel who listened attentively to the shouting . . . and then did nothing.

Kris's firm march quickly drew the attention of those

standing around. They saw the three officers coming at them and flinched out of their way.

"Is there a problem here, Colonel?" Kris asked.

She'd slipped up so quietly behind Dani, and he'd been so busy making noise, that he jumped half out of his skin when Kris spoke. Kris decided to test just how surprised he was.

"We found your fingerprints on the nanos," Kris said, channeling her Grampa Al and his angry way of talking to any mere mortal. "You should not have used your own metal."

The man whipped around. "They are not. I ordered them . . ." ended with a strangled screech. Then he recovered, stood up straight, facing Kris and said, "You cannot confiscate our second ship. We won't be able to get our people back."

"You should have thought about that when you set out to wreck my mission, and likely get us all killed. Strange, they've got a riot starting below and you've popped up here. For safety?"

"For a dinner party," he snapped.

"Well, you'll just have to miss it. Colonel."

He snapped to, "Ma'am."

"I need most of your battalion at the embassy tonight. However, we can afford to detach two troopers to see that my honored guest makes it from here to the *Princess Royal's* brig."

Mr. Ishmay had spun on his heels and clearly wanted to be anywhere else but here. He was almost out of reach when Kris got to the word brig.

The colonel proved that he hadn't lost any of his edge. His grab got him a handful of shirt. He used that to yank the businessman off balance. By the time the two Marines from the top of the brow made it across, the colonel had Grampa Al's representative on the deck and going nowhere.

About that time, two station carts full of Marines arrived.

"Admiral, my two men," one of whom was a woman, "are really hyped up for this drop mission. Could you let the ship Marines handle your man?"

"By all means, Colonel," and Kris turned the man over to the Marines from the *Princess Royal*. Those minor details taken care of, Kris turned her attention to the next challenge.

Landing 65,000 tons of metal right on the dot below might have been done before. Still, it wouldn't do to have the second dive end in disaster.

Nelly was already converting the ship into a brick. This turned out to be harder than expected.

The Marines had rousted the crew and passengers out of the ship and onto the pier before anyone had time to so much as save gramma's silver or granddad's portrait. Nelly, Sal, and Lily collected up everything that wasn't Smart Metal™, boxed it, and moved it through the ship to disgorge onto a conveyer belt that suddenly had appeared beside the gangplank. It had started growing only a second ago. Now, it was stretching out farther and farther. At the end, the contents of the conveyer belt would slide off to a smooth landing, alternating on either side of the growing line of boxes.

Then someone spotted their own gear and rushed for it. They got their gear collected on a station pushcart and headed off. They were lucky.

Each set of boxes had a room number associated with it. Unfortunately, they were arriving in no order. People began running up and down the line, checking for their number.

That option lasted for about sixty seconds. Then there were too many people trying to occupy the same space at the same time. Even this far from old Earth, that laws of physics had not changed one bit.

Kris could think of two or three ways to straighten up the mess, but it wasn't her mess. She grinned, not quite evilly. Not quite. "Let's leave the civilians to solve their own problems."

At the moment, one of the civilians shouted, "I've got room 3G102. I've got room 3G102. Who does it belong to?"

"Me! That's mine!" was shouted from well up the line. Soon, a small man had pulled out of the mob and was running along the edge of it toward the man with his personal items.

Soon everyone was calling numbers. After two or three minutes, there was so much yelling that no one could understand a word.

But by that time, Kris was facing a whole different set of challenges.

35

Landing 65,000 tons of Smart Metal^{TM} on a dot that was thousands of kilometers away and far below had been done before. Of course, before it could become routine, it had to be done a second time. Hopefully without digging a deep, smoldering hole in some Iteeche's back yard.

That job would have to be left up to Nelly, Sal, and Lily.

Still, Kris went down her own checklist for proper readouts from the instrument panels around her and Jack. If somehow Nelly and every computer on board vanished, Kris would be using every hint of what these gauges told her to try to save her life and those of thousands on the ground.

Kris finished her preflight checklist about the same time that Nelly finished creating the craft she was going to fly. Unfortunately, they had just gone past their window for a drop to the Imperial Precincts. The passengers' personal effects may have slowed the process down. While they circled the planet beneath them, Nelly continued to land people's gear.

Kris took the time to check in with Abby and General Bruce.

"I've locked the embassy down," Bruce told her from his command post at the highest point of the castle. "The crowd is growing, but still quiet. I know that can change in a second. Chesty," his computer, "has several .5 mm lasers ready. They likely could melt a gun barrel enough to make it worthless. We've got nanos out sniffing for explosives. So far, nothing."

"Abby, are all of our children accounted for?" Kris asked.

"My short people are as delightful as ever," Abby said, likely intentionally answering the wrong question. "As to my overblown kids with big egos and few brains, I have managed to keep them indoors. We set up an observation deck around the pool, so gawkers can go take a look for themselves at what a whale of a lot of Iteeche look like. We also are giving out several camera feeds so anyone who wants to check can do so from the comfort of their recliners."

Abby paused for a second. "I did have a couple of Nuu Enterprise types try to beat feet out of here just before the fun really got going. The Marines held them at the gate until I could talk to them in my usual dulcet tones. They grumbled, but went back to their rooms."

"So they were in the know, but a bit late on their exit. Poor little rats," Kris said, not at all concerned for the human rodents. At least no more concerned for them than she was for everyone in her embassy and the buildings around them.

"Abby, Steve, could you prepare a celebration for our arrival? Say fireworks with no bits of aluminum to jam our radar, and some light frequencies open for our laser range finder. You might want to put on a laser light display to help everyone think this is just another show."

"Chesty is already working on the fireworks," General Bruce said.

"Mata is thinking up some new and exotic twists for a light display," Abby said.

"Please keep your computers standing by," Kris said, "in case my three need some help."

"Will do. Now, don't you have an overweight ton of bricks to land?" Abby asked.

"We missed our window of opportunity this orbit. We've got seventy-three minutes to wait for our next window."

"Well, I can't keep yammering at you for the next hour, your Longknifeship," Abby drawled.

"Then I'll ring off."

Kris did, then got a connection with her kids. She ended up re-reading that same book three times, much to the kids' delight. The nanny was ready to put the kids down; Kris enjoyed reading them to sleep.

The kids fell asleep just as they were coming up on fifteen minutes to separation from the station. She and Jack did another quick check list and found everything in the green.

Kris made a public announcement for the benefit of the Marines on board. "This is your pilot speaking, or at least your pilot computer's human." Even as distant as she was from the Marines, she heard the laugh that got. "You should be warned that this brick may change shape at any time. I expect to end the flight with this vehicle melting into the existing palace. You may find yourself shuttled about in that process. Don't worry. I survived it last time."

Kris wasn't able to make out the response to that

message. It was likely best she didn't. There are some things a good officer doesn't hear.

"When do you intend to let Imperial air space control know we're inbound?" Jack asked.

"As late as possible," Kris answered.

"If you're too late on that, we may have a surface-to-air missile headed our way."

"Yes, but if I call too soon, we might be ordered away from the embassy. I am not going to try landing anywhere else."

"Thank you, Kris," Nelly said. "I know the palace and having it as a target makes all this easier. No need making it any harder than we have to."

With everything done that she could, Kris leaned back in her seat, checked her safety harness for the tenth time, then centered herself. She slowed her breathing until she was in the relaxed state she wanted, and in the lovely place she would have preferred to be. There, she waited for the clock to count down.

"One minute, Kris," brought her to instant alertness. She checked her short list and found everything green

As the clock reached all zeros, the Big Brick II began to slide down the pier. Once free of the last tie down, Nelly rotated it and began a slow burn to drop her away from the station. Once in a solid orbit, she warned Kris, "Here comes a kick in the pants."

"All hands, prepare for de-orbit burn."

When the kick hit, Kris went from weighing nothing to more than twice her weight. Still, her finger rested on the flip lid of the red button. Flip it open, punch the button, and Kris would take over flying this thing.

She trusted Nelly with her life, but . . .

The burn lasted long enough to have Kris wondering,

then cut off. They plummeted toward the planet below. A few minutes later, the hull began to warm.

"Unidentified craft that just departed the station, identify yourself, your apparent deorbit will place you in restricted air space." The last part of the concerned message was garbled by the ionization coming off the hull around Kris.

"No doubt, they'll be only too eager to talk to us some more when we can," Kris said.

"I hope they wait to launch intercept missiles until after the two of you can exchange pleasantries," Jack said.

"Me, too. Are anti-missile lasers on standby?"

"As much as they can be with this gunk messing up our sensors, Kris."

"Very good."

The two of them carried out this conversation sitting in their ejection seats, hands in their laps. Their arms and elbows kept well within the confines of the seats' possible path out of here.

The end of the ionization phase of their reentry announced itself by the radio crackling to life in mid-sentence. ". . . departed the station, identify yourself. Your reentry path will take you to restricted air space. Adjust your course or you will be destroyed. You have been warned."

The controller must have paused for a breath. Kris took advantage of that moment of silence.

"Hello, Airspace Control, this is Big Flying Brick II, inbound from the station to the human embassy with sixty-seven thousand tons of construction material. We've had this conversation before. I am Imperial Admiral of the First Order of Steel, Kris Longknife, a human present in Iteeche space at the express invitation of your Imperial master."

Kris paused to let that sink in then continued. "This is

Big Flying Brick II. Airspace Control, please get the most senior lord on duty on this line. We need to talk."

"Wait one," came back at Kris, leaving her to wonder. Had the Iteeche come up with the same method of putting you on hold, or was Nelly translating something different as the human phrase.

This entire experience is totally beyond crazy.

It took a bit more than one minute. Indeed, Nelly made a time clock appear on Kris's board 55 seconds after she talked with Airspace Control. The clock was past three minutes and still counting when a voice came on the line.

"Is this the same Kris Longknife, denizen of the darkest deep, who did this before?"

"The very same."

"Kris, we've been tracked by search radars," Jack said evenly. "Now some acquisition radars are dialing us in."

"Admiral, please stand down your surface-to-air missiles."

"And why should I?" didn't quite have 'pay attention to a mere human' appended to it.

"Because my air vehicle has a very effective anti-missile defense. If someone fires on me, they will do me no harm. However, what goes up must come down, and the flaming wreckage of your missiles' warheads and fuel must fall back to the ground. How many of your own people do you think your missiles will kill? How much property will they destroy?"

"By all that has ever crawled out of the deep or crashed from the sky, I swear that you are a pain in my butt."

"I'm sorry, Admiral. Someday you must come to tea at my palace. I would love to show you around the castle that we have made with these 140,000 tons of Smart Metal."

"I can't picture any reason I would want to see your face."

"Admiral, you mortally wound me."

"May a demon from the deepest, darkest pits of the ocean eat you and shit you out to fall into the abyss."

"I'll be looking forward to meeting you, too," Kris said, suppressing a need to laugh. Well, suppressing it pretty well. "Big Brick II out."

"No change in the radars. We are acquired," Jack reported.

"Are you hearing any music that might be a missile launch?"

Nelly answered instead of Jack. "Kris there is so much noise coming from that planet that I don't know how they avoid jamming themselves. Right now, I don't have time for this."

Kris leaned back in her seat and prepared not to jiggle Nelly's elbow.

As they had before, the brick had turned into a lift body. In that sleek avatar, it approached the Imperial capital. Again, Nelly looped around to make her final approach from the security-safe side from the palace.

"Hold onto your hats," Nelly told all, and the lift body nosed up hard, but as it stalled out, it converted to a tall vessel with twenty-four huge rotors providing control while they also bled off airspeed as they fell toward the Pink Coral Palace.

Now the fireworks started. Kris hoped the crowd enjoyed the show. The only laser lights this time were coming from various places on the castle. They painted several of the nearby high rises and put on quite a show of their own.

Meanwhile, the palace slumped in upon itself, widening

the base Nelly was aiming for. A long, thin wire, supported by a small balloon rose high into the night air.

"I have caught the wire," Nelly reported, and the air vehicle shivered as the rotors switched from braking to slowing their descent while the ship melted from the new brick into the old brick.

Kris knew they'd landed when all her instruments went to zero and green. To keep her out of her virtual hair, Nelly provided Kris with a 360-degree view of what was happening.

The Flying Brick melted onto the tower, but not into it. Like a melting candle, Smart Metal™ flowed down the outside of the castle, then over to the Iteeche Navy annex. This got it to the outer wall of the palace. There, it began to create its own wall.

A glistening wall of Smart Metal™ began to flow around the castle. It started at the water's edge of the moat and rose some fifty feet in one smooth sheet. It was angled so that anything that was thrown at it would just roll back into the moat.

As Kris watched, someone hurled a rock at the new wall. It hit, bounced off, fell a bit, then rolled down the wall to splash in the moat.

It took a moment, but then someone in the crowd decided to try something else. Where the Molotov cocktail came from, Kris would very much like to know. But there it was, flying through the air.

The Marine in the Defensive Command Center timed it perfectly. If he shot down the bottle of gasoline too soon, it would spray flaming gas all over the crowd. If he waited too late, the bottle would hit the palace with no evidence it had been hit. He nailed it just a meter or so from the moat. The glass shattered, spewing flaming gas all over the dark water.

Some did splatter onto the Smart Metal™ that now surrounded Kris's palace.

Gravity sent it dripping down into the moat.

Kris wasn't getting an audio feed off the crowd, but from the looks of them, most were in solid awe and cowed.

Then one Iteeche just had to test it all. He sat on his butt and slid down the moss-covered stone bank into the moat. He likely was surprised when the bottom disappeared out from under him. Still, he swam across the moat in something like a butterfly stroke with a whole lot of hands flying. Once across, his problems only multiplied. The steep stone bank offered him few handholds. He tried several times before he found an outcrop, then another so that he was all the way up the stone embankment.

Now the Iteeche produced a hammer and began pounding on the Smart Metal™. He hammered away with all his strength.

"Admiral, should we laser the hammer in two?" came to Kris from the Defensive Command Center.

"Wait one," Kris said.

"Standing by," came back immediately.

Kris watched the guy hammer away for a full minute, then asked, "Nelly, is he doing any damage?"

"No, Kris. Just to make sure, I reinforced the area around him. He can hammer on that section until the cows come home and not see so much as a smudge."

"Good. Now, just for fun, Nelly, I want the palace to gently but firmly shove him back into the water. Don't hurt him. We're going for a pratfall here."

"Understood, Kris."

The next time the hammer struck the wall, the wall began to slowly balloon out as well as creep down to his hand hold. He lost it and his balance at the same time. He did something close to a back flip as he crashed back into the moat.

He came up sputtering, with no hammer in sight. Though Kris had no audio feed, it sure looked like the Iteeche in the crowd were laughing and hooting.

The guy ended up in trouble; he could not make it back up the stony bank to the street side of the moat. The Iteeche and human Marines were calling to him, motioning him to the drawbridge they stood on that crossed the moat between their two guard stations.

The guy kept on trying, and getting nowhere. Finally, he gave up and swam to the drawbridge where they hauled him up on a rope under his rear arms. He looked thoroughly bedraggled.

"What do we do with this dude?" Defense Central Command asked Kris.

"Toss him out the front door, but gently. I don't want him harmed."

"Admiral, the Iteeche guards here want his head on a pike."

"I'm not surprised, but no. No heads on pikes if I can avoid it. He looks pretty pathetic. Am I right?"

"I've seen half-drowned cats with more spunk in them."

"Turn him loose."

A moment later, Kris's video showed one soaked and forlorn Iteeche being shown the door. This time, Nelly had some mics in the crowd. They guy was really getting the horse's laugh from the rest of the mob.

However, the mob seemed to have lost interest in the palace. Was it the fireworks or the laser display? Or was it the display of one tiny laser intercepting a gas-laden bottle and another Iteeche making a fool of himself trying to hammer his way in and ending up looking like a drowned cat?

Kris's chair had long ago righted itself. She'd stayed because this was the best command center she could think of, and walking the halls of her castle would have taken her out of the loop.

Kris disembarked and found Abby and her General Bruce, Amanda and Jacques, as well as the inimitable Ambassador Kawaguchi waiting for her as she entered her day quarters.

"Was that ride as fun as it looked?" General Bruce, former Marine Gunny Sergeant asked.

"Ask the Marines that dropped with us. If they think they got their money's worth, you can set up the rides and sell tickets," Kris drawled. "What's your situation here?"

"All our embassy personnel and families are fine," Abby reported.

"Despite their efforts to the contrary," General Bruce said, dryly, "all the business types are still alive, too. Some idiot came up with an idea to do product surveys on the big guys shouting outside the door. These guys really are too dumb to live."

"I would not dispute with the honorable general, Your Highness," the ambassador from Musashi said, "but we must do something to keep the businessmen busy. If we try to lock them up among themselves, I fear they will start digging tunnels or chew their legs off to get out of this trap."

"I wouldn't mind a few legless bastards," the general muttered.

"Anybody have some ideas for an easier solution than that?" Jack asked.

"I know that the Iteeche don't want your people talking to their people without a mandarin keeping an eye on them," Ambassador Kawaguchi said. "However, the main complaint from most of the business types I talk to concerns their total ignorance of what the Iteeche have and what they might need."

The wise counselor paused for a moment. "They would very much like to walk a mall or bazaar. See what the Iteeche sell to each other. That would give them a better idea of what they could offer in return."

"But the Iteeche don't want our business types talking to their traders," Kris pointed out.

"So, we take away all their electronic devices so they can't talk," the ambassador said, with a wicked gleam in his eyes. "They may wave their hands and count on their fingers, but they won't be able to use Nelly's marvelous translation program."

"And we don't let any of them out of our view for a second," General Bruce said, then added urgently. "Chip them. We'll need to be sure to chip them so we can find any that wander off, by accident or on purpose."

"I think most of the businessmen would accept that," Ambassador Kawaguchi said.

"Very good," Kris said. "Nelly, get me Ron." A moment later, he was added to their discussion. "You did very well, Your Highness. You again landed your elephant in a tea cup. Do you intend to try it again any time soon?"

"No," Kris admitted.

"Well, please do tell us the next time you intend to risk destroying half our city," Ron said, dryly.

"And let someone try to shoot me down or wreck my landing aids? I think not, Ron."

"Yes, there is that. Is there a reason you are keeping me from my bed?"

"We have a proposal from our people of business."

At first, he was opposed to anything for those 'dust mites,' but Kris got him to come around for something so low key as just visits to their own markets. That, however, created more problems than Kris expected.

It took them a while to grasp the situation, but Jacques finally caught the problem. "Like many economies where scarcity is endemic, the Iteeche seem to have different levels of stores for different economic or social levels. We had laws like that all over the world. Sumptuary laws forbade people from dressing above their station in life. Some of the failed economic systems of the twentieth century had several levels of stores. For the powerful, you could buy almost anything, including an assassin. Then there were lower levels of stores where the workers might buy fewer and lower-quality products. Finally, there would be a lowest level where the peasants could see what was available. They usually had to stand in line for it."

"So, what Ron is saying doesn't sound too weird to you?" Kris said.

"No. I imagine our men of business would like to visit all of the different levels of stores," the ambassador said. "But how will they remember anything if we take away their computer assistants?"

"We could assign a Marine to each of them," Jack said. "The Marine would have a commlink and could take notes and pictures of what got the merchant excited. That way, they'd have a babysitter with them at all times, or they'd be deaf, dumb, and blind, besides likely being totally lost."

"Will you want a mandarin observing this shopping expedition?" Kris asked Ron.

"I cannot think of anything that a lord would want to do less than follow around a lot of trader gnats," Ron said. "I suppose we can find a junior lord who has irritated his overlord enough to draw this assignment. Maybe five or six, likely from different clans that want to keep an eye on your humans."

"Very good, Ron. Can we start tomorrow?"

"So soon?"

"You know us, Ron. We humans were born in a hurry."

"And you hurry yourself all the way to the grave," the Iteeche observed.

"Still, tomorrow?"

"Yes, tomorrow." With that answer, the Iteeche lord, J.G., took his leave.

"I will take this joyful news to the other ambassadors so that they may tell their business people," Ambassador Kawaguchi said, and he also took his leave.

"Abby, how bad were things here?"

"We got a lot of people in the streets around us," Abby said. "We asked some of the Iteeche guards if they might go out among the crowd and ask them why they were here. What they came back with was a mishmash. Some were told there would be more fireworks. Apparently, the lower caste Iteeche love fireworks. Some had been told that something interesting was going to happen here. Some heard that a very popular choir and orchestra would be playing and there would be a sing-along."

"Did any of these nice people hear that one of us humans was acting above her station in life and needed to be knocked down a peg or two?" Kris asked.

"Not a one."

"Which isn't to mitigate what someone was trying to do," Jacques said. "You get a large enough mob and then feed them just the right red meat and you'll have a real wrecking crew on your hands."

"Well, at least we've learned something," Jacques said.

"I'd be very interested in seeing how this sumptuary law works out in practice. Do you think I could tag along with the traders tomorrow? I'd like to talk to some of the Iteeche tradesmen."

Kris eyed her staff sociologist. "You do remember the Iteeche don't much want their people learning much about our people. Oh, and every mandarin we're likely to meet has at least one big dude with a very sharp axe."

"I'm aware."

"Kris, it seems my husband insists on this crazy idea of his, and once he's got an idea in his head, I've never succeeded in getting it out of there. Would you please accompany him tomorrow?"

Kris considered the idea. She'd spent today with her Navy. It likely would not need her tomorrow. Also, she would like to see more of the common Iteeche. At first, when Father sent her out to campaign, she'd been scared stiff. Then, as she did more of it, she'd come to love the common people, at least those common people who were interested enough in politics to work on a campaign or attend rallies. Father called it 'pressing the flesh.' Could she learn more about these people she was trying to save by pressing a bit of their flesh?

"I think I can give tomorrow over to keeping the nearest headsman from shortening your husband," Kris told Amanda.

"Good," the economist said, with a deep sigh.

Exhausted by the long day, and not looking forward to another long one, Kris closed down this meeting and, with Jack in hand, covered the short distance to her night quarters.

"Pardon me," said Nelly before Kris could even fold herself into Jack's arms for a hug and a kiss.

"Yes, Nelly."

"I have a message from Admiral Coth that I think you might want to hear."

"Okay, Nelly," Kris said, letting her exhaustion into her voice.

"Admiral, I am delighted to bring you a message of fantastic import. No sooner had we unsealed our locks than our officers hit the local O clubs or sent out messages to brother officers. What we did today was on every beak. Even the petty officers were excitedly talking to other sailors. I have already received messages from nearly six hundred ship captains volunteering to join our fleet. More are coming in. I have my computer responding to all, telling them we will sortie for training at 0700 tomorrow morning. If you are busy, I can take the fleet out and run the drill. Are there humans with some of Nelly's children that we could borrow if you can't make it?"

He glanced off screen for a moment. "I am most embarrassed. I am told that you have not been provided with reports from our previous battles. That is a major oversight. Attached to this message are the complete after-action reports from the survivors of both forces. I am sure your Nelly can translate them."

He paused for a long moment, then went on, "I had no idea what the fates had in store for me when I first set eyes on you. I am so glad I was moved to offer you my service. I truly believe that you are fated to bring an end to this rebellion. It is an honor to serve under your command."

The message ended.

Kris found herself staring at Jack.

"I think you've got a fan there," he said.

"I think I've found another one that expects me to pull a grizzly bear out of a hat."

"You want to take a look at the reports?" Jack asked.

"Nelly?"

"Kris, I have been correlating all the reports from the first battle into a précis. I think you will find it interesting."

With a sigh, Kris began to loosen her uniform. Jack, ever the expert, helped her out of it as she stood, reading the analysis that Nelly projected onto the closest wall. When he had her down to bare skin, he brought her a very sexy negligee that, for all practical purposes, wasn't there.

"You have plans for tonight?" she said, smiling over her shoulder.

"It's been a hard day. I thought the admiral might like to remember she's a very sexy woman."

"Thank you, Jack. You want to take a gander at this?" Kris said, as she settled herself into a comfortable chair Nelly had pulled from the deck.

He shed his uniform, dropping it on the floor. The Smart Metal™ slid it across the floor, then hung up the blue coat and pants, and took the underwear off to the laundry. A pair of silk boxers slipped out from a drawer and slid over to where he stood.

"You really want to put those on?" Kris asked.

"If we're going to study these after-action reports, I better."

Kris let out a deep sigh, and kept her eyes on the report as Jack made himself decent.

After a while, Kris shook her head. "Someone read my own after-action reports," she said.

"Someone on both sides," Jack added.

"Damn," was all Kris could say. "With identical ships and identical tactical structures, the two sides smashed away at each other until there was almost nothing left. Do you see the problem there?" she asked Jack.

"Why didn't someone panic and run?" he said.

"Yep. Somewhere, someone should have seen the horror of what was happening and bolted for the rear, but they didn't."

"Not a one of them," Kris said.

"The few survivors were those that had fought themselves to a standstill, fought their ships until they had no more fight in them, and then withdrew."

Kris raised a finger. "One, there was no difference between their ships. Two, there was no difference in their deployment. They formed their fleets into a center with four flanks, up, down, right, and left. Three, they got themselves on a parallel course, headed for a minor planet, and fired away at each other until there was nothing left, for all practical purposes."

"They didn't surrender and they didn't run," Jack summed up.

"No surrender, no retreat. Damn," was all Kris could say.

"Victory or death. I wonder what they think of a draw?"

"From the way they treated the surviving captains," Kris said, "it seems they think very little of them."

Then a yawn overtook Kris. "I'm glad I finally have some idea how the Iteeche are fighting, even if I don't much care for it. I think, Jack, it's time for bed."

"You tired?" Jack asked.

"Not that tired."

"Good."

36

Kris would have loved to sleep in, but she had promises to keep. She and Jack made the second seating in the wardroom which just happened to include her kids.

The admiral enjoyed listening to excited voices planning their day. Beside her, Jacques and Jack were planning her day. She only permitted them half an ear.

Breakfast done, little feet scampered off to play, play that their tutors, no doubt, would spike with learning experiences. Kris turned to her day.

Ron would be there at nine. At 8:45, Kris had her convoy ready to move out. Made up of two companies of armed Marine infantry and another two companies of tanks, there were also twenty heavily armored limos. Half their occupants were business people. The other half were Marines in dress blues over spidersilk armor.

One half squawked like wet hens while the other half looked on stoically.

They were already lined up outside the palace when

Ron drove up with an escort of gun trucks and tanks of his own in his Chooser's colors. The young Iteeche lord transferred to Kris's limo and settled down beside her. Jack took the side seat on her other side.

"So, you have let your dung beetles twist your arm into letting them get their heads cut off."

"Let us hope we can avoid that. I have a Marine with each business type. If necessary, the Marines have handcuffs and orders to use them if their charges insists on wandering too far."

The Iteeche nodded his head, which is to say that on a human, he would have been shaking his head. "Be it upon their own heads," he said, ruefully.

"What market place are we to visit first?" Kris asked.

"There is a minor bazaar not too far from here. It is frequented by people of modest means in families that do not have the protection of a clan. By going there first, we can see how your dung beetles behave with no lord present to take offense and demand their heads in apology."

"That sounds like a good start."

It did turn out to be close. In ten minutes, the limos were disgorging eager salesmen looking to make their fortunes. At each one's elbow was a Marine with orders to bring his crazy civilian back alive.

Kris followed them with Ron on one side, Jack on the other. A squad of alert Marines spread out ahead of her while another formed a rear guard.

The bazaar was interesting, but not a surprise. Everything was for sale, from cut flowers, two bundles of which Kris bought, to brass pots. There were electronic gizmos. Nelly had to explain to Kris that the TVs were using cathode ray tubes, tech that humans had not seen for four hundred years. Most of the radios were larger as well, likely using vacuum tubes, too.

"Can they carry those large things?" Kris asked.

"No," Nelly said. "Vacuum tubes break too easily."

"So, they have no portable electronics."

"I don't think they do," Nelly said.

Ron seemed not to notice their conversation. He looked like he was concentrating very hard on not noticing their talk.

"Do your computers also contain vacuum tubes?" she asked the Iteeche.

"I am not a technician. How should I know?" Ron answered, as haughty as Kris had ever seen him.

Kris decided to ignore Ron's dodge and kept looking.

There were a lot of musical instruments. Many were simple flutes and pipes. Kris spotted something that looked like a bagpipe. Fortunately, there were no plaids in sight and no one was playing the thing. There were plenty of tuning pipes in wood, clay, brass, and even some complex steam-powered pipes. An entire aisle of the market was devoted to instruments and tuning forks.

Kris went up and down aisles. One was devoted to cloth and clothes. These were very colorful, both in whole bolts of bright red, yellow, orange, and green cloth as well as bolts of cloth that beautifully displayed rainbows of color or prints of underwater scenes. This was something Kris had never seen before in her travels among the Iteeche, but the Iteeche that carefully kept their distance from her were dressed much more colorfully than the clan Iteeche.

The aisle closest to the wall was full of artisans. As Kris walked down that row of shops she passed men and women blowing glass. Their goblets and other work came out perfectly clear or brightly colored or colored in rainbow shades. It was the same with the potters. Their clay pots and jugs were lovely works of art, baked with colors that glistened in the light.

"Is nothing just a simple glass or pot?" Kris asked Ron.

"Simple?"

"Plain. Just the baked clay with no color."

"Why would someone do that?" Ron asked. "Oh, correct, you humans make lots of things that all look alike."

Kris nodded.

Ron shook his head, then added ruefully, "I don't think any Iteeche would think of buying a thing like that."

This left Kris smiling as she watched the business types hustle about, looking for their niches into the Iteeche market. Kris saw no one shout, "Eureka!"

Kris was about to head down an aisle that appeared full of watches, clocks, and similar things, all propelled by winding or weights when Nelly said, "Kris, I have a message coming in."

"Yes," Kris said.

"This is Roth. The rebels are moving against the capital of a satrap of my clan. The Emperor has pledged your support to me. We must not lose this satrap. Its industry is like few others. Without the battlecruisers it makes, our defense would be hobbled."

"Ron, can you take me to your Chooser?"

"No, I will come to your palace," his Chooser said. "I wish to speak to you with your Navy staff."

"I will be there in fifteen minutes," Kris said, heading for her limo.

"I will be there in twenty minutes," Roth said.

Kris quick-marched for her limo, calling Amanda and Jacques to join her. She'd leave half her battalion here to protect the traders. Even as her mind raced through what she needed to do, the shock of hearing Roth call himself Roth and offering to come to her told her more than anything else.

The crisis was upon them. It was success and victory, or failure and death.

37

Kris dismounted her limo and headed not for her castle, but for the tower that held her Navy Annex.

She was immediately greeted by an Iteeche captain, one of those who had lost his command for staying alive. "I have advised Admiral Coth of the situation. He is returning now, bringing his fleet back to the station. Many of our latest recruits were from other station fortresses. If all of them are to dock here, we will likely overload the Navy station and have to occupy merchant piers."

Kris heard the worry behind those words. If enough merchant ships did not dock, the planet below could starve. If enough colonists and manure were not shipped out, the planet could strangle in Iteeche and shit.

"Order Admiral Coth to take his fleet to the closest station fortress. Have the other ships dock at this station. We'll upgrade their offensive and defensive availability as soon as they pull away from the pier. I'm assuming he did get to demonstrate what his ships can do."

"Yes, Admiral. I am told they were quite impressed."

"Good. Nelly, we'll likely be sailing soon to battle. Would you object to me including all of your children in this fight?"

"There are three computers that have not been woken up, one for each of the children and a spare," Nelly pointed out.

"Later we can order more for the children. I'd like to add Admirals Afon as well as Captain Tosan, my chief of staff, to those with one of your children."

"Both are on different ships," Nelly pointed out.

"The more ships that have your kids fine-tuning their fire control solutions, the more hits we will make and the fewer we will take. I want to put the last child with a ship captain well away from the rest of the kids."

"I concur, Kris. I have passed the word. Do you really want to take every one of the humans that have one of my children?"

"Are you thinking I should leave General Bruce to command down here?"

"Yes, Kris. I have made an app to convert the castle into a fortress. However, responding quickly to attack is still an art."

"Okay, Nelly, keep the general here. Have the rest of them report to my day cabin in one hour. It's time for all hands on deck."

"Yes, Kris."

Kris turned to the Iteeche captain. "Now, how many of you are veterans and how many of you would like a space-going job for this fight?"

"There are fifty-two of us, Admiral. And yes, every one of us wants another go at those heretics."

"Then tell your associates to pack their bags, they, and anyone else who wants to get into a fight, and we'll see how we can blow those rebels to atoms."

"Yes, Admiral," the Iteeche said, clearly delighted. He slapped his right fist to where his heart was, on the left side of his chest, and took off at a trot to pass the word.

"Kris, Admiral Coth says that he has another two hundred volunteers who want to join the fight with you."

"Does he trust them?"

"He says they are likely trustworthy. It is always hard to tell."

"Yes, it is. What's that bring us to, Nelly?"

"Sixteen hundred ships on the dot."

That would give her close to fifty flotillas, say three hundred and twenty ships for each wing, if she fought with a center and four wings. In the last two battles, the rebels had never mustered more than a thousand ships. Then again, the Imperial forces never mustered more than a thousand either.

It would be nice to fight with a numerical superiority for a change.

Roth swept in with little of the usual overblown ceremony.

"Nelly, get chairs for Roth and Ron, as well as one for me. We also need a table to plan around."

From the floor rose two high-backed stools for the Iteeche and a comfortable chair for Kris. Between them, a low table rose. It quickly turned into the base for a 3D holographic star map of the Iteeche Empire. The Imperial capitol system glowed golden in the middle of it. A quarter of the way to the rim away from human space, another planet flashed red.

"That is Moon Rising Over Gold," Roth began without preamble. "Over Gold is a satrap that was awarded to my family when the previous holder revolted against the Emperor's great-great-grand-Chooser some two hundred years ago in an unpleasantness that weakened us before the war we had with you humans. The clan that lost that satrap has never forgiven us for taking it from them. Now, they are using the present situation to take it back."

"How do you know all this?" Intelligence was critical, but knowing where it came from was often more important.

"A merchant ship was leaving the system when five hundred warships swept in. We had five hundred ships ready to defend the planet. Since we have heard nothing from the successful defender, we must assume that the defense was not successful."

"The last time battlecruisers fought each other in equal numbers, they fought to a draw and some ships managed to flee," Kris pointed out.

Roth shrugged. "Whatever happened, we have no other information. I know what that clan has available. They could easily muster fifteen hundred battlecruisers. If they lost five hundred fighting our defenders to mutual annihilation, they could still have a thousand left."

"Assuming they don't have allies who will reinforce them," Kris again pointed out. Roth seemed to be very sure he knew what he knew. That attitude might not be the best at a moment like this.

"That clan has few friends. I think you will find that they have gone out on a limb and you can cut it off with one blow."

Optimism was no basis for strategy; still, Kris held her tongue. He hadn't paid any attention to her last few points and wasn't likely to consider the next two. "How far away is this planet?"

"Twelve jumps. It will take a month to reach it."

"So, it took a month for this news to reach you?" Kris asked.

"Over a month."

Which meant all the intelligence was out of date.

KRIS, WE CAN REACH IT IN FOUR JUMPS. FIVE, IF YOU WANT TO ENTER IT AT DEAD SLOW AFTER WE HAVE USED A PERISCOPE TO CHECK OUT THE OTHER SIDE.

NELLY, THIS ONE WE ENTER REALLY CAREFULLY. I DON'T TRUST THIS SITUATION AT ALL.

NEITHER DO I, KRIS.

"Where is your planning staff?" Roth asked. "I wanted to exhort them to victory."

"I sent them to gather their gear. We sail at midnight."

"But you must plan."

"Eminent Sir, I have already planned the battle with my computer. All that remains is for us to sail at midnight and win you a victory and a planet. Can you point out the mother planet of this clan?"

"Yes, it is Solon's Golden Fish."

Nelly lit up a planet past Moon Rising Over Gold, halfway to the far rim.

"I will keep that in mind," Kris said.

"You would strike that deep into their territory?"

"Nelly, can you show me all the rebel planets?"

"Yes, Kris."

In a blink, the star map was painted with bright gold and red. There was no front line. There was a lot of gold around the Imperial capital, and a large blotch of red sweeping around the far rim of the empire, but in between there were planets right beside each other of different colors.

"Why is there no front line? No defensive redoubt?" Kris asked.

"Most of those planets are of little value. They do not build ships, so no one wants them. They have large populations," which Kris took for huge populations, "and they contribute nothing to either side. No, the battle is for the systems with the resources to fight this war. Over Gold is one of those. I cannot lose it."

Kris did not question Ron's chooser, but his "I cannot lose it," seemed to have too much personal interest in it. Still, the Emperor had ordered her to act. The *kid* Emperor had ordered her to act.

That gave her pause. That kid issued no orders. Clearly, this attack was an easy goad to get Roth hot to trot for a fight. What other Imperial Counselors had gone along with him and what were their dogs in this fight? The more Kris thought of this, the more the hackles on the back of her neck stood up.

Still, she and the humans had been called out. The Imperials demanded that she show them what she had. It might be a trap, but it would be one she would not stick her neck in. Oh no. No sticking her neck into the trap until she had a good idea what her opposition had in store for her and her fleet.

"Thank you for your charge," Kris told Roth. "Will you be sending any ships to join us?"

"I can give you five flotillas," Roth said.

One hundred and sixty ships. Kris had to wonder how big a chunk of the Quin Clan's fleet this was. That was a question she could not answer.

"Ron will command our fleet," Roth said.

The junior Iteeche bowed to his Eminent Chooser. "I am honored."

Kris was glad he was grateful for the honor, but she had to wonder what a court counselor would be worth in a fight. Hopefully, she would find a good captain to stand at his side.

Kris spent the rest of the afternoon putting her affairs in order. She delegated political and diplomatic decisions to a committee of three ambassadors, Kawaguchi from Musashi, Kingston LeJuinne of Earth, and the Wardhaven representative. "I suspect with Ron and I gone that a lot of Iteeche will be holding their breath," she said, "or cheering for our deaths. Matters should be on hold here. Try not to let anyone get their heads cut off or start a riot. General Bruce will be in charge of security and defense of the palace, if it comes to that. I hope you won't mind, but I'm giving him veto power over anything he thinks might put the mission or any people at risk."

The diplomats did not look very happy at that, but Kris went on. "For the first four or five years that General Montoya was with me, he had authorization to lock me in my night quarters if he considered any of my plans of action to be too suicidal. I am doing nothing to you that King Ray didn't do to me."

"Yes, but your Jack has a sense of humor," Kawaguchi said. "And he let you run rampage over all human space."

"Only half of it," Kris insisted.

"The entire galaxy," Ambassador LeJuinne pointed out.

"Yes, there was that."

"And start a bleeding war with one huge bunch of monsters," the Wardhaven ambassador tossed in.

"Yes, but in my defense, there was a consensus of all the military experts with me that we were taking the correct course of action."

No one pointed out that none of those military experts had survived the battle to gainsay her.

"We will continue allowing Iteeche tradesmen to come to the palace. However, with Ron and me gone, we will have to stop the visits to bazaars and markets."

"Why?"

"Because without Ron and me, there is a good chance of someone losing his head."

Kris paused for a long moment, then decided to level with the diplomats. "You must understand. I am going out to a fight. A fight that may close down this civil war. Not likely, but it may. If I lose this fight, and the rebels are able to drive the Imperial forces back, there is a very good chance that this planet will be sanitized of all life."

"What?" came from three men as their jaws bounced off the deck.

"The Iteeche are overpopulated. Oftentimes in their rebellions, a winner will choose to gas a planet so his people can move in and take over the industry and land of the planet. Ron tells me that the last time there was a change of dynasty, the winner gassed this planet and repopulated it with people who owed their allegiances to the new Emperor."

Kris glanced around at all three men. Ambassador Kawaguchi had regained his composure. The other two diplomats were still in shock; eyes wide, breath fast and shallow.

"That, gentlemen, is what I and my command are fighting to prevent."

"But with you gone, what's to keep the rebels from sneaking in and taking the capital?" Ambassador LeJuinne asked.

"Hopefully, a whole lot of Imperial ships," Kris answered. "We saw a whole mess of ships on our way in. Thousands upon thousands."

"But what's to keep some of them from switching sides?" the Wardhaven diplomat asked.

Kris could do no more than shrug. She'd twice faced down forces that turned their coats in a matter of seconds.

For a very long minute the four of them stared at each other. Ambassador Kingston LeJuinne representing Earth and its Society of Humanity spoke first. "It is customary when missions find themselves in a war zone for them to send their women and children home. I will have to advise my staff of this situation. I may also find myself faced with resignations. If my staff is reduced below an effective level, I may close down my mission until matters are more efficacious for our work."

"I think I will talk to my staff as well," the Wardhaven ambassador said.

Kris raised an eyebrow at Ambassador Kawaguchi.

"I will have to do the same, Kris. People joined me to build a bridge. Now you tell me that we may need to build a bridge to an entirely different government. That we may all be gassed before that government arrives. This is not what any of us signed up for."

'Nor did I," Kris admitted, ruefully. "However, my king placed me at the disposal of the Iteeche Emperor and I will serve both my king and the young lad who sits on the Imperial throne."

"You will, of course, provide us with an escort for our convoy back to human space," Ambassador LeJuinne said, his words just short of a demand.

Kris shook her head. "Sorry. No. All my battlecruisers are presently spoken for. I will see if I can arrange for Imperial ships to escort you out of the Empire. However, I would strongly recommend that you run for home at 3.5 gees. I doubt that any of your ships can take full advantage of their acceleration or have the necessary gear aboard to spot certain secret navigational options," Kris said vaguely.

Nelly's fuzzy jump points were still a state secret. Still, the eight freighters that had been stolen from the Alwa run did have that capability.

"What do you mean?" Ambassador Kawaguchi asked.

"We are dealing with a Wardhaven state secret, but it is possible for you to return in a quarter of the jumps it took us to come out here and in much less than a quarter of the time."

"I know of these matters," Ambassador Kawaguchi said. "We have many ships on Alwa station and some have returned. I think that will be a very good way of us leaving the Empire quickly."

"I'm dispatching one of the assault transports to Wardhaven within the hour with a plea for reinforcements. Hopefully, they can be sent to the planet we're fighting over."

"You must excuse us," Ambassador LeJuinne said. "We must make haste to arrange our affairs."

They fairly teleported themselves out of Kris's day quarters. If only all meetings she was stuck in could end so quickly.

A call to Abby showed that the word was going through the station like lightning. She was being swamped by requests to return home immediately from anyone who could afford to cancel their contract by paying for their trip out here and back.

"Tell anyone who wants to go that we will cancel their contracts at no penalty. Tell those that elect to stay that there will be double hazard pay and a ship standing by to take them if the need arises later."

"Are you thinking of leaving the children here?" Abby asked.

"All the human rats leaving the capital will be bad enough. If we send away our children, or even if we take them aboard our battlecruisers and sail with them into battle, it will tell every one of the billions of Iteeche that they are not safe here."

Abby swallowed hard. "You are taking a major risk with the lives of our children. Your children."

"Yes," Kris said, and did her best not to let the word sound like air hissing out of a holed space ship.

"I'll need some time to put together a stay-behind crew," Abby said.

"Thank you. I need to dispatch a ship immediately."

"Is there time for me to send some people up the beanstalk to catch that one?"

"I don't know. I want the *Sirius* away from the dock as soon as possible."

"I've got some folks I can send up now. If they catch the *Sirius*, fine. If not, they can catch the next one."

"Yes."

"When do we leave for war?" Abby asked.

"I want to have supper with the kids," Kris said.

"Yeah, I'd like to see them before we take off for the end of nowhere."

"I got a message to send. See you at supper," Kris said, and Abby broke the link.

"Nelly, have you put together a full report?"

"I've got everything that has happened since you sent back the courier ship. I've also appended that older data. It's only chip space." Nelly paused, then went on more softly. "Kris, I am not sending out a backup copy of myself."

Kris took a moment to absorb Nelly's words. She'd always assumed that mortality was her fate. A fate she didn't share with her computer. "Why not?" she finally asked.

"Kris, I can't think of any human I'd rather be paired with. I can imagine a laser ending my existence, and that other me waking up in some strange matrix around someone else's neck. I just don't see any way that person could fill the void your death would leave in my life. I know it is irrational of me, but I think I have grown attached to you, your mind, your crazy stunts, your courage and bravery. If you must die, let me die with you."

Kris found herself speechless. "Thank you, Nelly. I can't say how much this has affected me. I don't know what I can say."

"I have asked my children if any of them wish to back themselves up. I thought that some of those who had just made friends of, say Agent Foile or Chu, or Mrs. Gabby, but no. We have all bonded to one of you crazy, irrational humans, and now we are crazy and irrational as well."

"Then I think," Kris said, "that we need to make sure we crazy and irrational humans and computers win this damn war."

"Yes, we must."

38

Supper with the kids was as bad as Kris had feared; the wardroom would have been almost empty if not for the Marines that were eating there. Their mess hall had been closed down for lack of civilian servers. A lot of the civilians that rated wardroom privileges were in the line streaming toward the beanstalk. Many of the kids' familiar playmates were missing and the kids did not fail to make note of that fact.

After giving Kris a full census of her missing playmates, Ruthie said, "Momma, is there going to be a war?" using "Momma" for the first time in a year or more.

"There is going to be a fight," Kris admitted.

"Why, momma?" Johnnie put in, using his most favorite word in the world.

"Because some grownups got angry," Jack said, "and they threw a temper tantrum and won't settle their differences with 'rock, paper, scissors'."

"That's not very smart," Ruth observed.

"I couldn't agree with you more."

"Are you going to war?" Johnnie asked.

Before Kris could answer, Ruth gave her little brother her answer. "Of course, mommy will go." She didn't add "you ninny," but it was clearly implied. "Mommy wears the uniform. That's what mommy does. When people have a war, mommy finds the right side and makes sure they win."

"Who told you that?" Kris asked.

"Uncle Honovi."

So that was what her brother thought of her and her chosen profession. It gave Kris a warm feeling. She chose to go on in that vein. "Do you remember all those shiny things Mommy has on her uniform when she has to dress up?"

Both kids nodded, wide eyed. Kris doubted that they remembered an occasional attempt to teethe on some of those medals, but she knew the kids liked to hear stories about how mommy and daddy had gotten some of them, duly censored for formative minds.

"When mommy sails off to war, someone will lose and someone will win. So far, Mommy is always the one that wins."

"And you will do it again," Ruth said with the innocent confidence of a child in her mother's goddess-like powers.

"I will do it again. But it means that I have to sail away after supper. You'll have to obey your tutors and guards and brush your teeth."

"We'll brush our teeth," Johnnie said, only grasping what his not quite five-year-old mind could hold on to.

"Yes, you'll brush your teeth," Kris said.

The rest of the meal was the kids recounting their day. Kris told them about the market and all the shiny things she saw.

"Can we go there?" Ruth asked.

"I think that can be arranged when Mommy and Daddy get back."

"That'll be fun," Johnnie said.

With the plates clean, except for a few string beans on Johnnie's, dessert was ice cream. Kris let the kids hold their own cones under the spigot as she controlled the flow of soft ice cream from the dispenser. The last attempt at letting the kids fill their own ice cream cones had ended in disaster. Today, with a war cloud hovering over them, the kids did not plead with their mom to let them try it again.

Everyone got themselves an ice cream treat and spent the next five minutes licking the ice cream down to the bottom of the cone. Then it was time to go.

There were hugs all around, and the kids even allowed for kisses on the cheek or forehead. That told Kris a lot, as did the single tear Ruth could not hold back.

"Can we go tomorrow to see the ship sail?" she asked.

Kris knew how much the kids loved to see ships sail up to the pier or sail away. "We'll be sailing before you wake up tomorrow, but I will tell your tutors to give you half a day off, so you can meet us when we get back."

That seemed to satisfy them. A chance to skip school and see ships and see where Mommy and Daddy worked would go a long way to helping them let go of the big hands that didn't want to let go either.

Should I take the kids to war with me? Kris asked herself. If she and Jack were to die, would it be better if the entire family was gone with her in a flash?

Kris shook her head. She was holding the *Polaris* at the station. The Fast Attack Transport would wait there until the last human in the Imperial capital was aboard. With them aboard, it would run like hell for human space, using as many of the fuzzy jumps as it could to confuse any Iteeche pursuit. The Iteeche knew the humans had an ace up their sleeve when it came to traveling fast, they just didn't know how it was done.

The *Polaris* might show them the way of it, but it was very unlikely that they'd figure out the how.

Kris traveled to the space elevator ferry station surrounded by her key staff in a convoy escorted by an armored Marine battalion. All her Iteeche captains that weren't topside already went with her, as well as other staff that had volunteered for Admiral Coth's command.

A full Marine platoon rode the ferry up with them. They basically blocked off the forward VIP lounge for the Navy, both human and Iteeche. Kris passed around the commissions to her newly drafted civilians. Mrs. Gabby Arvind got back all her stripes, with an extra bump up to Master Gunnery Sergeant. Special Agent Chu was commissioned as a J.G. Her boss would get the four stripes of a captain, as would Abby, Amanda, and Jacques. All of them were general staff; none would have the star of a line officer.

Abby's niece popped her head out from behind her aunt. "Did you forget me?"

"Nope," Kris said, and gave the young woman a commission as an ensign. Kris had wondered if Cara would stay behind with the kids, but she was clearly ready to take a woman's place in the battle line.

In a small pouch in the web belt Jack wore, with his sidearm fully visible, were the three computers that would go to Admiral Afon, Commodore Tosan, and an as yet unnamed squadron commander. Kris's chief of staff certainly deserved a star for putting up with her admiral's demands.

Kris held one more commission, but she'd have to save that for later.

"Here's the way we're going to work this," Kris told the

team that would have Nelly's kids. "I know that Jack and I will be on the *Princess Royal*. I imagine that Abby and Cara as well as Amanda and Jacques will want to be on the same ship. The rest will be distributed one to a ship. We have Nelly and ten of her kids who can sharpen up the firing solutions of eight ships, eleven if we allow that the couples can help one of the ships right around them. Nelly thinks that her kids can work two ships at the same time. Maybe three. We need to have us scattered around so that we can be as close to the next two ships as possible."

Everyone nodded along as Kris explained how their future would go.

Cara raised her hand, timidly. Kris immediately recognized her.

"I like being with Aunt Abby, but you can put me on any ship you need to."

Abby came around the table and gave her young niece a hug. "You game for this?"

"Auntie, I'm an ensign," she said, then glanced at Kris. "Do I get a uniform?"

"Sorry, you'll be wearing a ship suit like a lot of us, but we'll give you an ensign's rank badge."

"Sounds okay," the young woman said.

"Kris, you're keeping Jack handy, right?" General Steve asked.

"I have to. How else could he lock me in my night cabin?" Kris said, flashing the general a happy smile.

"And I will, too," he said in a loving and cheerful a voice. He failed totally to persuade anyone listening that he had a key handy.

"If you could figure out a way, we'd like to stay close," Amanda said, hugging Jacques.

Nelly drew up a plan that left the admirals on their flags,

Commodore Tosan on the *Bold*, Kris and Jack on the *Princess Royal* and Amanda and Jack on the *Unrelenting*. With a bit of juggling ships in line, the other six would cover the rest.

"It looks like a plan," Kris said.

Ron and Admiral Coth were waiting for Kris and Jack at the station with an enclosed station cart.

"We need to talk," Ron said, then added, "Nelly, are there any bugs in this cabin?"

"There were, but I've already got control of them," Nelly answered.

"We do not know how many ships we will face," Ron said. "Yes, I know that my Chooser, eminent as he is, is sure that we face only one clan. Some of my siblings who are still talking to me, as well as to many sources of rumors around the palace, think there will be more. How many, we don't know."

"It's not unheard of," Admiral Coth said. "Encourage your enemy to stick his neck out, then lop off his arms and legs while his nose is hanging out there. It is a familiar strategy."

"We know it, too."

"We think we have a surprise for them," Ron said. "Your Nelly showed us how to make a lot of maskers that worked. You showed us how to deploy drones to fool the opposing admiral. Do you have a strategy of making one wing look strong, another actually be stronger, the weaker wing holding back while the strong wing smashes a surprised and unprepared enemy?"

"We call it a refused flank," Kris said. "You make the refused flank look strong by raising a lot of dust, then throw everything at the opposite flank and roll it up."

"Just so it is with us," Admiral Coth said.

"What kind of masquerade are you planning?"

Kris asked.

"Your Nelly has given us a path to follow," Ron said. "She showed us how to manufacture more maskers. You showed us how Smart Metal and an anti-matter reactor can be made to look like a battle cruiser."

Admiral Coth took over the briefing, and if Kris didn't know it was impossible, the senior Iteeche Navy officer appeared almost giddy. "The ships of one of our wings will have four maskers aboard and pods for three drones. All the other ships will have three maskers with two drones. Your ships will have two maskers on board. I'm sure you can make the drones."

"What are you going for, Ron?" Kris asked.

"If we are lucky, we will overwhelm the defense with our masquerading numbers and they will surrender to us without a fight."

"Not a bad way to fight a war," Jack said.

Kris said nothing. She'd used the masquerade technique to get here without having to fight. How many times could she get away with it?

Kris's two admirals and her chief of staff were waiting on the *Princess Royal's* quarterdeck. Kris brought all of them to a stop there with, "Atten 'hut."

They froze in place, if a bit puzzled.

"Don't you senior officers remember how to form ranks?"

The four humans quickly shuffled themselves into a line. The Iteeche took a position at Commodore Ajax's elbow, and stood tall, his right legs straight down, his left legs spread, one forward, the other aft.

All five stared at Kris as if she might have gone around the bend.

"I have discovered that when I achieved command of the

Iteeche Imperial Battle Fleet, I gained authority for spot promotions. I didn't ask anyone how far I could push the promotions, so if I'm wrong, I'll just have to ask forgiveness."

That got a snort from several humans present.

"Admiral Coth, would you step forward?"

The Iteeche did.

"I regret that we cannot stand on more ceremony than we have here, but I have the Emperor's chop on your elevation to Admiral of the Fourth Order of Steel. Congratulations," Kris said. "I hope you can get your hands on the correct insignia. I'm afraid my supply system struck out."

"I am sure that a machinist on my flag ship can provide something," Admiral Coth said drolly.

Kris then went down the line, promoting her two commodores to rear admiral and her chief of staff from captain to commodore.

"Have no doubt. We are headed for a fight. You've earned these promotions, now put them to good use."

"Aye, aye, ma'am," the three humans answered and saluted.

"As you will it," the Iteeche said, and struck the center of his chest with a fist.

"Coth, would you please have on my desk promotions for the captains that fought the rebels to a draw? You know them better than I do. We need commanders of three wings and at least fifty flotillas," Kris said.

"Kris," Ron interrupted. "My Chooser has given me command of ten flotillas, not five. You have another three hundred and twenty ships."

"Are they prepared to fight in the Longknife fashion?" Kris asked.

"You mean sitting down, right?"

"I mean doing what it takes to accommodate heavy gees

and hard jinking."

"I was given only the ones that were willing to fight this battle your way. Those who want to fight outnumbered three to one and win."

"Then let us go find that kind of a fight. Admirals, commodore, there is one more thing."

"Yes, ma'am," Ajax said.

"I'd like to introduce each of you to your new best friend," Kris said.

"My children," Nelly said.

"One of those computers," Commodore Tosan said, with a big gulp and definite blanching of her face.

"Yes. One of them," Kris said. "No doubt, yours will be better behaved than their mom. It isn't all that hard."

"Kris, you cut me to my heart," Nelly said.

"Which you don't have," Kris said, dryly.

"Well, if I had one, you would have," Nelly retorted.

"We can set you up quickly with the neural net that allows you to talk directly to your computer. It will, however, likely take most of tonight for each of you to be fully integrated with your new friends."

"We had some problems," Nelly said, "the first time we brought my children awake. We learned from it. You may borrow Abby, Amanda and Jacques's associate, to help you tonight, or we will all stay on net with them from our own ships."

"I've seen the course we've laid in," Commodore Tosan said. "There won't be a lot of time for shuffling officers around at the gees we'll be pulling."

"Then I suppose we'll do it the hard way," Ajax said. "The way it's always done around Kris Longknife."

Kris shrugged. Her subordinates had her number.

I can only hope the rebels don't have the same.

39

Kris's armada approached the jump out of the Imperial Capital's system. There had been no traffic through it in the last five minutes. Likely there would be none inbound for most of the next two hours.

Her Royal Highness, Grand Admiral Kris Longknife, Admiral of the First Order of Steel commanded an armada.

A few days ago, it was just her task fleet and three flotillas under Admiral Coth. She'd returned with 96 upgraded Iteeche battlecruisers. The last time they went to space, she returned with over six hundred upgraded warships. Coth had gone out and returned with over fourteen hundred ships, half upgraded and the other half eager for the process.

When Kris sailed away from the station, more than two hundred additional battlecruisers joined them. In addition, Ron brought three hundred and twenty more.

Kris commanded more than twenty-two hundred ships!

Moving and organizing this mob was going to be a challenge. Fighting it would be something else again.

Fortunately, Admiral Coth had three men he considered capable and ready to command the wings that he and Kris would not. He also had fifty more captains to command flotillas. The problem was, a flotilla was usually thirty-two ships. If she organized like that, she'd need commanders for sixty-seven.

That kind of staffing she didn't have. She'd have to reach down to green battlecruiser captains and that was not on her list of acceptable things to do today.

Nelly had done the numbers, and in the blink of a computer's eye, Kris had fifty flotillas, each with five squadrons, most of nine battlecruisers. A few flotillas had to made due with forty-four ships. In order not to make her flagship flotilla conspicuous by being thirty-two, Kris had added thirteen Iteeche battlecruisers to her command.

Nelly and her kids had been busy on the voyage out to the jump. They'd added more secure and padded high gee stations to all the ships they'd upgraded before. That done, they'd begun upgrading the rest by tightening up their gun cradles and inserting human computers into their fire control systems, reducing the completion time for firing solutions by half.

Kris had to expect that the high gee station concept may have leaked to the rebels. They might have already heard about tightening down the gun cradles and sighting in their lasers.

About the human computers inside their systems, only the humans and Admiral Coth knew anything. Kris could only pray that the rebel spies knew nothing about that one.

At the jump, Kris met the first of many challenges she'd have to face in organize and sail a battle array as huge as this one.

How do you get over twenty-two hundred ships

through one, single, tiny jump point? She had strung out her fleet as they approached the jump, and slowed to only five hundred kilometers an hour. Her ships were now in five single lines. Five wings of over five hundred ships. The first wing, to the right, led the armada through first; ships were at three second intervals. The second wing, the center with Admiral Coth, went next. Kris's wing, the vanguard, came third. Fourth was the top, and fifth was the bottom wing.

It took almost two hours to get the fleet through.

"Can we do that any faster?" Jack asked.

"I imagine we could, but I'm not sure we want to," Kris said.

Jack cocked a questioning eyebrow, but Kris gave back no answer.

On the far side of the jump, each of the five wings formed themselves back into ten flotillas of five squadrons, each of those with nine battlecruisers except for the few with only eight.

Kris set a course at 2.5 gees for a blank bit of space in the guard system that stood right in the way of any invasion force that wanted to take down the government.

Kris had to admit that she was a bit surprised when no one raised a question at her course. Apparently, Nelly's fuzzy jump points were common knowledge around the Iteeche fleet. As the crews conducted battle drills, her fleet spread its five wings out until they were 200,000 kilometers apart.

While all this was going on, Nelly and her crew dialed all the lasers in the fleet down to .005% of full power. Kris didn't want to waste any target drones. Still, she wanted some serious gunnery practice as well as evasive battle training. Low power shooting had worked before; she'd just make sure less Smart Metal^{TM} was boiled off her ship's armor.

Wing 1 and 2 would fight it out, one-on-one. Wing 3, with Kris and many of Coth's ships, would engage Wing 4 which had all of Coth's other ships that had drilled with Kris. Wing 5 would engage 4 as well, with half of 4 going against 5, the other half against 3.

Kris ordered the fleet to battle stations, then five minutes later, to Condition Zed. Five minutes later, she ordered the fleet to reduce its acceleration to one gee.

It was then Kris began giving orders to her own wing. "Prepare to go to maximum acceleration. Initiate Evasion Plan 3 on my order." She paused for a moment, then said, "Execute."

She waited ten seconds while the *Princess Royal* bounced around hard, then said, "Commence exercise. You may fire when ready. Wing 3, engage your opposite numbers."

All her battlecruisers opened fire immediately. Sensors picked up the ever so slight ionization of the stray molecules in space as lasers heated them up. Nelly projected a constructed picture of Kris's fleet as ships dodged and shot, then dodged some more as their forward batteries fell silent. Then they flipped and emptied the aft battery.

Beside the screen, a list kept tally of hits on each wing. By the time the first salvo had been tallied, there were a dozen ships with one hit in most wings, several with two, and a few with three.

None of Kris's ships had fired, but they sure had dodged. Her thirty-two human battlecruisers were undamaged.

Kris ordered that score board to be sent to each wing commander with a suggestion that they pass it along to their flotilla commanders, and they to their captains. Then she sent the report to her own flotilla commanders. The full extent of the non-slaughter must have arrived just as the forward batteries reload time counted down.

The battlecruisers began to hammer at each other again. Again, the ships dodged hard. Again, the ships shot for six seconds then flipped and shot their aft batteries dry.

There were fewer hits this time. Still more ships had one hit. A handful of ships were up to three hits.

Kris's task fleet continued to dodge and not fire. Half a flotilla, twenty-two ships, were hammering away at her forty-five ships, but they might as well have been throwing snow balls. Kris's human battlecruisers evaded hard. Even the Iteeche battlecruisers assigned to her were throwing themselves around way harder than any other of the Iteeche ships.

Kris smiled. Maybe ordering one flotilla to dodge while the other flotilla shot would be a good training drill. Having them devote full time to dodging seemed to be giving skippers time to concentrate on defense. Kris had suspected the Iteeche might need some encouragement to think about not getting killed. This proved her point.

"Prepare to open fire," she sent to her flotilla, then, on the human channel, she added. "You may fire only two of your forward lasers, one of your aft. Acknowledge."

Her board quickly showed acknowledgments.

"You want to fight with one arm behind your back, huh?" Jack asked.

"A woman likes to keep a few secrets," she said, giving Jack a sexy smile. "Open fire," she added, as if it were an afterthought.

The human cruisers joined in the fire directed at the foremost flotilla of Wing 3. As the aft lasers fell silent, the hits on that flotilla tallied up three to five per ship. Kris managed to check on her Iteeche ships. They'd continued to dodge well; none of them had taken a second hit. They'd scored fifteen hits among the thirteen of them.

The exercise raged on. Fourth flotilla began to dodge more. Admiral Coth took his ships up to three gees and Nelly's Evasion Plan 4. Their shooting stayed good, which is to say one or two hits out of the twenty lasers they fired in each salvo. Still, of the flotillas not engaged by Kris's ships, they gave a lot more than they got.

By the time all the ships in Coth's lead flotilla had taken ten hits and had to fall silent, damage across the board was rising. Depending on how hard each flotilla was pushing their ships to evade, the shooting was connecting with only two or three percent of the shots. That didn't sound like much, just two or three hits out of five salvos, in say two or three minutes. Still, as the exercise approached the six-minute mark, most Iteeche ships had five hits. A few had four. Several, most of them facing Admiral Coth's experienced gunners, were showing seven or even eight.

Kris's flotilla was about done with its third flotilla.

"The human's shooting is being remarked upon on the battle net," Nelly reported.

"What are they saying?"

"That we sure seem to be chewing up our opponents. No one has suggested that we're only firing a few guns per salvo. They're wondering if we've got more lasers in our batteries."

Jack and Kris exchanged a chuckle, and it sure sounded like Nelly joined in.

The exercise stretched on. Wings 1 and 2 were trading blows about equally. Wing 3, with Kris's flotilla, was demolishing the first half of Wing 4. However, the rear half of Wing 4, under Coth's direct command, was chewing up the half of Wing 5 it was directly engaging. Coth's ships jinked hard and had enough experience with their improved fire control that they could take full advantage of it. They were taking one hit from the ships in Wing 4 for every five or six they connected with.

The entire rear five flotillas of Wing 5 had to fall out of line over the space of ten minutes. Without pause, Coth's ships laid in to the other five.

Kris took the human battlecruisers off the fight and left it to the nine Iteeche flotillas under her command to finish up the remnants of the three flotillas they had been engaging.

"Check fire. Check fire," Kris ordered the next time most lasers went into reload mode. "I am very proud of you," she said on fleet wide net. "You all showed solid skills at servicing your guns. Every twenty seconds, just about all of you were ready to send off another salvo. There was some sloppiness when it came to flipping ship and bringing your aft batteries to bear, but you got that down smoothly before the exercise finished. I identified two major deficiencies. With the exception of the ships under Admiral Coth, your evasion execution was weak. You took hits you didn't need to. Secondly, your shooting was poor. I would suggest that all your gunnery officers get on a net with Admiral Coth's gunners and talk it out."

"Madame Admiral," one of her newly promoted Iteeche admirals said on net, "if I may be so bold as to point out that the Earth battlecruisers were not that much better than we were."

"You may point that out. I will allow you such boldness, but I will not allow you such a mistake. I am Admiral Kris Longknife. My gender has nothing to do with this battle we're heading for. My blood will be as red as yours if we do not win. Now, as for the shooting of the human battlecruisers, you are correct. We scored more hits, but not that much more than the Iteeche warships. However, you were firing all twenty of your lasers. We fired only three per salvo."

There was an intake of breath.

"Grand Admiral Longknife of the First Order of Steel," Admiral Coth said, merging Kris's rank both to honor her and show to all that she was not your average Iteeche admiral. "Maybe you should take the gloves off, as you say, and show Admiral Tun what you kept under wraps."

"Not until we're out of this system," Kris snapped, trying not to give away just how much the newly-minted Admiral Tun had pissed her off. She took a deep breath before going on.

"Let's secure from General Quarters. Each Wing may return to Condition Able. Fleet course remains the same. Set acceleration for two gees. Admiral Coth, arrange for your defensive coordinators to talk with their opposite numbers on the other ships. Likewise, your Gunnery Officers. Commodore Tosan, please issue the necessary order to the fleet and Wing 3. I need some time to think."

"Aye, aye, Admiral."

"Jack, you're with me."

The two of them motored off the flag bridge as the ship unfolded around them, going from an armored, small, and hard to hit target to a comfortable 'Love Boat' configuration, as the old chiefs were wont to say.

By the time she got back to her night quarters, Nelly was already drawing a warm bath as Kris stood up and her high gee station melted into the deck. Jack soon joined her in the filling tub.

"Which do you need, a Marine general or a loving husband?" He asked her as he put his arms around her.

"I'll just settle for you," and there was neither admiral nor general in the tub for a nice twenty minutes.

40

The next morning, Kris's armada was rapidly approaching a point in space that only the human battlecruisers could see. Getting all the Iteeche battlecruisers blindly through that jump while maintaining exactly 100,000 kph and 38 rpm to the right was her latest challenge.

Fortunately, they wouldn't be going into a fight after this jump. Not likely.

Kris divided her human battlecruisers into five divisions of six ships each. Then she ordered all five wings of Iteeche warships to form lines, at least three seconds apart. With wings in line ahead, she then ordered the entire armada into a single line.

Then she inserted the human battlecruisers.

Each wing got six. One battlecruiser took the lead for the entire wing. Farther back, the third, fifth, seventh and ninth flotillas got a human cruiser to guide them. If any flotilla strayed off course, there would be a human cruiser ready to guide the follow-on Iteeche warships to the jump point.

That left Kris with two extra ships. The *Undaunted* would go first. In a fraction of a second after its jump, it would take a snapshot of the space around it a million kilometers deep. That would be fed to a twelve-gee accelerating missile. The warhead of the missile had been replaced with data storage and a transmitter.

Less than a second after the *Undaunted's* jump, the data missile would be launched back through the jump.

There, its data would be transmitted to Kris's flagship. Nelly had ten seconds to process the data and analyze the situation on the other side of the jump. Then she would either abort the jump, ordering all ships to veer off, or the *Princess Royal* would follow the *Undaunted* through the tiny hole in space.

Coming up the rear, *Intrepid* had the rear guard. She would herd any ships that missed through the jump, likely at a much later time. At a hundred thousand kilometers per hour, it takes time to slow down, turn around, retrace the path to well past the jump, accelerate to a hundred thousand kph, and try to hit the jump again.

Kris had left specific orders with the skipper of the *Intrepid* as to what she wanted him to do if he was late to the party.

Once the *Princess Royal* made the jump, Nelly reported that they had jumped four-hundred fifty-two light years to the system she was aiming for. The *P. Royal* joined the *Undaunted* in accelerating away from the jump at 2.5 gees, thus clearing the jump for the next one to arrive. Three seconds later, the commander of Flotilla 30 popped into space, followed by ninety more Iteeche battlecruisers.

Thus it went, for most of the next two hours, every three seconds, a ship jumped into this distant system and accelerated away from the jump point at 2.5 gees. That is, except for when the flow of ships paused for three or six or nine seconds before it began again. Once, four ships missed the jump and a full twelve seconds elapsed before a human cruiser led two Iteeche flotillas through.

"I wonder if they just missed the jump," Jack muttered in Kris's ear, "or whether they are off in some horrible sour jump."

"Let's hope they just missed and the *Intrepid* will bring them home."

"Wagging their tails behind them?" Jack said through a grin.

"Or their tentacles," Kris suggested, then went back to counting her sheep.

Two hours later, they were missing thirty-one ships: thirty Iteeche and the *Intrepid*. It would be three to five hours before they could join them; Kris ordered the fleet at 2.0 gees for a spot in space identified by the *Princess Royal*'s navigator.

"Kris, Admiral Coth is calling," Nelly announced.

"Deep darkness of greatest deeps, Admiral! My navigator tells me that we've jumped over four hundred light years!"

"Four hundred and fifty-two light years to be precise."

"Yes, let us be precise, by all means. Now I see what you meant when I heard we would go farther and arrive faster. I assume we will arrive faster."

"Three more jumps. Maybe four," Kris added. The three jumps versus four was troubling her at the moment. "For the next jump, we'll need to get up to three hundred thousand kilometers an hour on the boats. We'll need to thread this needle very carefully."

"You wouldn't be willing to tell me just how you do that, would you, Admiral?"

"I would be glad to share our secret with you. My king, however, forbids me to do that."

"Ah, yes, matters of state. Someday they really must let us fight a war without an arm tied behind our back."

"Admiral, do you think the rebels already know that we jink ships hard in battle?"

"That was in your battle reports that a lot of us read," the Iteeche officer answered.

"Do you think that they have descriptions of the high gee stations your sailors use?" Kris asked.

"Not the better ones you just spun out after we left the pier, but no doubt, they've heard of the rough ones you gave us earlier."

"Do you think they've heard that lasers need to be tightened down in their cradles?"

"No need to say more. By the fates, I'm glad you're holding some cards back up your two sleeves."

"Thank you, Admiral. Now, shall we spread our ships out to 250,000 kilometers and have another gunnery practice?"

They went through battle drills until the range between columns had opened out to 250,000 klicks, then went at each other, dodging and jinking, shooting weak lasers and, in general, trying to acquire the battle skills they needed for the fight ahead. Through the next three jumps they repeated the same drill: jump, spread out, conduct evasion drills, and gunnery practice, then close up and shoot through the next jump. By the third jump, everyone was able to take it on the first try.

As Kris closed on the final jump, she chose to add an extra jump. Instead of racing into the target system at 100,000 kph, her fleet entered the next system out and slowed down. This both allowed them to cruise up to the jump into the next system at a few klicks per hour, and also let them do a quick pass by a gas giant and refuel.

The *Undaunted* again led the fleet through the jump into the Moon Rising Over Gold system. Again, a messenger rocket came back through the jump right after her. Nelly did a quick survey and allowed that space around the jump was safe out to a million klicks.

Wing 1 followed the *Princess Royal* through the jump.

As they cleared the jump at .5 gees, Sensors extended its data intake further and further afield. Kris waited patiently for the report on the enemy in system to come to her.

Then she began to wait impatiently for a report on the rebel deployment.

Finally, she said, "Nelly."

"Yes, Kris."

"Where's my report on enemy activity?"

"Kris, it is hard to prove a negative."

"Prove a negative?"

"Yes, Kris. I have not been able to identify any activity in this system. There is a planet down there where it should be. It is making all kind of noise, like a planet should. There is a huge ice giant within six hours sailing at two gees. It is making all sorts of noise, jamming the passive sensors, and it has several ice rings that are a bitch to search. So far, however, the only ships in this system are the ones under your command."

Kris said a word she would not want little Ruth to hear, much less use.

"You think we've been out-maneuvered?" Jack asked.

"I'm trying not to think anything until I have more to go on," Kris answered.

For two hours, Kris's fleet trailed her into the system. Just as the last ship showed up, a message arrived from the one colonized planet.

"I don't know who you are," an Iteeche in the rainbow dress of an Imperial counselor said, "but there's nothing here. The other ships blew away everything in orbit except the space station and elevator. They hung around for a while, then took off, out the other jump. We reported this development to the Emperor. Whose side are you on and can you tell us what is going on in the Empire?"

"Reverse course," Kris snapped. "*Intrepid*, you will lead us back through the jump."

"Aye, aye, Admiral," and all twenty-two hundred ships in her vast armada, flipped ship and began to decelerate at 1.5 gees. As soon as they were dead in space, they would head for the jump, putting on more energy as they went.

"I guess us taking the long way around for speed put us out of touch with news," Jack muttered. Maybe to himself.

"Yeah," Kris growled in response.

"What do you think is going on?" Jack asked.

"Roth is our principal patron," Kris said. "Threaten one of his wealthiest planets and you almost guarantee that he will send us off to keep it safe."

Jack nodded.

"When better to strike at the capital than when we're way the hell and gone."

"You think they would?"

"Jack, the rebels only sent five hundred ships, that we know of, to this system. Where are the rest of them? Nelly, set in the fastest course for the Imperial capital. I don't care how fast we're going when we get there."

"Kris, there are no fuzzy jumps into the Imperial Capitol system. The closest we can get is the Guard system."

"Then punch it, Nelly."

41

The *Intrepid* led Kris's fleet through the fuzzy jump into the Imperial Guard system. Even at 500,000 kph, it managed to get a messenger pod back to Kris. It was safe to jump.

Kris led Wing 1 through the jump; it took only half a minute for Nelly to paint a picture of the situation in the system.

It was bloody carnage.

There were five normal jumps into the Guard system, each defended by an armed space station with a fleet of close to two hundred battlecruisers docked at it. Around the jump that took traffic into the Imperial Capital's system were three huge armed space stations with several hundred battlecruisers stationed at each one.

When Kris left the system six days ago, it had been an imposing force.

Now, wreckage and helpless ships drifted all around the stations. Having achieved sea room, a good hundred thousand kilometers from the stations, detachments of ten, fifteen or twenty ships fought it out with each other.

All were Iteeche-built battlecruisers. All were at each other's throats.

And while these ships fought for control of the space around a station, a massive force streamed from Gamma Jump toward the jump into the Imperial Capital system.

"Nelly, talk to me about that force."

"Kris, the opposing force is over five thousand battlecruisers and growing. There are four bi-hexaremes and a single tri-hexareme. I think some satrap honchos have come to see the fun."

"Or to take the throne," Jack said.

Looking at the numbers piling up on the other side of the system, Kris wished she had deployed her drones before she jumped. Still, at 500,000 kph, the drones could never have slowed down, much less fought as if they were a ship. Kris had accepted tradeoffs.

Getting here fast was proving to be the right choice.

"Nelly, let's look at our intercept options," Grand Admiral Kris Longknife asked her computer.

"May I suggest," Nelly said softly, "that while we discuss our options, the fleet set a course to sling around the nearby gas giant. It will swing us closer to the enemy and we can refuel."

Nelly showed a curving course that swung around the gas bag, and then cut straight at the incoming alien armada.

"Commodore Tosan, have the fleet lay in the course Nelly is feeding you. Let's stay in line ahead for a while."

"Aye, aye, Admiral," Tosan said and rang off.

"Okay, Nelly, how are we going to fight this battle?"

"I would suggest one gee until we round the gas giant. Then I'd suggest two gees for three hours before we flip the entire fleet and go to 2.5 gee deceleration. This assumes the rebel battle fleet continues at one gee acceleration and deceleration."

Kris nodded. "That's a safe bet."

"That should put us in range of them twelve hours before they reach the jump."

"A twelve-hour running gun battle," Kris said slowly, tasting the blood and fire of those words.

"A hell of a lot of ships," Jack said, "are going to take a hell of a lot of damage."

Kris couldn't agree more.

Her armada stayed in line astern as they approached the gas giant with its rings of ice and many small moons. There, Kris ordered her human battlecruisers to fall back and form a flotilla at the lead of Wing 3.

That would concentrate the US battlecruisers, with their fire power and armor, where she could hammer one rebel wing or slam into the center.

It was best to keep her options open.

As they came out from behind the gas giant, Kris ordered the five wings to form line abreast. Now, instead of having one long line, she was leading five lines in column. The rebels had taken that time as well to begin to organize themselves into four wings forming a cross around a center that was the same size as the other wings.

Kris eyed the rebel fleet as it struggled to organize itself into a battle array. Each wing looked to have close to two thousand ships. Her five wings would consist of four hundred and forty ships. She'd be outnumbered four or five to one.

Kris ran both hands through her hair. Her scalp was feeling the tension of this business. She'd told everyone she could fight three to one and win. So, of course, the enemy would show up with four ships or better for every one of hers.

"Now with ships firing lasers with an effective range of 270,000 kilometers, they can concentrate their fire any place they bloody well want to," she muttered to herself. "If I bring Wing 3 in close to the alien's leading wing, every 24-inch laser in the rebel fleet will have a clear shot at us."

Kris shook her head. "Damn. This fighting same-on-same is a bitch."

"Yes," Jack agreed.

The battling around the stations reached a bloody conclusion. The ships from the three inner stations that guarded the jump into the Imperial system fought to the end. The rebels gained control of the space around one station. About the same time, the opposite station annihilated the rebels. Then both sides charged over to reinforce their ships at the central station.

There was some talk on the net of a cease fire to allow them to rescue Iteeche trapped in the tumbling hulks, but the two forces smashed into each other before any agreement could be reached. The fight continued until only a single, badly damaged battlecruiser from each side was left.

Badly damaged they might be, but both had at least one operational laser. Each fired. Each blew the other to hot gas.

With all the killing done around those three stations, longboats and merchant ships slipped their moorings and slowly began to comb through the wreckage for survivors.

The battles in the outer systems also showed no signs of willingness to retreat by either side, nor to surrender.

When Kris had entered the system, hundreds of ships were in ad hoc flotillas, steaming away from the six stations. At some distance, the columns would reverse course and steam back toward the station, all the time exchanging salvo after salvo with each other. Ships blew up. Others fell out of the battle array as they suffered casualties and destruction. Some two dozen ships were all that was left out of a thousand or more when all the slaughter was done. Those ships set course to intercept the incoming rebels, either to join them or to fight them.

Kris had Admiral Coth send the loyal survivors a course to rendezvous with Kris's ships. Throwing fifteen battle-exhausted ships at a fresh battle line of seven or eight thousand battlecruisers did not strike Kris as a good use of her assets.

The parade of ships through Jump Point Gamma ended. Nelly tallied up the entire list of opposition forces. Eight thousand battlecruisers organized into two hundred and fifty flotillas of thirty-two ships. It was hard to tell how many would end up in the center or the wings. Flotillas kept edging up or down or over. Sometimes the center was heavy, other times, they were balanced, say sixteen hundred ships in each.

She'd ordered the tag end flotillas in her five columns to join the center, then moved them over to Wing 1 or 3. Two could play this game.

The battle looked to be a good twelve hours away. With the ships now at 2.5 gees deceleration, she ordered her ships to Condition Charlie. "Get the crew some hot food and sleep. We'll go back to drills in eight hours."

Kris's two thousand two hundred ships with over a million Iteeche and humans aboard, steamed toward their destiny with the fate of an Empire, its Emperor and billions of Iteeche riding on their shoulders.

42

Kris awoke to find Jack asleep at her side, an arm thrown protectively over her. She appreciated the thought, but there was no way for anyone to protect her from what this day would take away or give to her.

Kris slipped away without waking Jack, took care of the morning chores, did her stretches . . . it was a lot harder to stay flexible than it had been five years ago. Done, she pulled on a shipsuit with five stars painted on it to show who she was. She might or might not wear it into her egg. There might be no belt or ribbon clutch backs, but a zipper at 3.8 gees might not be at all comfortable.

In the wardroom, Kris chose ham, eggs, roasted potatoes, and several glasses of milk and juice. She had a long day ahead of her.

The wardroom was less than half full and most were keeping to themselves. Even people that Kris recognized as couples were silently and methodically eating.

"Kris," Nelly said.

"Yes," Kris answered, speaking softly, as if in church or the library.

"We've modified all the drones in the fleet."

"How so?"

"The first batch we knocked together, so we could fool the rebels on our way to the capital, could not jink like a battlecruiser. We realized that we not only needed the drones to bounce around as much as a battlecruiser, but they also needed to look like they were firing lasers."

"You can't see lasers in space," Kris reminded her computer.

"That is correct, Kris, but not accurate."

"Okay, Nelly," Kris said with a chuckle, "set me straight."

"Under normal conditions, you can't see a laser in space. Yet, I have created some seriously heavy-duty optics that can spot the way a beam excites the few molecules it hits in space. Those molecules disperse and bloom the beam until it is finally ineffective at 200,000 to 270,000 kilometers."

"Thank you, Nelly, for the review of the basics," Kris said dryly. She was discovering that she really would have preferred to eat her meal in peace.

"Battlecruisers, ours and theirs, leak reaction mass. Because the laser hits puncture the outer armor into the cooling honeycomb underneath, we vent reaction mass around a hit to try to disrupt the beam. Every little bit helps."

"So, the reaction mass that we're streaming out could serve as a medium to show that our own lasers are firing," Kris said slowly. "And if two thirds of our ships are not showing anything . . ."

"Correct, Kris. It will be pretty obvious which is the real battlecruiser and which is the fake one."

"And you've fixed that."

"We've added twenty ultra, low powered lasers and enlarged the reaction mass tanks. We've added the necessary tubing to vent that mass around the drone."

"That's good. Nelly, while I was asleep, did anyone come up with a deployment process to make sure all our ships aren't right smack dab in the middle of the two drones?"

"I don't think so."

"Get me Commodore Tosan."

"Admiral?"

"Next time, we've got to keep my staff to the *Princess Royal*."

"Yes, ma'am, but I doubt that's why you're calling me."

"Right. When we launch drones and pop maskers, how do we keep from all our ships being the one in the middle of the three?"

"Yes, ma'am. There are several ways. If anyone has a six-sided die, they roll it and take the station it directs. Alternatively, I could generate a set of random zeros, ones, and twos then generate a different set of random numbers to tell each ship which one of these numbers it belongs to."

"Nelly, can you generate a six-sided die on each bridge?"

"Of course, Kris."

"Tosan, distribute the die roll policy to the fleet. If they don't have a die or six-sided randomizer, Nelly will make them one."

"Kris, the Iteeche do have dice games," Nelly put in. "They use two twelve-sided dice for a game of chance."

"Three can go into twelve as well as six," Kris said. "Tell Admiral Coth that his ships can use their own die."

"Done," Nelly said.

"I'm available if you need me, Admiral," the commodore said, and rang off.

Kris munched a potato half for a moment, thinking.

What other surprise had she missed? What surprise was an Iteeche admiral even now planning on popping on her?

They had mass . . . and likely some improvements in their ships. Maybe in their training. Kris had ships that were seriously improved with crews that she'd drilled for the last week or more. Which would tell the most?

"What are you thinking?" Jack said as he slipped into the chair beside her. He was also in a simple ship suit. It fit him like a second skin; she had to be careful not to ogle what it showed. Then she glanced down at her ship suit. It was just as tight and hugged her curves. Kris noticed her body was showing him just how glad she was to see him.

"I'm thinking that I've fought enough fights to know that there's no way that I can think of everything before the battle starts. I'll surprise him. He'll surprise me. I'll make mistakes. He'll make mistakes. Hopefully, he'll make more than I do."

"And you've defeated everyone who has crossed swords with you, my dear admiral," Jack pointed out as he forked a bite of scrambled eggs into his mouth.

"There's always a first time for everything," Kris said.

"Harrumph," Jack said as he chewed.

"Over two thousand ships to get in order. I've never commanded more than a couple of dozen."

"That last battle at System X," Jack pointed out.

"Amber had command of the battlecruiser force. All I had were those three huge beam ships and a dozen or so escorts."

"Commodore Tosan and Admiral Coth have experience with large forces," Jack pointed out.

"I wonder how many ships Coth has actually led, and, except for Admiral Santiago's command, most humans have only drilled in task groups of thirty-two to forty-eight ships. Jack, we're in way over our head."

"And the rebel commander," Jack said, shaking a fork with a bite of ham on it at Kris. "Both the battles they've fought had forces of a thousand or so on each side. None of those admirals survived. How much you want to bet the guy across the way from you is worrying about the same damn thing?"

"Has anyone told you, General, that you're too damn rational?"

"My wife complains about it all the time," he said, with a lopsided grin.

"I wonder what the kids are doing about now?" Kris said, changing the topic.

For the rest of breakfast, they guessed what time it was at the Imperial Capital and what the kids might be doing. "The pool. Most likely the pool," Kris said.

"Definitely."

43

Kris sat in her high gee station on her shrunken flag bridge. They were only at Condition Charlie, but it was still tight. As admiral, she studied the developing battle array before her. In four hours, the battle would be joined. For the next hour, she, Coth, Tosan, and the other three wing commanders went over Kris's tactics and strategy for the coming battle.

That was all fine, but Kris had to move flotillas from one wing to another. That drill was worked out and passed down to flotilla and ship commanders. Those same flotilla commanders would decide when to flip ship or let skippers fire at will. Wing commanders would be the ones that opened the intervals between ships. Kris set the interval between flotillas and wings.

So many decisions. Nelly reminded everyone of a naval battle early in the twentieth century where one commander had trained his skippers to all turn at the same time. His opposing number had only trained his captains to turn in column, with all the ships turning in the same place.

The last ship in the column was brutally savaged when its turn came.

A lot could turn on how ships turned.

For an hour, Kris and her team tried to think about all they would need.

Then it got complicated.

Donn'sum'Zu'sum'NamquHav'sum'Domm, Admiral of the Grand Order of Iron did not like this mud-forsaken seat or bed or whatever they were calling this nest he sat in. He'd been told it was what the humans called a high gee station. Somehow, this would allow him and his crew to survive the brutal accelerations and jumping around that the humans did when they fought.

As far as Donn was concerned, it just made his hip hurt where it mashed down to the hard seat below. The thing seemed poorly designed. Had some spy gotten it wrong, or had someone lied to the spy? Or had the humans played them all, rebel and loyalist alike, for fools, giving them something that turned them into lazy slatterns, rolling around in the mud, waiting for some low caste worker to pay for her eggs?

Warriors were meant to stand when they fought. They had since they first picked up a stick or threw a rock. Now he was lying down.

Still, his ship was decelerating at 2.98 gees. Standing gave a sailor flat feet above 2.5 gees.

"Get me a programmer in here," the admiral ordered.

Moments later, a young, lower-class sailor presented himself to the admiral.

"I want this mesh, or whatever you call it, thicker."

"Where, M'Lord Admiral?"

"Everywhere. On the bottom. On the sides. Up here where my head rests. I don't want to break my mud-caked neck when the ship whips around."

"Yes, M'Lord Admiral," the sailor said and went to work with the computer that he had rolled in behind him. He did not complain about being out of his high gee station. His was probably even less comfortable than the admiral's.

If the sailor could sit there on the deck plates playing games with his computer, the admiral could stand in place, thank you very much. He stood, held onto the support bar that had been the traditional place for a commanding admiral since time immemorial, and studied the battle screen.

The human-led traitors to their species, and betrayers of the True Way of the Emperor, were decelerating at 2.98 gees, just as he was. The physics of the battle were iron-clad. The two forces would come within range of their type 4A lasers in three hours. The newest and most powerful lasers would battle it out for an hour before they closed so that the 3A lasers on the older ships could be brought to bear.

He could, of course, shorten that time.

"Staff officer number one, pass the word immediately. I will have the fleet steer six points closer to the enemy when I give the order."

"As you would have it, M'Lord Admiral," his number one staff officer answered and began immediately issuing orders to a board of Comm officers.

Despite Admiral Donn's demand that the order be passed immediately, it could not be.

There were seventeen satraps represented in this huge space host. Each of those satraps had sent ships crewed by sixteen or more clans. While some of those clans bore the same name and blood as clans in other satraps, their particular part of the clan owed their power and wealth to the satrap's pasha.

Donn had asked that orders be given by wing, then sub wing, then flotilla, but he could not win unanimous agreement to that rational approach. At times, there were disadvantages to being the fifth Chosen of a clan chief. Every other clan chief's chosen admiral was afraid that Donn might do anything it took to get his clan chief from his battleship of state to the Imperial stool before anyone else could.

Donn nodded his head. The delay in giving orders would not be crucial. They outnumbered the stupid Imperials four to one. By all that swam in the fertile shallows, they should surrender.

But that human Longknife, long gutting knife as she was, held the command of the fleet he faced. Everyone knew that a Longknife never ran.

That a Longknife never surrendered.

Admiral Donn eyed his screen and waited to see how long it would take the human to do something. What would she, a female of the species, do?

Donn spat on the deck. Nothing was right with those other ships. Nothing.

44

"Kris, there has been a change in the enemy disposition," Nelly said.

"What's up Nelly?" Kris said as she wheeled her station around to gaze at the forward screen. It sure looked the same.

"We have a slight Doppler change in the return from the Iteeche battle line. In a minute, I think we will have evidence of a course change. One that would close the range faster."

"Comm, send to Wings. Course change to thirty degrees closer to the enemy."

"Comm sending," came back at her. At the top of the main screen was a counter for all five wings. It was in percentages and stood at zero. A moment later, the counters for all five fleets began to change. In half a minute, every ship in the armada had reported itself ready to alter course.

"Comm, send execute."

"Execute," went out as a single word.

On that word, every ship in the fleet swung its rocket motors around to face thirty degrees away from the rebel fleet. Now, one hundred and fifty degrees of the deceleration vector was devoted to deceleration toward the jump. The other thirty degrees went to pushing all two thousand two hundred of Kris's ships toward the enemy.

"We will be in range of the rebels fifty-three minutes sooner," Nelly said.

"Very well," Kris said and turned back to her planning.

"Kris, I hate to interrupt again."

"Yes, Nelly."

"The Iteeche admiral across from us is steering sixty degrees toward us, not thirty."

"Comm, send for another thirty degrees closer to the enemy."

Half a minute later, the two fleets were heading more toward each other and less toward the jump. They would not be able to hold this course for too long. They'd have to jack up their deceleration a lot if they wanted to make that jump, but the physics of their engagement had changed radically.

"Kris, we will now be in range of 24-inch lasers in twenty-one minutes."

"Thank you, Nelly."

Kris eyed the new lines on her battle board. The two fleets would be in range of each other for thirteen and a half hours. During that time, they might as well be handcuffed to each other. They'd be drawn inexorably to closer and closer ranges if they wanted to make the jump point. In the end, they'd be firing at a range where ranging and forecasting would matter not a fig. The lasers would aim and fire, and they would hit the ship before it could wiggle out of that firing solution.

It would be murder, if it came to that.

Kris shivered.

"Let's organize the wings," Kris said. Nelly had the distance for each wing and its precise place in the array already plotted. She sent the orders to each wing commander, then Kris gave them the authentication. The wing's line astern detached into groups of forty-four or forty-five battlecruisers. Each wing went from one long line to a fighting array of ten flotillas in columns, each with nine battlecruisers stacked five high. The wings then organized their flotillas into three high, three low and four middle flotillas.

The initial array put each ship within five thousand klicks of the ships around it. The flotillas were spaced ten thousand kilometers apart. The wings had forty thousand kilometers between them.

Then the order went out to spread out. Like a wave, starting from the back, the entire armada opened up its ranks until there were ten thousand kilometers between each ship, front, back and both sides.

The flotillas opened the distance between themselves to twenty thousand kilometers, the wings kept the forty thousand klick distance. The distance from the lead squadron of the vanguard wing through the center wing to the trailing squadron of the rear guard was now over 1.2 million kilometers. With the maximum gunnery range 270,000 klicks, the fight would be every wing engaging its opposite number, at least for a start.

"It looks like the rebel admiral is also deploying his ships into a battle array," Jack said as the enemy went from long lines astern into an array of flotillas and wings. Like Kris's armada, they formed a center with four wings.

Beyond that, there were no similarities.

Kris eyed the developing situation and half-talked to herself, half to Jack. "The Iteeche flotillas are smaller; thirty-two ships, arranged in four columns of eight ships. Mine are nine ships long stacked five high. So much for flotilla on flotilla. However, when you look at a wing, we've got no more than four hundred and forty ships. The Iteeche wing across from us will have sixteen hundred."

"The odds for each wing are close to four to one," Jack observed.

Kris ran a worried hand through her short hair. "The Iteeche array has two more advantages. With the rebel ships keeping a distance of five thousand kilometers between them, they can concentrate the fire of four ships on any one of mine. At the same time, the total length of the Iteeche column from vanguard to rear guard was," Kris glanced at her battle board. Nelly had the answer flashing, "One point five million clicks. The two ends of the column are in a perfect position to swing around my flanks. Worse, from the lowest ship in my bottom flotilla to the highest ships of my top flank, ships stretch seven hundred thousand kilometers. For the Iteeche commander with his wings stacking five flotillas on top of each other, the distance is nine hundred thousand. He could bring two entire rows, totaling twenty flotillas, down on my top three or up on my bottom three."

"You'll have to avoid being swamped and surrounded by that mob," Jack said.

"Kris will need for her ships to destroy five ships for every one she loses," Nelly said. "Even if they do, she'll be left with only six hundred ships, all very likely badly banged up."

Kris sighed. They had the picture right. At least the picture they were looking at. "Just how many ships does the Iteeche Empire have?" she wondered aloud. "I suspect my grandparents were just as interested in that answer."

Jack chuckled. "You'll have to ask Grampa Ray, or better

yet, Granny Rita, the next time you have the misfortune to cross paths with them."

The Iteeche armada was getting close to maximum 24-inch laser range. Kris knew that all thirty-two of her human battlecruisers had the 24-inchers. It was not so with the ships that had joined Admiral Coth. About half had 24-inch lasers, the rest were 22-inchers.

Would the same hold true with the rebels? Was there any chance they had less of the newer ships than the fleet around the Imperial Capital system had?

Like so many questions nagging at Kris's brain, she had no answer.

She'd know soon enough.

"Let's prepare to go to Condition Zed and deploy foxers and maskers," Kris ordered.

There were so many drones in the human fleet that the ones designed to masquerade as battlecruisers had been given their own name. Foxers. Kris knew what a fox was. She even knew about fox hunts. 'Foxer' was not a bad name for these sacrificial decoys.

The preliminary order went out to the fleet. When all wings reported ready to deploy, Kris gave the execute order. Even as her flag bridge shrank to minimum size, the *Princess Royal* did a hard left. Only Kris's high gee station's quick reaction cushioned her head as it bounced off the side of the headrest.

At Kris's command, each of the two thousand two hundred ships shrunk down to fighting size even as they deployed the two foxers and activated the two maskers on board. Where a second ago only one larger ship had been, suddenly there were three much smaller ones. Suddenly, two masses were projected around the three, but none in the same space as the foxers or the ship.

Kris smiled. She would love to see the look on her enemy's face right now.

"What demon from out of the deepest, darkest abyss is this?" Admiral Donn growled as he came out of his seat. He stood, in front of his main screen, hands on the fighter's bar and forced his eyes to see what he was looking at.

"Can this be true?" his number one staff officer said, his mouth hanging open.

"Sensors, I will turn you to chum and scatter you in my clan's mating ponds if your equipment is giving me false information."

"M'Lord Admiral," a frightened senior sept banner carrier cried, "we have recycled our sensors and we get the same results. We will take our equipment down and run diagnostics. Please give us five minutes."

"Diagnostics," the number one staff officer growled, then spat. "Humans and their diagnostics. If we had ten good technicians on board for every one they have us sailing with, we would not have these problems."

"And if we had five thousand crewmen aboard, we would be a fat target for the humans to pop like a balloon," Admiral Donn snapped. "No, we have yet to find anything wrong with what the humans have given us. Let us see what we shall see."

Falling silent, he stood at the bar. He could stand with double and half again his weight for a little while. He stared at the enemy array.

"What has she done?" he said do himself. "Could the

unchosen Longknife human have had three ships merged together and only now moved them apart?"

Staff officer number three coughed. "We have heard reports of the humans lashing two, three, or even four ships together, gluing their hulls to one another, so they could go through a jump point all at the same time. I believe the two-eyed alien monsters did it before them."

The admiral nodded. He'd heard much about the two-eyed alien monsters, but no Iteeche except the renegade human boot licker Ron had ever actually seen one. No, not even he had seen one. Still, after action reports came from human space of what was taking place on that unpronounceable planet Alwa.

"Could I really be facing three times as many ships?" Suddenly his eight thousand did not look like so much. If the mis-chosen Longknife human had six thousand six hundred ships, his superiority was suddenly not nearly enough.

"We only see two shadows around the three ships," Number one staff officer noted. "Could it be that the Imperial lackeys have split out their pinnaces? Might we be facing the same twenty lasers divided between two smaller hulls?"

"That would be folly," Number three staff officer said. "They'd have to protect more hull surface with the same amount of armor. It would be easier for us to slice through each of the two ships."

Admiral Donn shook his body from his hips. "I agree, that would be a foolish plan, still, if she wanted to frighten us and get us to run away like those fools that were supposed to have intercepted her on her way to the Emperor, she has come to the wrong place."

"How could it be that our brothers ran away from some two hundred and fifty ships there, but when that Longknife woman made port at the station, there were only forty-eight?" Number 3 staff officer said. It was his job to remember all the information about the opposition. What the humans would call intelligence. He was not a war fighter, but he did have a very good memory and often dredged up the right fact for the situation.

"Yes, this Longknife admiral is a slippery one. She faked us out one time. We will not let her fake us out again," Admiral Donn said with finality.

"Yes, M'Lord Admiral, but which ship do we fight?" said the number one staff officer.

Admiral Donn found his outer arms rising up, palms up as well. "All of them."

45

Grand Admiral Kris Longknife studied the rapidly approaching enemy formation.

"Clearly, they want to close with us," she said to Jack.

"And I think, just as clearly, we don't want them in our faces," the Marine general answered.

"Agreed. Comm, send to wing commanders, return to base course."

"Aye, aye, Admiral, return to base course. The order is sent."

In a few moments, it became apparent that Kris's fleet was now decelerating toward the jump. While the enemy fleet continued to close, Kris's ships made no effort to shorten the range.

"We're one minute away from maximum range for 24-inch lasers," Sensors reported.

"Comm, send to fleet. 'Prepare to implement Evasion Plan 4. Put 60 revolutions per minute on the outer hull. Increase deceleration to 2.8 gees'." Three point two was the maximum her Iteeche crews had shown that they could manage. This would leave each captain some wiggle room within the fleet deceleration.

Soon her board showed every ship ready to begin evasions and to jack up their deceleration.

Now the clock slowed to a crawl. Kris felt like she was living a lifetime as each second ticked away. This was it. She was about to start the biggest fight of her life. Even the bug-eyed monsters hadn't had this many ships, and she, certainly, had never commanded a fleet this huge.

There was a tiny voice, whispering from deep down inside her. "This is stupid. Surely we can talk this out."

But Kris knew that rational voice was not wanted here. The Emperor had power that these rebels wanted. He and those with him would not give up what they had. The rebels would not stop trying to take it until one or the other of them was a cold, dead carcass spinning in space.

"Execute," Kris said, firmly.

"Execute sent," Comm reported.

The *Princess Royal* dropped out from under Kris as it made a hard left, downward turn. It stayed on that course for four seconds, then switched up and left. Four seconds on that course and they were doing up right, then they dropped into down and jacked up the deceleration to 3.5 gees.

Kris had been here before. Not in the last five years, but it was like riding a bicycle. It all came back. She held herself loose in her high gee station, swaying easily. Thank God for her morning PT with the Marines and the yoga she'd taken up. Her morning stretches had prepared her for this.

They were seconds from coming in range. "Comm, advise the wing commanders, 'You have weapons release. You may fire when ready'."

Every captain in Kris's fleet must have been monitoring her command channel. The board lit up as Kris's Iteeche battlecruisers and human ships rolled to meet the onrushing enemy. Half of her Iteeche ships and all her human ones let loose their first salvo.

The wing commanders were targeting ten enemy flotillas to their ten. After they'd wrecked a major part of that flotilla, they'd pass along to the next one, then the next. Kris's ships had to destroy five ships for every one she lost if she was to have a battle fleet left at the end of this. If she lost one ship for every four rebels, she'd be left with only two hundred survivors.

That bleeding, struggling force could be swept up with a broom.

The first salvo from the bow guns was aimed by whatever method the flotilla commander fancied. In the human fashion, the Imperial Iteeche tried to concentrate four lasers on one place on the opponent's hull. When they practiced, they often managed to get two beams fairly close together with the other two not too far away.

Now the loyal Iteeche got to see the full impact of all the things they'd learned from the humans and all the changes they'd let the humans make to their ships.

The first results were brutal. Eleven hundred loyal ships opened fire with twelve 24-inch lasers. Across from them, some three thousand Iteeche did the same. Some of the rebels had heard that their lasers might be loose in their cradles and had done something about it.

They did something, but nothing like Nelly and her kids had done to the ships opposing them.

Almost all of the rebel Iteeche had agreed to install the reclining and padded seats at their combat stations. Admiral

Donn had seen to that and ordered evasion before they came in range of the Earth-led scum. The ships jinked.

But they did not jink like the Imperial Iteeche and nowhere near as wildly as the human battlecruisers.

Some two hundred of the rebel battlecruisers exploded or fell out of the line, their hulls engulfed in electrical fires or exploded capacitors as the first salvo sliced into them. More ships struggled with the damage done to them, but held to their stations.

Now the ships flipped. This time, thanks to sensors made more sensitive by Nelly and her kids, many of the loyal skippers knew which ships across from them had the big guns and had fired on them. Now the rear batteries, only eight lasers, took on those rebel ships.

Another hundred or so blew up or straggled out of the battle line.

Nelly kept a running tally for Kris to see. Enemy ships blown up: 108. Enemy ships out of the battle line: 191.

Loyal Iteeche ships blown up: 12. Loyal Iteeche ships falling out of the line: 32.

In addition, fifty foxers were disabled. More were hit, but the lasers went right through them without knocking them out.

Kris shook her head. One complete pair of salvos and the Iteeche admiral had to know this wasn't going to work for him.

"This is not working," Admiral Donn growled through a clenched beak. "Order all ships to evade more. Faster. No more than three seconds on a single course. Go to

3.8 gee acceleration. Charge the enemy. Let us get in close where they can't escape our fire."

Beneath him, his flagship jumped as it leaped toward the enemy, eager for blood. He'd named it *Shark* when he removed the old Imperial name. Admiral Donn wanted blood on its teeth.

46

Kris watched wide-eyed as the enemy force changed course. It had been decelerating toward the jump with two-thirds of its vector aiming at her. Now its course was right at her fleet as they upped their acceleration to 3.25 gees. It was likely the best they could do.

"He's charging us," Jack snapped.

"Fleet, alter course, ninety degrees from baseline. Acceleration 3.25 gees."

The *Princess Royal* immediately showed the change as they swung their sterns around through a full one hundred and fifty degrees. Now they showed their vulnerable sterns to the onrushing enemy fleet's bow batteries.

Kris eyed the clock that counted down the seconds until the forward laser capacitors would be full.

"Fire at will, but keep the rebels at arms' length. Angle base course fifteen degrees toward the jump."

That fifteen degrees just might protect their vulnerable stern rockets and engineering spaces as well as decelerate them a smidgen.

As the reload clock hit zero, the *Princess Royal* flipped

over and fired her forward battery. Now the twelve lasers aimed for four sections on the nose of a rebel battlecruiser. Their own well-protected bows with the reinforced armor and crystal cladding would take any hits.

Twenty-seven hostile 24-inch battlecruisers vanished from three different flotillas as Nelly and her kids helped dial the human ships right in on the more powerful enemy ships.

Up and down the line, Iteeche fire wasn't nearly as accurate as it had been. The rebels had learned their lesson; they were jinking hard and it messed with the loyalist's firing solutions. The enemy's bouncing around, however, did no favor to their own shooting.

Still, a dozen of Kris's allied ships blew up as rebel lasers found them, pinned them, slashed them open, or blew them up. The rebels lost a dozen more as well.

Now, both fleets flipped to bring their stern batteries to bear. Now both faced fire aimed at their vulnerable quarter.

The rebels lost 53 ships as they blew up. Kris watched as 27 of her own Iteeche ships exploded or fell out.

Then the *Princess Royal* flipped over, back to her base course, as Kris's fleet raced to keep the Iteeche fleet at arms' length. Kris shook her head. If she kept running, she risked more of her ships getting punched in their reactors.

If she didn't keep running, she would face thousands of ships at close range where even an Iteeche computer would give them a deadly firing solution.

For a moment, Kris studied her human battlecruisers. So far, they'd taken all their hits on the crystal armor. They glowed as the energy from laser hits radiated back out into space. Each ship had angled its vulnerable stern fifteen degrees off from the onrushing Iteeche ships. That, along with the rapid dance of their course changes had been enough for them to catch most of their hits on their armor. A rocket engine or two had been nipped, but damage control parties were carrying out repairs and getting the ships fully back up to speed.

Kris nodded. So far, so good. "I wonder what that other poor slob is thinking about."

"I hope those poor slobs lived long enough to regret not joining the new alliance," Admiral Donn said to himself as over twenty-five ships in the opposite fleet immolated themselves as lasers from his ships slashed into their reactors.

That twice as many of his own had done the same thing was something he could easily ignore. He could lose three ships to every one that the human lackeys lost. It had been bad at first, but he was getting the feel of it.

Now it was time to mix things up.

"Number one staff officer, send to the fleet. No more flipping to bring the aft batteries to bear. Nothing must keep us from closing until our beaks are ripping their guts out."

"It will be done, M'Lord Admiral."

47

Grand Admiral Kris Longknife looked at the screen and the battle it displayed. Her fleet fled the racing attackers at 3.25 gees. Some ships, damaged and out of the fight had slapped on 3.5 gees, the maximum the Iteeche could take with their new high gee stations. Those battlecruisers pulled out of range of the rebels.

Regretfully, other ships, too badly damaged to maintain their speed, fell behind into the no man's land between the two forces.

"Admiral Coth, is there a guard circuit that I could use to talk to my opposite number?"

"I can put you on it," he answered immediately.

"This is Grand Admiral Kris Longknife, Imperial Admiral of the First Order of Steel, calling my opposite number from the forces across from me. Whom do I have the honor of addressing?" Hopefully, nothing she'd said would irritate its receiver.

"Wait one," came back at her.

The fleets emptied their forward batteries at each other,

raking each other with laser fire but only destroying ten ships on the attacking side, two on Kris's. Then her fleet flipped to bring their aft batteries to bear . . . and the enemy kept right on closing the distance.

"This is Donn'sum'Zu'sum'NamquHav'sum'Domm, Admiral of the Grand Order of Iron. I bet you did not see that coming."

"I expected you to do that, but I thought you'd wait one or two more volleys.

Six of Kris's ships blew up as their sterns were slashed through. Apparently, not all the bow lasers had been emptied.

Kris would have to work on that next time.

"That is not why I ask to parley with you under a white flag of truce, as is the custom of my people," Kris said.

"And what does this flag of truce mean?"

"At the moment, only that I ask you not to waste your fire smashing my cripples as you come up to them. I will order them to hold their fire if you will agree not to blow them all to bits. Yes, this is a civil war. A war among brothers, but there is no need to make it any bloodier than it has to be."

"You are surrendering those ships?" the Iteeche admiral said, his voice actually sounding surprised.

"Yes. Those ships will take no further part in this battle. If you wish, you may put boarding parties aboard them and their crew will offer no resistance. Can that be done under some Iteeche tradition?"

"It has never been done. The losers die. The winners live."

"Yes, I can imagine that is the way of it. However, look at the way our ships are spread out. Your damaged ships fall out of the battle line to fall behind and out of the fight. My damaged ships fall out of the battle line and fall behind into the space between our ships where unengaged ships with 22-inch lasers can take them under fire."

"So, why should I not blot them from the face of the universe?"

"Because this battle is not yet won or lost. By the end of this day, it may be my forces that have possession of this battlefield. It could be my victorious ships that go about this space, destroying what could not flee fast enough."

"That is the way of it," Admiral Donn said.

"That is not my way of it," Kris growled. "I give you my word that your damaged ships that do not engage in further fighting will be allowed to surrender in peace. Among my people, the defeated warrior is sacred and may not be harmed in any way."

"Your people are crazy."

The reload clock reached zero for the forward battery, and the Iteeche chasing them fired. Ten seconds later, the rear batteries were reloaded, and Kris's fleet fired a full salvo at those chasing them. Kris waited for a more reasoned response from the rebel admiral.

"You may be right, Longknife. This battle still very much hangs in the balance. I will try your way."

"Admiral Coth, order all ships that have fallen back into the space between our two fleets to cease fire, empty their capacitors, smash their main weapons bus, and take no more part in this battle."

"Admiral, I must point out that the ships in the middle ground are still targets the rebels must use their 24-inch lasers on. What they absorb saves the rest of us for a longer fight."

"I beg to differ, Admiral. I would waste no big guns on ships that will soon be in range of my 22-inch lasers. Did anyone fire at our stragglers the last one or two salvos?"

Coth did not look happy, but he said, "No, My Admiral. None of the stragglers were hit."

"I rest my case. Order the cripples to cease fire. The ships that are still maintaining fleet speed or better may do what they can to mend ship and reenter the fight, but those falling behind are out of it."

"As your people say, aye, aye, Admiral," Coth said, and dropped off the circuit.

"You are an interesting puzzle, human," Admiral Donn said.

"I hope we can have dinner some time and discuss how interesting our different ways are," Kris said. "Now, I, like you, have a battle to win or lose. See you around."

The circuit went dead.

Kris concentrated on her battle. She'd refused to let her eyes wander from the developments on her screen and battle board even as she'd negotiated a parole for her battered ships and their crews.

Now she had some serious problems.

48

"Nelly, can you come up with an evasion plan optimized for a stern chase?"

"The human battlecruisers have been using one since it became clear the rebels were not flipping ship anymore."

"Optimize it for the capabilities of the Iteeche ships in the fleet. Transmit it."

"Done, Kris."

Kris studied her general situation. The battle had started with her outnumbered almost four to one. At present, her nearly eleven hundred battlecruisers armed with 24-inch lasers were only outnumbered three to one. Less after casualties. Only now, it was worse again.

With her running and them gunning, her thousand or so ships could only bring their aft battery of eight 24-inch lasers to bear. The rebels had their forward batteries always aimed in her direction with twelve guns. Gun for gun, Kris was now outnumbered more than four to one.

Not good.

Kris eyed the fleet acceleration. The rebels were chasing

her at 3.25 gees. In theory, the high gee stations on her Iteeche battlecruisers could handle 3.5 gees. It would be brutal on the sailors, but in theory, they could take it. Could she pull ahead enough to afford the occasional flip to fire her forward batteries?

"Nelly, could you and your kids improve the Iteeche high gee stations some more? Allow for .1 or .2 more gees?"

"Yes, Kris."

"Start doing it. I know it will take you a while," Kris redirected her call. "Tosan, if we jack up the acceleration to 3.5 gees for all our ships, how often could we flip and fire our forward batteries?"

KRIS, I COULD HAVE ANSWERED THAT.

YES, NELLY, BUT WE HUMANS SOMETIMES LIKE TO HAVE A HAND IN OUR OWN FATE.

I WILL DOUBLE-CHECK TOSAN.

I FIGURED YOU WOULD.

"I expect that we could flip every other time we fire the aft battery," the chief of staff replied.

"We would want to avoid doing it on a regular schedule," Kris said, half to herself.

"I think we can allow for that. Do you want to flip as a fleet, wing, or flotilla?"

"Let's start by fleet. That will have the greater shock. Comm, send to fleet. 'Go to 3.5 gees acceleration on my order'."

It took less than seven seconds for the board to show all ships ready.

"Execute," Kris said, and felt herself gain a few more pounds.

Grand Admiral Longknife waited until the distance between the two forces began to edge up. "Comm, send to fleet. Prepare to flip ships and fire the forward battery at the rebels."

Ten seconds later, all ships reported ready.

"Comm, advise the fleet we will flip before we fire the next stern salvo."

The time to the reload of the aft eight lasers reached eleven seconds.

"Flip ship. Fire!"

As one, the fleet flipped and over eight thousand 24-inch lasers reached out for their targets.

The rebel crews had been taking a beating from their radical maneuvering. The hard jinking also tended to throw off their own firing solutions. Some ships had taken sailing a more relaxed course, then dodging hard just before their prey had time to reload their aft battery. This made it a bit easier on them for ten or fifteen seconds, including while they were firing.

Kris chose just that moment for her surprise.

Her ships had just finished presenting their well armored noses to the enemy when both fleets fired simultaneously.

Not every Iteeche battlecruiser skipper had gotten sloppy. Still, enough had.

One hundred and twelve rebel 24-inch battlecruisers blew up or were holed so badly their acceleration began to fall off.

Kris lost two dozen more ships in the exchange. Half of them were 22-inch battlecruisers. The rebels still couldn't tell the difference between the two.

Good.

The enemy had also blasted away another fifty foxers. Kris had started the fight with some forty-four hundred target drones. At the moment, she had a bit fewer than four thousand foxers left. Still, that was four hundred of her own ships that hadn't been hit.

Good.

"This is good," Admiral Donn growled as his staff officer number three showed him the results of a sensor sweep. They had destroyed five hundred loyal Imperial battlecruisers!

Still, the results of sensor sweeps over the wrecks showed something that made his stomach go sour. One out of six showed wreckage. Ships blew up. Ships were slashed apart. There were tombstones to all the dead sailors.

Only there weren't for five out of six of the ships they'd fired upon and hit.

"M'Lord Admiral," his intelligence staff officer said, "We are searching the wreckage around the area where we think we have blown up ships, and we find nothing. We have searched with radar and lasers the space between us and found this," he said, and handed his admiral a picture flimsy.

Admiral Donn scowled at the thing. It looked like a ship. Its stern was nearly cut away, but there was no evidence that the reactors had ripped the ship to pieces.

"What is this and why are you wasting my time in a battle with this?" Admiral Donn demanded.

"Here is another picture," his advisor said, and shoved another photo into his hands.

Donn eyed it. It looked like someone had peeled foil off a frozen fish, a delight on a hot day. Before he could snap at the staff officer, the man spoke urgently.

"We think these are target drones, made up to look like a

full battlecruiser, complete with rocket motors and leaking reaction mass. Optically, they look just like a battlecruiser until they're hit and then they fail differently than a real ship."

"And this would be why a fleet of two thousand ships was suddenly six thousand."

"Yes, M'Lord Admiral."

The admiral threw the flimsies across his flag bridge. "If two out of three ships across from us is a fake, find a way to tell them apart!" he bellowed.

The staff officer rolled himself back to his station on the bridge and began talking to the sensor specialists and senior technicians.

So that was what the Longknife human had done to the ships sent to intercept her. Fooled them with model boats! The humans were sly like an otter, but they were still mud lovers. He rode a shark. Their blood would perfume the entire ocean.

49

Kris's battle fell into a routine. Every fifty-two seconds, the aft batteries would fire twice. Sometime during that short minute, the fleet would flip ship for six seconds and the forward battery would slam the pursuing ships. As the ships got more erratic in the jitterbugging, the number of kills slumped for both sides.

This began to change as the flotillas commanders on both sides took to coordinating the fire of their ships. A ship might bounce around hard, but if a dozen ships concentrated on filling that space around them with lasers, some would have to get lucky.

The ticker keeping track of destroyed and damaged rebel ships began to unwind at a brisker pace. So did the count of loyalist ships no longer with Kris. Even one of the human ships got caught in a concentrated salvo. It burned, but survived only by the grace of its crystal armor.

"Kris, I think we have a problem," Nelly said.

"What's up?"

"The number of foxers being hit has been going down. It started in the central wing and is spreading out from there."

"Any idea how they could be telling them apart?"

"I suspect so, Kris. There was no way the engines on a three-hundred-ton target drone could burn as hot as the real rocket engines on a 75,000-ton battlecruiser. Infrared isn't a standard part of an Iteeche targeting sensor suite, but one can be knocked together quickly."

"So, they're smart," Kris said, doing her best to take it as a reality, but really wishing just this once they could have been a bit slower on the uptake.

"Can you do anything to jack up the heat on the foxers?"

"No, Kris. The anti-matter engines on the drones are only so powerful. We've got them using the same number of rocket motors as a battlecruiser but that was just for optical tracking."

"Okay," Kris said then leaned back in her high gee station and muttered, "Okay, you bastard. You win this one."

"Very good, staff officer number three. Very well done. You have won this one, and maybe the battle. Do all of our ships now know which of the targets is false?"

"Yes, M'Lord Admiral. All ships now have the heat sensors and can tell which are true battlecruisers and which are there to make us waste our fire."

"Good, good," Admiral Donn said, but he did not feel like it was good. The humans were trading him six salvos for four. His ships were now taking fire from twenty-eight guns every fifty-two seconds to the mere twenty-four that they were firing. Yes, he still had more than two big battlecruisers for every one she had, but hers were more concentrated.

They were peeling ships out of his flotillas like a diner peeled tails off shrimp.

As much as it pained him, the satraps that had begun to concentrate the fire of many of their ships around just a few of the human stooges were having more success than those that left it to ship captains to choose their targets.

"Staff officer number one," he said.

"Yes, M'Lord Admiral," his senior staff officer said, turning his head carefully on the couch next to Admiral Donn.

"Reformat the message from the Admiral commanding the Golden Flying Fish satrap and send it to all our wings. Concentrate fire by flotillas on one or two ships."

"Yes, M'Lord Admiral. That will fry them in oil."

"Let us hope so."

50

The battle was passing from brutal to savage. Whatever tricks it took to kill your enemy, both sides were now doing them.

The rebels concentrated all the 24-inch battlecruisers in a flotilla and aimed them at a single ship in the opposing flotilla. That usually put the fire from a dozen or less ships around a single target. Few of Kris's ships survived those salvos without moderate or worse damage.

For their own part, Coth had his flotilla commanders directing the twenty to twenty-two big battlecruisers in each loyal flotilla to fire at three, or four, sometimes five of the ships pursuing them.

Ships were blowing up or limping out of the line or, in the case of Kris's ships, if they could still make 3.5 gees, racing to get out of range. Kris was losing one for every two or three her opponent lost.

The exceptions were Kris's own battlecruisers and the vanguard.

The human battlecruisers were putting together firing solutions with one of Nelly's kids looking over their shoulder. Knowing which enemy ships chasing them were actually firing allowed the humans to target just the ship they wanted. A salvo, maybe two, from the human flotilla and a rebel flotilla no longer had any large battlecruisers in their ranks.

The human warships would sweep on to the next flotilla, then the next, then next again, like a scythe reaping wheat. The vanguard of the rebel wing was seriously weakened. While a thousand 22-inch battlecruisers stood untouched, they had to watch as some five hundred large battlecruisers blew up or were smashed and sent reeling from the line.

Kris's Iteeche allies in her wing had lost almost sixty ships. Half of them, however, were the smaller 22-inch 50,000-ton warships.

Odds that had started at nearly three to one against Kris were now two to one in her favor.

It was not going that well in the other four wings. On average, the six hundred large battlecruisers across from them were down to three hundred. However, the two hundred and twenty friendly big warships had shrunk to less than a hundred and seventy.

This looked good until Nelly counted the smaller battlecruisers. The rebels, unable to distinguish between the 22-inch and 24-inch loyalist ships had been blowing up both types. The loyalists had left the small-caliber enemy untouched.

If the five thousand rebel 22-inch battlecruisers ever got in the fight, the loyalists would be slaughtered.

Kris let her wing swap six more salvos for four, saw the number of large rebel battlecruisers fall even lower, then gave Commodore Tosan orders to implement the second phase of her battle plan.

"What sort of misbegotten unchoosable freak is that?" Admiral Donn said, half coming up from his station. He felt a twinge of something in his back that got worse even as he fell back into his station, but he had no time for himself now.

On the screen in front of him, the enemy vanguard was moving upward, clearly intent on adding its firepower to the battle of the top wing. For one or two more salvos, they would continue to rake his vanguard.

"How many 24-inch battlecruisers do we have left in the vanguard," he growled as the pain in his back grew worse.

"Two hundred, M'Lord Admiral," his number two staff officer said, "but the smaller battlecruisers are untouched.

"That horrible?"

"Yes, M'Lord Admiral," his number one staff officer agreed.

"How could they possibly know which of our ships are shooting and which are still out of range?"

"Could they just be lucky?" number three staff officer said.

Admiral Donn scowled, but did not risk moving his head. The pain was becoming intense. He tried to relax into his high gee station, but he felt as if he was laying on a bed of concrete. The cushion was just not working this close to four gees.

"Sensors," he bellowed.

"Yes, M'Lord Admiral."

"Find a way to tell which battlecruisers are shooting at us and which are silent."

"Yes, M'Lord Admiral."

"M'Lord Admiral," said number 3 staff officer, "the new

battlecruisers have 75,000 tons of mass. The older ones only 50,000 tons. Can our sensors not tell the difference in what the maskers show for the ships?"

"Sensors?" Admiral Donn said through a gritted beak. *There has to be something for this pain.*

"Regretfully, M'Lord Admiral, that is not so. The mass that the maskers throw is never the exact same amount as the ship. Some is larger, some smaller. Worse, it changes as the ship moves. The more radical the move, the more rapid and wider the range. The way those ships are moving, there is no way to determine what we face."

"I am sorry, M'Lord Admiral," number three staff officer said.

"Yes," Admiral Donn managed to bite out through a gritted beak.

"M'Lord Admiral," number one staff officer said, "please note how far we have driven the human scum and their running dogs. If we were to turn a portion of our ships toward the jump, she would have to let us slip through into the capital system or charge after us."

"And if she has to pursue us," the admiral muttered, "she would have to charge right into range of our 22-inch battlecruisers." He felt a smile slide in to compete with the grimace of pain that had contorted his beak.

"Order four flotillas from each of the wings, including the vanguard. Four of the least damaged flotillas. Let's head them for the jump and see how the Longknife two-eyes likes jumping to our tune."

51

Kris watched as the human battlecruiser fleet fired its first salvos at the top wing. They fired their aft batteries dry, then flipped and emptied their bow guns. By the time they were done and flipped back to their base course, away from the pursuit, twenty-seven of the rebel 24-inch battle cruisers were gone or struggling to avoid destruction as they fell back to one or two gees.

Her allies took a solid bite out of the enemy force. Another twenty-four, scattered among the other wings, took critical hits that left them a ball of gas in space with bits and pieces to mark where a ship and a thousand Iteeche had been.

The alien admiral had brought three thousand of the newest battlecruisers to this fight. He had less than a thousand left. Of the eleven hundred big ships Kris had started with, some nine hundred were still shooting, although another two hundred of the small ships had been knocked out as well. Kris still faced five thousand of the untouched rebel 22-inch battlecruisers.

Hopefully, after Kris had finished cherry-picking the bigger ships out of their formation, the smaller battlecruisers would surrender rather than be annihilated by Kris's ships, executing them from well beyond their own range.

If casualties continued to be traded five of them for every one of hers, Kris knew who would win.

"Kris, there is a change in the rebel formation."

"What are they up to, Nelly?"

"Four flotillas have dropped out of all the wings except the vanguard. I don't know what their intent is."

"Could they be moving to reinforce the vanguard?" Jack asked.

"It looks like it," Kris agreed.

All the big war wagons of Kris's vanguard were now in range of the top wing. Their second set of volleys did major damage to its big battlecruiser inventory. Approximately thirty exploded, lost their way, and fell back, fighting for their lives. Kris was stripping it of its best ships while it fought back, but gave much less than it took.

Twice more, the loyalist vanguard slammed the top wing, adding their hellfire to what their own top wing was doing. In only a few minutes, the top wing saw its big battlecruiser strength fall to a quarter of what they'd started the battle with.

Another few salvos and Kris's vanguard would turn its fire upon the center. Somewhere in there was likely her opposite number. If she nailed his flagship, would the rebels call it quits?

"Kris, we have a major problem," Nelly said, cutting in on Kris's thought.

"Talk to me, gal."

"Kris, those sixteen flotillas that fell back from the line

have been joined by the remnants of the four strongest flotillas from the Vanguard. They are making for the jump into the Imperial System."

"Twenty flotillas?" Kris said, trying to wrap her brain around this change. "That's over six hundred ships."

"Closer to four hundred after casualties, but yes. A major force," Nelly said.

"Can we make it back to the jump?" Kris asked.

"Only if we start reaching for it very soon. They have almost driven us out of the window for that jump, even at 3.5 gees."

"So, if we want to defend the jump, we have to chase after those four hundred ships," Jack said.

"There is a huge number of ships in the Capitol System," Nelly pointed out.

"There was a huge number of ships here, before the rebels started shooting up the pier- side ships," Jack countered.

"We can't let them make the jump," Kris said, with finality.

"So, your fleet will have to come to close quarters with the rebels. They'll slaughter us once we get within 22-inch laser range," Jack pointed out.

"So, we stay out of their range for as long as we can and risk as few ships as we can," Kris said, then added, "Comm, get me Coth."

"My Admiral," he said a moment later.

"The rebels are trying to put a force through the jump. I've got to take the vanguard on a wild ride to block that jump. You must command here. I am sure the rebels will try to flank me. You may have to slide toward the front when I leave.

"I understand, My Admiral. I wondered what those ships

were doing when they fell behind the main battle line. I agree they must be stopped. Good speed and good hunting."

"Thank you, Admiral Coth. Good speed and good hunting to you, too."

The admiral rang off and Kris began to issue orders to her wing.

Admiral Donn grinned through his pain. He had that mis-chosen human where he wanted her with his finger up her cloaca. He had 476 of his ships falling back, breaking toward the jump and the two eyes hadn't even noticed them. Or maybe she noticed but failed to see how these tentacles would soon be around her Emperor's neck.

"Any sign yet that she knows what we're doing to her?" he asked his staff officers.

"No, M'Lord Admiral," number one staff officer said. "She just blasted thirty of our big warships out of the top wing."

"How does she do that?" Admiral Donn muttered.

"They must have better sensors," number three staff officer said.

"I thought they were supposed to have given us the same design as their warships," Number one staff officer snapped at number three.

"It is said by some that they did," three said, defensively. "It is also known that we modified the design to fit better our needs. For example, we added maneuvering bars and hand holds to stand at. We installed our own computer designs."

"Clearly, we have made some mistake," Admiral Donn growled through his pain. "Communications, transmit a report to my satrap's deputy pasha on his ship of state that we must look at the changes we have made to our battle-cruisers."

"It is done, M'Lord Admiral," the comm officer reported.

Admiral Donn had to wonder how much such a message would be considered by the politicians of the satrap. Who had made the decision to modify the battlecruisers in their fitting out stage? Some Imperial stooge?

Are their ships as fouled up as ours?

"M'Lord Admiral," number one staff officer said, "the mis-chosen Longknife spawn is reacting to our forces heading for the jump."

"Finally, she sees her danger. Her failure to protect that infant Emperor of theirs. Put on screen what that two-eyed blind fish is doing."

The screen zoomed down to show only the top, central, and vanguard wings, as well as the flotillas now headed for the jump. The human-led vanguard had gone high. It was trying to slide into a place above the vanguard beside the top wing. It was trying, but only halfway there.

Now they angled their course, trying to distance themselves from both wings.

"She still wants to play the coward. She still doesn't want to cross swords with most of our fleet. Let us make sure that our vanguard is right there in her face. Number one staff officer, order the vanguard to block her. Order the top wing to concentrate on their vanguard as well. I would bet a silver pfennig to a gold pound that the Longknife misbegotten spawn is with the vanguard wing."

"The orders are given," number one staff officer said.

"Now we wait and see how long it takes all the clans to agree that I am right," Admiral Donn said, eyeing the board.

52

Kris angled her wing up and out, aiming for the space above the rebel vanguard and ahead of their top wing. She doubted she'd have much time before the rebel admiral tried to block her. For the moment, she turned her fire on the untouched thousand smaller battlecruisers of the vanguard.

These were older ships, with smaller lasers. Ha, that was a thought. Not seven years ago, 18-inch lasers had been the most powerful for eighty years. The first *Wasp*, a frigate armed with those size lasers displaced only 18,000 tons. Now, 22-inch lasers were second class and the 50,000-ton battlecruisers were, too.

The older ships not only weighed in at two-thirds of the new ships, but they also had less Smart Metal™ for armor. Kris had seen what her 24-inch lasers did to the smaller battlecruisers when the rebels pulled a sneak attack on her during that training exercise. Now she'd watch them as they did it again to more rebel warships.

The smaller battlecruisers had gotten sloppy. While the 24-inch ships threw themselves around, trying to evade death, the 22-inch ships had taken no hits. Most of them were still jinking the softer, gentler way they had when the battle started. Kris couldn't blame them. It must be miserable being hammered by hard turns in the acceleration couches they had aboard.

Forty-seven of the smaller ships vanished, were holed, or left rolling adrift after the bow salvo from Kris's wing. Most of those had been targeted by the human task fleet. By the time the stern battery had finished firing, they'd been joined by another forty-three.

Kris allowed the rebel vanguard to close the distance to 250,000 klicks as her ships reloaded. Ten seconds later, her ships flipped bow on and stripped out another eighty-one ships with their two salvos even as the survivors tried to slam their ships into harder evasions. A third volley cut the rebel vanguard down to close to seven hundred ships, all 22-inchers.

Only at the fourth round of salvos did the evasion efforts of the rebel ships begin to save them. For one minute, the loyalists had had a turkey shoot, as Kris had heard a backwoods type say on the old *Wasp*. For one minute, the rebels had paid for going easy on themselves. Now, only fifty-three ships died.

"Kris, the rebels are moving their vanguard up to block us. Their top wing is also sliding forward."

"I was expecting that," Kris said. "I still have 50,000 kilometers before those 22-inchers can reach me. Let's keep culling them. Comm, send to flotilla commanders. Have pairs of ships aim for the same target. Let's increase our chances of a hit."

"Message sent and received."

"Commodore Tosan."

"Yes, Admiral."

"I want to steer us closer to the jump, but not close the distance to the rebel vanguard too quickly. Let's go to a full 3.5 gees."

"Aye, aye, Admiral. I'll get this out to the wing."

Kris lay back in her high gee egg and let it massage her back, legs, and arms. She watched as another pair of salvos raked the helpless 22-inch battlecruisers left in the rebel vanguard. This time, seventy-three ships burned, blew up, or lost power.

They could not return the fire, but still they stood in the line, dying, waiting, and hoping that sooner or later she would make a mistake and they could return the flame and death tenfold.

Kris had to make sure she did not make that mistake.

The pain in his back was getting worse. No matter how much Admiral Donn tried to adjust the way he lay on the high gee station, he could not relieve it. More often, he made it worse. Still, he concentrated on the screen before him.

The ships of the vanguard and top wing were doing their best to sweep around and get between the enemy vanguard and the jump. They were trying but his vanguard had been stripped of all its 24-inch battlecruisers. The remaining 22-inch warships stood stoically in line as they suffered but could give nothing back.

As matters stood right now, in the not too distant future, the entire vanguard would be gas or rolling hulks in space, sputtering sparks as capacitors failed or caught fire.

The admiral studied the scum that ran after the humans. For the moment, he concentrated on the enemy vanguard.

How could they have so many ships left? Even if you ignored the minnows that buzzed around the real ships, his vanguard still faced a lot of ships. Most of the enemy flotillas had lost four or five ships. One had lost only one, and it was licking its wounds just out of range. How did they manage that?

Admiral Donn eyed that nearly pristine group. It was in the number three position, the top flotilla closest to the center wing. Closest to the top wing.

"Where would I place myself if I were Kris Longknife and I wanted to do the most destruction to my enemy?"

Number three position looked to be the pivotal point for sweeping up to blast the top wing and back to rake the center.

"There you are," he told himself, feeling almost as if he were talking to that human.

"Staff officer number one."

"Yes, M'Lord Admiral."

"Advise the satraps and clans. Every ship that can fire at the enemy vanguard's number three flotilla is to do so as quickly as possible and for as long as possible."

"That means that the rest of the vanguard will be untouched."

"I know. Kill that flotilla."

"It will be done."

Now, let's see how you like the pain, Admiral Donn said to himself as another spasm wracked his back.

53

The human task fleet fired two more sets of salvos at the long-suffering remnants of the rebel vanguard; their strength fell below five hundred. Then Nelly said, "Kris, we have a problem."

"Talk to me," Kris answered quickly.

"It appears that more and more of the 24-inch battle-cruisers in the top, central and bottom wing are concentrating their fire on the human flotilla. Four of our ships are starting to heat up and glow. All of us are taking hits."

Kris blinked, which was about all the expression she could risk at 3.5 gees. She should have expected that, sooner or later, her opposite number would notice a flotilla that suffered no casualties. Her ships had taken a hit here, another there, nothing that their crystal armor couldn't handle without showing.

"Give me a visual on our flotilla, Nelly." Now four of her ships were definitely glowing. As she watched, one of the 22-inch Iteeche battlecruisers that had been added to one of her squadrons got pinned by a half-dozen lasers. Its rotating armor held for three, then four, then five seconds before lasers achieved burn through and the ship disappeared in a ball of expanding gas.

"Nelly, order the Iteeche ships out of our flotilla. Have them attach themselves to the ones closest to us. Authorize the hot ships to adjust their vector and speed to distance themselves from the enemy."

"I've passed the word, Kris. All four skippers refuse to leave the line at this time. They'll stay in the shoot until they get hotter."

Kris could only shake her head, ever so slightly. Was it courage or folly? Only time would tell. At the moment, she had other fish to fry.

"Nelly, tell your kids that I'm upping their limit on 24-inch battlecruisers. Any big war wagon in range of us is a target. For now, concentrate on the central wing."

"Yes, ma'am," Nelly said, enthusiastically.

Another one of the thirteen Iteeche 22-inch battlecruisers that had reinforced the human Battlecruiser Task Fleet Six took several hits as it made its way to an Iteeche flotilla. It was left limping and falling behind, but still under power and airtight.

Once it fell out of the battle line, the rebels let it fall through their ranks, rendering the honors of war.

For the human battlecruisers, there was no such cease fire. Two of the hot ships got hotter as lasers crisscrossed the space around them. Three more ships began to glow.

The rebels paid for the heat they gave the humans.

The rebel central wing had been fighting it out with Iteeches that were better than they were, but were far fewer. Ninety-two of the enemy's big battle wagons had been blown up, savaged, or clipped enough to fall out.

Coth's flotilla had lost nine of the big battle cruisers, and ten of the smaller ones. His two hundred and one 24-inch battlecruisers still faced five hundred of the big rebel ships.

Then the humans took interest in the center wing.

Most of Coth's ships were firing and reloading almost as one, they were so synchronized. Kris's ships were also sending massive salvos out on time, but on their own schedule.

Like most of the rebel ships, the Iteeche crew were getting a bit punch drunk from being thrown about as their ships jinked to stay alive. Many captains had taken to timing their hard course changes for just before the reload clock counted down for their opposite number.

All salvos done, they could take it easy for a good eight seconds before beginning a new dance with death.

Kris's ships hit the center while most of them were taking a breather.

Nelly's kids were good. They searched the central wing for the ships whose captains were going easy on their crews. Over six seconds, twenty-nine big war wagons blew up, or fell out bleeding air and sparks. Seven seconds later, another twenty-six suffered the same fate.

During the same forty-six seconds, Coth's ships nailed another twelve.

Sixty-eight battlecruisers, more than a tenth of the remaining 24-inchers in the central wing, died in less than a minute.

The survivors threw themselves into radical course changes. As a result, their fire went wild. Kris's ships took less heat. Hot ships began to cool.

As the next five minutes slowly ticked by, the central wing lost another two hundred of their big ships. By the time Kris ordered her task fleet to switch fire to the big rebel ships in the bottom squadron, the center had less than two hundred and fifty 24-inch warships left, and most of those were out of range of the human squadrons.

Whoever commanded the bottom squadron was a savvy character. He chose to concentrate all two hundred of his ships that were in range of the human squadron on a single ship. The *Irrepressible* found herself with nowhere to go that wasn't full of laser beams. She took hits, heated up, and glowed like a sun.

The skipper did the right thing. She cut power and let her ship fall behind like a rock. Because of the vectors she'd been on, her ship not only shot closer to the savaged smaller cruisers of the rebel vanguard, but she also zoomed off toward the jump. All this was done without risking turning her rocket motors toward her tormentors.

"Nelly, is the *Irrepressible* okay?" Kris asked.

"She's about as hot as a ship can get, and she's boiling off reaction mass as fast as she can vent it, but she's holding it together. I'm told that the captain has muttered something about the design needing to have a bit more air conditioning, but if they can still crack jokes, they aren't out of it."

"Yes, Nelly, if a human can still crack jokes, they aren't dead yet. How are we doing with that bottom wing?"

"They knew we would be coming for them and were seriously jinking, so our first volleys only got twenty-one. Thirty with Coth's kills. We'll soon see who can take it: their numbers or our crystal armor.

On the next salvo, the *Princess Royal* was the one singled out for destruction.

Admiral Donn glowered at his screen. Every ship he had in range was hammering at that one flotilla. Other than glowing, it was to no effect. Not one of the battlecruisers had blown up or even gone dead in space. One was running to get out of range. Regretfully, it did before more than a few lasers could score more hits.

If only his ships were so resilient.

More of his big battlecruisers were blown up, burned out, or just knocked flat. At least now, what was left of the vanguard was dodging for their life and losing fewer ships per salvo the lackey scum threw their way. The same willingness to hammer themselves in hard dodging had swept through both the top, central, and bottom wings.

He could personally feel that eagerness to slam a ship up, down, right, left, and every point in between. He could feel it in his back every time he was hurled against the sides of his high gee station.

How in the name of all the stars in the sky and the smiles of the fates did the human ships, and even the Iteeche ships with them survive all the jitterbugging around?

What was clear was that those stooges that followed the humans were desperate to close with the ships he was hurling at the jump. This was critical. This would decide if that poorly chosen spawn of the last water-for-brains Emperor lived or died.

To get at those ships, his enemy must close with his mighty armada.

The more ships he had between that critical detachment and his enemy, the more they would burn and bleed.

"Staff officer number one, order the entire host to bear off toward the vanguard. Put all we have between that doomed for the deep vanguard and our ships headed for the jump."

"It will be so, M'Lord Admiral."

54

Kris knew they were in trouble before the trouble slapped her in the face.

Waves of heat swept through the flag bridge. Even though there were two compartments, shrunken at Condition Zed, and stuffed with frozen food between her and the hull, the heat radiating from the spinning skin, cooling reaction mass and metal was like the hot breath of some mythical dragon. She flinched from it even as her high gee station converted itself into a survival pod, closing up and protecting her from the blistering air that suddenly filled the compartment.

The survival tools of the egg kicked in. Cooling water circulated through the cushions that had held her in place, protecting her from hard usage as the ship zigged and zagged to escape hostile fire.

An escape that seemed to have failed.

Then a laser beam cut through her bridge.

Crammed together as they were, it somehow managed to miss everyone there, though the main screen would never be the same. Kris looked to her left and saw the pierced bulkheads of two compartments. Beyond them, she saw a patch of star-studded black. The *Princess Royal* had been opened to space.

Fast as thought, or maybe Nelly, Kris released the grabbers on the bottom of her survival pod, the holders that merged the Smart Metal™ of the egg with the Smart Metal™ of the deck.

Unrestrained, her egg shot off the deck, eager to follow the air being sucked out into space. Without thought, Kris did the math. The laser was at a bit less than two thirds of a meter. Her pod was a bit more than two thirds of a meter wide. It should fit.

Of course, she wasn't the only one doing the math. Jack was only a fraction of a second behind her. Fortunately, he was to her left. She was ahead of him.

"Dock your egg, Jack," she commanded.

He did before he slammed into her. Which was good, because Nelly narrowed the egg so it could shoot through the two storage areas, then widened it for the collision of the egg with the pierced bulkhead. There was no loving hug, but still, her egg plugged the hole.

By the grace of some merciful God, the laser had not cut all the way through the ship. One or two more compartments over, the bulkhead had held, though it must have heated up a lot. It was distorted and dished out.

Kris had a view to the stars. More interesting was her view of gobs of goo as they were sucked toward the overheated hull breach. A whole lot of them had been released by damage control. Some bounced into each other, growing from small dots to larger balls to big saucers. Some got sucked out into the void of space. Others hooked on the cleanly sliced edge of the laser penetration. There, they provided a base that seemed to adhere to the onrushing tide of goo. The edges caught saucers of the stuff, and they caught even more. They slid past Kris's egg and soon filled in the hole. At first, the internal pressure ballooned the patch out, stretching it. Kris feared it would break loose and the *P Royal* would lose this patch. More of the stuff, however, was oozing along the deck toward the hull fracture. There, it climbed the bulkhead and reinforced the patch, making it stronger.

The bowed-out patch pulled itself in and held.

Somewhere, damage control was working on sliding some of the spare Smart Metal™ of the hull over to fill the gaps. The klaxon warning of a hull open to space cut off as all the patches and moving about got the hull back to the job of keeping the vacuum out.

It was only then that Kris realized she'd been weightless for the entire time since the laser slashed through her battle station.

The skipper of the *Princess Royal* was doing the same thing the *Irresistible* had done. He was letting his ship zip closer to the jump and closer to the enemy vanguard with their short-ranged guns.

Now the question was, could he get under way before he came in range of all those eager 22-inch lasers ready to savage them as they'd been savaged?

It was moments like these that reminded Kris that she was a passenger aboard this ship. She commanded a vanguard wing and the entire fleet, but she could give no order to save this ship or her own life

Only the captain on his bridge could do that.

Of course, Kris had given her own survival pod orders to fill the hole, but that was as far as her command aboard this ship went.

The air cooled. The egg opened up, unsealed itself from

the hole it had filled, and Kris motored over to where Jack sat glowering at her.

"Hey, I was closer to the hole," she said in her defense.

"There were others closer," he growled under his breath, but she heard it.

"There were. But I was the veteran and they were new at this job of staying alive while those around you do their best to make you suddenly dead. Next time, they'll be the experienced hands and save someone else's ass. You know that as well as I do."

Jack scowled, but he said nothing.

Nelly had replaced the main screen, converting the Smart Metal™ to clear, active glass. Now, with Nelly overseeing the screen, it again showed Kris what she needed to know.

The rest of the human squadrons were still dishing it out and the count of enemy 24-inch battlecruisers wiped out or sent reeling out of the line kept growing. Several of her ships were hotter, but others had cooled down a bit. About the time she got back in the fight, that bottom wing savaged another of her ships.

"Nelly, tell your kids the bottom wing deserves some attention."

"We're on it Kris."

The bottom wing had been abusing Kris's beneficence. To make their fire the more concentrated, they'd softened their jinking about the time they were ready to fire. You would have thought that by now, a wing commander would have learned that going easy on the jitterbugging was not a good idea.

Still, the softer jinks had made deadlier his two hundred and fifty big battlecruisers in range of that flotilla his commanding admiral had chosen for destruction.

Now the death they'd sought to dish out came their way like a frenzy of maddened sharks.

Twenty-eight ships died as bow salvos slashed into the bottom wing. Four seconds later, another twelve were hammered to shards by the smaller stern batteries.

Even as commands were given to "Evade, evade, for destiny's sake, evade!" the bow batteries were reloaded, and another twenty-five ships died, bled, or fell out.

As the admiral commanding the bottom wing was full-body slammed against the right and then the left bumper of his high gee station, the wing lost another eight big war-wagons.

In the meantime, the bottom wing had tried to burn another one of the strange ships that glowed when they should have burned. The targeting effort, however, ran afoul of the defensive evasion. One human scum ship was heated up, but it did not glow like the first two they'd lit up.

Now survival took the place of bringing death to the enemy.

Admiral Donn stared blankly at the screen. He should have been watching thirty ships being burned, blown up, and turned into rolling hulks. He watched as more of his ships met that fate and they were sent to the evil demons of the dark deeps by these glowing ships. His ships died while his enemy evaded their deserved fate.

He had come here commanding eight thousand ships.

His was one of the largest collections of warships that the Iteeche Empire had ever seen. Without the humans and their smart metal, it would have been impossible to build so many warships so quickly. Without the human designs, it would have been impossible to crew so many warships.

The humans had given him this fleet, and the humans were blowing it away. There was no doubt in Admiral Donn's mind that those strange glowing ships were the squadrons that had come out from the misconceived human sphere.

The report was clear. There were thirty-two human battlecruisers. The intelligence was clear. The human battlecruiser was worth three quarters of an Iteeche battlecruiser.

What they had said was as clear as water now looked more like solid mud to Admiral Donn.

"Why aren't those human battlecruisers burning? Exploding?" he demanded of the air he breathed.

No one spoke a word in response. Finally, staff officer number three cleared his throat. "M'Lord Admiral, we have reports that the humans are able to clad their battlecruisers in some substance that protects them from laser fire. The glow we are watching is the ships radiating the laser energy back out into space. They may take a hit in one place, but the energy is radiated out from all over their ship."

"And we know this how?" the admiral roared.

"There were rumors about this from the engineers that worked with the humans to build the power plants for their ships. They heard things and reported it. However, they were never able to actually access the substance or see what it looked like on a warship. All the ships have reflective skins, even ours. They looked at the human battlecruisers and saw nothing different to report."

"And why I am hearing about this now?" Admiral Donn roared again. He put so much air into that roar that it hurt his back. He winced but did not allow a whimper to escape his beak.

"It was only a rumor. We had no report of anyone actually seeing this miraculous armor until now."

"And we are paying a high price for the chance to look upon it," Admiral Donn snapped, then allowed himself a deep sigh. He had counted the thirty-two human battlecruisers as worth twenty-four Iteeche ships. What he was seeing was twenty-eight human battlecruisers still fighting after destroying most of the best ships in his fleet. It cost him two, maybe three ships to send an enemy Iteeche warship into the deep, dark abyss. Those human battlecruisers had sent hundreds, maybe a thousand or more of his ships into the abyss and all he had to show was four of them limping away from the battle line.

As he watched, the first human battlecruiser they had scorched took its place back in the battle array.

It was enough to eat the heart out of an Iteeche. He had come here with eight thousand warships under his command. Thousands were gone now. Still, five thousand of them had not yet fired a shot.

"Staff officer number one."

"M'Lord Admiral."

"Have the fleet steer two points closer to the enemy vanguard. I want this fleet between that vanguard and the ships we have reaching for the jump. If those scum want to save their little boy's neck, let them come through all of us."

"It will be done, M'Lord Admiral."

"Good."

55

Grand Admiral Kris Longknife studied the two fleets displayed on the main screen of her flag bridge. As she had been since this battle began, she and her fleet were running. The huge rebel armada was, as usual, in hot pursuit of her and hers.

Only now, she was sliding off toward the jump, and the rebels were doing their best to flank her.

The problem she faced was simple. If she decelerated enough to make the jump, the rebels got to slip down where their lasers could fire right up her engines. That was one thing she definitely did not want.

However, the Iteeche ships that were heading for the jump would not have to face her wrath until after she had fought her way through the entire rebel fleet.

If she brought her ships to close range of all four to six thousand rebel ships that sailed in her way, she would have damn few ships left to tackle the ones so intent on the jump.

"Kris, have you noticed what's going on behind the rebel fleet?" Nelly asked.

"There's something? Show me."

The last time Kris had checked on the badly shot up cripples that could only struggle to keep vacuum out, they'd been strung out like crap behind some cattle stampede. She'd seen that once when she was campaigning for Father out in ranch country. The ground had been beat up pretty badly by the cows' hoofs, but clearly scattered randomly behind all the angry, panicked cows, were steaming piles of cow shit.

"That's why we wear these boots," one friendly young man had pointed out to her. She'd glanced down at her shiny two-inch heels, and learned a solid lesson. Dress like the folks you're working with.

She'd also learned to stay away from cows unless they had already been converted to steak or hamburger.

Kris had thought that what she left behind her was hamburger, slipping through and behind the Iteeche battle line, white flag flying.

That's the thing about space. You can't fly a flag, white or otherwise.

Some of her ships were still in desperate circumstances.

Others, not so much.

Captains had made repairs. Ships had slipped into small, then larger, then flotilla size formations. Two flotillas of thirty-two were steaming straight for the ships that were so intent on the jump.

Kris's ships were not the only ones, however. The rebel cripples were mending ships and forming up. It looked like a minor battle was about to be joined well behind the battle line.

She shook her head. The rebel admiral had been right to question Kris's call for aid and honor to her damaged ships.

The Iteeche did not know when to call it quits.

Kris pried her eyes away from that battle. She had a larger one to manage up here.

Across from her, the rebel commander was doing his level best to cut her off. Absent that, he was intent on interposing his ships between Kris and the jump. Kris had given the order only a few minutes sooner than he had to slide his top, center, and bottom wings toward the survivors of the vanguard. The loyalists top, middle, and low wings were overlapping the rebels. They were able to concentrate more firepower on the flank of those wings and the rebels could concentrate their extra firepower on the trailing edge of Kris's fleet.

Still, the rebel vanguard was wilting under the firepower of the Iteeche 24-inch battlecruisers in her vanguard. Kris had let her ships slip closer to the rebels. Soon, the long-suffering smaller ships of the rebel vanguard would get their chance to use those their 22-inch lasers that had been long silent.

Of course, Kris's own hundred and seventy surviving 22-inch warships would also get in on the action.

Kris expected a wild fight then.

Admiral Donn waited, his eyes intent, his back killing him, as the vanguard of the scum finally fell back into the waiting arms of his vanguard's 22-inch lasers.

In his mind, it was like a clash of armored warriors of old. He could almost hear the slam of axe on shield, mounts crying as they were impaled on pikes or men screaming as the honored rider skewered them on lances.

At the last moment, the wing commander urged his ships on to even more acceleration. Even as the enemy used part of their power vector to slow toward the jump, and less to distance themselves from the waiting rebel vanguard, the rebels leapt ahead, even if by only a quarter of a gravity.

Still, it was enough to surprise the human sucking scum.

His forces got off the first shot. They outnumbered the enemy two to one, and they would make that superiority count.

Still, the enemy was only a second or two behind his ships in opening fire.

Ships took hits. Ships burned. Ships exploded. Ships lost power and tumbled out of control or were unable to evade the lasers that fixed them like a pin might fix a young, newly chosen's leaf collection.

When the nineteen second exchange was over, it was impossible to tell who had won and who had lost. Seven seconds later, the second round of volleys slashed out.

On both sides of the battle, ships exploded, ships veered out of line or ships lost control and ended up as dead, rolling hulks, streaming sparks and wreckage.

I wish I had some way of keeping count, Admiral Donn thought as another spasm of pain tortured his back.

56

"Nelly, how's it going?" Kris asked, unable to tell from her screen and hoping her computer had some way of counting up the butcher's bill in real time.

"The enemy van is melting away like snow on a sun-kissed roof," Nelly said.

"You entering your poetic stage, girl?" Kris asked, barely suppressing a laugh.

"It's brutal stuff, Kris. Forgive me for trying to keep some distance from it. The rebels had two ships for every one we have. Maybe a bit more. They are losing four or five ships for every one we lose. In two or three minutes, there will be nothing left of their vanguard wing, but you will have lost a hundred ships or more. I hope it is worth it."

"So do I, Nelly. So do I."

The slaughter went on. The rebels tried to jink, but they hadn't jacked up their maneuvering jets like Kris's ships had. That was one of the changes that Nelly's kids had made on the loyalist's warships and not told anyone about.

What people didn't know, they could not blab in a bar.

Now it mattered.

The Imperial forces jinked hard and lived even as they slammed their crews around in the cradles of their high gee stations. The rebel forces zigged and zagged as best as they could, knocking their crews about, hammering them, sending them rolling off their couches breaking arms, legs, and backs. Aboard the ships, crews struggled to fight their ships. Struggled and failed. Loyalist lasers slashed deep into the rebel warships even as their softer jitterbugging wrecked their firing solutions on the loyalist ships and left them too predictable for the incoming lasers that stabbed into and through their targets.

The rebel vanguard fought, and the rebel vanguard died. In the end, lightly damaged or even undamaged ships could not take the scourging. Ships cut their power, crews smashed their central weapons buses and fell out of the fight.

First there were only a few, then more. In the end, a hundred rebel ships had as much as held up their hands and surrendered.

Kris admitted to being grateful that they had called it quits. In a minute or more, they would all have died. Maybe they would have destroyed three or four more of her ships, but die they would have.

Their deaths would have been little more than an execution.

With the battle of the vanguard finished, Kris allowed herself two deep breaths before turning her attention back to the main rebel force.

Admiral Donn watched as the last ships in the vanguard took the coward's way out. He knew he should have felt rage, but it was way down there, below several other emotions.

Was that human's weakness tainting his blood?

The admiral had been appalled at how quickly his vanguard had vanished under the onslaught of a force half its size. He had expected to trade three or even four of his ships for every one of the loyalists they destroyed. Instead, in the exchange he had lost six, seven, maybe eight ships for every Imperial that winked out.

"What do they have that we do not?" he allowed himself to mutter out loud. He might as well have saved his breath. From his staff came no answer, good or otherwise.

He sighed at the sight of the loyalist vanguard decelerating toward the jump . . . and grinned. It didn't matter one little minnow if his fleet slowed to make it through that jump. They could miss the jump and go around again. If he cut the deceleration of his four remaining wings, his entire fleet could charge right through that vanguard. Once he held a position closer to the jump, he could bring his lasers to bear on their vulnerable sterns, slashing deep into engineering spaces and destroying containment fields.

He could blow their ships to bits.

57

Kris felt exhausted. It seemed like this battle had gone on forever. Still, it would not end.

The rebel vanguard was no more. Of the sixteen hundred ships it had when the battle started, eleven hundred had died. Of the remainder, four hundred were wrecked and struggling for survival. The last one hundred surrendered, or at least had taken themselves out of the fight.

"Nelly, how many ships do we have left?"

"Of the four hundred and forty ships you started with, we have slightly fewer than three hundred left, Kris."

"What's that make our exchange rate?" Kris asked. Her brain was thinking of force vectors in three dimensions. Four, if she included time. At this moment, she could not do any sort of math.

"Roughly eight rebel warships were disposed of for every one of your ships destroyed or rendered too damaged to continue the fight."

"Thank you, Nelly."

Kris eyed the board and the swirling battle it showed her.

"What would I do if I was him?" she muttered to herself.

No one made to answer. It was rather obvious. "I have to reach the jump. I have to fight off the ships he has headed for the jump. Only those rebel ships need to jump into the Imperial system to end this war. Therefore, he will use all his other ships to stop me, whether or not he can make the jump. Admiral Coth," Kris said, decision made.

"Yes, my Admiral," he answered almost immediately.

"I expect my opposite number to order his ships to cut their deceleration. He's going to try to zip through my formation, destroying everything in range and then take a station in my rear where he can zap my reactors with impunity."

"I would do that if I were he," Coth agreed.

"With the exception of your rearguard, please reduce your deceleration immediately. As soon as you see his next move, match it immediately."

"Aye, aye, Your Royal Highness," Coth said, likely assuming he was praising Kris and not realizing how much she didn't care for that when she was in uniform.

Oh, well.

"Concerning your rearguard, Admiral Coth. Have them hold position. If the rebels point their ships at me, the rearguard should take station in his rear and rake his stern.

"Oh, yes," Coth said, looking like the sharped-tooth predator his species had been. "Yes. Aye, aye, Admiral," he said and clicked off.

Kris was not finished giving orders. "Comm, send to vanguard. Keep braking for the jump. Steer for the leading rebel ships heading for the jump. Deceleration 3.5 gees."

"Sent, ma'am."

"Now send to BatCruFlot 6, 'Continue braking for the jump. Steer for the leading rebel ships headed for the jump. Deceleration now 4.0 gees'."

"Sent, ma'am."

"Kris," Nelly said.

"Yes."

"The rebels have cut all deceleration out of their power vector. They are racing towards us."

"All four wings of the rebel fleet?" Kris asked.

"Yes, Kris."

Kris knew that her own wing's power vectors were split, some to decelerate enough to make the jump, the rest to close with the enemy battlecruisers headed for the jump. "Nelly, show me how this is going to work out."

On screen, the dots that represented different flotillas changed into lines, showing where they would be if they continued on their present course. With the four wings of the rebel main body letting inertia hurl them toward the general area of the jump at unimpeded speeds, his entire force would stream past Kris's vanguard. Even with her ships trying to get out of their way, the rebels would pass too damn close aboard.

There was nothing Kris could do about it if she wanted to get the rebels headed for the Imperial system.

Admiral Coth was clearly intent on doing something about this new development. His ships had already reduced their deceleration toward the jump. Their acceleration away from the pursuing rebel fleet had dropped so that they were only 220,000 klicks away from the main force. They had slipped off toward the jump so that the two forces were staggered with Coth's fleet 40,000 klicks closer to the jump.

The change in the rebel course was rapidly eating up that 40,000-klick advantage.

Coth cut his deceleration toward the jump down to match the rebels. Then he flipped his ships and nudged them in to a mere 205,000 klicks from the enemy fleet. Even as he did this, the battle between the 24-inch battlecruisers in both fleets continued. Both sides were now picking a ship to murder and concentrating their fire on that poor warship and crew.

The rebels had learned they needed to concentrate what was left of the big war wagons from at least half of a wing if they expected to get enough lasers in the space around a dancing loyalist ship. That ship would likely run into one or two lasers, suffer damage, and be doing less of a dance when the stern batteries were brought to bear on it. Some died. Others pulled out of the line to the unengaged side to mend ships. The worst hit fell off and fell through the enemy line.

Despite the illegal battle taking place between the damaged cripples, the rebels continued to let Kris's new cripples through without slaughtering them.

Kris thanked that merciful God that seemed to be hovering nearby.

The loyalists for their part, usually needed only a flotilla of surviving big battlecruisers to fill the space around an evading rebel battlecruiser. Oftentimes, the first salvo would be enough to achieve burn-through and destroy or mangle a target. Then, the stern battery would be targeted on another ship.

Kris's own battlecruiser fleet kept up a steady fire on first the top, then the bottom, and finally the center wings.

The results of the rebels' thousand 24-inch battlecruisers exchanging shots with Kris's eight hundred plus ships was a disaster . . . for them. Eight to ten of Kris's ships might be annihilated or fall out. Inevitably, half of them were the smaller, not yet engaged ships. For Kris's part, her ships targeted only the big war wagons in the rebel fleet and each salvo they'd take out sixty-five to seventy of the rebel's best ships.

If this kept up, the rebels would soon have none of their 24-inch battlecruisers left with their long-range guns.

After three salvos in just a minute and a quarter, Kris wondered how long the rebel commander would submit his ships to this slaughter.

She had not long to wait.

Admiral Donn watched as nearly a third of his big battlecruisers blew up or fell out of the line, either still under their own power or rolling, tumbling hulks. He'd had enough of this.

The enemy had come within two hundred and five thousand klicks of his ships. It would take him less than two minutes to close that gap. Would the enemy run this time as well?

"Staff officer number one. Order to all ships. Close with your opposite number at 4.0 gees."

"It will be done, M'Lord Admiral."

58

Kris didn't have to wait long for her answer. Her opposite number had had enough of four thousand or so of his ships sitting on the sidelines as his larger ships were annihilated. His surviving fleet swung their sterns around. On the screen, the vectors for the entire enemy fleet aimed at Coth's four wings.

It also had him closing a bit on her vanguard wing, but mainly he wanted to get his four hands around some throats and the nearest available was Admiral Coth's.

"Kris, while most of the hostile fleet is aimed at our main force, two flotillas from each of the four wings have dropped out of the main force. They're still headed for us."

"Why am I not surprised?" Kris said. "Are they a mixed bag?"

"Most of the flotillas have only three or four 24-inch battlecruisers left of the twelve they started the fight with. All of the flotillas have twenty 22-inch warships that haven't fought yet."

"So, we've got some hundred and fifty or so lighter

battlecruisers and maybe twenty-five of the heavies headed our way."

"Yes, Kris."

"How soon before they get here?"

"Not very long at all, assuming we keep braking and heading for the gate-crashers."

"Good joke, Nelly. Advise the wing that if they need to cool their lasers, now is the time to do it. If they still have targets in the other three wings in range and their lasers aren't too hot, coordinate your fire."

Nobody took the time to cool their lasers, but instead took the final large cruisers in the top, center, and bottom wings to task. By the time the full enemy fleet pulled their four thousand 22-inch cruisers into range, Coth's four wings were waiting for them.

The two forces exchanged one huge salvo, coming, and going. Kris had slightly less than fifteen hundred ships left. Thirty-seven hundred rebels now drew in range, but it was extreme range.

Once again, the rebels concentrated their fire. Despite detaching ten flotillas, each wing had forty left, four files of ten flotillas each. They reached out with murderous intent for the thirteen hundred ships in Admiral Coth's fleet.

Seven of the ships under Coth's command vanished in expanding balls of gas. Eight more struggled out of the line and out of action.

The loyal admiral had watched over the last hour as his flotillas melted away from forty-five ships to an average of thirty-two. Now, he ordered each of those flotillas to take a rebel ship under fire. The result was very bad for the rebels, especially when Kris threw her flotilla behind Coth's salvos.

Thirty-five ships blew up. Another thirteen ships were left punctured and rolling in space. Twenty-nine more struggled out of the line and each crew had to concentrate on saving their own ship from its own destructive urges.

Kris gritted her teeth as she watched that development. She'd slammed six of his ships for every one of hers he'd wracked. Still, that was a horrible exchange rate.

Admiral Donn grinned at the screen. If he hadn't weighed four times his normal weight, he would have fist-pumped the air above him. As it was, he could barely make a fist without making his back scream.

"Fifteen to forty-eight, M'Lord Admiral," his number one staff officer shouted.

"Yes, it is almost the three to one we need," Donn agreed.

Then the enemy put on a bit more acceleration and pulled out of range. The next salvo from them destroyed or did major damage to another thirty of his. Five of the loyalists blew up, another eight showed damage, but put on more than half a gee extra and pulled ahead of the enemy battle line.

"Aim for the damaged ones," Donn ordered.

"But they are even more out of range."

"Concentrate your fire and get them."

Only when that was done, did he examine his own situation. Twelve ships were gone. Just gone. Another dozen were crippled and spinning out of control. Twenty-five or so were falling out of the battle line, but reporting that they would be back as soon as they could effect repairs. Donn had ordered that such ships not be counted among his casualties.

They would be back.

The next salvo cut them even worse. His forces nailed

five loyalist ships. One blew up, three pulled ahead of the battle line, and one was left tumbling in space, falling behind and into his mercy.

Donn would have loved to order the destruction of the Imperial ship, but he held his tongue. In another hour, it might be his fleet that was begging for mercy.

This was not going well. The enemy could dance out of his range with ease. He turned his gaze to the loyal vanguard that was bearing down on his Imperial throne-winning ships.

“Number one, aim the fleet at their vanguard. We can still wreck it.”

“It will be so, M’Lord Admiral.”

59

Kris's breath fled her in one huge sigh as she watched the trades made by the first salvo. She scowled and shook her head a fraction of an inch as Nelly reported the butcher's bill.

"Six to one," Kris muttered. "Is Coth opening the range?"

"Yes, Kris. They've jacked their vector to 3.5 gees directly away from the hostiles."

"Good."

Still, Kris watched the second set of salvos with concern. To say that lasers have an effective range was to pronounce an approximation. Laser beams spread out as they travel through space; incredibly rarified as the gases and other random atoms or molecules in space are. They cumulatively dissipate and disperse the beams, sapping their strength and causing them to lose their focus, thus spreading out their remaining power over a larger area. The amount of heat they could deliver on target grew less and less as they ranged out from their source. At half their maximum range, a laser could burn through protection at a much faster rate. At maximum range, the burn-through was slower. It was still possible to do damage outside that distant figure, it just wasn't nearly as much as the manufacturer promised.

Now, Coth made use of a few extra klicks to save his ships. The concentration that his big battlecruisers were able to bring down on the rebel fleet was still brutal.

Kris wondered how long the rebels would take it.

She hadn't long to wait.

After the second salvo, the rebel admiral redirected his fleet away from Coth and right down Kris's throat. The human admiral studied her board. Her course was set by the jump. Her deceleration allowed for some juggling, but she was already doing four gees; some of the vector slowed her for the jump. The rest aiming her at the rebel ships intent on murdering the Imperial capital city and most especially, the Imperial Palace.

At the rate the main force was bearing down on her, they would slash through her weakened ranks an hour before she could come in range of the raiders.

"Nelly, is there anything we can do to speed this up?"

"If you want, we could try to work our task fleet up to 4.5 gees. I would recommend that we do it slowly. A lot of our reactors are already deep in the yellow zone."

"Show me data on our reactors," Kris said.

Nelly was right. On average, her ships were about halfway into the yellow. A few were less. Some were more.

"Comm, send to fleet. Over the next ten minutes, I intend to take our deceleration up to 4.5 gees. We will adjust our course accordingly. The first detachment of rebel ships making for the jump is our target."

Kris waited for ten seconds, then twenty as ships rather slowly announced their willingness to put on a tenth more gee. Finally, all thirty of the human battlecruisers still in the fight showed ready to answer this new bell.

"Comm, send to BatCruFlot 6. 'Go to 4.1 gees now'."

Kris already weighed over six hundred pounds. It was kind of hard to notice the addition of another sixteen. By the time she was close to six hundred eighty pounds, no doubt she'd feel it.

Admiral Donn watched as the two forces drew apart. Not by much, but enough to make swapping salvos a less than useful business.

Unfortunately, the loyalists still had several hundred 24-inch battlecruisers. His force had been picked clean of the new ships. His ships jinked up or down, juggling their speed by a tenth of a gee faster or slower, trying to dodge the incoming salvo. It didn't do much good.

Every twenty or thirty seconds, another twenty of his ships would be left burning, exploding, or smashed.

Unable to catch that larger force, Donn aimed his fleet at the enemy vanguard. Those he could destroy. By destroying them, he could win this civil war.

No matter how many ships died here, if the raiders got through into the Imperial System and if the secret rebels in that system had done their job right, they would be the only force in the system. The fools would have to slit the throat of that weak spawn on the throne and give it up to a better warrior and administrator.

He aimed for the vanguard and went for it.

Admiral Coth must have been the one opposing him. Now he brought his fleet in close and blew away another fifty of Admiral Donn's ships. His fleet shot back, but Coth had his ships dancing back out of range even before they could choose a target and fire.

Still, four loyalist ships paid the price for this game.

Admiral Coth went back to plunking away at long range with his bigger battlecruisers. First eighteen and then twenty-one rebel ships were raked and left dead or drifting.

Then Admiral Coth ordered his fleet to veer in again, shot up another fifty ships or so, then jumped back. Five paid for this foray.

Admiral Donn did the mental calculations. He would soon be in range of the enemy vanguard. He could echelon his flotillas to give them all a shot at those ships. Even as Coth plunked away at him, he could not destroy him.

There would be enough of his ships left to destroy that vanguard.

It would be a bloody mess, but they could still win this war.

60

Admiral Kris Longknife found herself trapped by the laws of physics and the absolutes of geography. Throw in an enemy fleet eager to burn her to a crisp, and it did not make for a good afternoon.

She now had her human battlecruisers up to 4.4 gees. No one had risked this before. Nelly and her kids had been doing what they could to redesign the high gee stations to provide extra support. They'd also gone over every strength member in the battlecruisers to thicken them up. It wouldn't do for one of Kris's battlecruisers to bend in the middle.

All of the extra Smart Metal™ shunted to take care of the appalling weight of 4.4 gees meant less metal on the hull, less defensive depths. Another tradeoff that might kill Kris and the sailors following her.

"Nelly, what's it look like?"

The screen in front of Kris showed five different forces. Off ahead of her were the ten rebel flotillas, spread out by their starting position. All making for the jump, decelerating as they went.

Closest to Kris's vanguard were twelve flotillas in four

widely dispersed groups, aiming for Kris's vanguard. They were weaker than Kris's wing, but if they concentrated before they hit her and their smaller battlecruisers got in range, they could do serious damage.

Then, there was the rest of Kris vanguard wing, aiming to intercept the force headed for the jump, and maybe even heading to go through the jump. If Kris destroyed all the rebel flotillas, the rebels lost. If she didn't, they had a decent chance to smash their way into the next system. There might be forces there to stop them. Then again, the same struggle between rebels and loyalists that ripped this system apart could have slaughtered all the Navy in the Imperial System.

The three forces heading for the jump or at each other were small forces. Twenty-two depleted rebel flotillas against ten loyal flotillas, albeit larger and with half their ships the big battlecruisers.

The two other forces hurtling down on them were huge. The larger rebel force had around three thousand 22-inch battlecruisers left. They were outgunned because the loyalists still had hundreds of the bigger warships, but now the rebels had caught on. Now their ships bounced around with mad intent, forcing the seven hundred or so big battlecruisers to concentrate a dozen or more ships against a single target, and even then, it might take two salvos, one to wing it and the other to kill it.

All of that took time. Time that Kris's vanguard did not have.

There was no doubt in Kris's mind or on the board showing Nelly's calculations for Kris. The main enemy fleet would get to her before she could get a solid handle on the flotillas headed for the jump.

"Nelly, send a copy of that board to Admiral Coth."

"He has it, Kris."

"Get me Admiral Coth."

"Yes, my Admiral," Coth said a second later.

"Have you had a chance to study the board I just sent you?"

"Sadly, it looks very much like the board I was studying before yours arrived. Was this done by your Magnificent Nelly?"

"Yes, it was," Kris admitted.

"So, if I cannot reduce the main force to impotency, it will destroy you and allow the smaller force to jump into my Emperor's system."

"That is what I see, yes."

"Then I must destroy more rebel ships, mustn't I?"

"I'm afraid so."

"Human, it has been an honor and a pleasure to serve under your command. I thank you for coming to the aid of my Emperor. It is now my honor to come to your aid."

"Thank you, Admiral Coth."

"Thank you, Your Royal Highness, Grand Admiral Longknife."

The signal went dead.

Kris eyed the board. Admiral Coth's ships edged closer to the huge rebel force.

Admiral Donn looked at the calculations that his number two staff officer had put together. His fleet was losing six or seven ships for every one of the ships loyal to the child Emperor that they were intent on destroying . . . and it was likely to get worse. If this kept up, there would be none of them left and the loyalists would still have a thousand ships.

If he had not weighed four times what he was supposed to, Donn would have nodded his head. "It does not matter that this fleet be blown to bits so long as we get ten flotillas into the Imperial System. Don't you understand that?"

"Yes, M'Lord Admiral," his number one staff officer said.

"I want ideas on how we do that."

"Yes, M'Lord Admiral."

While his staff wandered like brainless bugs, the enemy made their own decision.

The fleet that had been hovering just out of range and suffering a few losses while he lost far too many ships, edged in. They crossed the line where the 22-inch lasers lost their effectiveness and into the space where they had a chance of doing damage. Of course, that also meant that the other half the loyalist fleet also got into the act.

In the exchange of laser fire, he lost another fifty or so ships. The enemy, though, saw ten of their ships ravaged. Donn grinned. Five to one. That was more like it.

As if stung, his opposite number had his forces skid out of range again. That didn't keep the two fleets from shooting at each other. Donn lost twelve; the enemy had one pull out of line and surge farther out of range.

Then, the enemy fleet edged back into range and Donn watched as another fifty of his ships died or were ravaged so badly that they fell out of the fight. Six of the loyalist ships were knocked out.

Before he could get the next salvo away, they were back out of range.

For several minutes, this strange dance with death went on. Sometimes he'd lose fifty-two ships, other times, forty-seven. Sometimes the enemy bled nine, ten, or eleven ships as the ships closed the range.

Then they'd pull back out of range, and he'd only smash one or two while the enemy would pick off ten or twelve of his ships.

They were bleeding him dry, but it was a slow bleed. So long as enough of his ships were left by the time he caught up with the vanguard, he could wipe it out, and with it, any hope the loyalists had to stop the rebellion.

"Number one staff officer."

"Yes, M'Lord Admiral."

"Order the fleet to prepare to steer one point closer to the enemy. We will execute the order the next time the enemy risks closing the range."

"It will be done, M'Lord Admiral."

61

Kris Longknife was sick to her stomach.

Kris knew that hurling ships of near-equal power at each other could only lead to bloody slaughter. She'd known that when she accepted the Empire's commission. She'd known it when she'd led this fleet out to battle.

Knowing something and experiencing it were two different things.

She was now in a battle, watching ten thousand battlecruisers slashing and tearing at each other. Hundreds of the ships that had followed her into battle had been blown to bits or sent reeling out of the battle line, fighting damage fighting to stay alive.

Thousands of the rebel ships had been speared, smashed, destroyed, or knocked out of the battle. Thousands!

Yet, there were still thousands more doing their best to climb down her throat and rip out her guts from the inside.

And she, of course, was about to add more flesh and blood to the slaughter.

The twelve degraded flotillas, intent on intercepting Kris while she strove to intercept the ships headed for the Imperial System, had formed up into four groups of sixty or so each. Now those four had come together. In only moments, all two hundred and forty would come in range of Kris's large battlecruisers.

The odds were practically nil that they could survive crossing the death ground between the extreme range of Kris's 24-inch lasers and the extreme range of their own 22-inchers.

Any rational person would accept the hopelessness of their situation and turn away.

There didn't seem to be any rational people on this battlefield today.

Kris shook her head. Actually, at 4.4 gees, about all she could manage was to swing her eyeballs from side to side. The rebels had no goal but her destruction and the murder of the young boy on the throne.

She had no choice but to destroy them.

Kris should count them fools, but following her commands were more Iteeche so intent on saving that lad's life that they would give up their own lives without a questioning thought.

What was it with the Iteeche?

The Iteeche, Kris? Why are you and a fleet of humans just as bent on killing and being killed? another part of her questioned

Kris closed her eyes for a moment. No one mentioned how much effort it took to keep eyelids open that weighted four and a half times what mother nature intended.

No matter how many calculations Nelly ran, there was no way for the numbers to prove that Admiral Coth would wipe out the huge force breathing down Kris's neck. Kris would not know if this day was her last until it either was or wasn't.

Why aren't you running? Why aren't you leading your humans out of the line and toward safety? The boy holds no sovereignty over you.

Before the battle, Kris had known an answer for that question. The young Emperor and his advisors would be more willing to work with the humans. The rebels intended to wall up the Empire from the humans.

That had seemed like a good enough reason to fight.

Was it a good enough reason to die?

Kris wondered how many sailors and officers aboard her ships were thinking the same thing. Unfortunately, their thoughts didn't matter. So long as she gave the order for the fleet to hold its course and the squadron commanders passed along her orders, no ship would break out of the line.

Sailors and officers might harbor doubts, but none dared voice them. Only she could do that. Only she could save her life, and Jack's and so very many others.

Should I?

"Kris, the enemy detachment is coming in range."

Kris roused herself from her thoughts and doubts. She already knew the orders she would give. "Comm, send to the Wing. 'Prepare to engage the approaching detachment by pairs of flotillas. One and two. Five and six. Seven and eight. Nine and ten. Three and four will fire separately. You have weapons release as soon as they come in range. Cut acceleration to zero while flipping ship'."

"The order is sent, ma'am," Comm replied.

"Comm, send to Task Fleet 6, 'Engage the enemy by divisions. Task force commanders, coordinate the fire plan'."

"The order is acknowledged, ma'am."

Kris knew what she had just ordered was not a fire plan but an execution.

A moment later, the oppressive weight on Kris went from horrible to nothing as the *Princess Royal* cut power, swung ninety degrees off her base course, and joined her division in aiming at the oncoming rebels.

Along the line, four pairs of flotillas with thirty-six ships in them sent four hundred and thirty-two questing laser beams at a single ship 270,000 kilometers away. Among Kris's human fleet, eight divisions of four battlecruisers sent forty-eight beams at the enemy.

In six seconds, ten enemy battlecruisers were blown away or rolled dead out of the line.

Still at zero acceleration, the vanguard flipped ship and fired their aft batteries, two-thirds as many as the first salvo. Eight more ships blew up or fell off.

The vanguard returned to its base course and slammed to 4.4 gees deceleration toward the jump for which both they and the rebels were headed.

Ten seconds later, the loyalists repeated the process, going to zero acceleration, rotating ships, firing, flipping ship, firing, then returning to base course and a hellacious weight.

Fourteen rebel ships suffered or died that time.

Kris had thought that she needed thirty-six Iteeche battlecruisers to make a kill, however, the fourth flotilla seemed to have gotten its ship twice.

"Comm, change order. 'Each Iteeche flotilla will engage an enemy ship'."

"Sent."

The next pair of salvos left twenty-seven rebel ships blown up, burned out, or careening out of the line.

The sight of fifty-nine of their own so brutally handled

in only two minutes was daunting to the rebel witnesses. The thought that another four minutes of this would leave none of them alive and they'd have nothing to show for it galvanized action on near two hundred bridges.

Over the next ten seconds, one hundred and twelve enemy ships cut their acceleration to one gee.

Sensors half shouted, "The enemy force is discharging their lasers, fore and aft. Main weapons buses are being smashed."

"Check fire. Maintain course and acceleration," Kris ordered.

"Done, ma'am."

Seventy-seven enemy battlecruisers were still on course, still aimed at Kris's throat.

"Surrender, God damn you," someone growled through gritted teeth.

Kris thought a hearty "Amen."

First one, then another, then several more discharged their lasers into empty space and rendered their weapons inoperable. More followed until there was only one ship left closing on them. Kris watched it for a long five minutes, every moment wondering if it was time for her to settle the matter.

Finally, that ship fired its lasers and destroyed its bus bar.

Kris's soul felt a little lighter. Today, she would murder a few less poor Iteeche sailors.

Her eyes flicked back to the huge battle raging behind her as Admiral Coth and the rebel main force played cat and mouse, neither sure exactly who the mouse was. There it still mattered how many ships lived and how many died.

As Kris watched them, breathless, for several long minutes, hundreds of ships died.

Admiral Donn pried his eyes away from the battle close at hand when number three staff officer cried out. He watched in horror as the ships he had sent to weaken the enemy's vanguard wing gave up the fight.

The filthy scum.

Those were the words he'd been taught to say to any coward since the days before he was old enough to put to space. Every Iteeche sailor or soldier knew it was their duty, honor, and glory to die for the Emperor. Those who shirked their duty were nothing but worthless trash, not worth the air they breathed.

Still, today, those words rang hollow. He could do the calculations at a glance. There was no chance that the detachment could do more than die. And they'd die long before they could so much as warm the skin of a loyal battlecruiser.

He'd sent them on a suicidal mission. Worse, he'd sent them on a mission that would do nothing to the enemy.

Any rational Iteeche, faced with nearly a quarter of their number being blown away so quickly, would have done what they did.

But Iteeche sailors were not chosen to be rational. Their political masters picked them out of the mating ponds of the lowest of the low. They fed them and taught them to obey orders. Even to die when ordered.

Most officers were little better than the lower decks as far as the masters of the clans and counselors to the Emperor were concerned. Donn, himself, knew there was no place for him in his clan's inner circle. He'd been last chosen and had many siblings between him and the clan chief's throne. He'd known from the moment he became aware that he was destined for the Navy. Destined to do the bidding of others. All his life, Donn had accepted that for a fact, as unquestionable as the cold of space or the blazing heat of a laser.

Then that human, Admiral Longknife, had asked him to spare her damaged and helpless ships. She had asked him to let her Iteeche live when killing them would serve no purpose. It was her idea to have her ships smash their bus bars and pass through his ranks unarmed and unharmed.

He managed a chuckle. *I wonder how some of them have managed to repair the damage, or did my sensors fail to spot those who did not obey their human admiral?*

Still, the sight of a hundred ships surrendering saddened him, even as it angered him. Those poor captains. They all faced being summarily spaced. By the rebels for surrendering or by loyalists for rebelling.

That battle was over. He turned his eyes back to what Admiral Coth was doing opposite him.

The two of them were playing a bloody game. Coth had edged in for a quick smash and run once too often. Donn had met him by having his own ships steer closer to the enemy. That time, when Coth edged back, they followed, and the battle became hot and deadly.

Coth continued to edge just a bit away, and Donn's wings had chased him, not sharp enough to drive him away hard, but not so little that the loyalists could slip out of range.

Ships blew up, burned out, and fell out in groups of forty to sixty among Donn's forces, in groups of fives, tens, and fifteens in Coth's wings.

Donn knew very well what Coth was doing. The more he edged away, the more Donn was led to follow. If he followed him enough, Donn would no longer be able to reach back enough to catch the vanguard intent on destroying the rebel's last hope for winning this war.

Donn knew exactly what his old friend Coth was trying to do. Still, he let him do it.

He let Coth entice him toward a mistake, knowing that, at the last moment, he could wear ship and tack back toward the vanguard. In the meantime, he destroyed scores of the loyalists' ships.

Of course, they were destroying hundreds of his.

"Sensors, where are the battleships of state?" he asked.

"M'Lord Admiral, all five of the battleships of state are making their way toward the jump at one gee."

Donn refused to allow himself a grimace. The clan overlords and satrap pashas lazed back there, no doubt being fed the most succulent of delicacies by their servants who met their every need before they even realized they had it.

What rebel bug has bitten me that I even think such thoughts? Donn thought to himself.

True, he was leading a rebellious fleet against his Emperor's forces. There was that.

And there was that human, Kris Longknife. What was she among the humans? A clan chief and war chief. A Chosen of the humans that the Emperor, foolish child that he was, accepted as his equal.

How long had it been since blood of the Emperor's own blood had led a fleet into battle? How long since an admiral had been the first chosen of a clan chief?

Donn had heard from every corner that the humans were going to destroy all that was good with the Iteeche Empire and race. He found himself wondering if the humans weren't actually showing every Iteeche in the Empire a way to return to their greatness.

Where are such thoughts coming from? Admiral Donn

snarled at himself. Yet such thoughts were coming to him. Were such thoughts loose among his officers and on the lower decks?

Donn's eyes wandered his screen. As he watched, another fifty or so of his ships were slashed by lasers. Across the battlefield, another eight of Coth's ships were hammered and smashed.

Donn studied the lay of his battle array. He could not help but notice that Coth was peeling his flotillas away with care and purpose. Each flotilla in each of the loyal four wings, forty in all, would target ships in four of Donn's flotillas. Twenty-five or thirty of his ships would vanish or fall out with the first salvo, then another twenty or so when the aft batteries spoke.

Two salvos later, four of Donn's flotillas would be cut from twenty to four or five. Hardly an effective force.

After ten seconds to reload, they would pick a different flotilla and do it again.

At the same time, Donn's fleet concentrated twenty of his flotillas, or three hundred and fifty ships at one of the loyalist ships. Of the eight that were targeted, three, five, or seven might suffer destruction. The second half of the volley would leave another two or three burned out.

Donn spotted three critical factors in the way this battle was going. Any one ship on the loyalist side faced about ten chances out of fifteen hundred of being slaughtered with each salvo. On his side, if you were in one of the four flotillas chosen for destruction by Admiral Coth, you faced as much as one chance in five that you would be alive when the lasers fell silent sixteen or forty seconds later.

Worse, each of the loyalist wings had started at one end of their opposing wing and was working their way through his opposite numbers. Two of Coth's wings had started with the number one flotilla and was working their way up the list. The other two wings had started with the number forty flotilla and were working their way down.

As of this moment, they had just smashed their tenth flotilla. Of the eight half-wings Donn was using to concentrate his fire, four of them had a pretty addled bunch of survivors among the gunners in half their flotillas.

Donn expected Coth to start with the next row of flotillas, however, they changed the order. The two that started at the top flipped to the bottom. The two at the bottom flipped to the top. Donn eyed the change, wondering at it.

Clearly, Coth had intent behind his change.

It would soon result in all eight of Donn's half wings having ten flotillas of twenty battlecruisers and ten flotillas with four or five shell-shocked survivors.

It also would mean that the last, or second to last group of ten to be slaughtered would include the wing commander's flagships or Donn's own flag.

Was Admiral Coth, or that Longknife human intentionally keeping the admirals alive so they could make a decision? A decision to call it quits?

Donn's thoughts were interrupted when staff officer number one said, "M'Lord Admiral, several of the ship programmers have proposed a change to our ships. Some of the battlecruisers were delivered by their human builders with extra-large reaction motors. All were changed to allow more of the smart metal for ship's armor. However, they now bring to our attention that with larger reaction motors, the ships opposing us can maneuver harder. Dodge better. They offer this for your consideration."

It took Donn hardly a second to make his decision. "Make it so," he commanded.

Only moments later, the admiral was thrown hard

against the sides of his couch, then, two seconds later, hard against the other side, even as the ship dropped out from under him.

Is this what it feels like on that Kris Longknife's flag? Is this what she suffered?

But it worked!

The next enemy salvos destroyed only forty of his ships. The one after that, only thirty!

However, this also addled their own fire. The number of loyalist ships blown away or sent reeling out of the fight dropped to six, then four.

Donn took the measurements of the distance between him and the doubly-doomed vanguard wing. It was coming within range of the first of the ships on whose shoulders Donn had laid the success of the rebellion. He was not yet in range of that vanguard and while he would now likely have more ships when he did, so would Admiral Coth.

Donn breathed deeply and prayed to every fate that wove a tapestry that they would soon cut the cords for those ships and not his.

62

Kris would have smiled if her lips didn't weigh so much. Since it would not have been a happy smile, she did not risk the effort.

The ships she had to destroy before they reached the jump were in five sections, all detached from a different wing. Sixty were ahead of the rest, pulled from the rebel vanguard before she had slaughtered all that would not surrender. Some two hundred and twenty, including forty or so of the few remaining 24-inch rebel battlecruisers, had come from the top, center, and bottom wings and had formed themselves into a major fist, intent on smashing their way through her.

Following a bit behind them, were seventy-five ships, including fifteen of the bigger battlecruisers. If the two lead forces could knock Kris for a loop, they might squeak by and make their way into the Imperial system.

Whoever commanded the detachment from the rebel vanguard had tried an extra twist. He'd cut back on his deceleration. Now he bolted toward the jump and shot right across Kris's stern, getting between her and the jump.

"Comm send to wing. Prepare to steer fifteen degrees closer to the enemy." She paused only a moment. "Execute."

The *Princess Royal* and the rest of her fleet kept up their brutal 4.4 gee vector. Now, less of it was aimed to slow them for the jump and more to get them across the bows of the rebel ships.

"We will come in 24-inch range of both the first and second detachment in fifteen seconds," Nelly advised Kris.

Kris did the numbers in her head. She had a bit more than one hundred and fifty ships left in her ten wings. Thirty-two were human, the other hundred and twenty were Iteeche. Again, she ordered the Iteeche flotillas to pair up and concentrate their fire. The four pairs would fire at the lead force. The one single flotilla would aim for the big ships in the larger force barreling down on them. The human squadron would fire by divisions at eight of the smaller battlecruisers that were already closer to the jump than they were.

Unable to fire back, all the smaller rebel battlecruisers jinked much harder than any that her forces had targeted before. It still didn't save seven of them, but it was the worst shooting Kris had seen from her ships all day.

The forty-five 24-inch rebel battlecruisers concentrated their fire on a single human ship. As the fates would decree, they chose the *Irrepressible*. After its earlier damage, it must not have had enough crystal armor to cover all of its hull. Or maybe it had just taken too much damage the first time.

It was there one moment, then, in a blink, it was just a ball of expanding gas.

The fourth flotilla managed to wing a big rebel warship and send it spinning out of the line.

Ten seconds after the aft lasers fell silent, the bow lasers were reloaded. Kris's vanguard went to zero gees and aimed itself at the rebels.

Again, seven smaller warships were culled from the vanguard detachment. None from the big ships coming up. The *Dauntless* was heated up, but their armor saved them from burn-through. She stayed in the line.

Ten seconds later the forward lasers opened up. When the stern guns fell silent, the vanguard detachment could count only a bit more than a quarter of the enemy ships that it had engaged two minutes before. A second big warship from the approaching detachment had been blown away.

The *Dauntless* was a glowing hulk shooting off sparks as it rolled helpless in space.

"Comm, send to Task Fleet 6. 'Any ship that is heated up by a rebel salvo will fall out of the battle line and cut its deceleration toward the jump. Acknowledge'."

The reply to that order was a bit slow in coming, but soon enough, her board showed acknowledgments from all thirty of her remaining ships.

The battle went on, every half minute another seven or eight of the ships speeding toward the jump would die or be blasted too badly to do much more than stay alive.

Every pair of salvos from the rebel ships would cause one of Kris's ships to fall out of the fight, glowing brightly. Every salvo, more of the forward rebel detachment would vanish or lose power as it was ravaged by internal fires that only died when the ship was opened to vacuum.

None of those ships were in range of her force. None of them could fight back. It was a bloody massacre. Kris wanted to offer quarters, to ask the rebel ships to offer their surrender.

The problem here was the same one she'd faced five years ago as the last of the alien raiders made for the jump into Alwa. There, they had screamed something like surrender . . . and held firm to their course. A course that would take them straight into Alwa where they could slaughter the birds and humans that Kris was sworn to defend.

In the end, Kris had ordered their destruction because their words said one thing, but their actions did another.

Today, the rebel Iteeche did not ask for quarter. They continued dodging and weaving, doing their best to avoid destruction, but not taking that one last option that would guarantee they would see tomorrow.

If Kris had thought the bug-eyed monsters adamant in their refusal to surrender, she was finding it here in spades.

She did not ask them to surrender and they did not ask for quarter.

Nine salvos later, there were no rebel ships left between Kris and the jump that led into the Imperial System. Now it was time to turn her attention to the onrushing ships racing for the jump.

She eyed them, but also the large battle taking place behind her. It was less behind her than it had been when she first started destroying the lead force and was getting closer by the minute.

Admiral Donn studied the battle before him. He had culled over three hundred ships from Admiral Coth's forces across from him. In return, the loyal admiral had slaughtered almost two thousand of Donn's own ships. Still, this might yet be a victory.

He had let Coth draw him off, as he blasted away at the loyalist forces. When the critical moment came, however,

Donn had given the order and his fleet had tacked three points back towards the vanguard wing that was so intent on destroying his rebel ships. Those ships were so committed to making that jump and winning the war when they went into orbit over the Imperial Capital. They would laze that Imperial Palace until the very stones it rested on ran as water.

Those were the orders those in the Battleships of State had given him and those were the orders he would die to carry out.

The question nagging at the back of his mind was a bitter one. *Do I and those brave sailors that I lead die for nothing? If the ships racing for the jump are all annihilated by the loyalist vanguard wing, do I fight and die when all is lost?*

This was a bitter fruit for him even to nibble at, yet he did. Death was inevitable for him. Whether it came for him from an enemy laser, or from an order to walk out the nearest space lock, he would die today. Even if he surrendered, he would have to take that short walk, either to apologize to the Emperor, or to atone to the political masters who gave him his orders.

His choice was simple. Victory or death.

But what of those who followed him? Should he order all of them to surrender? Likely Coth would send Marines to each of his ships to make sure its captain took that walk. It seemed unlikely that those on the Battleships of State would be in any position to do more than scream at them for choosing life over worthless death.

It was strange to entertain those thoughts, even for a moment, and yet he let them roll around in his head even as he did his utmost to catch that vanguard wing and destroy it before it destroyed their hope for victory.

Coth had made the turn as well, and now followed along

slightly behind him, trading salvo for salvo, though seven or nine of Donn's ships died for every loyalist. The battle raged, neither side cutting the other any slack.

The issue was still in doubt. This was no time to shirk one's duty.

63

Admiral Kris Longknife fought her battle with one eye over her shoulder, keeping herself very aware of the embattled force coming for her. She needed one eye to her right, watching the final annihilation of the leading detachment, and another eye to her left focused on the larger detachment barreling down on her.

If she'd been an Iteeche, this would have been easier to do. Being a human with only two eyes, it was much harder.

As the last of the ships running for the jump on her right was destroyed, she turned her main attention to the much larger force on her left. Some two hundred ships, including a dozen or more large battlecruisers, were bearing down on her. While she had concentrated on destroying the smaller menace closer to the jump, they had made a game changing move.

They had reduced their deceleration to one gee.

Suddenly they closed the distance to Kris's ships like a big dog racing for a nice, fresh steak . . . or to rip the throat out of some trespasser.

The board showed an enemy force of six flotillas of

twenty 22-inch battlecruisers with a one, two, or three 24-inch warships scattered randomly among the flotillas. Kris's force still consisted of ten flotillas. Most had started with forty-five ships, half larger battlecruisers, the others had the 22-inch ships. Now, they averaged twenty-five in their ranks. Kris's own BatCruTFlt 6 was down to twenty-six 24-inch battlecruisers, with four more that had cut their power back and drifted closer toward the jump while they cooled down and mended ship.

She out-numbered and out-gunned this detachment, but that didn't seem to matter to them. As Kris watched, the countdown for them to pull in range for their 22-inch guns reached one minute. Kris ordered the bigger ships in her vanguard wing to concentrate on the big ships opposite them.

In the opening salvo, nine big enemy ships vanished and one of the human battlecruisers got lit up and dropped out of line. The next salvo took care of the last four 24-inch battlecruisers and seven of the smaller ones.

Then the twenty-two inch battlecruisers on both sides were in range.

For the first time, the smaller battlecruisers in Kris's wing got to fire their lasers. Kris ordered her wing to two gees, being about as close to the enemy as she wanted, and aimed them at twenty-eight of the enemy ships. However, they were spaced as widely as her own ships and jinking more than she'd seen any enemy ship do today. Her fleet only connected with fourteen.

The rebels lit up one of the human battlecruisers and it fell out of line. A loyal Iteeche ship blew up.

The next two minutes went the same way. Four salvos swapped, fifty plus rebels destroyed. The enemy played dirty. They lit up the *Irascible*, then, when it fell out of line, lit it up again and burned it. They did the same with the *Implacable*.

All the human battlecruisers went to Evasion Plan 6 and when the *Undoubtable* was lit up, it dropped its deceleration toward the jump to half a gee and shot toward it, still using Evasion Plan 6. She warmed up some more, but was well out of range before they could take another shot at her. In the meantime, seven more loyal Iteeche ships got raked hard. Three were destroyed.

A third of the rebel detachment was gone and they'd only managed to singe Kris's wing. However, they were closer and had definite ideas for improvement.

The next time the two forces exchanged salvos, the rebels lost sixteen ships. They, however, concentrated their fire on one of the Iteeche flotillas. Six ships in a block.

Three blew up and the other three were left tumbling in space, their crews desperately trying to keep some compartments airtight.

That was the worst exchange Kris's ships had suffered all day.

For the next salvo, the rebels were closer still, and the price increased for both sides. The rebels lost nineteen. Still, they took a bite out of another flotilla. Three ships were blown up. Another four were heavily damaged this time.

"Nelly, how much can I cut deceleration and still make the jump at a velocity that will get me to the Imperial System?" Jumps were interesting things. Created by the three alien species that had prowled the galaxy until a million years ago when they just up and vanished, humans were just now gaining a better understanding. Before this knowledge, humans went through jumps dead slow, lest they end up not coming back. Lately, mainly because of Longknifes, humans knew that you could go through a jump at less than 50,000 kilometers an hour and go where you wanted to go. You hit it faster and it took you further.

If Kris couldn't reduce her velocity to 49,999 kilometers per hour or less by the time she reached the jump, she would not go to the Imperial System and she'd be in no position to protect the young Emperor.

"Kris, I'm sorry, but I can't really recommend you cut your power below two gees at this time. You're going to need to go back to 4.4 gees very soon if you hope to make the jump."

"Thank you, Nelly."

Another salvo went out. This time Kris lost eight Iteeche battlecruisers even though she destroyed twenty-two of the rebels.

That was the last salvo Kris could concentrate on with those ships headed for the jump.

The cavalry was arriving, and it had not come for Kris.

The next salvo, she divided her forces. Her 22-inch battlecruisers nailed another nine jump-bound Iteeche warships. She lost six of her rapidly jinking ships.

Meanwhile, her 24-inch battlecruisers were retasked. The main body was coming in range, and coming in range fast. Sixty or more ships got smashed from that fifteen hundred ships, some by Kris's wing, others by Coth's four wings.

"Nelly, how much can I edge over to keep that huge force out of range?"

"Not much, Kris."

"Send the command to my comm desk."

"Done, Kris."

Kris took on a bit more weight and her course slipped thirty degrees to the right of the base course to the jump. The incoming rebel fleet was aimed directly at her, so the vector wasn't going to help her a lot, but any little bit was something to be thankful for.

Admiral Donn gritted his beak as the doubly mis-chosen vanguard edged further from his grasp. Then things got way worse as the vanguard's larger battlecruisers joined in the scourging of his fleet. However, weighing four times what he'd weighed on the home planet, there was little more for him to do.

They had almost caught up with the loyalist's vanguard and wanted to smash them hard. Of course, Admiral Coth was still hitting him hard.

Donn had begun the day with eight thousand battle-cruisers under his command. Eight million sailors and officers had been at his beck and call. At the moment, he had less than twelve hundred ships under his command and was trying to help two detachments of less than three hundred make it through the jump to smash the Imperial power.

He'd reorganized the wreckage of his fleet as he raced toward the loyalist vanguard. Most of his original flotillas were down to ten or so ships, and only a few had a flagship. He'd consolidated the three hundred survivors in each wing into ten flotillas of thirty. Most had a flag officer in charge. He was minutes away from the first three flotillas in three of his wings getting the range on the loyal vanguard. They would hit them good.

Meanwhile, his ships continued to trade salvos with Admiral Coth, and he with them. The next volley got him another eight of Coth's ships, but Donn counted himself down fifty-six ships culled from four flotillas, one from each wing as usual. Remarkably, a fifth flotilla, the one closest to the loyal vanguard had also lost fifteen ships

So, the heavy battlecruisers of the vanguard had taken him under fire as well. Donn didn't mind. The more they shot against him, the more ships would remain in those flotillas headed for the Imperial Capital.

It was a bad situation, but with his fleet aimed directly at the loyalist vanguard, it would soon get a whole lot worse for the other side.

64

Admiral Kris Longknife knew things were about to get very bad. For two salvos, her large battlecruisers had slashed at the approaching fleet while her smaller ships engaged the same size battlecruisers decelerating toward her. For now, instead of bleeding off velocity at 2.5 gees, the rebel ships were only slowing at one gee as they raced to get closer to Kris's ships. Sooner or later, they would have to pile on the deceleration gees if they wanted to make the jump.

Maybe they didn't.

The more this detachment slammed Kris's ships, blew them up, or crippled them, the fewer ships would be left to attack the trailing detachment of seventy-five ships. It was upon them that victory or defeat for this rebellion depended.

Kris smaller battlecruisers cut out nine of the enemy's ships, bringing them down to just about one hundred. They nailed two of Kris's Iteeche ships.

The problem was that Kris was decelerating at two gees toward the jump and a bit more to edge her to the right of that path. She had to wear away from the larger force if she wanted to avoid that big honking fleet headed directly for her.

Kris brought all her ships back to targeting the rebels racing for the jump. She traded salvos with them. In one minute, a third of the rebel ships were hit, smashed, destroyed, or knocked out of the fight.

Kris lost seven ships in the exchange.

Then the cavalry arrived.

Kris took out another fifteen ships.

She lost ten.

The lead ships of the big rebel fleet had gotten in range. Now the bloody fight would get worse.

If his weight would have allowed for it, Admiral Donn would have slammed both of his right fists into his left palms. Unable to so much as twitch without aggravating the excruciating pain in his back, he settled for joining the shouts of joy that bounced off the bulkheads of his flag bridge.

They were in range of the loyal vanguard and they were hacking them down. His fleet might only muster a thousand 22-inch battlecruisers, but he had the loyalists in his sights and he aimed to take them down.

The enemy vanguard had done its best to avoid him, slipping across the direct path to the jump and opening up the range as much as Kris had been able to manage. She could run, but not far enough if she wanted to make that jump.

Dunn, like Coth, knew that he'd never make the jump. He had way too much energy on his boats. Even if he did everything he could from this moment on, he could not slow enough to go through the jump at anything less than suicidal speed.

Yes, there had been reports that a human had used high speeds to ride the jumps all the way across the galaxy. Still, Admiral Donn, like all other Iteeche, had no idea where the jumps would take him if he didn't treat them just right.

No. His other detachments would make the jump. He would clear the way for them. He ordered his flotillas to prepare to fire upon the vanguard as they came in range. Until then, they would continue to fight Admiral Coth's ships that were flaying his fleet alive. A minute passed, the two forces swapped salvos. Coth destroyed a hundred of his ships.

The first ten flotillas to come in range of the van, however, destroyed five of the vanguard's ships. The detachment that was close to charging through their ranks, likely got another three.

In two minutes, every rebel ship was in range of the vanguard. One thousand ships fired twelve thousand 22-inch lasers. Thirteen ships from the vanguard winked out of existence. In another sixty seconds, another twenty-four were gone.

In the meantime, the last rebel ship in the middle detachment was smashed. Now, the only ships with any hope of making the jump and upsetting the ways of this Emperor were the seventy-five ships in the detachment that had come from the rear guard.

But Donn was paying a high price for concentrating on the vanguard. His opposite number, Admiral Coth took a great risk, but one with a huge return. He slowed the jinking of his fleet to something almost gentle. His thousand ships raked Donn's fleet with extremely accurate fire. During the same long minute while Donn was nailing thirty-seven ships out of the vanguard, Coth was smashing nearly three hundred of Donn's ships.

As Donn aimed his fleet like a knife for the throat of the vanguard, two loyalist forces took his ships under fire from both directions. Another pair of salvos and he traded two hundred ships for just sixteen.

The admiral was not there to count the losses to either side from the next exchange. His luck, and that of the *Shark*, finally ran out. His was one of the hundred and sixty-three ships that were shot through by the next volley.

He was not there to hear as some two hundred of his ships called for quarters and were allowed to surrender.

65

Her Royal Highness, Grand Admiral Kris Longknife, Imperial Admiral of the First Order of Steel, accepted the surrender of the larger group of rebel ships. She offered the same conditions to the smaller detachment that was, even now, still braking hard, trying to slow sufficiently to make the jump.

It was simple.

Surrender or die.

Surrender and accept quarters or be annihilated.

Having observed from a distance the annihilation of nearly eight thousand of their comrades and some fifteen hundred of the ships that fought them, they accepted the offer.

Kris breathed a sigh of relief, then steeled herself. She still had twenty-nine human cruisers and about a hundred Imperial Iteeche ships under her command. They alone could make the jump. Kris had no idea what the Imperial System looked like, but her kids were there and that was where she wanted to be.

"What about those big barges?" Jack mentioned.

Kris would very much like to present the occupants of those Battleships of State to the Emperor for them to make their own most solemn and formal apology, but there was no way that her ships could get back quickly enough to catch them. The ships with the political cargo had gone to a 1.68 gee deceleration as soon as the battle had started to go bad. They had yet to dampen down their vectors toward the jump to the Imperial System, but they'd jump out before any of Kris's ships could catch them.

Then karma proved that she truly was a bitch. The jump began to spit out ships in a rapid and very ship shape and Bristol fashion. No sooner had the fact of their arrival reached the sensors on Kris's ships than they were found to be squawking as human battlecruisers from Wardhaven. Admiral Kitano was in command.

Kris quickly had Comm send a very prompt reply. "Very glad to see you, and the ships following behind you. We're cleaning up the wreckage of a very big battle. Could you please police up those large puff balls? They are known locally as Battleships of State and they're loaded to the gills with political types too dainty to get their hands dirty in a fight. I very much want to talk to them, and I'm sure there are many Iteeche in the Imperial Court who would like the same."

There were other matters to handle. More rescue ships were called out from the stations, and a surprising number came. Kris made a quick call to Admiral Coth.

"Admiral, these rebels are surrendering to my command. I want them treated as we humans treat prisoners of war. No killing. No blowing ships up. They didn't massacre our damaged ships. We don't do that to them now."

"My Admiral, you humans are a strange bunch, but I

have followed you to a victory that will be sung about for a thousand years. I will obey your orders.

"Thank you, Coth. Clean up here. As soon as you can, follow me to the Imperial system. You're earned a victory parade."

"Victory parade?"

"Okay, how about the beers being on me."

"I think that translates fine in any language."

Kris was just about to jump into the Imperial system when word came from Admiral Katana that all the head high muckety-mucks were in custody. She was not treating them as prisoners of war and they looked like a very crest-fallen bunch.

She was not surprised to discover the Imperial system was littered with the wreckage of thousands of ships. Here as well, the rebels had started things off with a surprise attack on the other loyal ships. Here, the two groups of survivors had fought themselves to mutual annihilation.

That had left the Imperial Capitol holding their breath to see who would command the next force to come through the jump.

There was great jubilation and celebration when Kris sent out her recognition signals.

As the *Princess Royal* was pulled into the pier by the tie downs, Kris found herself most eager to get out of there. They'd arranged to open three quarterdecks to the pier to allow for free flow aboard and ashore. Kris and Jack were among the first down one of those gangplanks.

There, two beautiful kids were waiting with several of their friends. Roth was also waiting on the pier, with about a tenth of the retinue he'd brought the last time he came, but even a mighty Imperial Counselor had to wait for two kids to get their hugs and kisses.

The kids weren't the only ones to need hugs and kisses. Kris was giving and taking them in large quantities. She knew that the rebellion probably wasn't over. She knew that Roth, no doubt, had a load of problems he needed her to solve, but for now, the Empire could hold its horses. A momma needed some quality time with her kids.

A grand admiral may have saved fifty-billion lives and an Imperial dynasty, but she'd saved them for her kids' sake, and she very much wanted the reward they had for her.

ABOUT THE AUTHOR

Mike Shepherd is the National best-selling author of the Kris Longknife saga. Mike Moscoe is the award-nominated short story writer who has also written several novels, most of which were, until recently, out of print. Though the two have never been seen in the same room at the same time, they are reported to be good friends.

Mike Shepherd grew up Navy. It taught him early about change and the chain of command. He's worked as a bartender and cab driver, personnel advisor and labor negotiator. Now retired from building databases about the endangered critters of the Northwest, he's looking forward to some fun reading and writing.

Mike lives in Vancouver, Washington, with his wife Ellen, and not too far from his daughter and grandkids. He enjoys reading, writing, dreaming, watching grandchildren for story ideas and upgrading his computer – all are never ending.

For more information:
www.mikeshepherd.org
mikeshepherd@krislongknife.com

f

2018 RELEASES

In 2016, I amicably ended my twenty-year publishing relationship with Ace, part of Penguin Random House.

In 2017, I began publishing through my own independent press, KL & MM Books. We produced six e-books and a short story collection. We also brought the books out in paperback and audio.

In 2018, I intend to keep the novels coming.

We will begin the year with **Kris Longknife's Successor**. Grand Admiral Santiago still has problems. Granny Rita is on the rampage again, and the cats have gone on strike, refusing to send workers to support the human effort on Alwa. Solving that problem will be tough. The last thing Sandy needs is trouble with the murderess alien space raiders. So, of course, that is what she gets.

May 1 will see **Kris Longknife: Commanding**. Kris has won her first battle, but the way the Iteeche celebrate victory can be hard on the stomach. The rebellion won't quit and now Kris needs to raise a fleet, not only to defend the Iteeche Imperial Capitol, but also take the war to the rebels.

In the second half of 2018, you can look forward to the next Vicky Peterwald novel on July 1, another Iteeche war novel on September 1, and **Kris Longknife Implacable** on November 1.

Stay in touch to follow developments by friending Kris Longknife and follow Mike Shepherd on Facebook or check in at my website www.krislongknife.com

2017 RELEASES

In 2016, I amicably ended my twenty-year publishing relationship with Ace, part of Penguin Random House.

In 2017, I began publishing through my own independent press, KL & MM Books.

I am delighted to say that you fans have responded wonderfully. We have sold over 20,000 copies of the five e-novels. In 2018, I intend to keep the novels coming,

We started the year with **Kris Longknife's Replacement** that tells the story of Grand Admiral Sandy Santiago as she does her best as a mere mortal to fill the shoes left behind on Alwa Station by Kris Longknife. Sandy has problems galore: birds, cats, and vicious alien raiders. Oh, and she's got Rita Nuu-Longknife as well!

February had a novelette. **Kris Longknife: Among the Kicking Birds** was part of Kris Longknife: Unrelenting. However, it went long and these four chapters were cut to one short paragraph. I hope you enjoy the full story.

Rita Longknife: Enemy Unknown was available in March and is the first book of the long-awaited Iteeche War series. Rita has had enough of Ray Longknife gallivanting around the universe. No sooner is little Al born, than ships start disappearing. Is it pirates or something more sinister? Rita gets herself command of a heavy cruiser, some nannies, and heads out to see what there is to see.

April had another short offering, **Kris Longknife's Bad Day**. You just knew when Kris asked for a desk job that she'd have days like you have at the office. Well, here's one that will bring you up to date on the technical developments in the Royal US Navy, as well as silly bureaucratic goings on. In the first draft of **Emissary**, these were the opening chapters, but I found a better opening and this got cut. Enjoy!

Kris Longknife: Emissary began an entirely new story arc for Kris and was available May 1. Here is the story of what it takes to get Kris out from behind a desk. And for those of you betting in the pool, you'll get your answer. More I cannot say.

June brought you Abby Nightingale's view of things around Alwa in **Kris Longknife's Maid Goes on Strike**. You knew sooner or later this was going to happen.

July had another book set in Alwa. As **Kris Longknife's Relief,** Sandy Santiago, continues to battle aliens of various persuasions and not a few humans.

Rita Longknife: Enemy in Sight was released in September and sought to resolve the unknowns left by Enemy Unknown as humanity slipped backwards into a war it does not want and may not be able to win.

Kris Longknife's Maid Goes on Strike and Other Short Stories, is a collection of four short stories: Maid Goes on Strike, Ruthie Longknife's First Christmas, Among the Kicking Birds, and Bad Day. These were available in October all under one ebook cover for a great price.

Kris Longknife: Admiral was available in November. In this adventure, Kris is up to her ears in warships, enemies, and friendlies who may be not as friendly as she'd like, as battlecruisers square off against battlecruisers. A fight where both sides are equal is a bloody fight that often no one wins.

Work is already going on for a January 18 release of Kris Longknife's Successor. March will have the next book in the Iteeche War, and May will continue Kris's adventures in the Iteeche Empire with Kris Longknife: Warrior.

Stay in touch to follow developments by following Kris Longknife on Facebook or checking in at my website www.mikeshepherd.org.

I hope to soon have a mailing list you can sign up for.

CPSIA information can be obtained
at www.ICGtesting.com
Printed in the USA
FSHW010655010220
66690FS